SEA GOLD

"A first-rate, crisply told adventure story."
—Toronto *Globe and Mail*

"Thrilling, fast-paced . . . *Sea Gold* combines a high sense of adventure with excellent character and story development. . . . An out-and-out winner."
—*The Hamilton Spectator*

"Full of furious action."
—*Quill and Quire*

AIR GLOW RED

"Provides page-turning thrills that should leave even the steadiest hands shaking."
—*The Toronto Star*

"One of the top suspense writers in North America. His plots are intelligent, well thought out, and have the eerie specter of reality hanging over them like a rain cloud on the horizon."
—*The Hamilton Spectator*

"One of the most riveting chase sequences in recent fiction."
—*Midland Free Press*

By Ian Slater

published by Ballantine Books

WW III
PAYBACK

A NOVEL

IAN SLATER

BALLANTINE BOOKS • NEW YORK

WW III: Payback is a work of fiction. Names, places, and incidents are either products of the author's imagination or are used fictitiously.

A Ballantine Books Mass Market Original
Copyright © 2005 by Ian Slater

Published in the United States by Ballantine Books, an imprint of The Random House Publishing Group, a division of Random House, Inc., New York.

Ballantine and colophon are trademarks of Random House, Inc.

ISBN 0-345-45376-X

Printed in the United States of America

Ballantine Books website address: www.ballantinebooks.com

OPM   9   8   7   6   5   4   3   2   1

As always, for Marian, Serena, and Blair

ACKNOWLEDGMENTS

Among the unsung heroines in the world of writers are those women who unselfishly give of their time and talent in support of writer husbands. Such is my wife, Marian. Without her, these books would simply not appear. I would also like to thank David Leask, Peter Petro, D. W. Riley, and Charles Slonecker for their help and support, and Tim Ross, map librarian at the University of British Columbia.

In the Defense Science Board (DSB) study on Special Operations and Joint Forces in Support of Countering Terrorism, the study suggested that "a robust cadre of *retirees*, reservists, and others who are trained and qualified to serve on short notice" be retained for possible call-up when needed. [Italics added.]

—*Jane's Defense Weekly*, November 6, 2002

WW III
PAYBACK

CHAPTER ONE

Fort Lewis, Washington State

"YOU TENSE, DOCTOR?" Air Force Chief of Staff Michael Lesand asked the chief scientist from DARPA, Defense's Advanced Research Projects Agency. A dozen military and civil VIPs had gathered in the open in the ice-cold, pine-scented fall morning for the final test of DARPA's latest expensive and most secret equipment project. If the test was successful, it would save countless American lives and justify the American taxpayers' unwitting subsidization of the multimillion-dollar program. If it failed, heads would roll.

"Of course I'm nervous," said the DARPA man. "I don't know why you people from the Pentagon don't trust us. We could've done this back in the Seattle lab."

"*I* trust you," said Michael Lesand, with an ill-concealed smirk. "It's just that some of the Joint Chiefs and my other colleagues here have seen the difference between a controlled lab situation, where ideal windage, humidity, and a perfect dummy are used, and a dummy in typical outdoor battle conditions, like this morning, when you can't jig with the variables. No offense."

"None taken," said the engineer, his forehead creased with worry lines as he looked around at the other VIPs and the small crowd of assistants and Humvee drivers who had con-

1

gregated by a copse of Ponderosa pines, a group of four Fort Lewis infantrymen assembling, or at least wrestling with, what at the moment was still known only as Item A-10437-B/215 in DARPA's inventory. The engineer did a double take when he saw General Douglas Freeman, immediately identifiable in his long Russian Army coat, amid the invited guests.

"What the hell's Freeman doing here?"

"A mistake," said Lesand. "Apparently some kid in Fort Lewis's admin thought he was still on the active list and issued an invitation. While this equipment was his idea before he had to retire because of his age, someone in admin forgot that he's no longer on the active or even the reserve roster. But it was too embarrassing, I guess, for Fort Lewis's CO to send a 'stay away' letter, so they let it ride. When the young go-getters at the Pentagon heard about him being invited, the joke was that there must be a 'has been' list."

"I'll go with that," said the engineer. "His day is done."

"I agree," concurred General Lesand. "Uh-oh, here he comes. Get ready for a lecture on how this item was all his idea or a lecture on the damned superiority of the Russian Army greatcoat." Lesand was smiling at Freeman as he approached, but while the retired general was still out of earshot, Lesand said, "What an eccentric. Should have been put out to pasture long ago."

"Morning, gentlemen," said General Douglas Freeman, the man who had so often been mistaken on the street as a look-alike for the late actor George C. Scott, who had portrayed Patton, one of Freeman's heroes, in the movie of the same name.

"Morning," said Lesand, smiling. Freeman had already extended his right hand toward the civil engineer. "I'm Douglas Freeman. And you are—?"

"Dr. Klein," responded the DARPA scientist, unsmiling. "We've met once before, I think. You were giving a lecture at the Naval Postgraduate School in Monterey. 'Soldiers on Water' I believe was the title of your presentation."

"You've got a damn good memory," said Freeman, obviously pleased.

"What are you doing these days, General?" asked Lesand. "I seem to remember you used to put on the odd golf tournament for your old Third Army officers?"

Freeman ignored Lesand's baiting tone in his use of "odd" and "old." What was it Kipling had advised? "If you can fill the unforgiving moment with sixty seconds' worth of distance run . . ."

"Yes," said Freeman, his breath turning to mist the moment it hit the cold air that had been sweeping down eastward from the majestic mountains of Washington State's Olympic Peninsula. "I used to organize the occasional golf game. But as for the game itself, I was never really a big fan. I take the Scottish view, gentlemen, that golf is a good walk ruined." Neither Lesand nor Klein would give him the courtesy of a laugh. In fact, Lesand was out to bait him further, to fill the time during which the restive invitees were stomping their feet to keep warm while the Army foursome continued to have some difficulty assembling DARPA's dummy.

"Tell me, General," said Lesand, as if the thought just happened by. "You still believe that George Washington stood in the prow of that boat while he crossed the Delaware? Someone mentioned it in the mess here this morning."

"Mentioned what?" said Freeman. "The painting?"

"No, no—someone was chuckling about you still believing that, uh, Washington actually stood in the prow as that painter portrayed him. I was just wondering whether you still hold that view." Lesand smiled condescendingly. "I mean, that Washington actually stood up in the prow with all those great chunks of ice floating around?"

"Yes," answered Freeman decisively. "And I'll tell you why, General Lesand. That artist, Emmanuel Leutze, painted the wrong damn boat, and everyone—including you, I presume—fell for it. Fact is that Washington used a Durham boat, which was sixty feet long, three times the size of that little boat in the painting. And besides, a Durham's a damn sight heavier than that weensie rowboat Leutze depicted."

Dr. Klein nodded with newfound respect, a scientist's respect, for Freeman—if not for the man whom the Pentagon called a "loose cannon" then for the man's encyclopedic grasp of myriad details.

Freeman, not usually one to turn the other cheek when a smart-ass had tried to set him up, nevertheless decided to move off before his blood pressure ignored Kipling's poetic line to take a deep breath and walk away from needless argument. "I'll see you after the demonstration," he said, and walked away.

"Well," said the Army Chief of Staff, who'd overheard his Air Force colleague's baiting of Freeman. "He made a fool of you, Mike, about that painting."

"The day's young," said Lesand petulantly. "He'll trip over his ego—it's as tall as that ankle-to-crown coat he hauls about. He looks ridiculous."

Perhaps the general did look a mite quixotic in his long Russian coat, but Douglas Freeman, who had fought the so-called Soviet advisors in Vietnam, had learned a thing or two about coats and all manner of things during his now-legendary exploits overseas. He wasn't a man who'd turn against the tradition of his own country, indeed he loved tradition, but he had a markedly objective mind when it came to evaluating tactics, strategy, and equipment. He'd learned that the Russian Army greatcoat was unique in its ability to keep a soldier warm in the worst of winters. A Russian soldier who knew how to wrap himself up properly in the ankle-to-crown greatcoat could spend a night outside in the normally killing subzero temperatures of the Russian taiga and survive to fight the next day. The general remembered how in the sixties, when a Soviet infantryman got hypothermia and died while on a winter maneuver and news of the man's death filtered up to the Kremlin, a bemedaled Soviet marshal, a veteran of the great winter offensives against the German Wehrmacht, banged his fist on his desk, declaring, "Have Soviet soldiers forgotten how to sleep in their overcoats?" and summoned over 170 generals for an emergency meeting. The "meeting" was a refresher lecture by the marshal himself on how a soldier could sleep out in the bone-numbing Russian winter and survive if he knew how to use his greatcoat properly. To make sure his generals got the point, the marshal promptly issued each of the generals with a regular soldier's greatcoat and ordered them out into a bitterly cold Moscow night. They would stay warm or die. For his own part, Freeman had once ordered his officers in the Third Army to spend a week in the Sonoran Desert, learning how to cope if, through either accident or faulty manufacture or failure or resupply, their boots were no longer useful. They were ordered by Freeman to negotiate an attack route in their bare feet. Freeman, also in bare feet, led from the point, which was precisely why he believed, contrary to "expert" opinion, that General George Washington *had* stood in the prow of the long Durham boat. It was just the kind of command stance, Freeman believed, that Washington's men, who had been led out of near utter defeat to victory in that dreadful winter of 1776–77, had come to expect.

"What's the holdup?" demanded the Chairman of the Joint Chiefs, strolling over from his warm Humvee.

"I don't know," said Dr. Klein apologetically. "The instructions for assembling the dummy are so simple, I don't know what the problem is."

"Then maybe you'd better go and have a look," said the chairman. "We've got ten million bucks invested in this and somebody doesn't know how to put up the damn dummy?"

"I'll take a look," said Freeman nearby, taking his gloves

off and making his way down toward the pines, at which point DARPA's Klein strode after him, passing him as Freeman stopped for a moment to chat with a couple of the military policemen who'd been called on to escort Item A-10437-B/215 from the DARPA aircraft that had delivered it a few hours before to the SeaTac—Seattle-Tacoma—Airport.

When Dr. Klein, trying to find one of the bolts that held the dummy together, looked up and saw Freeman walking toward him with the Heckler & Koch sidearm the general had borrowed from one of the military police, he asked bluntly, "What the hell are you doing with that, General? You going to shoot me because we're running late?"

"The thought had occurred to me," said Freeman, grinning. "No, I thought we could test the son of a bitch right here."

"Well, if you don't mind," said Klein, "we're going to need a few minutes before we get the dummy set up. I don't know what these guys have been doing, but there's supposed to be an assembly diagram here and I don't know where the hell—"

"Murphy's Law," said Freeman good-naturedly. "Right, guys?" he asked, looking at the four harried Army privates who had been searching in vain for some kind of diagram that was supposed to be in the item's box. Freeman stuck the 9mm in his waistband and told one of the privates, "Hand me the vest, will you? It's time we got this show on the road." Freeman took off the Russian greatcoat, strapped on the vest, and walked back to General Lesand, handing him the 9mm. "I think you'd like to shoot me, General. Go ahead."

Lesand looked about. No one said anything. They were struck dumb by Freeman's braggadocio.

"Go on!" Freeman urged Lesand. "Pull the trigger."

Lesand licked his lips nervously. "No way."

"Anyone?" asked Freeman, looking at the others. "I'll take full responsibility."

"Don't be foolish," Dr. Klein warned him.

"Oh, hell," said Freeman impatiently, "you're just a bunch of ninnies." With that, he took the gun from Lesand, reversed it, and, using his thumb as a trigger finger, fired at his chest. Point-blank range. Three times.

"Jesus—," began Lesand, abruptly stepping back, almost tripping. "What the hell—"

"It works," said Freeman casually.

Every one of the VIPs was agape. As Freeman took off the vest and returned the 9mm to an equally astonished MP, he thanked the man and, buttoning up his Russian greatcoat, the steam of his breath looking momentarily like the fiery nostril exhaust of some tall, hitherto unspecified *Matrix* hero, he paused by the VIPs and pulled the coat's high collar up around his ears. "So, now we know that the fibers in hagfish slime have, as I suggested in my initial report, a molecular structure that gives it a tensile strength and toughness better than the old Kevlar. Now we've got to face the problem of globalization. Once this hagfish-slime composite starts being produced, the thing you've got to watch out for will be offshore, substandard knockoffs, which some son of a bitch'll try to sell to our DoD—if DoD isn't awake." He was pulling his gloves back on, flexing his fingers. "So, gentlemen, quality control is the name of the game. Any sublicensing contract is going to have random slime tests written into it, otherwise some cheap bastard somewhere will try to use slime from any kind of fish or other slime-producing creature, like a politician." Freeman glanced at his watch. "Now if you'll excuse me, I have to do my ten-mile run, then catch a plane at SeaTac. I'm supposed to be in Monterey for dinner."

As the Great Russian Coat and legend walked off, Michael Lesand finally found his voice and demanded, "How in the hell does he know all that stuff? Hagfish slime, Durham boats, all that crap?"

"Well," answered the Chairman of the Joint Chiefs, "he

reads and he's done a lot of things, knows a lot of people, inside and outside the service. He keeps current. And—" The chairman paused, looking directly at Lesand. "—I think that's the second time this morning he's made a goat out of you, Michael."

Michael Lesand muttered an obscenity to the effect that he wasn't going to forget it, but his words were lost in the sound of the VIPs' Humvees and other vehicles' engines coughing to life. Dr. Klein was still looking at the vest that Freeman had thrust at him as he passed. The results were even better than he'd expected. The 9mm slugs were so flattened, they looked as if they'd run into—well, a wall of solidified composite of hagfish slime, not penetrating even a quarter of the inch-thick vest.

CHAPTER TWO

YOUNG MICHAEL O'SHEA, like so many of the other two hundred students from all over America who were aboard the new state-of-the-art American Airlines Stretch Dreamliner, was literally on the edge of his seat with excitement. Most of the children, like Michael, had never been near an airplane, and although the bus trip through Manhattan's canyons en route to JFK was a tremendous thrill, now, buckling up for the President's annual sponsored trip for pupils from low-income families, the children were in a dream coming true. Each of the lucky ten- to thirteen-year-olds had been selected from all fifty states for the best oral or written presentation on "Why I'd like to go to London."

Of the other fifty passengers aboard, twenty were teachers in coach with the children, eighteen were in business class, eight, including the Secretary of Education, her secretary, and her public relations handler, were in first class, and four sky marshals had been stationed throughout the plane. Everyone, including the Secretary of Education and her staff, had been closely vetted by Homeland Security, especially anyone of Mid-Eastern descent. Suicide bombers, America had learned on 9/11 and in Iraq, came in all sizes and ages. Seventy-two virgins apparently awaited twelve- and fourteen-year-olds as well as the grown-up martyrs of al Qaeda and its ilk, whose rationale for detonating their dynamite-belted bodies directly on their targets was not simply to terrorize Israelis and Americans but to force countries, almost exclusively democracies, to push Israel to yield land, as it had in Lebanon, land that the terrorists believed was rightfully theirs.

Students and teachers alike had photo IDs around their necks. One of the Secret Service sky marshals, Angela Medved, who had immigrated to the U.S. as a child in her teens, had suggested that four sky marshals might be a little excessive, given that everyone aboard had already been thoroughly "backgrounded" by Homeland Security.

"Hey," Angela had been told, "this is the President's trip, with a high-level Cabinet member on board. So we have more than the usual marshal allocation. Nothing goes wrong. Understood?"

"Understood."

Angela and her fiancé, Rick Morgan, a fellow sky marshal who, because of Secret Service rules, was never assigned the same flight as Angela, had met during small-arms training down in Quantico, Virginia, and had decided that when they were married they'd want kids, but not right away. She had seen too many of her girlfriends exhausted by the time they were in their mid-twenties, bags under their eyes from not enough sleep, and marriages under permanent strain from trying to be the all-American supermom. They were worn out, racing from day care to midnight, balancing careers and motherhood with car payments, a mortgage hovering over them like the sword of Damocles, and what investments they'd managed to put away for the kids always on the brink of a precipitous economy in a world that since 9/11 had become increasingly uncertain.

Even so, both of them wanted children—never mind one girl, one boy. Don't be so demanding, they'd told themselves—they'd be satisfied with two girls, two boys, "whatever," as *Seinfeld*'s George Costanza would say, so long as they were healthy. Then two months ago, while they were still just engaged, it happened. She found out that despite their precautions, she was pregnant. Abortion was—well, it was "a bridge to cross," she said, "if the scan shows up something so serious—"

Rick had responded, "A scan means you already agree with abortion. Otherwise, why have the scan?"

"It does not!" she'd replied tartly. "If you know, then you can plan...special meds—you know, that sort of thing. Anyway, *I'd* be carrying it, not you."

"*It*. Carrying *it*. I'm *half* of it. Don't I get a say?"

That exchange was the beginning of a furious argument that had all but finished the engagement, but they'd agreed to drop the subject for a few days and came back to it with cooler heads, acknowledging that you probably didn't know what you'd do in such circumstances until you were actually in them. "Like combat," Rick told her. "In Iraq we all used to try to figure out what we'd do if this or that happened, but all your preconceived notions—well, things change, Angie."

Angela had remained shaken by the argument, but friends told her that the fact she and Rick had postponed further "discussion" until they'd had time to reflect on each other's viewpoint was a good sign. Marriage was compromise—life was tough enough with what you had to deal with, potential hijackers and terrorists included. Leave the what if's in your life out on the street and get busy, get the best home in a nice suburb—tree-lined—good medical coverage, and go on doing what you had to do.

Right now, Angela was having second thoughts about having *any* kids. The noise from the excited horde of two hundred young "jet-setters," as the head teacher referred to his delighted charges, was ear-throbbing. Several of the first-class passengers were not amused.

"I pay for first class and this is what I get?" asked an elderly, short, balding passenger in 10A. "I should go deaf for buying a ticket?"

"Motrin time," joshed his wife, whose bulk dwarfed him.

"They'll settle down," a petite, curvaceous blond—and transparently unconvinced—flight attendant assured him.

"No," the man replied, looking up at her. "Kids never give up. They keep going and going and going till you're dead."

"He's right," enjoined his wife, her earlier jocularity giving way to spousal support. "It's true, young lady," she told the blond flight attendant. "You worry about them when they're born, when they go to school, when they finish school, when they get married. You never stop worrying."

"I'm not *worried*!" said the husband, turning to her. "I'm *mad*. I save all my life for London, to see my brother—to go *first class* to see my brother—and I'm assaulted by this noise. I live in New York—I haven't had enough noise already? I should get more?"

"I'll have a word with the teachers, sir," the attendant told him. "I'm sure they'll calm down."

"Teachers?" He turned back to his wife. "What do they teach them? They should teach them manners, that's what they should teach them." He looked across the aisle at Agent Angela Medved. "Am I right?"

Angela smiled, a strictly by-the-book sky marshal, her smile apolitical, friendly but strictly "no comment." The old complainant in first class had a point, but his tone was embarrassing several of the other passengers, including the Secretary of Education, Norma Peale, the first African-American woman to hold the post. These people seated in the new condensed foam seat/bed recliners were habitual first-class flyers and for some, if not the Secretary herself, such a plebeian outburst was as unsavory as observing someone trying to sneak into their more plush and sedate domain from coach class. First class was occupying itself with magazines and newspapers, this privileged group feigning unawareness of the FASTEN SEAT BELTS signs and the chief steward's announcement to make sure all seats were in the upright position, hand luggage properly stowed, et cetera. It was a purposely nonchalant contrast to the hyperactivity and noise from coach and that of the loud, complaining man from Brooklyn and his large wife.

"Ladies and gentlemen!" announced the tour leader, a young principal of a grade school in Dayton, Ohio, who was standing in front of the coach section's screen and holding the intercom mike while patting the air for silence. "Ladies and gentlemen," he repeated to the students, "we can't take off until you're quiet!"

A chorus of "Shhs" hissed through coach's 220 maroon-upholstered seats. The image of the cheery-faced, thirty-year-old principal in a short-sleeved blue polo shirt and casual tan trousers, his matching blue Gap jacket draped loosely over the back of his seat, was in marked contrast to the more formally attired airline personnel. "That's better," said the principal. "Now, whether you've flown before or not, you need to watch the screen in the back of the seat in front of you in a moment."

"Where else would they look?" a colleague nearby joked with his fellow teacher.

"You'd be surprised," the teacher laughed, adopting the same holiday spirit.

"No, I wouldn't."

"Now," continued the principal, cabin lights intensifying as the sun disappeared below the skyscrapers of New York, "for those of you who've not flown before, the first thing we want you all to know is that your arms might get tired from flapping them!"

"Sheesh," said one of the other teachers, but the kids loved it. What normally would have been greeted by them with hoots of "Ha-ha!" derision was now accorded a sprinkle of laughter and giggles, even by the would-be sophisticated youngsters excited by their anticipation of the seven-hour flight to London, of seeing the changing of the guard, Buckingham Palace, and the Houses of Parliament, where, one teacher had told them, Britain had made the decision to be the first to stand up and fight side by side with the Americans against Saddam Insane.

"Thank you, thank you," said the principal, bowing to the smattering of applause for his weak attempt at humor. "Second thing for those who haven't flown before is not to be freaked out by the noise of the plane as we taxi down the runway, and the thump of the undercarriage, that is, the wheels, as they're brought up." He leaned forward, reading the name of a ten-year-old fifth-grade student, the beautiful contrast between her white teeth and ebony skin set off by a cherry-red blouse, and asked, "Emily, what's another word for bringing up the wheels, pulling them in?"

"Re—," she began softly, tentatively, "—tracting."

"*Retracting!* Excellent, Emily. Everyone hear that? Retracting."

The principal heard the word "penis," followed by raucous laughter from a gaggle of seventh-grade boys, huddling several rows back, in front of Michael O'Shea, his assigned flight buddy, Tony Rivella from Astoria, Oregon, and the chaperone of the seventh graders, Susan Li.

"Okay, guys," the principal told the seventh graders, "behave yourselves or you get to carry all the girls' luggage." There was more laughter, from the girls, the lights dimmed against the wavy painted turquoise interior, and the Boeing Dreamliner began its full-power run.

"You know, miss," Michael O'Shea informed Susan excitedly, "they call this new plane 'the Porpoise.' You know why?"

"Yeah," cut in Tony. " 'Cause it's supposed to look like one of them smiling fish."

"Yes," said Susan Li, deciding that this wasn't the time to correct Tony Rivella's grammar. "And the way they've painted the inside of the fuselage, that's the body of the plane we're in, looks so graceful, like a porpoise."

"They say," said Michael O'Shea, his eyes sparkling with anticipation, "that this Dreamliner can reach point eight five Mach."

"That's not fast," said Tony. "Not even the speed of sound. This crate's no faster'n a jumbo."

Michael was stymied for a second, and Susan Li felt sorry for him. The gap of a missing tooth in his upper row from a recent Rollerblade argument with a brick wall, together with his crestfallen look, evoked the mother in her—she had a boy of her own—and she wanted to embrace him, hold him. But these days, no way. You didn't dare touch a child. "I didn't know that, Michael," she said instead. "Point eight five Mach. It sounds pretty fast to me."

Michael, rallied by her response, felt emboldened enough to parry Tony's disdain further by adding, "Yeah, and the Dreamliner only needs two engines. Old jumbos used to need four."

"So," retorted Tony, "what if one catches fire?"

"Tony!" Susan Li cut in. "Don't say such things."

Michael O'Shea wouldn't be outdone. "My dad says the airlines have ordered, like, a hundred and fifty Dreamliners and that a Dreamliner can fly on one engine and—"

"You'd crash and burn, man!"

"You two!" Susan scolded them, "stop arguing and watch your monitors."

Tony's aggressive retort to Michael, who was an inherently shy boy, upset Susan Li more than she cared to show. She hated any kind of petty one-upmanship because it reminded her of the mean-minded verbal bullying she had been forced to endure as a Taiwanese immigrant to the U.S.—the daily gauntlet of "slant eyes" and other racial epithets she had run into every day. The worst of such abuse, she knew, was that you never knew when it would be un-leashed against you. You'd just start to feel safe, accepted by your peers, when out of the blue "Chink!" would be hurled at you and you'd feel like melting into the floor. When it was just you and your tormentors, it was bad enough, but ironi-cally that was much easier to deal with than when you were with friends. Even now, at twenty-nine, the memories of the childhood humiliation made her face burn with indignation.

Oh, to heck with the paranoid, no-touching rules. She put her arm around young Michael. "What are you looking for-ward to most, Michael?"

His smile was golden, and it struck Susan then that the boy was starved for affection at home.

"The guards at Buckingham Palace," he said, "with the big bearskin hats."

"Not bearskin!" cut in Tony. "Can't kill bears anymore. It's artificial fur. I read about it."

"Well, before artificial fur came along," said Susan, "peo-ple had to keep warm in the winter with animal skins and fur."

"Gross," riposted Tony.

"Tony Rivella," she said in a tone seldom heard from her, "what is your problem? Aren't you looking forward to see-ing London?"

He glowered up at her. "Yeah."

"Well, what would *you* like to see?"

Tony shrugged. "Dunno. Big Ben, I guess."

She turned to Michael, raising her voice above the high scream of the engines approaching full pitch. "How about you, Michael? You want to see Big Ben?"

"Yes."

"I've seen it in the movies," boasted Tony, but his tone was suddenly less pugnacious.

Susan put her other arm about Tony. "We're going to have a great time. Right?"

Both of them said, "Right." As the Dreamliner lifted off, Susan instinctively held them closer.

Michael glimpsed the buildings of JFK rushing by, the Manhattan skyline in the distance and headlights coming on along the expressway, a wink of one bright light pretty against the purple dusk.

It was the last thing he saw, the missile slamming into the starboard-side engine, fragments penetrating and igniting the wing's fuel tank. The pilot had no chance. The 7E7 plummeted hard right from seventy feet, the wheels not yet retracted, their spinning throwing off burning fuel like a grinding wheel spitting sparks, the fully loaded and fully fueled plane slamming into the tarmac at 122 miles per hour; the time elapsed between the Boeing taking off and it crashing into an inferno, 3.8 seconds. It was 4:48 P.M., Eastern Standard Time.

In Los Angeles it was 1:48 P.M. West Coast time. Japanese Airlines Jumbo Flight 824 taking off from LAX was struck on its port-side number-two engine. At Dallas/Fort Worth, the terrorists, in the final act of simultaneous horror, brought down a Brazilian Air jumbo bound for Rio.

Unbeknownst to the general public, as CNN's anchorwoman Marte Price explained during the network's sensationalist "Triangle of Terror" report on the New York–L.A.–Dallas/Fort Worth hits by the three MANPADS—Man Portable Air Defense System—missiles, modern jet engines and their mountings are built to contain a wide range of explosions. But what had presumably happened in all three crashes, as Marte Price's audience of 14 million were told, by virtue of quickly generated computer graphics and by aeronautical experts, was that shrapnel had probably penetrated the wings, and thus the fuel, which in LAX's case the air traffic controllers saw spewing out of the starboard wing in a plethora of high-pressure leaks, had been ignited by sparking nine seconds later. Exit stairways were deployed by flight attendants on the JAL plane, allowing some people to temporarily escape, even though most of these perished in the flash fire that swept under the fuselage from starboard to port, once the flood of fuel had been ignited, the flames fanned by the brisk San Fernando breeze.

"Tragic though it is," Marte Price continued, "those nine seconds probably saved some of the two hundred and fifty passengers aboard." She paused. "Unfortunately we cannot say that about either of the attacks on the Boeing 7E7 at JFK or the Brazilian Airlines Boeing 777 flight out of Fort Worth/Dallas. For more details of the attack at Los Angeles International, we go to Adrienne Alamada."

"Marte, the scene here, as you can tell, is horrendous. The smell, smoke, and confusion..." Alamada covered her left ear in an attempt to muffle the screaming of sirens as dozens of fire trucks and ambulances sped away from the remains of the JAL 777 Jumbo, only its blackened, smoking tail section and cockpit resembling anything like the remains of an aircraft. "Marte, it's too early for any details, but ground crew who've asked to remain anonymous have suggested that many of the dead probably succumbed from lack of oxygen because of the dense black and white toxic clouds. There have been reports of people in the airport hearing an explosion prior to the crash, but this has not been confirmed."

Some burn victims had mercifully died while waiting on the tarmac for medical attention, which was slow in coming because of what initially had been a paramedics' strike against the city. The labor protest, however, collapsed the moment the alarm bells began ringing in the various precincts, but by the time the fleet of ambulances arrived at LAX, more burn victims, many of them children, had died from shock and/or multiple burns, others expiring en route to area hospitals.

Half an hour later, Marte Price announced on CNN that while precise numbers were not yet available, airline officials had confirmed that there had been at least a thousand passengers and crew aboard the two fully loaded jumbos and the one fully loaded Dreamliner.

CHAPTER THREE

AS THE NATION and the world watched the first reports from Marte Price and Adrienne Alamada, stunned by the three—obviously simultaneously timed—attacks, they heard the usual unthinking comments of survivors who proclaimed that they'd prayed to God—as if those who had lain dying hadn't—and that "He was looking out for me." On FOX, there were near-distance shots of the unidentifiable dead being carted away.

Numbness and sadness momentarily took over the nation, flags at half-mast, forlorn impromptu roadside monuments sprouting overnight. The one image in particular that filled the country with disgust, simultaneously arresting the attention and inciting the rage of everyone—except the terrorists and their apologists—was the black-and-white photograph of three black, charred bodies sitting together, the remains, a coroner said, of a woman, who had obviously been pulling two children protectively to her at the moment of their death. It was impossible to tell until further tests and passenger list verification were completed, but the coroner said he thought that the two children—the trio had been aboard the JFK Boeing 7E7 flight bound for London—were boys. National Transportation Safety Board investigations hadn't been able to get inside the burned-out hulk of the $130 million Dreamliner for an hour and a half, the tangle of superheated alloys and melted materials that had earned the 7E7 fame as the first all-composite-wing aircraft still too hot to approach.

Within hours of the three shoulder-fired missile attacks, during FOX's 10:00 P.M. newscast, it was announced that a group calling itself "Army of Palestine," loosely allied with Hamas, claimed "credit" for the triple attack "against the Great Satan, the United States."

"Army of Palestine, my ass!" thundered retired general Douglas Freeman, punching his TV remote back to CNN.

"Douglas!" came an imperious command from his sister-in-law, who was busily preparing dinner. "I've asked you before, please watch your language!"

Douglas Freeman, the legendary and voluble general made famous throughout the armies of the world for his outspokenness and for what had become celebrated as his brilliant WUA—withdrawal U-turn attack—against state-of-the-art Russian-made main battle tanks in a U.S.-led intervention around Lake Baikal, now said nothing, sitting like a chastised boy, glaring at the TV screen, mouthing an obscenity at CNN's BBC hookup in the Middle East.

"What's wrong now?" asked his sister-in-law, Margaret, a woman who, in her mid-fifties, still possessed the striking beauty of a gracefully aging film star and whom he was obliged to visit once annually, in Monterey, fulfilling a promise to his beloved wife, Catherine, who had died years before.

"Douglas, what's the matter?" Margaret pressed. She knew his silence usually betokened disapproval. "You aren't sulking, are you?"

"Certainly not! What's wrong is that I'm listening to the latest anti-American sh—nonsense from the BBC. They're yapping about 'root causes' again. Root causes for butchering hundreds of Americans, many of them children on these three planes. Canadians have had a free ride for the last fifty years under our defense umbrella. The damn root causes now are the same as the root causes on 9/11—those Arab loonies who hate Israelis more than they care about their own 'martyr' children hate us and the Brits and the Aussies so much, they're obsessed with killing us. Not our military, mind you—oh no, blowing up a plane full of poor kids whose big crime was going to visit London. By God, if I had my way I—"

"Turn the TV off," advised Margaret. "It's bad for your blood pressure. There's nothing you can do about it."

And wasn't that the truth, he thought. He'd done some great work for the government. They knew it, he knew it, but, crises aside, they didn't want him. "A loose cannon!" the State Department had said. "George Patton's ghost," the doves had called him. "Out of control."

Well, yes, all right, he wasn't always that diplomatic, but, goddammit, in the field he was at his best.

Marte Price was back on-screen, but it was a few seconds before he consciously registered her appearance, the general momentarily lost in the reverie of old memories, Marte Price's words unheard as he remembered her breaking the news of how on coming up against the crack Siberian Sixth Armored Corps in the dreadful depths of a minus-sixty-two-degree Lake Baikal winter, he'd ordered his armor to retreat "with all possible speed." Not since the withdrawal of the Marines from the Chosin Reservoir in the Korean War or the withdrawal from Vietnam had the United States seemed so humiliated. But at least the Marines had been true to the Corps' *Semper Fidelis*—Always Faithful—and had refused to leave their dead, and it was a heroic, fighting withdrawal along the valley road from the reservoir, with the Chinese Communists swarming down on the bedraggled American column from the snow-covered hills on either side. Their commander would deny it was a retreat, characterizing it instead as "an advance in another direction." But when the American public had heard during the U.S.-led intervention in the Far East that Freeman—he whose favorite military dictum, like that of Patton, was Frederick the Great's *"L'audace, l'audace, toujours l'audace"*—Audacity, audacity, always audacity—had ordered his armor crews to retreat in haste from the Siberian Armored, there was a similar mood of shame that had not been experienced since the frantic withdrawal of the U.S. from Saigon. As Freeman's M1 Abrams, to the disgust of his tank commanders, fled the Russian T-80s, which, sensing fright, only increased their rate of pursuit through the taiga's deep snow and forest, Freeman had kept asking his meteorological officer for the temperature. The general's action, reported the American division's psychiatrist later, had seemed to fit the classic definition of avoidance behavior under pressure. His apparent obsession with the temperature was typical of people under extraordinary stress, like anxious travelers who, laden down with anxiety about flying, bookings, and business meetings, will suddenly turn all their attention to some inconsequential detail of clothing, where an errant piece of fluff or tiny stain on a jacket is seized upon as a worry bead in order to find temporary refuge from the far more seemingly unmanageable problems at hand. In Freeman's case, the psychiatrist saw the general's obsession with the temperature of the "damn forest" as Freeman's second in command put it, as a classic example of "extreme" avoidance behavior. Several of the U.S. tank platoon commanders were in tears of utter frustration as they were commanded by Freeman to run away, at full speed, from the pursuing Russian armor. Yes, it was true that they were outnumbered by the Russians two to one, but for the Americans, the descendants of the men who fought up the slopes of Mt. Surabachi, fighting Japanese every step of the way before planting Old Glory atop it in the hell of the battle for Iwo Jima, the humiliation of this U.S. retreat at speed, as snow and forest whipped by, was too much. With the wind-chill factor, the temperature hit minus sixty-seven, and while several M1s were taken out by the T-80 hounds despite the M1s' evasive twists and turns, the thermometers dropped to minus sixty-nine, at which point Freeman abruptly ordered his M1s, through his second in command, Bob Norton, to make a U-turn en masse and engage "targets of opportunity." Sensibly, the Russians slowed, so as not to overrun and risk "blue on blue," or, in this case, "red on red."

"What changed his mind?" yelled a tank commander, bringing his 125mm to bear on the hitherto pursuing Russian T-80s.

"Dunno," said his driver. "Maybe Bob Norton shamed him."

But no one had shamed Douglas Freeman. He had sprung a trap born of the kind of attention to detail, to the kind of crucial minutiae for which he'd become known over the years. He knew that at minus sixty-nine Fahrenheit the waxes in the T-80s' more poorly refined Russian lubricating oils would start to settle out, *despite* the heat of the engines. This meant that whereas the American M1 Abrams would keep running, the Russian T-80s' fuel and hydraulic lines at minus sixty-nine degrees would quickly gum up, the waxes like cholesterol-clogged arteries. So that now the American armor made sweeping U-turns in the snow, the full-fledged retreat of only minutes before becoming a full-fledged attack against the Russian T-80s, which were coughing, spluttering, and stopping, "sitting ducks," the T-80s not only unable to turn on their tracks but unable to rotate or swivel their 125mm main gun turrets.

It was a slaughter not seen since the crushing defeat exacted by the Israeli armies against the numerically superior divisions of Arab armor in the ferocious Six-Day War.

Overnight, "Freeman the Runner" had become "Freeman the Fox." But that was years ago, and although he and his SpecFor team of Aussie Lewis, Choir Williams, Sal Salvini, and Medal of Honor winner Captain David Brentwood had done brilliant work since, all over the world and at home in the Pacific Northwest in the world war against terrorism, he and his team were "demobilized" as quickly as he'd been called to serve in crises. For while, like Patton, he had a genius for war, he was, in the words of National Security Advisor Eleanor Prenty and others in preceding administrations, an "unmitigated disaster" in peace.

Though a man capable of deep reflection, Douglas Freeman was in the main a man of action and a persistent advocate of his own ideas. Which was why he was more than surprised now to receive a call from Eleanor Prenty, who, after reading Jenkins's elegant biography of Winston Churchill, found herself repeatedly struck by the differences *and* similarities between Douglas Freeman and England's greatest prime minister. Churchill, like Freeman, at times annoyed others with the pushy side of his personality, but this side was always balanced by an unfettered willingness to dive into danger or, as Churchill's cousin on his American mother's side would have said, "into harm's way" for his country as well as for his personal ambition. But there the analogy ended, for while Churchill brilliantly excelled in politics, Freeman did not. His place was in the field.

Eleanor said nothing about the Churchill analogy, flattery not her strong suit.

"General Freeman. Eleanor Prenty here."

"Douglas, please," he said, switching the TV to Mute.

"Douglas, you've no doubt seen the news?" He could feel the fatigue in her voice.

"I have. Those—bastards."

"Any ideas? I thought I'd pick your brain—pass your ideas off as my own at the next National Security meeting." It was nice of her, he thought, to say that, and a courtesy—it must have been terrible at the White House as the news came in, worse than 9/11 in some ways, three simultaneous widely spaced hits, an east-west-south triangle of catastrophies, the vulnerability not just of New York but of the entire nation on show, which was no doubt, Freeman told Eleanor, why al Qaeda had done it.

"You think there's any possibility it's not al Qaeda?" she asked.

"Maybe a branch plant, like Hamas, but these hits, same time . . . Look back at the attacks on our embassies in Africa, the USS *Cole,* et cetera. Terrorists like the number three. Question is, Ms. Prenty—"

"Eleanor."

"Question is, Eleanor, does it matter what name the scumbags use? We've been hit again."

"You've had a lot of experience combating these people. Any chance that there might be a home-grown element involved? You know, a Timothy McVeigh, Oklahoma City type?"

"No, I don't think so. Right-wing, left-wing nuts may be against the government, but when someone from abroad hits Uncle Sam, they draw together against the common enemy. I'm pretty sure what we're looking at are raghead—offshore terrorists."

"Well, Gen—Douglas," began Eleanor, "I'm glad I picked your brain." She paused. "How's retirement?"

"Dreadful. This goddamned rule of ours that anyone in the military over sixty has to be put out to pasture is nuts. I'm fitter than when I was in my forties. Look at Doug MacArthur. He was seventy when he made the landing at Inchon. And that professor, Barzun, wrote *From Dawn to Decadence* at ninety-three. They still give him an office and—"

"Yes, Douglas, I take your point. But Professor Barzun isn't expected to lead men into battle."

"Goddammit, Robert E. Lee was fifty-six at Gettysburg, and had three horses shot from under him, and—" Freeman paused and took a breath. "Sorry, Eleanor. You've been courteous enough to seek my advice and here I am carrying on like a prima donna."

"Well, Douglas," she said good-naturedly, "you *are* a prima donna."

"Yes, but I'm damned grateful to you for making the call. I appreciate that. I'll put my thinking cap on and if I come up with anything that might be useful to the administration, I'll give you a bell."

"A bell?"

It was a Limey expression Freeman had picked up years before when doing a refresher Spec Ops training session with the elite British Special Air Service SAS at Brecon Beacons in Wales, a course that another American legend, Colonel Charlie Beckwith, a Green Beret captain at the time, had adopted for instructing U.S. Special Forces personnel.

"I'll give you a bell," the general explained to Eleanor, "call you."

"Fine."

"Ah, may I ask," Freeman ventured, "did the Joint Chiefs suggest you call me or—"

"It was on my own recognizance," she said.

"Huh. Well, that's the nicest 'no' I've heard. So, I'm still in the doghouse with that bunch?"

"You're not the *only* prima donna, Douglas. *They* like recognition too."

"Touché! Bye!" he told Eleanor as they ended the conversation.

The point was that Freeman hadn't had any recognition, any publicity, for at least a year. What was it, mused Freeman, that General Simons, a young Turk, a go-getter brigadier general at the Pentagon, had called him in a memo? "Granny Freeman." Anybody over fifty-five in America was relegated a has-been.

"By God—" Freeman had begun as he put the phone down.

"Nice chitchat," said his sister-in-law from the kitchen. Was it a question or a criticism? She had this tone that permanently fluctuated between disdain and bland observation. Freeman was never sure.

"It was the White House," he told her. That should rock her socks.

"I don't like garlic," she replied, ignoring the White House remark, "so I've made a Caesar salad with romaine and low-fat egg. You can fill up on bread rolls."

"Fine," he said, mumbling subversively to himself, *"Making a damn Caesar without garlic!"* Besides, he was a high-protein, low-carbohydrate general, something he insisted on, *used* to insist on, in his armored division's mess.

"What was that about, Douglas?" asked Margaret.

"Nothing," he lied, his sister-in-law one of the few people to whom he found it more expedient, and less troublesome, to lie, something he normally despised, but he'd always found it particularly difficult to deal with what he characterized as overbearing women, unless they were in the military, in the same world. Which had made for his on-and-off romance with the famed, tough-minded, if beautiful, Marte Price of CNN, a woman against whom, many interviewees had concluded, "there was no known defense."

Freeman thought of Marte now as a counterpoint to his sister-in-law, against whom *he* had no known defense and who, on his annual obligatory visit, caused him more irritation than the Siberian Sixth. Marte Price, veteran correspondent of many wars, was outwardly tougher than his sister-in-law, but once the dust of her hard, unyielding battlefield interviews settled, she left the fighting behind, and in Iraq one night had presented a softer, feminine persona in the metamorphosis from khaki, flak jacket, and goggled Fritz to perfumed lace. As battle had raged in the distance, the tough, world-wise face of someone who'd seen and reported on the worst of war took on the gentle smile of a woman who unashamedly confessed her need to receive passion with the same urgency as she was willing to give it. She had taken him by storm that night, giving a new meaning to his axiom of *L'audace, l'audace, toujours l'audace.*

"Was this a planned mission, General," she had asked sweetly in the quiet that had followed their tryst, "or a target of opportunity?"

He had never answered, any reply he might have been formulating stymied by a fierce salvo of Republican Guard artillery. Two hours into a fast U.S. Armored counterattack, the Republican Guard was quickly silenced. But by then Marte was back on air, and in the way that some of the most important questions are put in abeyance by events, Marte had never asked the question again. Had she been asking if he loved her? He didn't know for sure, and if that is what she had meant, he still didn't know the answer. He liked her, of course, but was she, as she jocularly, if basely, put it, a "target of opportunity"?—good sex for a legendary general whose secret was that he was inwardly shy of women unless they, like him, were fellow warriors? And thoughts of his late wife, Catherine, interceded now and then, causing him to question his loyalty. In his soldier's heart he held loyalty as the preeminent virtue, and although it had been years since Catherine's death, he still missed her, despite the fact that she'd liked Jane Fonda even after the actress happily posed for a North Vietnamese photo op, sitting on one of the AA guns they used to shoot down Americans. Freeman had suggested Ms. Fonda should have sat on an antipersonnel mine instead. It was one of the few political arguments he and Catherine had had—something that he and Marte Price had avoided under the most ancient military axiom of "no shop in the mess"—in his and Marte's case, "no shop in the bed."

He'd expected a call from her before or during a commercial break in CNN's coverage of what was fast becoming known throughout America as the "Triple Play." In fact, he had thought it had been Marte calling him, for his "military take" on the attacks for CNN, and was surprised when he'd heard Eleanor Prenty on the line.

"We have to do what the Israelis do," Freeman told the TV. "Hit 'em back. Fast. 'Course, the goddamn namby-pamby liberals'll start whining about root causes again."

"Must you always be so blasphemous?" said Margaret. "Really, Douglas, for a man of your supposed talents, you're appallingly vulgar."

Freeman rose in heat, his anger pumped up not only by what the terrorists had done but by the impotence of his retired status, as well.

"I'm off. This is the last visit, Margaret. I've kept my word to Catherine religiously, visiting you every year. But you are a royal pain in the butt! I consider my duty to Catherine fulfilled."

"A man of your word, I see."

He paused at the kitchen door. "I don't understand you. You insult the hell out of me. You obviously don't like me visiting. What possible reason..." And then she looked at him hard, unhesitatingly into his gunmetal-blue eyes, and her firm, discipline-red lips quivered. In that second Douglas Freeman understood the meaning of her emotional hurt, the tremor passing through her. This real Margaret beneath the always immaculately dressed woman in her meticulously kept house. And he flushed with embarrassment, finally realizing that his sister-in-law's hostility, her often cold demeanor, had all been a front to cover the guilt she obviously felt for having coveted her sister's husband. Like a hitherto blurred picture snapping into focus, the sudden sensuousness of her mouth explained at once something that had always perplexed the legendary warrior—why his sister-in-law had never asked him to stop his yearly weeklong visit, why she hadn't released him from his wife's deathbed request—to "keep an eye out," as Catherine had phrased it, for her sister's well-being. He stood there, guilty of one of the shallowest assumptions of callow youth: that aging invariably erodes sexual desire, that a woman—in this case, in her mid-fifties—could not possibly yearn for the kind of passionate intensity that he and Catherine had known when they were young and that he still longed for.

She was in love—only the quivery lip asking him not to go had revealed it, giving the lie to her usual buttoned-down sense of propriety.

"Stay for tea?" she said, the banal phrase pregnant with import, her normally stern gaze and bearing having given way to a schoolgirlish nervousness, her entire sophisticated frame seeming to have collapsed under the admission of her eyes.

"Thank you," said Freeman gently, as flummoxed as she was about what to say next. "Perhaps later." He paused, and the legendary commander, who had never been known to be at a loss for words, couldn't think of anything else to say other than to make a vague hand gesture toward the living room.

"Yes, of course," she replied, her voice having quickly recovered a tone of indifference. She turned abruptly to the sink. "I'm sorry."

"No, no." He went in to watch the TV again. FOX network was running a special.

"Huh," grunted Douglas, clearing his throat awkwardly. "FOX put out a call for any amateur videos of the planes taking off."

"Oh."

The legend was tapping the La-Z-Boy's armrests nervously. "Ah . . . yes. Got a whole bunch of videos—from parents, friends, and the like, I guess . . . you know, seeing loved—you know, relatives and stuff taking off. 'Specially those children on the President's trip to London, you know."

"That's terrible." It didn't sound like her. Her tone now

had much more warmth and was relaxed, or at least trying to be. Freeman was castigating himself for being so damn inarticulate, three times using the phrase "you know," which he'd always forbidden his officers and men to use, the general opining that it was a sloppy avoidance of the need—indeed, what he believed was the obligation—to be as specific as one could. It was a lazy phrase and one that could cost lives in urgent combat communication.

FOX was airing two video sequences on a split screen, which in one half showed a quarter second or so of the missile streaking toward the other half of the screen, in which he could see the doomed 7E7 at JFK. The plane had reached takeoff speed and had just started to lift when the MANPAD's warhead detonated against the alloy of the upper superstrong wing skin. The strength of the new composite wing, as the FOX Network's aeronautical expert explained, was probably responsible, together with the strong carbon fibers embedded in the 7E7's vertical and horizontal tail sections, for buying the plane's frame a few vital seconds that allowed some of the passengers to exit from the aircraft's port side.

When the expert mentioned "embedded," Douglas Freeman, video-recording the telecast, immediately thought of the "embedded correspondents" in the second Iraq War, and Marte Price in particular. Momentarily he felt guilty, an affliction that rarely even showed up on his mind's inner radar screen. It was as if his sister-in-law could read his thoughts of Marte, of his infrequent but intensely sexual rendezvous with the correspondent.

FOX was rerunning the videotapes obtained to date, one a copy of a video offered to the National Travel Safety Board by a naturalized American Latino in Dallas/Fort Worth who had been filming his mother's departure on the 777 for Rio, another showing the hit at LAX, acquired, FOX said, from an American host of a Japanese exchange student leaving LAX on the JAL flight bound for Tokyo. And there were two videos, bought or confiscated—no one seemed sure—that the NTSB had obtained from parents of two of the boys on what was supposed to be the President's sponsored "trip of a lifetime" for the 220 teachers and disadvantaged students of New York.

FOX, having replayed the videos ad nauseam, now varied their presentation, making up for lack of any more information at the moment by playing the videos in slow motion, resulting in the switchboard at FOX, and other networks who were doing the same thing with the FOX-accredited footage, lighting up as thousands of outraged viewers charged the TV stations of "gratuitous" cruelty to those who'd lost loved ones aboard the 7E7 and the two Jumbos and to those distraught families who were still in the agony of trying to find out whether family members and others had been among the victims of what one announcer on a FOX feeder station referred to again as "the terrorists' Triple Play."

"It's not a game of baseball!" Freeman snarled.

"I agree, Douglas." It was Margaret, the first time Freeman could recall that she had concurred with him about anything he'd said. It gave him a start. Unbeknownst to him, she had quietly entered the living room and sat on the low-slung velour-upholstered love seat across from the La-Z-Boy. He leaned forward during the replay, something suddenly having attracted his attention, so absorbed by whatever it was that he hadn't responded to Margaret's agreement with him about the callow description of the mass murderers' act as a "triple play."

Margaret felt acutely embarrassed. Having finally, albeit unintentionally, revealed her true feelings for her late sister's husband—did Douglas know she'd felt like this since the first time Catherine brought him home?—she now felt the vulnerability that often follows the revelation of one's deeper feelings to another. His only feeling now seemed to her to be one of utter indifference. At the very least, she interpreted his silence as the beginning of the end of any hope that he would continue his annual visits. For a woman whose trademark was absolute control over her emotions, it was the most abject kind of humiliation. And for a woman of such refinement it was as if she'd flung herself at him like some brazen slut. Had he any idea of what she had fantasized about them doing in bed, of what raw sexual desire lay hidden beneath the demure, sophisticated respectability of the mid-fiftyish spinster who had pleasured herself in the lonely darkness of her room, calling his name, biting her arm until the pain smothered her urge to scream what she ached for him to do, to fill her so voluminously that she would swallow and take him until he was bone dry. She had taken courage from a woman, a retired elderly schoolteacher, the very figure of propriety, who, realizing, indeed shocked by, how quickly life was passing her by, had placed an ad in the classifieds in *The New York Review of Books* saying she was attractive, graying, and that she wanted sex, determined to live the rest of her life enjoying sexual pleasure of a kind she had denied herself for so many years.

"You see that?" asked Douglas.

"What?" she asked, her usually more formal, even stern, tone replaced by a new, at least for Douglas, inquiring tone, as if wanting to share his excitement. Or was it alarm? He pressed Rewind to see the entire footage again.

"That missile. The LAX plane. Watch. I'll rerun it."

There was an expectant air in the living room that transcended any unease between them, their momentary sense of awkwardness with each other sidelined by what they were seeing on the TV screen, an event of such moment that, as Bogie had said in *Casablanca,* suddenly the problems of two people didn't amount to a hill of beans. The world war against terrorism had invaded everyone's living room.

"There!" said Freeman, stabbing the DVD's finicky Pause button—she needed a new DVD—quickly rewinding, advancing, stopping the disk milliseconds earlier than he had the first time. The image, however, was still blurry. "A *shoulder*-fired missile," he said, sitting forward on the very edge of the recliner.

In the next few minutes Marte Price had one of CNN's "on call" stable of instant experts talking about a "Stinger" MANPAD—Man Portable Air Defense—missile. Margaret, though little interested in military affairs, had, like most Americans, heard of the Stinger. Anyone who had lived through the Cold War and who had seen the nightly broadcasts of the Russian invasion of Afghanistan in 1979 knew what a Stinger was—a long 5.5-inch-diameter pipelike missile fired from a one-man shoulder-buttressed mount, which for the invading Soviets had the nasty habit of downing their HIND attack and troop choppers that tried in vain to dislodge the Afghan "freedom fighters" from the mountain fastness of the Hindu Kush.

While most of the Stingers the U.S. had issued to the anti-Soviet forces had been used against the Soviet Air Force, the CIA, England's MI6, France's DST, and Germany's BfV, all suspected that there were still stockpiles of unused Stingers. But for Freeman, the fact that the missile he now had freeze-framed on Margaret's outmoded DVD was *not* a Stinger catapulted the danger to the United States and her allies to an unprecedented level.

Freeman zoomed in on the freeze-framed streak, which he could now see was a long, thin missile about five feet in length with a diameter of three inches. "That's not a Stinger! Length's about the same, but the Stinger's thicker. Like comparing a man's wrist to a woman's."

"Does this mean this one's weaker?" asked Margaret. A few hours before, such a question would have been perceived by Freeman as yet another wry jab at his macho vocabulary, a comment to get a rise out of him, but now her tone was one of genuine interest, a question that came out of respect for what Douglas knew.

"Powerful enough," he began. "An Igla, I think. Type 2C—proximity fuse MANPAD." Pausing and zooming the DVD with some difficulty onto the nose section of the missile, he walked up to the screen, thrusting a forefinger at the front of the long, wrist-thick missile. "Can you see this?" If Margaret couldn't, it was unlikely anyone at the White House could. "Like looking at clouds."

"Clouds?" Margaret asked. "I don't—"

"I mean you often see what you are looking for, particularly when the image isn't sharply defined. You know, someone says they see a face, a recognizable shape in the clouds. You look up and you say, 'Oh, yeah, I think I see it.' Guys on watch are sometimes so hopped up with excitement, fear, or with just wanting to do a good job, they see things that aren't really there." He peered at the screen. Without his reading glasses, for which he was feeling his pockets and about which he was mumbling, he furrowed his brow, giving him a distinct Mr. Magoo–like appearance. He was, as he'd tell anyone who'd listen, as fit as many a thirty-year-old marathoner, but momentarily the Magoo-like expression— no doubt a politically incorrect analogy these days, Margaret thought—gave him an endearing, vulnerable look. "Yes," she said, "I understand. People do see what they want to see. But can you give me a clue as to what I'm supposed to be—"

Now she was peering at the frozen image of the missile, following Douglas's finger. But the background was made up of heat waves rising from LAX's tarmac.

"No hints," Freeman said. "You either see it or you don't."

"I'm sorry, Douglas, I can't see—"

"A thin probe, like a thin wire just visible in the nose. May I use your phone? Long distance. I'll use my card."

"Of course." She smiled unabashedly, as if having let her guard down once, she was resigned to go all the way—the new Margaret coming out. "The house is yours."

The general called "Aussie" Lewis, who was the longest-serving member of Freeman's once-elite SALERT—Sea Air Land Emergency Response Team. There was no answer, so he left a message to ring him back.

Next he phoned Sal, Salvatore Salvini, one of Freeman's toughest and most experienced SALERT warriors, who also didn't answer the phone. Freeman glanced at his watch. By now it was about 10 P.M. in Brooklyn. The general left a message on the voice mail to call him. Next he dialed the Washington State number for "Choir" Williams, the Welsh-American who was one of Freeman's ex–Special Forces SALERT.

Choir, who'd been channel-surfing following the reports of the three terrorist attacks, was delighted to hear from his ex–gung ho commander. "Lot of planning on this one, General," Choir opined in his soft-spoken Welsh voice, which could rise to a Pavarotti high C when called upon.

"You mean lots of planning for these *three* attacks," Freeman corrected him. "Particularly given the fact they were simultaneous."

"That's what I mean. Acquisition of the Stingers is one thing, but organizing—"

"They're not Stingers, Choir," cut in Freeman. "Least not from that video from LAX. Looks like an Igla to me. Russian MANPAD."

"Well, whatever they used, it took some planning, right? But DHS'll get whoever launched them."

Choir's easy, informal tone between the ex-NCO and officer, typical of so many ex-SpecFor types, nevertheless annoyed the general this evening. No one was in a good mood, given the tragedy wrought by the attacks, but Choir, uncharacteristically, seemed to be missing the point. Oh sure, have DHS, Department of Homeland Security, go after the scumbags who fired and organized the "Triple Play." Choir was correct there—the meticulous planning necessary to effect three simultaneous attacks on three of what were presumably the most secure airports in the U.S. must have left some kind of computer/paper trail for DHS to follow. Of course the bastards had to be hunted down—that was a tactical, political imperative—but to protect the nation in the long run, Freeman knew that catching the trigger men of the three MANPADs wouldn't be enough, merely a Band-Aid.

"Have you seen any tape on the other channels of the Dallas/Fort Worth or LAX hits?" the general asked impatiently.

"No," said Choir. "NBC's saying it has something coming in from JFK but that could be more shots of the wreckage—howling relatives, usual media-stoked drama."

To anyone else, the Welshman's comments might have sounded callous, but Choir disliked the way news, through multichannel competition, had become "infotainment," each network vying for ratings with the most gruesome footage available. Those CBS-shown shots in '04 of Princess Diana in her death throes were obscene. And he was annoyed with himself for watching. But while normally eschewing the usual sensationalist "film at eleven" reports, he, like millions of other Americans, had been drawn to the tube by the sheer magnitude of the latest attack against his country, his sense of patriotism, like that of so many immigrants, felt more passionately than that of many native-born Americans.

"So what's your take on the transport?" Freeman asked him, the general once again exhibiting his willingness to seek advice from fellow pros, despite the marked difference in rank between the four Special Forces vets.

"Pickup trucks for sure," answered Choir. "Or a flatbed."

Freeman nodded, adding, "Then they left the vehicles?"

"It's what I'd do," said Choir. "Airports' perimeter cameras should have picked up the backblasts, zeroed right in on the vehicle. Dollars to doughnuts, General, none of those lads had beards. No mustaches either. Terrorists have become very careful about that. Still, you'd've thought that our agencies would have been on to at least one of the teams."

"No," said Freeman gruffly, his annoyance not so much with Choir not seeing the long-run problem as impatience with not yet having seen any comparable missile flight tape from Dallas/Fort Worth. "Every damn agency in the country missed the signs leading up to 9/11. One guy, just one, an FBI agent, warned the agency about Mid-Eastern guys taking lessons on how to take off in a commercial jet, but no lessons on how to land it. But the FBI guy's message couldn't be passed on to the CIA because some liberal ass congresswoman had written a law forbidding too much cross-agency sharing of personal information."

Choir murmured his disgust.

"Problem is— Hold on, Choir. CNN's cutting in with more New York tape. I'll call you back."

The pictures were of pandemonium at JFK—police everywhere, pallid-faced relatives being ushered in by walkie-talkie-wielding airport officials, more ambulances. The general felt his cell phone vibrating. It was Eleanor Prenty. "Douglas, the man is desperate for information." She meant the President. "Homeland Security, FBI, CIA—nothing. Absolutely zilch. He is not happy, Douglas. We've spent billions on antiterrorism and—"

"A convertible," cut in Freeman. "Near LAX. Tell our guys to look for a convertible—its hood up. Rope off all motels, hotels, in the area. Have the FBI's garbage can, Dumpster guys sweep for cordite deposits and discarded clothing, especially coveralls. Motel, hotel details should sweep the showers for cordite, sulfur residue, et cetera. The terrorists will try to shower themselves clean of any trace chemicals from the MANPADs. Backblast from those things is the same as a shoulder-fired antitank round. Throws crap everywhere. Discarded goggles are also a giveaway. Look for goggles."

"Hang on, Douglas. I can't take all this down. I'll put you on speaker."

"Fine."

"Before I do, why didn't you call me on all this stuff?"

"Standard procedure. Thought your guys would already be doing it."

"Convertible?" she said. "Is that standard—for terrorists?"

"No, that's mine. I've been watching the LAX tape. The background. A lot of convertibles are there. Hollywood. I think it's a good bet. Hood down, fire, hood up. Ditch."

"All right. That's smart. But have you any idea about what we can do to prevent another attack?"

"That's what I'm working on. Have the Pentagon, NSA— anybody—gotten pics of the missiles' exhaust trails, apart from the LAX video?"

"We're working on that. Trouble I guess is that some people don't know what they've got till they rerun their tapes, take a close look at the background. Some haven't got the equipment to go into the background. Truth is, CNN'll probably have bought them all, see them before we do. Like the Zapruder film of the JFK assassination."

"Your guys should have confiscated them at each airport!" he said gruffly.

"We're doing that. We're not letting any video cameras out of the airport. But have you seen the size of some of those mini video cameras? You can slip them into your handbag."

"I wouldn't know," replied the general. Besides, some of the women's handbags he'd seen could carry enough gear to launch a Saturn rocket. "And," he continued, "they download it to their home computer first via cell. *Then* give you the cameras."

"Yes," said Eleanor dishearteningly.

"Can you send me anything you have?"

"Of course," she assured him, "though some of the gang won't like it."

"I'm not politically correct."

"You have the man on your side on this one."

"I do? Then send it."

He'd no sooner put the phone down and entered the bathroom than the phone rang again.

"Douglas," Margaret called. "A Mr. Aussie Lewis would like to speak with you."

Mr. Lewis. Freeman smiled at the contrast between Aussie Lewis's renowned informality and Margaret's polite form of address.

"Aussie?"

"General. Thought I'd pop around for breakfast first thing tomorrow. Nothing fancy. Coffee and scrambled eggs?"

The general was normally doubtful that the line of an old retiree was being tapped or scanned by terrorist cells, but with National Security Advisor Eleanor Prenty having contacted him, and terrorists, courtesy of bin Laden's millions, equipped with some of the most sophisticated wave-band scanners in the world, he had to be careful and let Aussie know they were not on a scrambler. "No eggs, I'm afraid," he told Aussie, using the old SALERT phrase for "Be careful, the line could be tapped."

"Righto. Just coffee'll do. This product you're intending to buy from us. Is it domestically produced or an import?"

"What was that?"

"I was saying I thought the product you were interested in is an import."

"Can you hear me all right?"

"Fine."

"I'm having trouble hearing you." Margaret, in the kind of informal move she would never have made before she'd unwittingly signaled to Douglas Freeman that she was in love with him, pointed to the cordless phone the general was holding, whispering, "You can turn up the volume."

Freeman nodded but didn't do it. "I'll give you a call later," he told Aussie, "from a call box. Have to get this phone seen to."

"Okay, mate," Margaret heard Aussie Lewis say. There

was nothing wrong with the volume at all—the flat Australian drawl perfectly audible.

Freeman hung up the phone and turned to Margaret. "Thanks, Margaret, but I'm going to make some calls from a public phone."

Margaret looked surprised.

"Ironically," he explained, "a public phone is more secure. I know, probably no one's listening—after all, as far as the Pentagon and the press are concerned, I'm a has-been—but I don't want to run the risk." He smiled at her, looking pensive. "On the off chance someone has been watching me, I don't want you to be in any danger."

"I'm always careful," she assured him calmly, but she was reveling in his concern for her, trying not to exaggerate it in her mind as evidence of some deeper feeling he might have for her. She kissed him on the cheek. "Bless you."

As he left to walk down to the call box by the local 7-Eleven, he saw the blue flickering of TV sets in the houses. It seemed as if everyone was watching the news. Passing by a group of youths drinking and watching a set from a condo balcony he heard "Holy shit!"—the same phrase of alarm and surprise Freeman remembered hearing uttered by a New York fireman witnessing the first hit on the Trade Towers on 9/11.

"Another attack?" Freeman called up to the youths.

"No," one of them answered. "New footage of the Dallas/Fort Worth hit."

"Damn!" Freeman said, and hurried to the call box. As he dialed quickly, he wondered whether Aussie had seen it.

He had. "Nasty stuff," he told the general. "Andra's rewinding the video now so I can watch it frame by frame."

"Fine."

"Andra" was Aussie Lewis's nickname for his Jewish wife Alexsandra, whom Freeman's SALERT team had rescued from the JAO—Jewish Autonomous Oblast—region during the U.S.-led U.N. intervention in what was the old far-eastern USSR when Alexsandra had provided vital intelligence. She loved America, her only real irritation being with those who were naive enough to believe that since the fall of the Wall in '89, Gorbachev, Yeltsin, the breakup of the USSR, Putin, et cetera, Russia had forgone its dreams of empire. There were, she knew, anti-American terrorists in Russia. Didn't her fellow Americans realize that the collapse of the USSR by no means meant the end of Russia's drive for hegemony in the Far East? In the short run, the Soviet Union did suffer an economic and military disaster. But, as after a terrible fire or a great flood, and after having gotten rid of the nonproductive, parasitic elements, the new Russia, doing as Japan had done after the U.S. bombers had destroyed all her factories, was now building newer state-of-the-art manufacturing plants and a computer infrastructure that would allow Russia to regain her power.

Alexsandra viewed all this with a marked ambivalence. She applauded Russia's advance, but she feared the terrorists. It was not just the Muslim fanatics, but the old guard, Communist diehards who, temporarily pushed into the background by the surge of economic activity, were patiently waiting to once again seize the reins of power—with, if necessary, the help of terrorists.

Aussie was watching the rewound tape on frame-by-frame advance while listening to Freeman describe the thin, wire-like probe and other features of what he believed had been an Igla 2C missile, which in 4.2 seconds had ended the lives of 375 people in the LAX attack, and which, with the other two missiles fired at JFK and Dallas/Fort Worth, had now shut down every airport in the United States and Canada, stranding millions, and causing so many cancellations—computer banks literally burned out—that two-thirds of the airlines were facing immediate receivership. The impact on the economy, especially on the airline industry and its dependent industries, was as immediate as it had been following 9/11. But insofar as foreign carriers—JAL at LAX and Brazil Air at Dallas/Fort Worth—were involved, the impact on the airline industry worldwide was far more dire than on 9/11. Indeed, it was such that Alan Greenspan's heir at the Federal Reserve said that to describe the terrorist attacks as having a ripple effect "would be disingenuous, to say the least. Another tsunami," he said, "has hit the American economy. Every single person in America, from newborn to the most aged, has been directly and catastrophically affected in the financial network that binds this country together, from passengers to subcontractors who provide the important services that a modern aviation industry requires."

"Is it another Igla?" Freeman pressed Aussie impatiently.

"No, General," began Aussie, replaying the Dallas/Fort Worth video. "I don't—"

"Don't tell me it's a Stinger?" said Freeman. "One of our own—"

"It's a Vanguard," replied Aussie.

"Damn!" said Freeman. It was a Chinese MANPAD. Momentarily he was back in England, early nineties, at the Farnborough Air Show, the biggest and best in Europe. The Chinese were alarming foreign military observers with the claim that their MANPADs were now much faster, their warheads more powerful, their TARSCAP, or target-seeking capability, vastly improved, even against the latest LAIRCOM—Large Aircraft Infrared Countermeasures—and were also superior, their killing and slant ranges being greater than America's state-of-the-art Stinger. In particular, Freeman, then only a brigadier general, remembered seeing the face of one of India's military reps, the wing commander's eyes widening to saucerlike proportions as he watched the Chinese NORINCO—PLA—industries' rep and a Pakistani general speak excitedly to each other. The Chinese salesman, eschewing the stereotypical reserve of Chinese officials, had returned the Pakistani's garrulous, back-slapping bonhomie in full measure. The salesman had obviously sensed, as the CIA later confirmed, a lucrative sale of a Chinese Vanguard shoulder-fired surface-to-air MANPAD.

"You said it was a Vanguard," said Freeman. "Mark Two or Three?"

"Mark Three D, I think," said Aussie, getting a further close-up with the zoom. "About the same diameter as a Stinger. Dual thrust by the look of the segmented exhaust trail on the video. I'll do an overlay of the video of the airport. Or do you want to do that yourself, General?"

"Can't. I'd like to, but I'm on a landline away from my laptop. You do it. I'll wait."

"Roger, I'm doing it now," Aussie told him. Freeman could hear the clacking of Lewis's PC keys in the background. It was a noise that the general found intensely irritating. An Igla and a Vanguard—Russian and Chinese missiles. What in hell was going on?

As Aussie Lewis enlarged the airport map and superimposed it like a transparent sheet over MSNBC news shots taken from an NBC affiliate feed, he was able to quickly compute the distance back from the black, burning hulk of the jumbo at Dallas/Fort Worth and the island of ambulances, fire trucks, police, and assorted vehicles to the point at which the video had caught the bluish-tinged yellow light that had been the MANPAD's fiery exhaust.

"General, it's difficult to pinpoint the speed, given we can't be sure of the exact point of firing. But given the slant angle on the video, I'd say we're looking at about two thousand feet a second."

" 'Bout the same as our Stinger," commented Freeman. "Mach one point seven."

In fact, subsequent videos that came in—"patched" by the

airport's perimeter security cameras—revealed that the terrorist's firing location at Dallas/Fort Worth was in fact closer than Aussie Lewis's estimate. The information being communicated to the White House by the FBI and Department of Homeland Security was that the missile that had struck the Brazilian Airline jumbo had been traveling at 2,268.5 feet per second. *Mach 2.*

And so, when Douglas Freeman, still relying on the greater security of the pay phone's landline, called the White House and was put straight through to an exhausted Eleanor Prenty, the National Security Advisor already knew the speed. With the ego that, along with moments of unexpected compassion and empathy with his men, had made him such a legendary figure, the retired general felt deflated. Despite his fast work he'd been preempted by the FBI and DHS.

"Well, of course," he told Eleanor, "whatever the speed, the real problem is that there were two types of missiles used."

"Two types?" inquired Eleanor, the previous tiredness in her voice replaced by a tauter tone. "What do you mean?"

"Well, one being Chinese, the other Russian."

The silence at the other end told him either she didn't know there'd been two different types of missiles used, that they weren't Stingers as reported by the press, or that she hadn't grasped the ominous implications.

"Chinese and Russian?" she repeated.

"Yes, ma'am," Freeman told her. "The one that hit the JAL at LAX was an Igla 2C, a Russian-made shoulder-fired surface-to-air missile for pinpoint antiaircraft protection of Russian troops. It's ARFIR-3 capable, that is, against approaching and receding fixed-wing jets, helos, or cruise missiles. Engagement range is between five hundred and fifty yards and three miles. It's also all-airport targeting, which means its optical seeker can outfox antimissile flares and alternate infrared sucker deflectors. The other missile was a

Vanguard. It has a range of seven miles up. At around twenty-four pounds total weight of missile and shoulder-launcher, it's a lot lighter than the Russian thirty-seven-pound Igla."

"General," Eleanor cut in, "these *have* to be terrorist attacks."

"Right."

"Then what's it matter where the missiles come from? I— Hold on, General." He heard her conferring with someone in the background, not clearly but enough to pick up "MAN-PADs...thousand bucks...anyone..."

"General," Eleanor cautioned, "I'm told there are an estimated five hundred thousand MANPADs in existence. Many of them unaccounted for. On the black market. Apparently of all the Stinger missiles we shipped to Afghanistan, we're missing at least forty."

"Forty-eight," said Freeman.

"Well then, Douglas, the source hardly matters, does it?"

"It matters one hell of a lot if you know where they're stored, don't you think? Shut it down. Destroy the inventory."

"Of course," she said, her tone of alarm suffused with impatience. "But if there are over a half-million MANPADs in the world—"

"I believe I know where these terrorist MANPADs are stored. At least the Russian Igla. But I haven't seen the close-up of the Chinese Vanguard yet. I'm calling from a public phone booth. Soon as I get back, I'll watch it on the video of the third attack."

"Can you do it quickly, General?"

What happened to "Douglas"? he wondered. Stress? Or was she in the Oval Office, surrounded by pooh-bahs who would resist any advice from the "outsider" or "Loose Cannon Doug," as some of them called him?

"If it's a good video the networks are airing," he continued, "I should be able to tell you more in an hour or so. I'll have to do some cross-checking in my files." These weren't

computer files but well-thumbed three-by-five-inch Rolodex
Organizer cards, some of them typed, most written on in a
scrawl so appalling that when his second-in-command, Norton, had first seen them during the Russian campaign he
thought it was some kind of ancient Sumerian hieroglyphics,
the scrawl including symbols that subordinates referred to
impolitely   as   "chicken   shit."

"Surely Russian missiles come from Russia?" said Eleanor.

"I'll call you as soon as I confirm my suspicions," he
promised.

Back at Margaret's house, he found her watching CNN.

"Worst of all," CNN's Marte Price was saying on her
"Target America" special, "is that all three airliners were apparently equipped with antimissile defenses." She was talking about Northrop Grumman Corporation's LAIRCOM, the
Large Aircraft Infrared Countermeasures System. From the
background panel of instant experts, a talking head elabo-
rated to the effect that the countermeasures relied on a modulated high-intensity laser beam that had been touted by
industry experts as state-of-the-art. The LAIRCOM's laser
beams, he added, had had a better than 95 percent success
rate in trials, the system's laser beam blinding various MAN-
PADs, including the U.S. Stinger's missile "seeker," that is,
its guidance system.

"None of these missiles," said a painfully puzzled aeronautical guru, "should have reached their target."

"I guess," said one of the other experts on the panel
"they're making better missiles." This otherwise banal line
amid the numbing reruns of the amateur videos was seized
upon by the detail-starved networks as both an explanation
for the American public and a challenge to the administration.

FBI, Homeland Security, NSA, CIA, and all other government security and defense agencies were stymied by how
such MANPAD technology could have become so advanced

and so hidden from U.S., British, and other friendly agencies whose agents were supposedly at the forefront of antiterrorist intelligence.

Upon hearing the expert's nonchalant response, Eleanor Prenty called Freeman again and asked him what he thought about the prognostication.

"I think he's probably correct," said the general and, though careful on Margaret's home phone not to mention the missiles he'd identified to Eleanor earlier from the phone booth, he added casually, "If so, the product we're talking about is being held in a very secure place. If we find out where they are—"

"General," Eleanor cut in, "FOX is broadcasting another video from JFK. Stay on the line." He did and, while waiting, clicked to FOX, feeling a moment of empathy for the President, knowing that, contrary to public belief, the Chief Executive of the United States seldom if ever had enough hard intel to make a 100 percent clear decision. All his perks notwithstanding, the President, like most other folk, including generals in the field, sometimes had to make tough decisions without having as much information as he'd like but was forced to react by the unyielding pace of the market and pressing national security concerns.

The new FOX video from LAX was the clearest yet, with the alert photographer, whoever he or she was, having the smarts to immediately reverse the left-to-right direction of the camera that was following the missile's yellow streak, filming back right to left immediately after the hit. Where the bluish-tinged yellow smoke trail ended was the point of firing. The missile's speed could be accurately put at Mach 2.2.

While he was still on hold with the White House, Freeman's cell phone rang. It was Aussie. "Have you slowed down the JFK tape?"

"No. I just got back to the house. Margaret's been taping. Why?"

"Video shows *four* canards on it, General."

"A Stinger?" said the general, visualizing the four steering vanes.

"Mach two point two? Dunno. Got me beat. But one eye-witness on the freeway who was going out to LAX said the missile, whatever it was, was fired from a pickup truck. He also said the 'launcher' had a kind of— Just a mo, General." Freeman could hear Aussie calling out to Alexsandra. "What that bloke call it, Andra?"

Freeman heard her in the background. He loved the sound of her Russian Jewish accent, had ever since the moment they'd got her out of the JAO.

"He zed," intoned Alexsandra, "it had like two metal ears on ze front—like sluts."

Despite the tension on the line, Aussie couldn't help but laugh. "Slats, not sluts!"

"Zat's what I said, metal sluts."

"Sounds to me," Aussie told the general, "like it was a box antenna. Like a Stinger's."

When Freeman reran the JFK video and slowed it frame by frame, he could see the blurs of three of the flight guidance canards, or steering vanes, the fourth hidden by the angle of the missile's flight path to the amateur photographer. He also glimpsed the slatted, "boxy" antenna. It could have been a Stinger, but again the angle revealed only part of it. He had a prodigious memory but there were so many different types of MANPADS and their subspecies, SHORADS, Short Range Air Defense Systems, and VESHORADS, Very Short Range Air Defense Systems, designed to answer every infantryman's dreams of a quick, light, "fire and forget" antiaircraft missile, that he knew he'd have to consult his scores of computer and old Rolodex files. The worrying detail—the part that didn't fit the Stinger profile, given the evidence of a full air sock, that is, a head wind at JFK at the time—was the Mach 2.2.

As Freeman and Aussie were considering the possibilities on the general's cell phone, he heard the White house line go dead. Must've been accidental.

He was correct. In the excitement of the White House receiving an on-the-spot discovery by the NYPD's JFK detachment, Eleanor's aide, in trying to contact the Pentagon, had killed the Prenty-Freeman connection. She rang back within minutes. "General, I'm sorry you were cut off." She sounded breathless. "NYPD have found what they believe is a missile launcher. LAPD have also found one near LAX."

Freeman wasn't surprised. The moment you unleashed a "fire and forget," you ditched the launcher and walked, as Oswald had done after he'd fired the shot at President Kennedy, though the general was astonished by the number of people who, though they didn't know the difference between a rifle and a toy cap gun, naively believed that Oswald was the only shooter. In any event, Freeman was in no doubt that all three airliners had been downed by shoot-and-scoot teams. Another launcher would probably turn up at Dallas/Fort Worth.

"Painted blue?" he asked Eleanor Prenty.

His know-it-all nonchalance annoyed her. "*Blue?* I don't know. Why?"

"Ever since the attack on the Israeli Arika plane in Mombassa back in '02, terrorists have been painting the launchers blue, the PDC, practice designation color, for all U.S. MANPAD launchers when dummy warheads are being fired. So," Freeman continued, "if any other—real—U.S. troops had seen the blue-colored launchers, they would have thought they were just more practice dummy warheads."

"Hold on," she said sharply. There was a ten-second wait as he heard her ask someone, "JFK and LAX launchers, yes—were they both blue?

"Yes," she told Freeman, "apparently they were."

"Shooters might have been in U.S. Army uniforms," added Freeman.

"So zero chance of finding the shooters or the launchers?" said Eleanor.

"Not necessarily." The general was ransacking his memory for MANPAD hits. In Afghanistan against the Soviet, the U.S.-Stinger-supplied mujahideen had brought down 270 aircraft, and they weren't big 7E7s or jumbos but agile close-air support attack helos, including the highly maneuverable Soviet Hind gunships and fighter aircraft. For the mujahideen there had been no need to jettison the reusable launchers, but for terrorists audaciously attacking American civilians in three of the nation's biggest and most heavily populated airports, ditching the launchers of course made more sense.

Then he recalled an attack by Chechen rebels on the sleek, updated international terminal at Moscow's Vnukovo Airport. He clicked the mouse to bring up the file on his laptop but remembered the details of the attack before the computer had it on-screen. The crucial point had been that though the Chechen terrorists had fired MANPADs, they'd ditched the launchers and vanished. How? Freeman went to the NYPD's overhead traffic cam on the expressway and saw the gridlock of traffic—none of it moving except for police and security vehicles—their reds, whites, and blues flashing frenetically all around JFK's perimeter.

"I've got it," he told Eleanor, recalling the details of the Chechen attack. "They're hiding out in a safe house close to the airport—waiting until the hullabaloo dies down and…" Switching the computer screen back and forth between the NYPD cam window and the Chechen file, he suddenly announced to Eleanor, "Chechen terrorists were belted," by which he meant they had had dynamite belts beneath their battle tunics, as Iraqi Shiite "martyrs" had later armed themselves against the Americans in '03 and '04. "And they could be in NYPD uniforms."

"Shit!"

"I don't want to depress you further, but from the firing point position I saw on the video—"

"Which one?"

"The one with the eyewitness—guy who thought it was fired from a pickup. The point of firing looks close enough to the airport that they could be changing clothing *in* the airport."

"My God!" said Eleanor. "It's a zoo out at JFK."

"Not to mention LAX and Dallas/Fort Worth," said Freeman.

Eleanor Prenty knew from her experience of crises involving airport delays that passengers would put up with it overnight, but then would start demanding that they be put up in hotels, be transported back to the city. And there'd be added pressure from delivery trucks and taxis, and toilet facilities would be overloaded. "By the time there are enough cops to cope," she told Freeman, "it'll be like a sieve of escape hatches out there."

"Those two discarded launchers," Freeman said. "Have we got their MIDs?" It was obvious she didn't know what he meant, and so he added, "Manufacturer's identification numbers. Without them you can't keep track of inventory in a factory. Do we have them from the launchers?"

"I don't know. But I'll find out."

In fact, the FBI field forensic lab was already examining the launchers for MID numbers. It had proved helpful in the past—the same launcher used in the near-miss against the Arika Airlines' Boeing 757-300 of November '02 had been used in other attacks.

"If we can find out where the launchers came from," said Freeman, "we could pay it a visit."

"The President's already determined to do that, but we've had so much stuff coming in, I don't know whether anyone's determined the actual source, even if they've got those MID serial numbers. My God, Douglas, how are they getting them into this country?" Eleanor asked exasperatedly.

"Through slimeballs like unlicensed arms dealers."

"I'll press the agencies for the serial numbers."

"If I can be of further help . . ."

"Don't worry, Douglas. The Pentagon might have exiled you; I haven't."

He was at once gratified and humiliated that his only conduit as a "retiree" to the halls of power was not via his reputation, his *past* reputation, as a gung-ho leader of Special Forces in America's defense, but only through the goodwill of Eleanor Prenty. A *civilian*.

"I appreciate what you said," responded Freeman, then said good-bye, his tone, one of a forgotten champion, noticed by Margaret—who, getting ready for bed, passed by in her robe, beneath which she was wearing a brand-new translucent pink nightgown, of a kind that her mother would have condemned as "blatant." And Margaret would have agreed, but the awful carnage of today, the sight of the black, smoldering heaps that only seconds before had been hundreds of human beings pulsating with life and hope, had been an epiphany in Margaret's life, provoking a determination to no longer simply exist, to vegetate in a lonely world of restrained, reined-in spinsterdom, but to cast off her uptight, buttoned-down feelings of guilt about the love she'd felt for her sister's husband all these years. Catherine was long deceased. Anyway, wouldn't she have wanted Douglas to be, well, comforted? Margaret felt it was time for *her* need to be comforted. And today they had broken the ice, through the deep freeze she had built up between them, but she was afraid that now that the ice of her guilt had cracked, she would be—well, she would be humiliated.

She said good night. He was still working at his laptop but gave her a smile. "Good night, Margaret. You've been a great help." After all this time, it was as if he'd kissed her.

"Don't—," she began, quickly aborting the phrase "stay up too late" and instead encouraged him. "Don't forget there's lots of food—in the icebox."

He laughed. She smiled, but was nonplused. "What's so funny?"

" 'Icebox.' It's—such an old-fashioned term. I like it."

"You do?"

"I do."

"God bless," she said, and went to her bedroom. "Icebox," she said softly. Well, she wasn't going to be an icebox. She searched in her dresser drawer for a small six-by-one-and-a-half-inch square white box purchased in a moment of fantasy years ago in an out-of-town drugstore. She took the tube of viscous liquid from the box and, removing her robe, admired her figure in the mirror—full breasts, firm tummy and bottom, front *and* side-on beneath the slinky film of pink silk. "Not bad," she dared whisper, "for an old-young girl of fifty-five."

Beneath the covers she squeezed a bead-sized drop of the K-Y lubricant on her right index finger and, careful to replace the tube's screw-on top so as not to get any on the sheet, she slowly applied it, working it in gently. She couldn't fit a minnow in there. One of those dreadfully sex-obsessed women's magazines—*Cosmopolitan,* if she remembered correctly—at the hairdresser's had had an article in it about how virgins needed to use one of those "things" to widen the entrance.

It seemed such a lot of bother, but then sometimes alone in bed, or working alone in the garden, alone on her daily walk, she just ached—there was no other word for it—she ached to have a man inside her, hard and gentle and forceful until . . . until what she'd never known from a man would happen. How so-called modern women would laugh at her, she thought, a woman so traumatized by a fundamentalist upbringing that even satisfying yourself was such a mortal sin that she had always felt guilty—you had to save yourself, wait for marriage. She *had* waited—fifty-five long, aching years. Dear Lord, wasn't it time? The awful vision of the dead from the plane crashes was before her, their lives ended, snuffed out like candles. Life itself was so tenuous—you never knew. If Douglas walked through her bedroom door, she'd cast her bedcovers aside and be blatant for once in her life. He could do what he wanted with her. He would be her lover. Her first.

The very thought of the word "lover" made her catch her breath, her eyes closing, then wide-awake in fright. The article in *Cosmopolitan* said you would need to insert one of those wax things daily for a week or two, or use your fingers with some lubricant, to ensure you were wide enough, because if the skin tore, it would hurt like the devil, as too many honeymoon-nighters had apparently discovered, a terrible way to start a relationship—and worse, put the man right off. Surely her lubricated fingers would serve to—

She tried to relax. Of course he wouldn't approach her tonight. What was she thinking? They'd just broken the ice. Besides, he'd be too busy trying to help track down the unspeakable creatures who had murdered all those children and other passengers at JFK, at Los Angeles, and down in Dallas/Fort Worth, hundreds of people who'd been alive only hours before. Tomorrow she would go see a doctor—no, not her usual MD, but someone, a young woman doctor perhaps? No, a married middle-aged doctor, who could advise her. Surely there must be a quicker, more modern way to widen herself than one of those things *Cosmopolitan* talked about. Ugh.

The phone rang and she glanced at the clock on her bedside table. It was just after midnight as she picked it up. She heard a man's voice—an Australian accent. "The products' MID numbers—" Margaret replaced the phone.

In the living room, the kitchen's cordless phone beside

him by the laptop, Freeman was pressing Aussie Lewis for details. "What's the problem?"

"Scuttlebutt from my buddies at the Pentagon is that there's a jurisdictional scrap going on between National Transportation Safety Board investigators and the FBI over who has primary responsibility for detecting serial numbers."

"For God's sake!" thundered Freeman. "What are those suits doing? The President's spent millions with Homeland Security, trying to get those wankers to stop competing against each other and start cooperating. Pride, Aussie, pride cometh before a fall."

"You got it," agreed Aussie, thinking of another adage, something about the pot calling the kettle black. Freeman's legend, like Patton's, was based on solid and, at times, brilliantly unorthodox tactics, such as the famous Russian tank-oil maneuver in the U.S.-led NATO mission in Siberia. But the legend was also built on an ego and a pride that, like Patton's, thrived on media-fed public acclaim. What was it General Omar Bradley, Patton's onetime subordinate, then his superior, had once said about the legendary Patton when his Third Army had broken out of the heavily fortified bocage, the hedgerow country in Normandy, slashing through the Nazi defenses? "Give George a headline and he's good for another hundred miles."

"Where do you think the product is coming from, General?"

"Don't know. If we catch any of those bastards maybe we can have a little *talk* with them."

"Roger that," said Aussie with feeling. "I'd like to have five minutes with one of the bastards. I'll keep in touch. By the way, General, no need to be hesitant about what we're saying on the blower anymore. The networks are all yakking about MANPADs."

Freeman had no sooner put the phone, or "blower," as Aussie called it, down than he was thinking again about the MANPADs' backblast. He immediately called Eleanor

Prenty, explaining to the National Security Advisor something that the mujahideen and later the anti-U.S. Taliban had never had to do in Afghanistan: change clothes after firing their MANPADs. The terrorists' drill, having fired their weapons in such a high-density area, would be first to dump their launchers and disappear into the airport crowds, as he'd already told her; then they'd probably try to shower down before they donned their replacement clothing, in order to get rid of any scent of cordite, sulfur, et cetera, lest a K-9 dog squad sniff them out at the airport.

The general advised her to order NYPD and their counterparts in LAX and Dallas/Fort Worth to immediately shut off all water flow to airport shower stalls, detain anyone who was found using one, and go over them and the washbasins with the police's handheld NBC sensor. Even if the terrorists had dumped the clothes they'd used while firing the MANPADs, the backblast was so pervasive it was like passing another vehicle on a dusty road with your windows open; particles wedged themselves into ears, nostrils, and especially in your hair. Even if their hair was shampooed, the particles could still be detected in trace amounts by the handheld sensors and, if necessary, analyzed by spectrometers either in the FBI's portable field labs or in Homeland Security's downtown forensic labs.

The order from Eleanor Prenty was out to all three airports within two minutes, and within another seven to ten minutes—it taking longer because of the endless corridors at Dallas/Fort Worth and an argument over who had first call on the electric carts, federal or local police—dozens of astonished, irritated, and some downright outraged citizens, most already fatigued by long flights from Alaska and South America, found themselves being ordered out of executive club and public coin-operated shower stalls into Immigration holding rooms, where they were being "swept" by NBC sensors and searched—some would complain violated—by no-nonsense AO, all-orifice, examinations.

Meanwhile, all waiting passengers, air crew, and airport staff were being sniffed by K-9 squads. At Dallas/Fort Worth, two Guatemalans, seeing the dogs approaching, made a dash through a packed waiting lounge for the nearest exit, police running after them, converging on them. One of the pair, a dark, mustachioed man in his early twenties, stopped and threw up his hands. The other, an older man, held a tubular map case close to his body with his left hand, one end on the floor, his right hand grasping the tube's other end, which seemed to be either a screw- or pull-up top. "I have bomb! Nobody move!"

Nobody did, except for a terrified elderly woman who made to get up from her waiting-lounge seat but couldn't un-aided. A cop eased her back into the seat. "Don't worry, ma'am. Just stay still. It'll be fine. Just stay still."

"It's a bluff!" an FBI agent on the periphery of the over-crowded waiting lounge whispered into his voice-activated shirt-button mike to the just-arrived SWAT team, which had been swiftly summoned from patrolling the airport perimeter. "Ten to one he's carrying dope."

"You certain?" came the SWAT team's CO's response.

"Not a hundred percent."

"Then we do it by the book. Bomb squad and negotiator are en route. Tell this guy someone's coming—we'll work it out. How's he look?"

"Like they all do, sweating like a pig." The agent held up his hands and called out to the Guatemalan, "Just relax! We're gonna work this out, okay? You understand? We'll work it out."

"Nobody moves," shouted the Guatemalan.

"Nobody moves," the agent assured him. "Absolutely."

The other Guatemalan with his hands up wasn't moving,

but he was talking rapidly to his partner in Spanish. But one of the words he used was "SWAT," so then the one with the map case told a half-dozen passengers to "come here." Most of them were taller than he. He told them to stand face-out in a circle about him, and told his ring of hostages, "Anyone turns around, anyone touches me, the bomb goes. You understand?"

Everyone understood, and it meant that for the SWAT team moving quickly, quietly into the airport, it was going to be virtually impossible to get a head shot—or any other shot, for that matter. Now the other Guatemalan, seeing how his buddy had brought temporary immunity with the threat of a bomb, got cocky, put his hands down, and moved over to his map-case friend.

"Shit!" said the FBI agent into his wrist mike, a profanity that would never have been condoned in Hoover's day. "His accomplice is getting a ring of more people around them. Now we've got double trouble. Who's our negotiator?"

"Ralph Fiennes," cut in the SWAT commander. His real name was Ralph Fine but they called him "Fiennes" because he had the same lean build and intense eyes as the movie actor.

"We don't want him," snapped the FBI agent. "We need casual cool with these two, not Sigmund Freud."

"Here he is," cut in the SWAT commander from behind a ticket counter. "He's riding a cart. No necktie—looks like he's gonna do his casual serious bit."

Fine was undoing the top button of his shirt. "This place stinks like a locker room. Everybody's sweating. Where's the bomb squad?"

"En route," the SWAT commander told him. "What's the matter? *You* sweating, Mr. Fine?"

"Just a little," Fine said. "It's hot. You think you might get a shot at him?"

"Dunno, there's a lot of people around him."

"Around *them*," cut in the FBI agent. "Don't forget the second guy."

"I won't," said Fine. "We'll know more when—"

"Hey!" shouted the second Guatemalan. "Those cameras. Turn those stinking cameras off."

"They *are* off," said the FBI agent.

"No, they're not," said Fine, alighting the cart about thirty feet from the ring of terrified hostages, his body language that of a golfer approaching the nineteenth hole, his eyes, however, never moving from the Guatemalan with the map case. "We'll duct-tape 'em—the cameras. How's that?"

"Yeah," said the one with the map case. "You do that. Duct-tape 'em right now."

"That wasn't any help," said Fine, talking to the FBI agent who was standing off to his right. "You lying about the cameras. Makes them nervous. Let me handle this. You go over to that newsstand and get some tape, plastic carrying bags, anything, to stick over those security cameras. Stand on someone's shoulders if you have to!"

"It isn't a bomb," said the FBI agent. "He's a druggie. Saw the sniffer dogs and panicked. Nowhere to run."

"You might be right," said Fine. He looked over at the one holding the map case. "I'm Agent Fine. Mr.—?"

The Guatemalan hesitated. "Gonzales."

"What do you want, Mr. Gonzales?"

"I want you should get a plane for me an' my frien'. Right now. These people come with me—us—to Cuba."

Ralph Fine scratched his head. "That's going to take a little while to organize, Mr.—"

"Bullshit! I wan' that plane. Honda jet, eh?" The Honda Executive jets had displaced the Lear as a status symbol. "Half an hour," he added. "Half an hour." His friend whispered to him. "Yeah, an' two million dollars!" The friend whispered to Gonzales again, who nodded eagerly, his voice infused with bravado. "Yeah, an' no dye, no sequential noombers. You understan'?"

"I understand, Mr. Gonzales, but you don't," said Fine, his arms unfolded unthreateningly, his hands clearly visible, to show he wasn't holding anything. "We can get you the plane, but the money—that's two hours minimum, Mr. Gonzales."

"Bullshit. *Half* an hour or these people are gonna die. You understan'? *Half an hour.*"

"Impossible," said Fine calmly. "An hour, we can do it."

A putrid smell invaded the air, a not unusual occurrence in a group of hostages terrified that they were going to die.

The two Guatemalans conferred. "Okay," said Gonzales. "One hour maximum. You understan'?"

CHAPTER 4

IT WAS 4:00 A.M. at Margaret's house in Monterey when Douglas Freeman saw the *CNN Headline News* story of the "alleged" bomber in Dallas/Fort Worth. Marte Price, looking her usual unflappable sexy self, even at this late hour, revealed—in the absence of visuals—that the two "Central Americans," believed to be either Guatemalan or Honduran, were rumored to be holding a map case that they were claiming was a bomb. Freeman tried to get through to the CNN newsroom to speak to Marte during a commercial break.

"General who?"

"Douglas Freeman, General Douglas Freeman." These kids, he mused, didn't know squat about American history or any other history. He recalled the latest "National Geographic" test given to eighteen- to twenty-four-year-old high school– and college-educated kids throughout Europe, the U.S., and Russia, asking them to identify ten countries on a world map. The U.S. kids came second last. And the present generation's knowledge of history, of their own country's history, was even worse. If they knew squat about the Civil War, they sure as hell weren't going to remember *him*.

"Douglas?" It was Marte on the line. "I've only got thirty seconds till I'm back on air. What's up?"

"Marte, that map case this nut at Dallas/Fort Worth is holding. I need to know how long it is."

"How long—oh Jesus, you think it could be another

shoulder-fired—amber light's on, Douglas. Gotta go. I'll try to find out."

"Don't broadcast it. It'll freak everyone out."

"And a bomb wouldn't?"

She was right. Hostages at the airport'd probably feel safer if they thought it was a missile. A missile doesn't blow up on the spot. It had to travel before exploding. Hell, it didn't matter; the waiting room in question at the Dallas/Fort Worth terminal was tightly packed, including the protective double ring of hostages. Shrapnel alone from a missile fired in such a confined space and hitting a wall would cause carnage. Freeman's indomitable pop-up icon in the margin of his new laptop was smiling, bowing in joyful obsequiousness, informing the general that he had mail.

The e-mail was from Choir Williams, in response to the general's e-mail informing Choir about the general and Aussie identifying the Igla and Vanguard missiles.

"Police, Homeland Security, et al.," wrote Choir, "are saying that they're looking for three-man teams. But the missiles you and Aussie have ID'd—a Chinese Vanguard 3D and a Russian Igla 2C—are *one*-operator MANPADs. We maybe should be looking for two-man teams at each airport? A spotter-driver and a shooter. What do you think, General?"

Freeman shook his head in admiration at Choir Williams's observation, and while he waited for CNN to take a commercial break so that Marte could call him back about the size of the map case, he forwarded Choir's conclusion directly to Homeland Security while keeping one eye on Marte. She was easy to watch, had a figure like Margaret's. Both examples of women who, to borrow a self-righteous yuppie phrase that he'd grown thoroughly sick of, had not only "worked out, eaten right," but had also protected their alabaster skin from the ravages of the sun.

He was tired, but wanted to wait for Marte's call or e-mail about the length of the Guatemalan's so-called map tube be-

fore he informed Eleanor Prenty that the airport at Dallas
Fort Worth might have another MANPAD on their hands, or,
just as likely, an empty MANPAD-launcher case, because if
you were a terrorist and had fired off a missile, surely you
would have already dumped the case, like the launchers
found at JFK and LAX?

The general moved quietly through the living room, past
the vase of hothouse roses and into the kitchen to pour himself another coffee. It was the best Columbian java he'd ever
tasted. Margaret ground the beans with the same thorough-
ness with which she did everything else. Dangerous stuff—
so velvety, not a trace of that iron-filing detritus crap they
brewed in every church basement and military camp in
America. Margaret's coffee was so smooth, you'd drink
three or four cups before you knew it. Keep you up for a
week. Strange thing—while standing there looking out at the
dark, star-spangled sky, he experienced a psychological phenomenon he'd undergone before, following long stretches of
high-tension fatigue at HQ or in the field—the more dry-
eyed exhausted you were, pumped up with caffeine, the
harder your johnson would become. He'd once asked his division's chief surgeon about it.

"Quite common, General," the doctor had told him.
"Nothing to worry about."

"I'm not," Freeman had responded. "Just surprised. Would
have thought fatigue—you know, long hours—would send
the dragon into rest mode."

"Sometimes," the doctor conceded. "But any kind of stim-
ulant can pump it up stiffer'n a cucumber—no letup. In combat, as you well know, Douglas, it shrinks to nothing. Same
with your anus, right? Pucker factor. But after, the tension
inside has to get out."

Now, watching Marte Price on CNN, Douglas, sitting back
in the recliner, felt the cucumber starting to ache.

Margaret appeared with more coffee, the flickering television's light silhouetting her momentarily, her perfume washing over him. "Everything all right?"

"What?—oh, yes," he said, straightening up in the sofa and pressing the remote's Mute button. "I'm sorry. Did I wake you? Meant to keep the noise down."

"No, no, I don't mind," she said, adding, "but I'm worried about you," before realizing she'd violated her own noninterference rule. He was a big boy—a legend like Douglas Freeman didn't need a nanny, for goodness' sake. He could see he'd kept her awake but had obviously attributed it to his networking rather than realizing the truth, that her tossing and turning had been occasioned by her worry and excitement. She feared that somehow all these missile attacks would take him away from her, to ensnare him in yet another of his sudden trips "abroad," as he used to euphemistically describe his sudden Special Forces deployments to Catherine. Margaret knew Douglas wasn't liked by jealous colleagues at the Pentagon, but in times of national crisis—such as Bosnia, 9/11, and the two Iraqi wars, reserves were badly needed from the pool of retired officers and National Guard personnel.

There was a moment of silence, Margaret sitting down beside him on the sofa, the images on the TV a collage of JFK, LAX, and Dallas/Fort Worth. "The country should have been prepared for this," Freeman said. "We should have seen it coming." He gave Margaret an enigmatic smile. "I'm an old Boy Scout. Be prepared."

Margaret inexplicably, at least to Freeman, blushed. "Be prepared" had been a phrase she'd read over and over again in the embarrassing but helpful *Cosmopolitan* article on what every virgin should know—a ten-step guide on how to best prepare for one's first—nonpainful—sexual encounter.

She was worried about whether her long-suppressed desire for intimacy would be thwarted by her embarrassing lack of preparation "down there." Oh Lord. She recalled the poem about the salmon: "... to ponder with his dying bubble, 'Why is sex so damn much trouble?' "

Marte didn't call. She was broadcasting yet another story from a bystander who'd seen the SWAT team going into the Dallas/Fort Worth terminal, Marte obviously having decided to run with a "possible bomb" story—whether the bomb was in missile form or not. News was news. She was concluding her newscast with "... the tube, which looks like a map case"—still no pictures, she was obviously on a phone feed—"is reportedly about five and a half feet long."

"Damn!" said Douglas. "Launcher length."

"What can they do?" Margaret asked him.

"Us or the Guatemalans?" he asked her.

"Us."

"Good question." Freeman paused, drawing on his past wisdom as a commander. Like Montgomery who went to sleep once his 8th Army's thunderous and momentous six-thousand-gun barrage at El Alamein had begun against Rommel's Afrika Korps, Freeman knew there were times when you could do nothing more than wait and see what happened. Whether, come the morning, his advice would once again be sought by the White House—or rather, Eleanor Prenty—or whether he would merely be thanked and sidelined while the younger West Point "desert smart Turks," as the Iraqi war veterans were called, would take over the field, moving fifty-five-plus grandpas like himself politely, or not so politely, to the bench, he didn't know. It was time for bed.

He saw Margaret gasp—it had been an entirely unintentional reaction, as one might respond to seeing a close friend with their teeth missing. But in this case it was the unexpected sight of the bulge in his trousers, which simultaneously evoked shock and excitement.

"I'm sorry—" She blushed. "—oh dear, I'm so sorry—" Then she fled to her room. He turned the TV off, and the next moment was standing by her door.

"There's nothing to be sorry about. It's the oldest compliment in the world." He paused. She had never heard him speak so gently. "May I come in?"

She began to speak but couldn't, the covers drawn tightly about her. He touched her hand. She was wide-eyed, heart racing.

"I'll be gentle, Margaret."

"I—I don't know. I've never—I mean . . ." He saw tears in her eyes as she said, "I'm not prepared. I want to, but—oh, Douglas, I'm so embarrassed, I—"

He sat down on the edge of the bed in the peach glow of her bedside light. "I don't have to go in, if that's what you're worried about. We can still enjoy each other."

She had no idea what he was talking about—or perhaps she did. Those wretched magazines . . .

"If I do anything you don't like," he said, "anything—I won't do it. I won't hurt you."

No, it was too much, she thought—the awkward physical details, the paraphernalia. It wasn't supposed to be like this at all. Those people, the young women in the films, always made it seem so simple—you just did it! No fidgeting nervously, naively, with lubricants, sponges—she'd been too mortified to ask the druggist. But now it was all too overwhelming. Everything was happening too fast, but along with her heart pounding—so clichéd, she thought, but it *was* pounding as though about to burst from her with her desire—she saw the picture again of the black, smoking debris of the hundreds of dead, the huge engines blackened and twisted, just sitting there on the runway. He drew her toward him and she murmured with pleasure, her throat so parched, she was barely audible. "Please, be gentle."

"I will," he promised.

He lay beside her, talked softly to her, held her without once moving his hands beneath her waist, now and then caressing her silk-covered breasts, her jasmine perfume insistent and seductive, and in their quiet he could hear the sound of gulls and foam-crested breakers thumping hard on the Monterey shore.

It was perhaps no more than fifteen minutes. But to the general, ever impatient for action, it seemed like an hour, his right arm crooked comfortingly about her neck aching from cramp. In a sniper's hide his arm could have stayed immobilized for hours. Was he getting old, or was impatience the catalyst for his pain? No, he wasn't getting old—it had been the same on his first date a half century ago, his arm around the girl at the Roxy movie theater. He didn't want to take it away, for fear she might think he was tiring of her—but sufferin' catfish, he no longer had any feeling in his arm. What even a legend, all right, an *ex*-legend, would do to get his rocks off! He could tell she was worried about how they could do it and he instinctively knew she wouldn't let him use his hand "down there." But if he didn't move soon, his trigger arm would radiate into lockjaw.

"Sweetheart," he told her, "lie on me, honey." It was more instruction than request, and before she knew it he had extended his arm down her side, rolling her atop him. Immediately she felt the hardness of him against her and he began a gentle to-and-fro motion, his member sliding easily back and forth on the slinky rustle of silk. She was in awe of the sensation, completely devoid of pain, no tearing, no mess. There was only the contact of their two bodies and the hardness that she wanted to be even harder as she now, to her astonishment, became the driving force, waves of ecstasy building, swelling, like a giant surf, reaching such voluptuous crests of hitherto unexpressed emotion that she knew, God willing, it would crash in an uncontrollable release, her lover pacing it, timing it, so exquisitely that she heard a voice—hers—imploring, "Now, now, now!" her grip about him so powerful as they climaxed he could feel her fingernails clutching his neck and shoulder with viselike intensity

as she shuddered, again and again, and cried what the satiated general knew were tears of joy, his own mixed with
hers.

For a full half-hour, caressing her, kissing her breasts, he
told her truthfully how wonderful she'd been and how, when
time allowed, which, given his sidelined military status,
would be plenty, they would spend as much time together as
they could. She spoke about going for long, lazy walks together by the sea.

He knew she loved the sea, Catherine had told him that,
but now Margaret told him about the sense of eternity, the
sense of peace it gave her, the sea so reassuring that she
didn't feel insignificant by its vastness but rather felt her soul
was part of it. Freud, she told Douglas, called it the "oceanic
feeling," the sense of oneness with everything and everyone
around you.

"But I don't want to walk by the sea," he said. "I want to
stay here with you. Forever." It was a moment so magical for
her, her satiation so complete, she suddenly felt sad that it
would end. Douglas said nothing. She murmured, and soon
fell asleep in his arms.

Slowly, with all the care he would have used extricating
himself from a booby trap, he slipped his battle-scarred arm
from beneath her and started quietly toward the bathroom.
He stopped, retraced his steps, and, adopting that "I'm not
here" technique that hide-and-seek children instinctively
know and soldiers relearn and refine so as not to give away
their presence, he unplugged her bedside phone and, once in
the bathroom, used reams of toilet paper and quietly ran the
faucet, rather than use the shower, whose noise might waken
her. In the kitchen, he closed the door and turned the volume
on the cordless phone way down before he poured two large
breakfast glasses of juice, noiselessly searching the cup-

boards for a breakfast tray—she'd be as ravenous and thirsty as a SpecFor warrior back from a snatch and grab.

The kitchen phone rang as he dropped bread into the toaster. "Freeman."

"Morning, General." He'd expected it to be Aussie Lewis or Choir Williams, but it was neither. The line was a bit fuzzy. "Sal here, General."

"Oh—hello, Sal. Sorry, didn't recognize you. What've you got?"

"I got a call from Aussie. He and Alexsandra have gone down to some fucking Wal-Mart sale. Furniture and—"

"Don't you bad-mouth Wal-Mart, you Brooklyn hick," the general joshed. "Wal-Mart's got stuff on shelf that takes quartermasters two years to get!" It was true. SpecOps had often gotten "off shelf" stuff from commercial outlets that the Pentagon bureaucracy would have taken months to procure and for which it more often than not paid exorbitant prices with taxpayers' dollars. Especially for electronic gear.

"My apologies to Mr. Wal-Mart," said Salvini.

"So Alexsandra's buying patio furniture," said the general. "Is that why you called me?" He grabbed two eggs and held them under a lukewarm faucet so they wouldn't crack when it came time to start boiling them.

"Aussie just e-mailed me. One of his mates at the Pentagon says all three discarded launchers—you ready for this?—are North Korean MIDs."

Initially the general was disinclined to believe it, yet if there was one leadership outside that of al Qaeda that would have the balls to openly attack the United States—or rather, be crazy enough to openly give al Qaeda MANPAD launchers—it would be the oxymoronically named *Democratic* People's Republic of Korea, whose "Dear Leader" Kim Jong Il was as much a psychopath as Kim Il Sung, his equally crazy American-hating father, who'd started the Korean War all by himself.

"You said all *three* discarded launchers. I thought only *two* have been found."

"No, three. Just found one at Dallas/Fort Worth. All have North Korean manufacturer identification numbers," continued Sal. "But it's an Igla launcher from JFK. A Russian-made launcher, which means a Russian-made missile. 'Course, I know that doesn't mean dick in terms of where it came from. Any terrorist or dictator with the bread can make the things under license. Same as we sublicense our aircraft parts—everything, that is, except the wings."

"Well, I can tell you one thing, Sal," responded the general in the understatement of the morning, "those DPRK serial numbers aren't going to go down well at the White House."

"President's gonna go ape," said Sal. "First North Korea's been taunting us with their nuclear WMDs and my Pentagon buddies say they're already making Chinese and Russian MANPADs under license from China and Russia. It's a shopping bazaar for terrorists over there, General."

"Well," said Freeman, "I know what the Koreans'll say— that they manufacture the MANPADs under *sub*license, same as we sublicense the Stingers made in Germany. Whoever buys them, it's not North Korea's problem."

"Yeah," said Sal, "but the Krauts don't sell our Stingers to terrorists. 'Sides, the President'll have to do something. These attacks can't stand. 'Specially not now after this Guatemalan thing."

"What do you mean?" asked Freeman in alarm.

"You know," said Sal. "On CNN. FBI agent, or maybe it was the SWAT guy, ran the Guatemalan and he fired the friggin' thing. Must have had it wired to bypass the trigger circuit. An old terrorist trick in case they get caught in transit. Over twenty killed and wounded, glass and blood everywhere."

"My God!" said Freeman, switching on the small kitchen

TV. "You're right, Sal. We're going to have to launch a major payback on this one. Problem is exactly where?"

"Wherever the MID numbers take us to in North Korea," said Sal. What the hell was the matter with the general? Salvini wondered. Sounded as if he'd been laid—*dopey*. It was a word Salvini had never thought of before to describe the general, even after he'd reportedly "embedded" CNN's sexy Marte Price.

"In a way it's worse than 9/11, Sal. I don't mean in the number killed or airlines involved, I mean the triple play these bastards have been able to pull off, thousands of miles apart."

"That's what I mean," said Sal. "If we can't catch all the terrorists that slip into the country, we have to at least take out their source of supply."

"Of course," the general agreed. "But where in North Korea? Dammit, it's the size of Alaska."

"I know," said Sal.

CHAPTER FIVE

DOWN IN THE White House's situation room, so often erroneously, if sensationally, described as "the war room," the President, with full concurrence of the Joint Chiefs and an exhausted Eleanor Prenty, had indeed decided on a retaliatory strike, the kind they'd so often condemned the Israeli government for during the Palestinian Intifada's suicide attacks against Israelis. But as with most of the Israeli public, the Americans were infuriated by this murderous attack against their own civilians, so many of them children, the public in no mood for half measures, endless fruitless gabfests in the *United* Nations General Assembly or Security Council.

Doves at the State Department argued forcefully, along with the French, Germans, and Belgians, that there was no evidence it had been a North Korean attack, only that North Korean–*made* launch equipment had been used. Indeed, the *New York Times* editorial argued that the attacks could well have been by al Qaeda or any other group that could just as well have used stolen U.S. Stinger missiles. The paper suggested that the post-hostage situation at Dallas/Fort Worth might reveal some vital intelligence that had not yet been discerned that would *not* implicate North Korea. Such intelligence, the paper contended, would avoid the possibility of a "nuclear exchange," which, given the treaty of friendship between North Korea and China, could quickly escalate into a full-scale nuclear war, notwithstanding Russia's de facto associate membership in NATO. Yes, the U.S. could expect immediate help from Japan, at which North Korea had already fired nuclear-warhead-capable-missiles to demonstrate that it could strike Japan at will.

The *Atlanta Journal-Constitution*, on the other hand, made much of the "strained relationship," to put it mildly, between Tokyo and North Korea's capital of Pyongyang, citing how Kim Jong Il had ordered the kidnapping of Japanese off Japan's bathing beaches over the past forty years by North Korean special forces. These Japanese abductees had been on a beach one moment, disappearing the next. Taken back to North Korea by submarine, they had been forced, by threat of murdering their families back in Japan, to train North Korean spies on how to infiltrate Japan's large Korean workforce. It was a technique, the *Atlanta Journal-Constitution* pointed out, that the North Koreans had borrowed from Japan's wartime use of Japanese immigrants to Hawaii, these spies having relayed vital information to Japanese headquarters for the stunningly effective attack against Pearl Harbor.

The *Washington Post* weighed in with an editorial that doubted the likelihood of the North Koreans being involved, knowing as they did what had happened to terrorist groups who dared to blindside America on 9/11. With this in mind, the *Post*, one of the most powerful newspapers in the world, advised caution. Meanwhile, the *Wall Street Journal,* which since the 1990s had become America's most widely distributed and read newspaper, stated something that for it was uncharacteristically radical, arguing

There are times for action. Caution stayed President Clinton's hand when he'd been given the precise coordinates of Osama bin Laden's motorcade in Afghanistan. Instead of giving his CIA field officers the "Go" signal to attack with pro-American Afghanistan fighters, he said no; he thought there would be an international uproar if Osama bin Laden was assassinated. This is not a time for fear of international uproar; this is a time for America to strike, not with recklessness but in our good time wherever the terrorist perpetrators and their bases can be found.

It is our view that insofar as the launchers found at JFK, LAX, and Dallas/Fort Worth were clearly North Korean, whoever the terrorists are, the base or factory from which these missiles came must be found and destroyed, even if it takes us years—as it did following Libya's destruction of Pan Am flight 103 in 1988 over Lockerbie, Scotland.

In addition to the appalling loss of lives, from those of our children so viciously murdered aboard the 7E7 at JFK to those who perished so horribly at LAX and Dallas/Fort Worth, these three cowardly acts of war against civilians constitute an acute blow to the heart of our economic well-being. That prescient man George Orwell, long before he wrote his prophetic warning against the growth of totalitarian states, cautioned that "freedom essentially means the freedom to move to and fro across the surface of the earth" and warned us that, rather than adopt what he called the "sit on your bum and do nothing" philosophy of all those well-meaning but hopelessly naive pacifists, the fanatical totalitarian minds of the kind that assaulted this country on 9/11 must be fought against.

We do not propose the use of a nuclear threat against terrorists, but at this moment we need a Churchillian resolve, for whether or not these deadly attacks against America have been launched either directly by their perpetrators or by proxy, those responsible must be dealt with without compunction. We of course need time, perhaps months, to prepare, but inaction on our part would signal nothing less to our enemies than weakness, and only encourage further attacks.

*   *   *

As the battle for public opinion in the press and amongst the talking heads, such as Marte Price on TV, raged, opinion on the street was equally divided but no less passionate. In the White House's basement situation room, however, there was by contrast a somber calm. Two decisions had been made by the President. The first, based on the fact that the CIA had determined that all three discarded launchers had MIDs on them that indicated a warehouse on the outskirts of the North Korean coastal town of Kosong, was to attack the warehouse.

"Why," posited Air Force General Lesand, "don't we just bomb the hell out of it? One B-2 out of Diego Garcia and we could obliterate the damn thing."

"Excuse me," said Eleanor Prenty, her National Security Advisor voice authoritative but testy with fatigue. "Who is it you'd like to declare war against, General? Just North Korea or China as well?"

"I—," began General Lesand, his tone already defensive.

"Have you any *idea,* General, any *idea* at all, of what the political implications would be of an air attack? What a bombing attack, an invasion of air space, would mean for us on the most highly militarized peninsula on earth?"

"I wasn't suggesting a massive bombing," said Lesand. "One laser-guided BLU—"

"One hand grenade, General," Eleanor snapped. "One hand grenade dropped by a U.S. plane on North Korea could precipitate a full-scale war against South Korea, which, might I remind you, is barely eleven miles from Kosong. And over there on the demilitarized zone between South and North Korea, hair triggers and tempers are the order of the day, every day."

"What's the difference between a bomb and, say, a—"

"A Special Forces attack?" suggested Eleanor.

"Well, yes," replied Lesand.

"General," said Eleanor, "covert attacks by our special

forces, those of our allies, and those of the terrorists are happening even as we speak. They won't make the evening news. But any kind of invasion of *airspace* in what the guys over in State call the 'China Arc,' that is, everything from Hunchun in northeast China off the Sea of Japan past the Korean Peninsula to the big Chinese naval base at Qingdao on the Yellow Sea, could precipitate a general war between the United States and China, let alone North Korea. We cannot risk violating North Korean or Chinese airspace, as it is, and we sure as hell can't go dropping bombs on them. Besides which, we need hard evidence of MANPAD storage at Kosong. Bombing won't help us get that. It's out of the question. The Chinese military leadership went slack-jawed when they saw how easily we knocked out Iraq's air defense in the '91 war. Suddenly they realized that their cold-war theory of massed tanks and troops couldn't overcome Western technological expertise, so they've had a big push on for early warning air defenses. As you know, General, a Stealth bomber may have no bigger radar signature than a sparrow, but the ChiCom's new coastal Sa, or Kill, radar, could get a lock on it and that is all the evidence Pyongyang and Beijing need of an enemy air attack. Besides which, whether a bomb is dropped by Stealth or non-Stealth airplanes, a bomb announces its arrival."

"So," cut in the Air Force Chief of Staff, "you're talking about sending in Special Forces."

"General Lesand," explained Eleanor, her patience running thin, "a bombing attack caught on ChiCom radar will be on CNN in half an hour and in the U.N. General Assembly tomorrow. The political ramifications are—"

"Okay," said Lesand. "So what are we doing, sending in a Special Forces company?"

Eleanor and the others looked at the President.

"I agree," said the President. "Drop them in, do the job, and get out. Not too messy but messy enough to get the job done."

* * *

The second decision, on which there was also unanimity among the Joint Chiefs, the President, and Eleanor Prenty, was that the White House must disavow any intention of doing what it had decided to do—namely, to attack the warehouse from which, it was believed, the MANPADs had come and where others were stored. It was situated ten miles north of the DMZ, or the demilitarized zone, that had separated North and South Korea since the armistice had been signed at Panmunjom on July 27, 1953, at the end of the fierce three-year-long fighting that the Useless Nations had declared a U.N. "police action." In fact, the fighting between North Korea and the U.S.-led U.N. alliance had been a bitter full-scale conventional war. An armistice was signed, but it was only that, an armistice, a ceasefire, the two countries remaining technically and at times literally at war since 1953, so that any attack anywhere in North Korea by U.S. forces, large or small, ran a high risk of initiating full-scale warfare. The President was prepared to take that risk—as JFK had done during the Cuban Missile Crisis—but his second decision was that everything must be done to allay North Korean suspicion of any such impending retaliation by the U.S.

"It won't matter," said the Air Force Chief General Lesand. "It'll be like Iraq. Whatever we say, they'll be expecting a hit. They'll be on high alert."

"They're always on high alert," countered Marine General Taft sharply.

The President's eyes searched the room. "Can you do it? That's the question, gentlemen."

"Casualties could be heavy, Mr. President," cautioned Lesand.

"I mean Special Forces. In and out. Can we do it?"

"Yes, sir," said Taft.

"All right," said the President wearily. "Anything else?" He was as exhausted as everyone else.

"Mr. President?" said National Security Advisor Eleanor Prenty, albeit tenuously. "May I suggest we call on Douglas Freeman for some out-of-house advice on this one. He's very knowledgeable about this MANPAD stuff."

"Fine with me," said the President easily. "Gentlemen, any objections?"

"He's very opinionated," put in Lesand. "Troops used to call him 'PR'—Patton Resurrected."

"I know," said the President. "And they used to say he's the spitting image of George C. Scott, but the other political party in this country used to call *me* an obstinate son of a bitch."

"They still do," ventured Eleanor Prenty gamely. The ensuing laughter subdued the high tension in the situation room, but only temporarily.

A Joint Chief's career, like that of any other executive officer, was not enhanced by disagreeing with the boss, nor was it advanced by being a sycophantic yes-man if you had serious reservations about a president's decision, in this case attacking what most armed forces field commanders considered one of the most, if not *the* most, dangerous places on earth.

The danger that both the Clinton and Bush administrations had been most concerned about was that with North Korea's harvests failing several years in a row, over two and a half million of its people would face starvation. The situation was made worse by the North Korean government's insistence on spending 31.5 percent of its gross domestic product, as compared with South Korea spending only 2.9 percent of its GDP, on its armed forces. As a result, North Korea's military belligerence was fast approaching what the CIA and the Senate Intelligence Committee designated a "use it or lose it" situation, that is, a quick, overwhelming invasion of South Korea to get secure food supplies, the NKA leadership seeing this as a concomitant reason for its desire to dominate the whole peninsula.

South Korea's capital of Seoul lay only twenty-five miles south of the ten-foot-high barbed-wire and mine-infested DMZ, a two-and-a-half-mile-wide scar that ran for 148 miles from coast to coast, all the way from China's Yellow Sea in the west to the beaches fronting the Sea of Japan in the east.

The Air Force Chief of Staff pointed out how this meant that the South Korean capital was well within range of over nine thousand North Korean heavy artillery guns, five hundred of them specifically aimed at Seoul. And that the abundance of food and industry in the relatively rich South Korea, one of the Asian economic miracles, made it a prime target, in many analysts' eyes, waiting to be attacked by the North. A Special Ops "in and out" would make a political point, Lesand agreed, but to even invite gung-ho Douglas Freeman to give his *opinion* could be a spark that might quickly turn the President's idea of an "in and out" payback raid into a brushfire that would swiftly engulf the entire Korean peninsula.

Lesand also reminded the President and his National Security Advisor that just as the Wehrmacht had kept detailed files on Patton, Eisenhower, Montgomery, and the other "stars" of the Allied powers, all North Korean brigade intel units maintained detailed profiles on the U.S.'s leading lights past and present, which would include Freeman.

The General of the Army also spoke against seeking any advice whatsoever from Freeman, driving home to the President just how extraordinarily volatile North Korea was.

The President knew both men had a point. American soldiers manning the DMZ with their South Korean allies and the North Korean guards had glared at each other 24-7 at the Panmunjom "truce village," where absurd rituals of pettiness, manifestations of the hatred between the two sides, had occurred daily. In one instance, the North Koreans had sawed off several inches from the legs of the chairs on the

U.S. side of the negotiating table so as to make their U.S. counterparts look small and silly. And when North Korean guards, deliberately and, they thought, undetectably, came to the negotiating tables with stubby-stocked AK-47s hidden under their jackets in clear violation of armistice rules, the Americans, pretending not to notice, prolonged the meeting while having the room temperature ratched up to well over a hundred degrees, thoroughly enjoying watching the North Koreans' acute discomfort as the profusely sweating stone faces of Kim Jong Il's officers endured the inferno rather than removing their jackets and losing face. In 1976, North Korean guards, enraged by two young U.S. officers felling a tree near a North Korean machine-gun guard tower, went berserk and beat the two young Americans to death with ax handles.

"Since the armistice was signed in 1953," said Taft, "theoretically ending the police action that killed over 33,000 Americans and 2.5 million Koreans, continuing 'incidents' along the DMZ have killed over 1,500 Americans and Koreans. It's a tinderbox, Mr. President. I agree something has to be done. We can't stand by and let them get away with the murder of over a thousand Americans in these MANPAD attacks, but Douglas Freeman, who, I admit, has one hell of a lot of experience in such missions, is a loose cannon. You can ask him anything about MANPADs and other state-of-the-art equipment—he does keep up with the technology, I grant you that—but strategically speaking, as I say, he *is* a loose cannon."

"I agree," put in the CNO (Chief of Naval Operations). "He's been a good man in the past, but this is a new century. He still thinks old school. If you ask him, he'll probably recommend we invade the entire country."

But Eleanor Prenty valued loyalty. Douglas had been a well of information when she needed it, surrounded as she was by the Joint Chiefs who, she knew, almost to a man disapproved of a woman having anything to do with military decisions. The President saw the look in her eyes—his wife got the same irritated look when some of his older male advisors feigned polite interest.

"Well, let's at least hear what he has to say," said Eleanor. "He's sure as hell not going to talk me into anything against your collective wisdom, gentlemen. But after all, he's done a stint in Korea, right?"

"He *did*," confirmed Lesand, while emphasizing the past tense.

"Good," said the President. "Get him on the blower, Eleanor."

Lesand thought the President's use of "blower" was particularly apt for the ego-driven Freeman, and added, "I'm sure he'll have something to blow about." There was a ripple of laughter in the situation room as Eleanor dialed.

CHAPTER SIX

SURELY, MARGARET THOUGHT, she was still in her postcoital dream. The epitome of the American soldier, the kind of man for whom a baby boomer's concern over the thread count of a bedsheet would seem incomprehensibly effeminate, was bringing her breakfast in bed: "soldiers" of toast set in a star pattern radiating out from her blue-and-white windmill-patterned Delft china eggcup. And as well as receiving a large glass of freshly squeezed orange juice and a cup of fresh coffee, there was one of her hothouse roses on the breakfast tray. The rose, though having been quickly decapitated and plunged, rather than arranged, into an eggcup, nevertheless retained its fragrance.

"How sweet!" she said, sitting up, hurriedly fixing the pillows behind her with one hand, clutching her pink nightie close to her with the other.

The kitchen phone was ringing and Douglas thought it would be Aussie or Sal.

It was Eleanor Prenty. Naturally, she couldn't speak to him about the upcoming and necessarily highly classified SpecOp against Korea. The White House, she said, meaning herself, appreciated his expertise and readiness to help with the MANPAD "incidents."

"MANPAD *attacks*!" he corrected her. His immediate correction of her use of "incidents," typical of his outspokenness, showed the lack of the kind of diplomatic finesse that had resulted in General Marshall in 1944 giving Dwight Eisenhower command of D-Day rather than Ike's fellow West Pointer George Patton. Patton, despite his superior command of the language of Lafayette as well as an encyclopedic knowledge of Caesar's chronicles, couldn't overcome such linguistic habits as referring to his Soviet allies as "commie sons of bitches"—to their faces. But if at times Freeman was as direct and as rough with the language as a drill sergeant to a recruit, he could be elegant in speech and manner if the mood took him. Most important to Eleanor, as National Security Advisor, he was also smart.

"Douglas," she asked, "I'd like your opinion on something. I'm sending someone over from an office in Monterey for a chat. Strictly verbal." He knew she meant the FBI.

He wasn't fooled for a second. Maggie Thatcher and Indira Gandhi aside, the fact, as Douglas Freeman saw it, was that women were far more reluctant to commit bodies to action than were men. For most women, like Catherine, God rest her soul, and Margaret, intuitively wanted, *believed,* there could always be peaceful resolutions. A sexist view, he told himself, but true. Yes, there were female fighter pilots, naval aviators even, and damned good ones, such as those on Admiral Crowley's *McCain* carrier battle group, but they remained the exception that proved the rule. Most women didn't like to fight, and Eleanor, he could tell from her tone, her firm grasp of realpolitik notwithstanding, wanted to be sure of something, which Freeman suspected had something to do with the ever-rising public clamor for a Freeman-like "in, hit, out" op. She needed moral support.

"When can I expect your courier?" he asked Eleanor.

"About noon your time in Monterey."

"Very good. And Eleanor ..."

"Yes?"

"I appreciate you bringing me in from the cold."

"Oh, Douglas, you're not in exile."

He almost said, "Sure as hell feels like it sometimes," but that was nosing into self-pity country, and that, in the general's eyes, was as contemptible as being a yuppie thread-counter.

"I haven't had breakfast in bed," began Margaret, "since..." She paused, dabbing her lips with the paper-towel napkin that Douglas had made into a sort of triangle and plopped near the edge of the tray. "I can't remember when," she continued joyfully. "You're so gallant."

She knew she would never forget the unselfish way in which he had lain with her *after*. In almost everything she'd read or heard about sex, the man so often just rolled over or left. Or snored.

As he removed the tray, telling her someone was coming to the house at noon, she started. "My glory!"

"I'm sorry," he said, recalling how giving Catherine such short notice of an impending visitor had always jolted her into a cleanup frenzy, with expectations of her having to prepare a first-rate lunch into the bargain. "Don't worry, sweetheart," he told her. "I'll take him out to lunch. You won't have to—"

"No, no," Margaret said. "You don't have to be sorry." He had completely misunderstood her reaction. She was staring at his pajamas. It was as big as it had been last night. "Does it take days to—well, you know..." She giggled. "To go down?" She was blushing in her surprise at his size, but enjoying it.

"It's hard to get it down," he said, smiling, "when there's such a beautiful woman around."

There was a strained silence; then suddenly she beckoned him, open-armed. "Oh, Douglas, I've never been so happy. I didn't imagine—"

"Shush," he said, and this time threw the bedclothes aside with abandon.

She was thrilled and alarmed. "I haven't showered, I haven't—"

"To hell with showering," he told her. "I want to smell you, every part of you—I want to consume you, every inch of you."

She drew him to her with such violence and speed, it excited him even more and, lifting her translucent nightie, he began kissing her thighs, moving quickly from one to the other and then, suddenly, shockingly, she felt his tongue in her, at once hard as steel, soft as velvet, its fierce probing and sucking of the warm juices between her legs sinking her into paroxysms of pleasure, her head lolling side to side in a surrender so wildly complete she knew she'd do whatever he wanted. She cupped his hands on her breasts, crying, arching her body, and begging him to go further, deeper, praying it would never stop. The thought, albeit fleeting, of him leaving her, going away, was an unbearable torture. She wouldn't let him.

CHAPTER SEVEN

AT THE WHITE House, the press conference was minutes away, the President's press officer, Melvin Spinner—a name made in hell for a White House press officer—quickly briefing him on a Gallup poll that revealed the American people's major concern was the presence of terrorist sleeper cells within the United States.

The President met the problem head-on in the media scrum: "This administration is doing all we can to flush out these terrorist cells, but, as this latest outrage against the American people has clearly demonstrated, it's the weapons they are using that pose an equal danger."

"Mr. President," asked the *New York Times* reporter, Steve Loren. "There's a rumor in the intelligence community that the missiles used to down the three planes are indisputably North Korean. Can you comment on that?"

"This administration doesn't formulate policy on rumors, only on facts. As I'm sure you can appreciate, Mr. Loren, the debris caused by such attacks makes it extremely difficult to identify the actual missiles used in the launchers we've found, and their country of origin. It'll take time, possibly several months, to make that precise determination, if indeed we can find an identifiable weapon part in the rubble."

"Excellent!" said the Chief of Naval Operations, watching the telecast on the Oval Office TV.

"Yes," agreed the Army Chief of Staff Kruger. "This way,

those bastards in Pyongyang won't expect a hit for about a year."

The other Joint Chiefs, the Air Force's Lesand and the Marines' General Taft, also approved of the President's adroit political—indeed, military—sleight of hand.

"Eleanor," said the CNO, "I suggest we arrange a leak in a few days that we suspect the launchers are from Iran, or Syria. Give our North Korean thugs an even greater sense of security."

She nodded. "We should feed it to Loren at the *Times*. Show him one of the Syrian launchers we captured in Africa."

It made Eleanor uncomfortable, lying to the press, and she only ever did it when absolutely necessary. Now, any reservations she might have had were squashed by the need to avenge the mass murder of so many Americans, in the same way the Clinton administration had to lie about an "accidental" bombing of the Chinese embassy in Belgrade in May of '95 when NATO intelligence discovered the Chinese were using their embassy to forward Milosevic's orders to the Yugoslav embassy.

As she left the Oval Office to pass her note to the President, the Joint Chiefs were having their own ad hoc council of war. The CNO initiated it with a sudden turnabout suggestion, while Eleanor Prenty was attending the press conference, to conscript "George C. Scott" into unofficial service for the Joint Chiefs. "Why not," the CNO suggested, "invite him to *lead* a SpecFor payback attack on Kosong in the next two to three months, seeing as how the CIA's confirmed all three launchers have come from there?"

Lesand concurred, but added, "He'll have to plan it carefully to the very last detail. We don't want to be even peripherally involved in a repeat of Jimmy Carter's 'Operation Rice Bowl' fiasco when our Special Forces flew into that talc-fine dust storm—"

"The *haboob*," cut in Kruger.

"Well, whatever kind of boob it was," said the CNO, "it downed our Sea Stallions at Desert One and scuttled the whole damn mission, so instead of getting our hostages out of Iran, we only worsened the situation."

Lesand nodded gravely. "Rice Bowl" in 1980 had ended in disaster as a Delta Special Ops helo, choked by the talc-fine dust, collided with one of the big C-130 Hercules. The aborted mission had not only failed to rescue any of the American hostages in Tehran, 250 nautical miles away, but had also left the Iranian Muslims with five state-of-the-art Sea Stallions, which, because they'd been abandoned intact in the desert rather than being "sanitized"—gutted of highly secret codes and equipment—meant that the Iranians also garnered an enormous intelligence coup. It had cost Carter the presidency, and scores of Pentagonians their careers.

"Why not?" said Lesand, seizing the CNO's inspired APM—ass-protecting maneuver—of letting Freeman take all the risk. "Douglas is always champing at the bit, a warrior born and bred. But where do we get the team? No one in his right mind—"

"Douglas," said the CNO, his use of Freeman's first name contributing to the apparent reasonableness of the proposal, "has his own SpecOp team."

"In service?" pressed Lesand.

"No. Ex-service Special Forces guys." Which was as pleasant a way as any of pointing out, without actually saying it, that if nonservicemen with no ID, using off-shelf weapons of choice, the weapons' MID numbers removed—not by some half-assed-qualified ex-armorer behind a pawnshop cage but laser-removed by the agency—were caught, it could be officially "deniable" that these were U.S. troops, but rather that they were renegade former soldiers, like the patriotic readers of magazines such as *Soldier of Fortune*, which had once offered $50,000 to anyone who could get a piece of the Communists' celebrated 600-pound red, white, and blue North Korean flag that flew over the heavily NKA-patrolled sector of the DMZ. The flag, standing over 500 feet high, was the tallest in the world and was situated in Kijong-dong, a so-called North Korean village in the 148-mile-long, 2½-mile-wide demilitarized zone. The village was in fact completely deserted, nothing more than a "Ptompkin Village"—Hollywood-like facades built to create the impression of order and prosperity, its flag a continuous challenge to soldiers of fortune.

In short, the Chief of Naval Operations, Lesand of the Air Force, Army General Kruger, and the Marines' Taft were agreed that unlike "Operation Rice Bowl," or "Desert One Slaughter," as the media and public had understandably dubbed it, this payback operation against North Korea could not be officially sanctioned or made up from any "active list" of Army, Air Force, Marine, or Navy personnel. And they agreed that the public pressure for the President to do something should mean the President would go for the idea of a strike in a month, rather than two to three months. If Douglas Freeman and Co. succeeded, the payback op would be an unambiguous message to the North Koreans that, their 832 nuclear-warhead-capable rockets notwithstanding, the United States would in no way cower before terrorists, as Chamberlain had against Hitler and the Nazi terror.

On the other hand, if the attack failed, U.S. policy would be to officially deny any involvement, the President already having made the shrewd observation to Eleanor and the Joint Chiefs that in the press of world opinion, those who were vehemently hostile to America were going to think the worst of the United States whatever happened. And if North Korea, God forbid, captured any of the SpecFor team and paraded them before international media crews, there would be nothing to prove an officially sanctioned raid.

The generals conceded it would be a weak denial—but well within the modus operandi of the diplomats in Foggy

Bottom—and official records would show Douglas Freeman's team were not on the active list.

"Yes," said the President upon his return from the press
conference ahead of Eleanor, who was still answering questions, "I think Douglas would be the ideal man, though I'm
not sure I want him to physically be involved in the attack.
After all, he *is* officially retired."

When Eleanor returned from the press conference, where
she had reiterated the possibility of there being a plethora of
MANPAD bases in other hostile countries, in order to draw
attention away from North Korea, she was taken aback by
the Joint Chiefs' mercurial turnaround. Having at first resented the National Security Advisor's seeking the ex-
legend's advice, they now actively sought his involvement in
a SpecOps attack. She was angry. Had the "boys," as she
called them whenever she sensed a "gang-up," really thought
that Eleanor Prenty—even if she hadn't gained her Ph.D. in
political science and international relations or attended the
postgrad intellectual marathon "War and Society" course
that they and Freeman had—wouldn't be able to see through
their ass-saving plan? If the raid against the launcher warehouse near the port of Kosong, which lay at the foot of the
wild and rugged Taebek Mountain range worked, the chiefs
would claim much of the glory. If it didn't succeed, they'd
disown it—in keeping with the traditional military axiom
that victory has a hundred parents, while defeat is an orphan.

"General Freeman'll see what you're up to in a flash," she
chastised them, trying to contain her disgust, though she recognized that in the hard world of realpolitik, the generals
did have a point in that the U.S. could simply disown Freeman and his team if he failed, disavowing any official U.S.
involvement.

"You think he's the only one who's been asked to go in

sans ID to serve his country?" the Marine commandant chided her.

"No," she admitted. "I don't." She'd seen the commandant's service record. He'd done such unofficial missions— like the SEALS who, disembarking from U.S. subs in what was clearly the sovereign North Vietnamese coast zone, had swum up from the littoral sea into the rat-infested sewers of Hanoi and planted what were still referred to in "Eyes Only" files as "devices."

"What d'you think?" the President cut in as he watched the networks broadcasting his news conference. "Think I convinced them North Korea isn't our target?"

"I think so," said Eleanor, trying to cool down. "I saw Steve Loren of the *Times* adding the usual suspects to the list—al Qaeda, Libya, et cetera."

"You can read upside down from twelve feet away?" the CNO asked her lightheartedly.

She smiled. Not even the Joint Chiefs knew about the pinhead-sized overhead cam that took in the reporters' notes from behind the press gallery. A sign of the times.

CHAPTER EIGHT

DOUGLAS AND MARGARET lay satiated once more, but something had changed in him, his lust now expended in the *petit mort,* the little death, that so often followed the physiological climax. The momentary emptiness, for some, the search—the yearning—for meaning, however brief, that at times attaches itself to sexual exhaustion, visited him, and he held Margaret closely. For a moment she became Catherine, the woman he'd loved, and who, like so many military wives, had sustained him through the vicissitudes, the multitudinous trials, of service life so alien to the public they protected.

A pang of guilt assaulted him. Was he using Margaret as a surrogate Catherine? Or was he merely indulging in that near-obsessional compulsion he had to overanalyze, a disposition that had been at the heart of his success as a career soldier? He stroked her hair, an attempt to repay her sincerity, her obvious love for him, in kind. For the first time in a long while, General Douglas Freeman, retired, was confused. War, for all its myriad details, was a simpler thing all round than love. What he needed, he told himself, was clarity, to get back into the war, for he believed that ultimately it was what a man did outside of bed—his *job*—that defined who he was. For Douglas Freeman and his ilk, the politically incorrect, honest-to-God truth was that peace is hell.

But at least now, he mused, he had contributed something in a military sense to the White House's understanding of the weaponry unleashed in this latest terrorist blitz of the war. He was also harboring the conceit that despite his retirement status, his body belied his age. His abs didn't have the hard, washboard look of the 24-7 gym fanatics, but rather exhibited the solid no-flab toughness of a Special Forces warrior ten years younger, despite the occasional "guerrilla" attack, as he described an occasional weakness in his left knee, brought on by the kind of subzero cold he'd experienced during his command of the U.S.-led U.N. force. But the knee had never bothered him with his occasional sexual liaisons with CNN's Marte Price, or now with Margaret.

For a moment he felt boyishly self-congratulatory, as if what in fact had been his relatively rare sexual adventures with the two women had been more regular occurrences. And his mind was in good shape too. The White House— well, maybe just Eleanor, but she was the President's National Security Advisor—was sending an FBI agent to confer with him. That was something.

Staring at Margaret's diamantine-studded ceiling, his postcoital mood growing into one of self-satisfaction about his knowledge of things military, he failed to remember his late wife's gently reminding him of St. Paul's First Letter to the Corinthians, that "knowledge puffeth up!" And so, it was an embarrassing blow to the legend's ego when Margaret, albeit gently, suggested that he might want to—well, brush his teeth, before the government man arrived.

The general didn't simply blush; his face turned beet red in a surge of embarrassment, exacerbated by the fact that, necessary body odor during missions notwithstanding, General Douglas Freeman was known as a stickler for personal hygiene. "My God!" He sat up. "I'm sorry."

"I think it was the onions you had."

"But," he spluttered, "they were Walla Walla!"

The name sounded so funny, she burst out laughing. "Walla what?"

He'd never seen her so girlish, so playful, so wonderfully relaxed. "You betcha," he avowed. "Walla Walla. World famous. So mild, you can eat 'em raw. My old man used to eat them like an apple."

"Oh, toosh!" she laughed.

"Toosh yourself!" he said, throwing her pink lace panties at her.

"Oh," she said, "you bully!"

"Bully's better than bad breath!"

"Silly, it's not that strong. I just thought I should tell you before your meeting. Honestly, Douglas, I don't mind." She'd been laughing so much that she placed her right palm against her bosom as if to steady her heart, her breasts rising and falling rapidly, revealing her nipples dark and sharp against the pink silk, so that he was ready to go again.

"Well *I* mind," he said. "Walla Wallas aren't supposed to stink." He was cupping his hand in front of his mouth to get the full effect. She was right. It wasn't that strong a smell but there was a distinctly off-putting odor. "That's it. I'm through with Walla Wallas!"

"You can eat a ton at lunch," she joshed.

"No I can't. How could I be—," he began, with mock shock, "—be *intimate* with you, smelling like this?"

"Oh, Douglas," she said, clearly touched. She watched him as he walked into the bathroom, where he vigorously brushed his teeth and took a strong swig of blue mouthwash, his gargling the most frightening sound, like some mechanical monster chewing up a swamp. She giggled again. No man had ever shown her such prompt consideration. A small thing to others, perhaps, but for her, in a world of terror and unspeakable vulgarity, it was the immediacy of his response that was the act of a true officer and a gentleman. She felt so extraordinarily young. It was true: you were as young as you felt. In the mirror you saw the body you inhabited, the bone and flesh that confined your youth, your hopes and dreams, like prisoners in a cell, but at last her passion was wild and free. She felt so happy, it seemed as if her heart couldn't contain her joy. She burst out laughing again, "Walla Walla!" holding her panties as a veil against her face. All he could see was her eyes, their sparkling aquamarine in vivid contrast against the filigree of pink lace she held cheekily against her mouth.

CHAPTER NINE

MONTEREY'S FBI AGENT Patricia Grant was taken aback. Never in her fifteen years with the agency had she had an interviewee phone up her regional office to check out her ID card number and insist on a detailed physical description—distinguishing marks, eye color, et cetera. So this was the guy they called "George C. Scott," "Patton," and a "has been" prima donna. What's more, he asked her—not impolitely but certainly directly—why she hadn't asked *him* to see *his* ID, driver's license, Social Security number, et cetera.

"I checked your file before I came, General," she lied. She could have said she'd heard all the good things about him, but to hell with it—she was miffed at Freeman for checking her out.

"No offense," he said, extending his hand, smiling graciously. "And it's not because you're a woman. I check out everybody. A sign of the times."

He was right about that.

"I'm to chauffeur you to our office," she told him.

En route along the Pacific Highway to the FBI HQ office in Monterey, the general was admiring the endless blue of the Pacific, struck by the agent's insistence that all the windows in the unmarked black Ford sedan be closed.

"I like to smell the sea air, even if it is a bit chilly," said Douglas.

"Same here," said Patricia Grant, tempted to add, " 'specially when the car reeks of Listerine." Instead she proffered, "But rules are rules, I guess. These days, windows have to be up. Agency regulations."

She was right, but he thought it one of the most distressing comments he'd heard, along with the babble of network "experts" who obviously couldn't tell the difference between an Igla, a Vanguard, or a Stinger. Distressing because she was right. Americans who, perhaps of all nationalities on earth, prized the freedom of the open road and the quintessential American invention, the convertible, the most had retreated, turtlelike, under a hail of bureaucratic alerts and concomitant rules into speeding cocoons of darkened, bulletproof glass in paranoid dashes between destinations, for fear of attack in their own country. It was a surrender of a kind, an undeniable admission trumpeted by foreign media that already the terrorists and affiliated scumbags had won a significant victory over America.

On the radio, Freeman and agent Patricia Grant heard that all commercial flights were being suspended for the next seven days.

"For the airline industry," said Patricia, "today's worse than 9/11. We have to do something."

Freeman heard her but her words didn't really register, the general experiencing a moment that was referred to in the work of the famed Austrian clinical psychologist Dr. Ernst Riefelmann as a *rückwärtige Verbindung*—a "reverse connection"—during which we work back from an apparently innocuous remark, a remark seemingly unconnected to our present overriding concern but which is in fact an unconsciously bred connect, "a mental bridge" by means of which two events that initially appear to be unconnected are actually intimately linked. Great investigators, including great generals and captains of industry, Riefelmann had pointed out, are invariably skilled, whether they consciously know it or not, in this *Zusammenschmelzen*, or "fusing," of the two or more parts of a bridge or "connect" between seemingly unrelated events.

One of the best known and frequently cited examples of Riefelmann's "reverse connection" theory had been George Patton's recurring and disturbing dream in the bloody spring of 1944, a dream in which Patton was haunted, or, in Riefelmann's terms, obsessively *verblüfft,* "puzzled," by the apparent disconnect between the hand carts Patton had seen in his dream and scores of dead Wehrmacht soldiers. For a time, Patton could make no sense of these two seemingly unrelated elements, but eventually it came to him: the once invincible mobile spearheads that formed the second stage of the Blitzkrieg, after artillery and screaming aerial bombardment, were out of gasoline, the carts being the Germans' only way of moving the dead and, more vitally to Patton's Third Army, their supplies. The message of the connect?— the German Army was finished, literally out of gas, no longer mobile, at the edge of total collapse, which Patton realized was an unprecedented chance for the Allies to surge ahead instead of following Montgomery's more cautious and time-consuming advance, during which, Patton feared, the Nazis might get their second wind and thus draw the war out much longer.

With General Douglas Freeman it was Margaret's apparently innocuous remark about the onions that hinted to him the first part of a possible connect. What the other half was, he didn't know, only that he had the sense that whatever it was, it was important.

Some people, Riefelmann wrote in his seminal paper, "Explanations for the Reverse Connect," attributed the source of their "moment of connect recognition" to God, others to fate, others to extrasensory perception, others to the phenomenon of remote viewing. The precise neurological trigger, however, remained obscure in much the same way that

Western clinical trials showed that Chinese acupuncture, as practiced for millennia by the Chinese, clearly worked, while the neurological explanation continued to evade clinicians.

Ironically, Freeman, though well read in all things military, had never heard of Dr. Riefelmann. All he knew, like those who benefit from acupuncture without knowing anything of complex explanatory theories, was that Margaret's comment about the Walla Walla onions had had a definite effect on him.

"You ever heard of Walla Walla?" he asked Agent Grant.

"Walla—?"

"Walla Walla."

"No," she said, daring to add, "Sounds kind of funny!"

It did sound funny, but Freeman was thinking "funny peculiar," not "funny ha-ha!" arrested by the conviction, as Patton had been by his dream, that whatever the connection was, it transcended the merely personal and was of enormous significance in the MANPAD imbroglio.

As they slowed for the light by Custom House Plaza, Freeman's cell phone was ringing.

"Excuse me," he told Patricia, who was looking apprehensively around. Stopping at lights wasn't something the FBI or any other of America's security agencies cared for. Stationary targets.

"Freeman," he said, flipping down his cell's mouthpiece.

It was a familiar husky voice, speaking much more slowly than the nation usually heard her. "Douglas?"

"It is."

"Oh." There was a pause. "You've got someone with you."

"Yes."

"Not the jealous little hussy I got at your other number?"

Marte Price's description of Margaret as a "little hussy" elicited a wry smile from the general. "No—another one," he told her.

"My, you're quite the old stoat, aren't you?"

"*Old?* You mean compared with all those adolescent gofers you have satisfying your every whim?"

"Not *every* whim, General. Now and then I like someone with experience."

"Hmm. What do you want, Marte?"

Marte. Agent Grant recognized the famed CNN voice the general was sparring with. Maybe he'd let Marte Price's name slip, thought Patricia, hoping that FBI agent Grant would be impressed. She was. And she could tell the blond newscaster was using flattery to pump the general for a scoop on what was being done behind closed White House doors about the MANPAD problem.

"I know," Marte told the general, "that you've been summoned to Monterey's FBI office. Which, I'd say, means your girlfriend at the White House wants to get you on scrambler-secure. Hush-hush. I'd guess they're going for a counter-strike and they want an old four-star's view on the proposed DA. Right?"

God, it was great to be in the game again, he thought. Well, all right, not exactly in the game, but at least advising the manager/owner in the box on the play.

The car stopped at another yellow light, and the general decided to have a little fun—an escape from the damn onions going around and around in his head like a song you've heard and just can't evict. "Proposed DA?" he replied, affecting confusion. "I know nothing about district attorneys."

"Very droll, Douglas." She knew he knew she meant a Direct Action mission: to go in, cause maximum damage, and get out. Fast. "I know it won't be for a month or two but—"

"I know nothing," he said truthfully. "And quite frankly, I'm surprised you're using a cell. Hardly secure, is it, given your eavesdropping competition, not to mention national security." In fact, the general wasn't at all surprised; an anchor with Marte's clout hadn't got where she was in the shark-infested waters of network and cable TV without taking risks, and the fact remained she had been able to help him in the past. And with the number of enemies he had in Washington, D.C., an IOU from the press was never a bad investment. Also, he knew she never broke her word.

"If I can," was all he'd promise, "I'll tell you."

"Exclusively?" She paused. "Bamboo in the wind." It wasn't a question but a promise—the expression they had both learned during U.S. interventions in Southeast Asia, the phrase describing what the Italians called "fellatio." Her brazenness took him aback. For all his sudden enjoyment with Margaret, he, like so many of the senior officer corps, was inherently conservative in discussing matters of sex. Marte must have sensed his shock at her openness. "Douglas?"

"I'm still here."

"What do you call a man who likes sex?" she asked, then answered her own question. "Normal. Now, what's a woman who likes sex? A slut, right?" Her old joke about the double standard between the sexes was lightheartedly delivered, but there was an edge to it nevertheless, the resentment of centuries of women.

His answer was from the heart. "I have never thought of you that way. And I never will."

"Thank you," she said. "You're a very sweet man. I hope we see each other soon."

He was about to say, "Me too," but saw Patricia Grant smiling. "I'll tell you whenever I'm cleared to do so," he said, adopting a slightly censorious tone and flipping the mouthpiece shut.

As the car slid into its reserved spot, Patricia Grant exited with relief. It had been a simple pickup and delivery for her, its sheer uneventfulness a luxury in this war where "sleeper cells" were daily being ordered out of their hibernation to launch another murderous attack against innocent U.S. citizens, resulting in workloads for agents that pushed law enforcement personnel to the limits of endurance. On top of responding to ever-changing threat levels, they were required to keep tabs on illegal immigrants, which in itself was a full-time job.

On the way up to the regional DHS/FBI/CIA liaison conference room, Freeman was wondering first if he would be talking to one of Eleanor Prenty's aides on a conference call, given that as National Security Advisor she must be exhausted, having been on her feet continuously since the attacks.

Before going in, he asked Patricia Grant whether he could use her PC to send an e-mail to Choir Williams, who, although he lived farther north in Washington State than Walla Walla, could do an IPS, intel profile search, about the place, vis-à-vis any possible connect between it and the terrorist attacks. The general knew little about the town in the wine-growing area in south-central Washington State other than that it was on the Walla Walla River near the Oregon border, and that it lay in the rain shadow east of the snow-crested Cascade mountain chain. He was aware that the latte legions in Seattle thought of Walla Walla as the back of beyond, like New York thought about the rest of the country.

After the comfortable warmth of the car, the conference room, to which only Patricia Grant and Freeman were allowed entrance, felt like a sauna. Yet he noticed Patricia Grant didn't remove her jacket, the redhead apparently in slavish obedience to the FBI's attempt to reinstate a strict dress code.

A second later the general understood the real reason for her obvious tension. The President of the United States appeared on the teleconference screen.

Freeman, belying his own penchant for the more relaxed Special Forces style, immediately stood to attention, conveying such ramrod alertness, as well as his runner's all-round fitness, that he looked no older than a man in his mid-forties.

It was the kind of transformation into a younger self, Patricia Grant mused, that one achieves in the moment of pleasant surprise—meeting an old flame, high school reunion— especially when it involved the kind of ego boost that everyone experienced in the presence of the most powerful leader on earth. The FBI agent realized she too had unconsciously straightened up. Freeman saw a note, presumably slid in from off camera by an aide. Perhaps it was Eleanor, if she was still on her feet.

"Agent Grant," said the Chief Executive, flashing a smile at the redhead.

"Yes, Mr. President."

"Thank you for bringing in General Freeman. He's on our most-wanted list."

It was a nice comment, simultaneously putting everyone at ease and making the subsequent presidential request that Patricia Grant leave the room sound more like she would be doing him a favor than obeying an order.

"Take a seat," the President invited Freeman. "Eleanor says you've been very helpful corroborating our security agencies' identification of the types of weapons used in those three terrorist attacks."

Corroborating, thought Freeman. He'd told the White House *precisely,* albeit through Eleanor, what two types of MANPADs had been used, the same types that would no doubt be used again if the U.S. didn't go after the terrorist base from which they came.

"Well, Mr. President," Freeman responded, at least trying to strike a middle ground between his ego and respect for the Chief Executive Officer of the United States, "we know they used a Vanguard 3D MANPAD and an Igla-2C, but I wouldn't vouch for the third."

"Ah," interjected the Air Force Chief of Staff, Lesand, whom the teleconference cam now showed was sitting to the right of the President, "the third missile was a Stinger, Douglas. Launcher's not in hand at the moment but we're pretty sure its MID will be one of those missing from our Afghan Donation List." *Donation!* Freeman could barely subdue his disdain for such euphemisms—donation! In the late eighties the U.S. had given the mujahideen scores of the missiles to kill Russians. Nor did Freeman like Lesand's use of "Douglas." The Air Force guy was a Johnny-come-lately, had seen one war—against the Iraqi Air Force, which wasn't there—and now it was *Douglas.* To Freeman, the flyboy was sounding like one of those overly familiar teenaged doctor's receptionists who start right off calling you by your first name—we're all buddies. You *could* run a small Special Forces team like that. Indeed, he had done so in the past, but let Michael try running his *Air Force* on a first-name basis.

"Ah, how do you know the missing launcher belonged to a Stinger, *Mike*?" asked Freeman.

Eleanor Prenty, the fatigue bags under her eyes looking even worse on the TV screen, was still trying to appear calm—after thirty-six hours without sleep—but inside she was on the boil. Freeman, she knew, wanted, ached, to be recognized for his ability rather than being shunted aside, like so many, by mandatory retirement rules and regulations which all too often assumed you became brain-dead at an arbitrarily, bureaucratically imposed age. But his combatively delivered *"Mike,"* Eleanor knew, was precisely the kind of petulance that quickly shifted people's attention away from the kind of respect Freeman had earned on the battlefield to his reputation as a diplomatic disaster.

"The videos we've seen, General," the Chief of Naval Operations told Freeman, "and the several eyewitnesses we've spoken to so far would seem to indicate pretty conclusively that the missile in question *was* a Stinger. The twin rectangular flap-ears antenna and—"

" '*Seem* to indicate' is the operative phrase, Admiral," cut in Freeman. "Now, I'm no flight engineer like Mikey here, and the flight angle on those videos may make it *look* like it's a boxy antenna, a Stinger, that we're seeing, but it could be another enemy-made MANPAD." He was recalling what Aussie Lewis had said about the similarity of the Stinger antenna to that seen on the missile in the Dallas/Fort Worth video. The missile that Mikey Lesand and the admiral were convinced was a Stinger could well be an improved Chinese Anza.

"How about the eyewitnesses, General?" retorted the CNO, the President, listening intently, giving no indication how much this Stinger/non-Stinger debate counted in what would ultimately be his decision following the Joint Chiefs' and his National Security Advisor's input.

"These eyewitnesses," asked Freeman, "civilian or military?"

"Civilian, I believe," answered Eleanor crisply.

"Not worth a damn," said Freeman. "They're not trained."

"One was a member of the press," the CNO retorted.

"Huh!" grunted Freeman, sitting back in exasperation, but in what Eleanor, her nerves frayed, was afraid might look like plain insolence to those in the Oval Office.

"Media types are even worse than civilians," continued Freeman. "If I had a dime for every time some correspondent called an armored car or a Bradley a *tank,* I'd be a wealthy man. The State Department's made serious foreign-policy blunders believing some radio report of enemy 'tanks' invading some foreign burg."

"So, General," cut in Eleanor, her no-nonsense tone reinforced by her stony stare into the Oval Office's camera, "some witnesses make mistakes. But let's get back to the point, shall we? Even if this third rocket, MANPAD, or whatever you call the thing that murdered over three hundred Americans at Dallas, is a Stinger, the CIA tells us the launchers we've found for these—" She glanced down at her notes. "—Vanguard and Igla, both come from the same source. North Korea, a place called Kosong."

"Yes," said Freeman, charmingly agreeable, as if he'd known the name of the place all along. "Kosong."

"Good!" said the President, relieved by Freeman's unqualified concurrence with his Joint Chiefs of Staff.

"I just don't want you guys to go into Kosong," said Freeman, "and have the attack get into trouble because of incomplete CIA intel, Mr. President."

The Joint Chiefs were trying to conceal their surprise with, and their resentment of, Freeman. The gall of the man! How in hell did he know they had already decided on an attack, before the suggestion had been finalized, the CNO in particular noting that Freeman had said *the* attack, not *an* attack, as if the self-assured son of a bitch could read their minds.

"I just thought it prudent," Freeman continued, "that it should be a matter of record for the administration that, if anything was to go wrong with the mission, the White House had to act on the incomplete information it had at the time, but with due deliberation. Like the allied attack on Iraq. The WMDs."

The general's phrase, "incomplete information," and his mention of WMDs, the supposed weapons of mass destruction in Iraq, produced dead air in the Oval Office, the silence pregnant with the WMD nightmare.

"You think," said the President in a tone of deceptive calmness, "we should wait—try to find the third missile's remnants? We already have the three launchers and their MIDs."

The President and the Joint Chiefs were expecting the usual unequivocal answer from the no-holds-barred general, but instead Freeman replied, "I don't know, Mr. President. I'm a soldier, not a politician—and I say that with respect, sir, for you and the awesome responsibility you have." And the general meant it. He was thinking. He habitually railed against government ineptness as much as any other taxpayer in the country, but he was too smart not to know how different a politician's lot was, trying to legislate in a sea of competing interests.

"Personally, Mr. President, I don't think we'll ever find the missile fragments after the kind of heat generated by the explosion of the planes' fuel tanks. And..." He left his sentence uncompleted until the President, sensing Freeman's as yet unspoken reservation, asked him to continue. The general wasn't a man who normally held back. "Sir, you know how sometimes—maybe during a campaign—my uncle was a congressman—"

"Yes, I know. Go on."

"Well, sometimes something bugs you, like a grain of sand in your sock. You search for it but you can't find it." He paused. "I'm not putting it well, but the truth is, every time I think about those missiles I think that something's wrong."

"Hundreds of Americans dead," put in the Air Force's Lesand. "That's what's wrong."

That did it for Freeman. No way was he going to tell them about the onions. They'd think he was nuts.

"A hunch," pressed the President.

"Yes, sir."

The President nodded, his fingers pressed together like a church spire as he thought. "I appreciate your honesty, General. I do know the feeling—a hunch that something's not right." He paused, then looked directly into the cam. "Up in Topeka, Kansas, in one rally, I had a gut feeling something was out of whack. Tell you the truth—" He turned in his swivel chair to the Joint Chiefs and Eleanor. "—I thought there was going to be an assassination attempt." He turned back to face the camera. "But nothing happened, General, despite my hunch. Everyone's on edge. Times in which we live."

"I won't argue with that," agreed Freeman.

"What we need, however, *if* we do an in-out job on Kosong, is launcher evidence brought back from that damned warehouse. Or something else concrete that nails the bastards, like the U-2 photos Kennedy got of the Cuban missile sites that were pointed right at us. Something that we could present publicly, as our U.N. ambassador Adlai Stevenson did with the U-2 photos in the U.N. just after the Soviets had denied it to the world. 'Course," the President continued, "half the world's not going to believe us, and never will, but it's our allies I'm thinking of. They should be shown hard evidence."

No one said anything for a moment, Freeman glancing at Eleanor Prenty, both of them knowing that everyone in the room recognized the importance of hard evidence, given how the difficulty of finding evidence of weapons of mass destruction had proved to be a massive headache for George W. Bush during the Iraqi war. The President turned back to Freeman. "Would you organize such an attack, General?"

Eleanor saw the sudden fire in Freeman's eyes. "Yes, Mr. President. Gladly."

"Good." There was an audible sigh from the Joint Chiefs.

"Good man, Douglas!" It was the CNO, any previous sharp exchange forgotten.

"General," said Air Force General Lesand, "we've picked you because you're not officially on the books. You're retired."

Freeman was ahead of them. "I understand, Mike. No ID. And nontraceable weapons—off the shelf, commercial."

"North Korean if we can get 'em," put in Marine Commandant Taft.

The voice-directed camera in the Oval Office panned to the President, his red-and-blue Yale tie against the pin-striped navy blue suit immaculately matched. "I'm going to leave all the details in your hands, Douglas, which of course means I don't want you in the raid itself. I want you at mission control offshore, making sure everything comes together."

Son of a bitch. Freeman was stunned. He had expected to be on the point, but here they wanted him in some damn CCC, Combat Control Center, his eyeballs turning red from staring at one mini TV monitor after another, staying in constant contact with his men, who would be doing the tough, physical commando action, the "hard yakka," as Aussie Lewis called any on-ground combat, where you actually saw the enemy's faces, or the begoggled gas masks that protected identity as well as gas-porous skin.

"General," added the President, seeing Freeman's acute disappointment, "the Joint Chiefs think you're the perfect man to set this up. I concur. Your experience and knowledge of that part of the world are as legendary as your military successes."

"Thank you, Mr. President," said the Legend graciously, but his face was funereal. He craved action. Yes, he understood the need for a high degree of coordination, that a team without a good coach on the bench could fail, but he craved the battle, the ear-dunning sounds, the smell of shot and wrenching clash of steel that terrified most men and terrified him. But it was there that he sought reassurance, reaffirmation that he still had it, still possessed the internal fortitude that, like the great hidden bulk of the enormous bergs that were calved at the ends of the earth, he could sustain himself through the roughest seas that either man or nature could throw against him.

"When can you have a force ready, General?" asked the President, adding, "you're on the retired list, which politically speaking is good if, God forbid, anyone gets wind of it. We can simply say truthfully that you're no longer on the active list. But having said that, I must emphasize that no one else on your team can be on the active list either. I'm giving you carte blanche regarding supplies and transport from Special Operations Command in Florida. Given that, when's the earliest you can go? I can have General Lesand here get you a ride as second man on a Raptor trainer." The President added, smiling, "*If* you're not afraid of heights?"

"I'm ready to go now. Could be at MacDill in Tampa within three hours, Mr. President. But the mission itself, training, equipment, et cetera—earliest would be six weeks. Absolute minimum, given the distances, the—"

"Tell you the truth, General," the President cut in, "I was hoping for something closer to a month, given the public's outrage, but I guess we can live with six weeks. If you run into any bureaucratic crap," he said, glancing purposefully at the Navy, Air Force, and Army Chiefs and the Marine Commandant, "call me."

When the meeting ended, the telescreens blank, there was some mumbling in the Oval Office about Freeman's tendentious argument over the make of the third missile and whether it really mattered. Clearly, whatever it was, it had been fired by terrorists.

"That's unimportant," commented the CNO. "At least we've got a loose cannon out of our hair. And we've told him not to take anyone on the active list. If anything goes wrong—"

"If anything goes wrong," interjected the President, "we'll be in the soup along with the general. We can deny it all we like, 'not officially sanctioned,' et cetera, et cetera, 'soldiers of fortune,' but unless Freeman's team brings back a clearly identifiable launcher and missile from Kosong as proof positive for our allies that we're up against the North Koreans, we'll have the U.N. and every other America-hater all over us." He paused and looked hard at each one of them. "That's why your 'loose cannon' was nice enough to say, 'I don't want you guys getting into trouble because of incomplete CIA intel,' like the Bay of Pigs or another WMD problem.

You're right—diplomatically Freeman is a loose cannon. I wouldn't make him ambassador to Tonga, but he understands the danger of a credibility gap. He did well to warn us. Some other generals," continued the President, "would have given me 'yes sir, no sir, three bags full.' He's not a yes-man, whatever you say."

"My apologies, Mr. President," said the CNO.

"Not necessary, Admiral." The President smiled. "I didn't say he was wasn't a pain in the ass." The ensuing laughter cut through the tension and fatigue. The President asked his National Security Advisor to stay behind. "Eleanor," he told her, "you're to go home, give young Jennifer and that stuffed piglet of hers a big hug, then go to sleep for twenty-four hours. You look done in. I won't call you unless something urgent comes up."

Eleanor smiled at the mention of the stuffed piglet, "Billy Bush," a name suggested to Jennifer jointly by Eleanor's husband, Tom, an ardent Clinton fan, and Eleanor, who'd voted for the first President Bush in college. It had been a fun political compromise by a couple whose marriage, friends had said, wouldn't last more than a year because of Eleanor's stressful position as an advisor in the White House. They were wrong—it had lasted eleven years, five months, and four days, the couple's mature approach to "no politics at home" having held until the 2003 war against Iraq. The strain over that one was too much. What had begun as a domestic "spat" over what neighbors would cattily refer to as the "flowers" incident, seemingly patched up between Eleanor and husband Tom Prenty, in fact marked the beginning of a fissure in their relationship. In time it became a gulf between them into which poured a flood of recriminations and mutual complaints hitherto put on hold and subsumed by the sheer pressure of Eleanor's work as National Security Advisor and Tom's job as critic of the administration for a Washington think tank.

Eleanor and Tom Prenty had tried to stay together for that most ubiquitous of reasons, the children—in their case, Jennifer—but a bright young psychiatrist had emphasized what they already knew, that the effect of the constant guerrilla warfare at home, which had already caused one nanny and two temporaries to quit, was undoubtedly having a much more severe effect on their only child. A trial separation, "to cool down, regroup," the doctor suggested, might be in order.

"Won't that hurt Jennifer even more?" Tom had asked.

"Not if you explain your absence as job-related and if you part on amicable terms. Half of upper-income earners in the Beltway spend long periods away from home. If you get back together, fine. If not, we'll discuss how to proceed further."

"How about—you know, weekend visits?" suggested Eleanor.

"In my experience," responded the counselor, "children—Jennifer's eleven, right?"

"Yes."

"Yes, well, ironically, they see these weekend visits as the end. Dad or Mom away on business keeps hope of reconciliation alive. And if that doesn't happen, then they've already been weaned somewhat for the divorce. Besides, she'll be busy at school. St. Andrew's, right?"

"Yes," said Eleanor, with a twinge of guilt. She was a big proponent of public schools—publicly—but St. Andrew's was private.

"And there's another benefit," the psychiatrist continued. "Time out will give you two a chance to get things into perspective. Absence may not make the heart grow fonder, but it tells you how important or not it is to have the other one around."

They had agreed reluctantly and with Valda, a British au pair, age twenty, whom Jennifer adored and who was taking a year off from international relations at the London School of Economics "to see just what Americans were like," things were working out pretty well. But there were nights— Eleanor's feeling of loneliness exacerbated by her lack of sleep—when gazing down at her daughter and Billy Bush held tightly to her, she wanted Tom there, just to share the joy of looking at their child, silently reliving the excitement and sheer terror of the first weeks.

She'd read every prenatal book she could lay her hands on, and when Tom had brought her and baby Jennifer home and Eleanor had seen the profusion of congratulatory flowers and cards, she'd taken Jennifer into the luxurious *Consumer Reports*–prepared nursery, placing her down with exemplary care, and burst into tears. She didn't have a clue what to do with this little human. Tom had tried to reassure her, but when he picked up his child he did so with such apprehension, so slowly, holding his breath, it looked to postpartum Eleanor that he could have been lifting a bomb ready to go off.

"Oh God!" she'd said suddenly. "Tom—Tom!"

He'd turned, whey-faced. "What's wrong?"

"Get those flowers out of here." She remembered a little girl in the French town of Grasse, when Eleanor and the busload of tourists were being shown through one of the small but famed perfume factories in the Côte d'Azur. Suddenly there'd been a terrible commotion. The young girl was frantic. She couldn't breathe, the perfume aromas, combined with the smell from a purple rush of lavender growing by the roadside, so intrusive that they were overwhelming her lungs, her face starting to turn blue, becoming cyanotic.

"Tom, get the flowers out!"

A neighbor watering his lawn, though loath to interfere in a domestic dispute, hearing Eleanor screaming, dropped the hose and ran to the Prentys' door to see if he could help. Eleanor opened it. He'd been shocked by her distorted features. "Get rid of the flowers!" she'd shouted.

The neighbor, Nick Jensen, took one look at her face and did as she ordered, rushing past her, grabbing the bunches of flowers, and dumping them on the front stairs, which quickly became festooned with the variegated bouquets. Nick Jensen was fined $225 for disobeying Rockville's watering restriction ordinance: "failing to attend sprinkler."

"But it isn't a sprinkler, it's a goddamned hose!" Nick told the stern female conservation official.

"It's a sprinkler when you leave it running by itself," the resolute officer had replied sternly.

Nick explained that he hadn't had time to turn it off. "There was this emergency next door—"

"Right!"

"No, go and ask them, miss. Go and ask them."

She did. It didn't matter. "You should have turned off the hose first," the official told Nick. "We're experiencing a very severe water shortage."

Nick, a banker, gave up, but Tom insisted on paying the fine. The banker refused. They were good neighbors.

"How'd she know about the hose being on?" asked Tom. "I mean, it was beside the house. You can't see it from the street. Did someone phone it in?"

"That's what I thought," said Nick. "But apparently it was spotted by a police chopper."

"*What?* I never heard a chopper."

"Neither did I. They've baffled the engines so much now that you can't hear them above three hundred feet till they're right on you." The banker looked around, making sure no one was within earshot. Even then he'd spoken so quietly that it was difficult to hear him. "Everyone's being watched, Tom." He'd paused, forcing a smile. "Have Eleanor tell the White House I'm not a terrorist, will you, Tom? That the flowers weren't bombs."

"I will," Tom had said.

"Y'know, Tom, seriously, I tell all my people at the bank—

unofficially, of course, nothing on paper—that when they're on the road, if they want to have any poon tang, never do it in a hotel or motel room. Go out in a field, a barn, but not inside a hotel or motel."

"You think it's that bad?" Tom had asked, looking around again before he spoke.

"Tom, this country is wired like you wouldn't believe. Cams—you know, the digitized pinhole cameras they put on everything from a Grand Prix driver's helmet to bunging them into a quarterback's helmet? Revolutionized sports coverage. It's also revolutionizing spying. The people doing it call it 'surveillance.'"

The bank executive glanced about. He had the hose going again, *attending* it, its pulse jet making a soft, stuttering noise. "One of my guys, mortgage assessor, got a knock on his door one night 'bout a week ago. Two FBI guys wanted to have a 'chat' about my mortgage guy having once reportedly said that the administration is full of loonies, that they sell arms to the Arabs, then the Arabs use them against us. And that he also said, 'Gee, Olly, what's going on?' and they wanted to know what that meant." Nick had paused and then asked Tom Prenty, "You remember the old Laurel and Hardy movies?"

Tom had thought about it. "No, why?"

"Well, in the old black-and-white movie days, Stan Laurel was a thin, dopey-looking screwup and Oliver Hardy was a big, overweight straight man. Laurel was always screwing up, and Olly'd go ballistic. Anyway, point is, the FBI guys asked my mortgage assessor what he'd meant. My mortgage guy explained about the two comedians—earlier generation, right?—but what he didn't tell them was that the only place he'd mentioned screwup Stan's line, 'Gee, Olly, what's going on?' was in the rental car he was driving months before. He was too embarrassed to tell the FBI agents he'd been talking to himself while listening to some report about how security experts were worried about some of the Stingers we gave the Afghans years ago possibly turning up in America sometime in the future." Nick paused again, then asked Tom Prenty, "You ever talk to yourself in the car?"

Tom Prenty hesitated, then shrugged, a little embarrassed. "Yeah."

"So do I. I talk back at the radio—and the TV, when I'm a passenger—all the time, like when they reran an old documentary made in '03 about that Dixie Chick telling a Brit audience how ashamed she was to be American during the Iraq War. I'm yelling at the screen and my wife says, 'They can't hear you!' But you know, sometimes you get so pissed... Anyway, my mortgage guy was listening to this talk show and talked back sarcastically at the radio, about the U.S. doing a Laurel and Hardy bit with Stingers in Afghanistan, and he says to himself, 'Gee, Olly, what's goin' on?'"

"You're telling me," Tom had said, "the rental car was *wired*?"

"Yeah, like those cars the cops use to catch car thieves."

"Bait cars," said Tom.

"Yeah. That's it. Bait cars. What I'm afraid of is that the water police bitch is gonna write about me and the flowers in her report. You know, about Eleanor screaming to get the flowers out and her being on the White House staff—"

"You told the water bitch *that*?"

"Hey, I'm sorry, but I was so pissed about the hose fine, I was just explaining how it was I had to leave the hose running."

Tom had put his hand reassuringly on Nick's shoulder. "Ah, don't worry about it."

The banker's face was creased with concern. "You think they're winning?"

Tom looked at his neighbor, trying to parse the neighbor's question. What did he mean by "they're winning"? The government's invasion of every American's privacy? Or did he

mean the terrorists were winning the war by turning America
into a quasi–police state, a country of spy cameras, hidden
recording devices, and informers?

"Tell Eleanor to make a joke of it or something at work,"
Nick advised. "You know, how—"

"Otherwise they'll think she's nuts," proffered Tom.
"Cracking up. Is that what you're saying?"

"It's the times, Tom."

"You sure your mortgage guy only said that about Laurel
and Harley—"

"*Hardy.* In the rental car. Absolutely. He's positive."

"I'll tell Eleanor."

He did.

She was recalling the incident now, back home by order of
the President. While her postpartum blues hadn't torpedoed
the marriage, they hadn't helped. Unable to sleep, and feeling an acute need for junk comfort food, she got up, went to
the kitchen, sniffed suspiciously at a "best before" date on a
lump of cheese, decided to chance it, made herself a decaf
tea, and wandered into the flickering blue light of Jennifer's
bedroom; the TV was still on. There was no sound, CNN
showing pictures of the National Transportation Safety
Board investigators treading painstakingly through reassem-
bled bits and pieces of aircraft from JFK, LAX, and Dal-
las/Fort Worth.

Eleanor switched off the TV and looked down at Jennifer
and Billy Bush, the two of them seemingly grafted together,
the room redolent with the same soft, warm smell Jennifer
had had as a baby. Had it been eleven years? It was just after
the flowers incident that Tom had bought the stuffed "Gotta
Have a Gund" pig. She'd taken his advice and made a joke
about the flowers incident to several of her female colleagues at the White House. They'd all had a big laugh, several of the women swapping their own postpartum stories,

funny now but not when they'd happened. No one thought she was losing it, but it transpired that Tom, who had seemed to be so kind and empathetic at the time, was more annoyed about it than his conversation with their neighbor indicated, and soon his annoyance grew into a sullen anger, exacerbated by Eleanor's increasing attention to Jennifer, which, Tom charged, was robbing their marriage of any spontaneity. It meant he wasn't getting enough sex.

She wanted to bend down now and pick Jennifer up, even though Jennifer's baby days were long gone. Instead, she kissed her daughter, patted Billy Bush—then started in fright as the kitchen phone rang shrilly. She dashed out, for fear the ring would wake Jennifer. It was three in the morning, for crying out loud. It had to be the President. What now? "Hello?" she began in a whisper, pulling the sliding kitchen door closed so she could talk to the President in an ordinary, nonhushed business tone.

"Eleanor, I'm sorry to call at such an ungodly hour." It was Freeman, calling from SOCOM—Special Operations Command—in Florida after an exhilarating two and a half hours en route from Monterey in an F/A-22 Raptor trainer on "super cruise" high above the western deserts. And yes, Eleanor agreed with Freeman, it *was* an ungodly hour. Besides, she'd been decompressing, as it were, from the tense teleconference during which Freeman had so tendentiously cautioned the White House that any payback mission would involve the President going ahead without conclusive evidence that the third missile was from a North Korean stockpile, a stockpile that, the CIA's list of MANPAD MIDs had assured the White House, was in Kosong—just north of the DMZ.

"I wanted to apologize," began Freeman, "for being a little—"

"Rude!"

"Ah, yes, well, I suppose that's a fair description, but I don't like that Air Force whiz kid."

"Oh, I would never have guessed."

"It's a character flaw."

"Yours or his?" she snapped.

"Mine," he said sheepishly.

But she knew that in his own brusque way the general had "covered their collective ass" in the Oval Office. As he'd pointed out, should something go awry, the CIA should rightly take some of the fallout. But why was he calling her at 3:00 A.M.? "You having second thoughts?" she asked.

"Hell, no!"

She'd been careful not to mention anything specific on the phone, knowing that even the National Security Advisor's phone could be tapped—but she knew the general knew she'd meant second thoughts about the in-out "snatch and grab" mission. "Ah," she said, her tone lighter now, appreciating his apology. "So you've been so guilt-ridden by your response to Michael, you couldn't sleep, is that it?"

She heard a snort of derision from the other end. "I want to call you at fourteen hundred tomorrow. I know how busy you are, so I wanted to reserve a straight-through call, on scrambler, no matter whether you're in conference or whatever."

Eleanor shook her head—the man was impossible. An apology, immediately followed by a demand to have her office cleared for a call at 2:00 P.M. tomorrow: "No matter whether you're in conference or whatever." The nerve of the man, thought Eleanor. He wasn't even on the active list, a man who'd been put out to pasture, really, and now this demand to drop whatever she was doing at the White House tomorrow the minute he called. Cradling the cordless between her left cheek and shoulder as she reached over to open the fridge door, she took out a jug of orange juice then turned to reach up and take a glass from the cupboard.

"Douglas, do you remember Paul's letter to the Corinthians?"

"Which one?" he asked. "There are two."

My God, he can be annoying, she thought.

"First Corinthians, eight, one," she said. " 'Knowledge puffeth up.' "

In response, he quoted Frederick the Great's *L'audace, l'audace, toujours l'audace.* "I'll call you at fourteen hundred hours tomorrow," he said.

Light-headed with fatigue and hunger, despite the hit of the orange juice, Eleanor was feeling faintly hysterical.

"General, what do you call a Scotsman with three hundred girlfriends?"

"Don't know."

"A shepherd," she said, giggling.

"That, Ms. Prenty," the general replied with mock gravitas, "is politically incorrect."

"Oh," she responded. "Then why does a Scotsman wear a kilt?"

"Why?"

"Because a zipper would frighten the sheep." She howled with laughter. "Are you still there, General?"

"Combat fatigue," he joshed. "You get tired enough, you get silly. Major problem with flyers."

She was so tired, she thought for a moment he meant junk mail flyers.

"I'm not in combat!" She yawned.

"Yes, you are," he said, his tone suddenly changing. "We're all in this war, civilian and enlisted." It was a chilling comment, which sidelined her Scotsmen jokes, and she thought immediately of Jennifer . . . and then Tom, whom she and Jennifer saw only occasionally when he drove in from his Georgetown think tank. "I guess you're right, Douglas."

"Good night."

Too tired to shower and change into her nightgown, she lay down on the tan velour love seat in the living room, the phone beside her, and tried to sleep. She couldn't. Douglas

Freeman's comment about the flyers made her wonder why he'd mentioned them—perhaps because he'd been given carte blanche by the President he might be thinking of sending his team in on a HALO—high-altitude, low-opening—jump from one of the big Hercules transports. Even as she pursued sleep, she knew that there were dozens of U.S. flyers aloft in the darkness on combat patrol for America, some of their missions so long that their fighters and bombers had to be refueled two or three times during flight. One such long-haul Air Force transport would carry Freeman and his team of SpecFor warriors into harm's way in—how soon did Douglas say?—six weeks at the earliest. The only way such crews were able to stay awake, Eleanor knew, was because of an open secret that armed forces public relations officers were forbidden to discuss when it came to long-haul "insertion" of a SpecOps team, namely that crews were popping five- to ten-milligram Dexedrine "go pills."

CHAPTER TEN

MacDill, Florida

INSERTION TO TARGET was one thing, extraction from target was another kind of beast altogether. This was especially true if things, in Choir Williams's understated phrase, got a "bit sticky." It was a phrase that came up as the general briefed his assembled team about the "macro," or 3-D computer map, he'd selected for SOCOM's Direct Action Mission 134, against the out-of-town Kosong launcher/missile warehouse. Freeman's laser pointer moved south on the three-dimensional map from Kosong down along the North Korean coastline to the DMZ eleven miles away and back again to the location of the warehouse, a rectangular building that lay north-south between the two arms of a Y-shaped path that led up from a crescent-shaped beach. "Gentlemen," he addressed the eight-man team, pausing to say, "that doesn't mean you, Aussie." There was a loud guffaw from Salvini who, with Choir Williams, was delighted with the general's friendly jab at Aussie Lewis.

"Oh, very amusing," said Aussie wryly, the give-and-take familiarity between the general and his team surprising Gomez and Eddie "Shark" Mervyn, two of the five SEALs Freeman had drawn from the nonactive list. The other three "nonactives" were "Bone" Brady, a six-foot-six African-

American ex–college basketball star; Lieutenant Johnny Lee, a multilinguist; and a burly chief petty officer, Samuel Tavos.

Like most Special Forces, the five SEALs Freeman had chosen to join himself, Aussie, Choir, and Sal were used to the informal camaraderie of Special Forces, but it was obvious to them that Freeman had established a remarkably close bond with his former comrades.

"What we've got here," explained Freeman, "is a quarter-mile-wide north-south fishhook-shaped harbor on North Korea's rugged east coast. I emphasize *rugged,* gentlemen, and Aussie." Salvini grinned, elbowing Aussie in the ribs.

"Harbor entrance is narrow," continued Freeman, "less than a quarter-mile wide. Coastline along the southwest aspect of the harbor continues out seaward for a half mile, forming the shank of a fishhook shape, and ends up with an "up yours" finger of land jutting northward into the Sea of Japan, which *all* Koreans insist on calling the East Sea. The North and South Koreans are at one another's throats, but they all hate Japan. I don't want to excite you too much, but we'll be entering the most dangerous space in the world. The crescent beach we'll use as the point of insertion is a half-mile-long curve."

Aussie Lewis glanced at the five "retired" volunteer SEAL combat swimmers. If you saw a Jimmy leg, a nervous up-and-down knee motion, it was a sure sign that the owner was anxious. There was no movement, however, among the five "Sheilas," as Aussie had cheekily but good-naturedly dubbed them. In fact, if anything, the Sheilas looked bored, impatient for more details.

"General," inquired Gomez, "has it occurred to anyone that the North Koreans might guess that our CIA forensic guys could have traced the MANPADs' MID numbers to the Kosong depot?"

"Good point, Gomez. I'm pretty damned sure they know

our CIA labs would detect the launchers' numbers sooner or later, but that we wouldn't dare risk a hit on Kosong because we'd know they'd be ready for us."

"Either that," put in Eddie Mervyn, "or they wanted to deliberately taunt us like they do every day along the DMZ and in Panmunjom. Dare us to do something, so they'll have an excuse to resume their nuke reactor program. So they'll have a reason to cut off nonproliferation talks."

Freeman was pleased his specialists had kept savvy with the political situation, something that, like their foreign language training, distinguished them and the Green Berets from regular forces.

"Who can tell?" said Aussie wisely. "The North Korean Communist Party in Pyongyang is one of the most psychotic the world's ever seen. Right up there with Saddam, Pol Pot, and Adolf."

"Could be," posited Choir, "that they don't expect our guys to trace the launcher MID numbers at all. I mean, it's one thing to put a launcher under an electron microscope, laser, or whatever, but they might not know we can match the number to a specific depot. That would mean we had a spy in North Korea tracking Kosong inventory."

"Do we?" asked Aussie. "Have a spy in Kosong?"

"You think the agency's going to tell me?" asked the general.

"No," said Shark Mervyn, so called because of his swim speed attained with the Jhordan flippers, the revolutionary rubber swim fins that the U.S. Navy typically rejected when they were initially offered them by the ever-innovative Freeman but which had now become de rigueur for many combat swimmers, and mandatory for any combat swimmer on a Freeman mission. Aussie, Choir, and Sal, as well as Shark Mervyn, knew that not even the legendary general would be privy to whether the CIA or any other allied intel agency had a man "in place" in Kosong, and they didn't resent it, because Freeman was playing the same kind of "need to know" game when he'd told the President, in the presence of the Joint Chiefs and Eleanor Prenty, that "Operation Payback" couldn't begin in under six weeks.

The problems of planning such a mission were so myriad, they reminded Johnny Lee, the multilinguist on the team, of a set of *matryoshka,* Russian dolls. At first there seemed only one thing to look at, to understand, but inside each doll there was another.

Freeman sighed. "So we're faced with a thicket of variables. Only one thing's certain." He turned his wrist over and glanced down at his no-glare combat watch. It was 50 hours, almost time to call Eleanor Prenty. "And that," he continued, "is that the sooner we hit the pricks, the better chance we have of a successful mission. Any country in its right mind wouldn't launch an attack from halfway across the world for at least a month—and not until it had the U.N. on its side."

Aussie folded his arms tightly and smiled enigmatically at Choir and Salvini, or at least it appeared so to Gomez and Mervyn and the other three new boys, who suspected Aussie, Choir, Salvini, and perhaps the general, of having some private agenda. But far from Aussie's grin being a shared expression of smug self-congratulation between the general and his two fellow veterans, his reaction was one of admiration for the general's deft appraisal of the complex political and military variables involved and his signature grasp of detail. Indeed, Aussie's smile was simply one of appreciation for the way in which General Douglas Freeman, with his Rolodex cards, had succinctly prepared them all for what Aussie could sense was about to be a "shocker."

The latter, in this case, was the call the general was now making to the National Security Advisor in Washington, D.C. It was precisely 1400 hours, the time he had told her he would call. Heightening the attention among his audience of eight SpecFors, the general asked Eleanor Prenty if she was the only one in her office.

"I'm the only one," she assured him, and he told her he'd brainstormed the attack and, pending her approval, was about to go from "macro" to "eyes only" superclassified "micro" details with his eight-man team.

"Eight?" One of the five new boys, Lieutenant "Bone" Brady, could hear her clearly. And then, sounding as if she thought she'd misheard the general, she said, "You mean *eighty*?"

"No," replied Freeman. "Eight, plus me."

"But—but surely, Douglas, you need more men than that?"

"Not for an in-out quick demo."

"Demo?" She was still tired, having gotten only three hours sleep, and for a second she misinterpreted the general's abbreviation as "demonstration." It was an easy mistake to make, as there'd been ongoing demonstrations outside the White House ever since the missile attacks, most signs demanding retaliation against the terrorists, others proclaiming that "Violence Begets Violence," "Two Wrongs Don't Make a Right." Noticeably there were no signs accusing North Korea, the majority of the American public having assumed that the terrorist attacks on the three aircraft had been unleashed by al Qaeda and Co. sleepers.

"Demolition," explained Freeman.

"Oh, yes, of course."

"I've been on the blower and computer," he informed her. "Transport's all set."

"Uh-huh," said Eleanor, moving past her illuminated globe, closer to her office window—a Secret Service no-no—and gazing at the protesters ringing the south lawn. If they only knew what the White House knew, she mused.

One of her assistants knocked on her door. She didn't answer, honoring Freeman's request—demand—that she set aside this time exclusively for him. He told her he'd been working his old network nonstop since his Oval Office meeting the day before. So what did he want? wondered Eleanor. Brownie points for working hard? Working hard was de rigueur in the White House, and anywhere else in America if you wanted to survive. Besides, Freeman, his ego and pride notwithstanding, wasn't the self-congratulatory type. There was no doubt about his self-confidence, but he wasn't like one of those men Eleanor knew, such as her estranged husband, Tom, who expected a medal every time they performed an extracurricular task, like loading and unloading the dishwasher or putting a clothes wash in the dryer.

"I'm glad everything's coming together," she responded, her attention wandering back to the protestors' signs, one of which, "NUKE 'EM!" she hadn't seen before. What scared her was that there were people around like the onetime head of the Air Force, General Curtis Lemay, who had pressed the administration to nuke the Soviet Union and China in the crucial window of opportunity during the Korean War.

She saw another "NUKE 'EM!" sign, and realized how prudence favored a retaliatory commando in-out attack. Such a strategy would satisfy the public's demands for action against the terrorists without giving in to the extremists who had come out of the woodwork, urging a nuclear strike against North Korea. "If I can do anything," Eleanor told Freeman, "to help meet your six-week deadline, just tell me."

"Thanks," he said, "but we're good to go. Now. We'll be on a bus in four hours. Loaded for bear."

Eleanor was suddenly aware that Freeman had said something about a bus, Special Forces jargon for transport aircraft.

"Ten hours for shut-eye on the way in," the general continued. "My boys have earned it. They've been in-house at Bragg around the clock." He was telling her that his team had been practicing nonstop in the "kill house" at Fort Bragg, where even the most experienced Special Forces were periodically required to hone the in-bam-out techniques required either in urban fighting or in any building from which terrorists had to be removed—alive or dead.

"Douglas—," she began, glancing at her calendar and the hard copy of the CIA's SITREP map of the DMZ, North Korea, and its larger-scale inset of the Kosong area. It was Tuesday, Earth Day on the calendar given to children like Jennifer all across America, each day of every month bearing the names of the deceased 9/11 victims. "—are you telling me you're going to attack this Friday night?"

"No, ma'am," he answered. "*Thursday* night."

"Douglas, I don't understand. You told us it would take six weeks minimum just to prepare!"

"Well, I know the President wanted it earlier."

"Yes, but *you* said six weeks. "I mean—"

"Ma'am"—he had dropped the familiar "Eleanor" in front of the team—"we had a guy from the 101st Airborne pull a pin on a grenade in Kuwait. Killed two of our officers 'fore they even had a chance to go into combat."

She remembered the case. It had shaken America—one of their own against their own. Not a civilian traitor like the man who had gone over to train in bin Laden's al Qaeda camps in Afghanistan, but a U.S. soldier killing his own.

"What's your point, Douglas?"

"That guy was a Muslim," said Freeman. "An American Muslim, a sergeant. You know how many Muslims are in our armed forces, ma'am?"

"No, but I suppose you do."

"I do," the general replied, "seventeen thousand eight hundred, and 99.9 percent are probably as loyal as any other American, but we need only one weak link, just *one*—from SOCOM down to a bus driver's ground crew—to get wind of our intention, and we're toast. Our best defense isn't just offense. It's *speed.* I want you to tell the President my timetable. No one else."

"My God, General," said Eleanor, taken aback by the force and exclusivity of the general's request, delivered in the tone of an order. "You don't even trust the Joint Chiefs?"

"Yes, I do," said Freeman, "but one overheard remark at the Pentagon after our conference at the White House could've tipped our hand." The line seemed to go dead. "Ma'am, you still there?"

"Yes—yes, I'll tell the President," Salvini heard her tell the general. "But you realize he'll have to give the final green light."

"That's why I'm calling you!" said Freeman, his tone one of annoyance. Didn't she get it—why he'd set up the phone call to her at precisely 1400 hours, how it had to be on scrambler from MacDill, how he'd insisted she be the only one in her office now?

Salvini, whose acute hearing was well known in Freeman's old group, listened for the National Security Advisor's reply. There was none. Sal could see the general's phone hand turn white, he was gripping the receiver so tightly. The prospect of the general not being given Presidential authorization for Operation Payback against Kosong after so much painstakingly detailed preparation, together with the adrenaline coursing through the general's veins at the thought of commanding a punishing hit against the MANPAD storage facility, would be akin to Eisenhower's refusal to let George Patton be part of D-Day. It didn't bear thinking about.

"Ma'am," pressed Freeman—it was a plea. "Could you *please* ask the President *right now*?"

"Can you hold?" she asked.

"Like a bulldog," the general replied.

As the team waited in the nondescript hut off one of the

runways at MacDill, the general imagined he could smell onions in the way that as smells often trigger the memory of one's experiences, one's memory of an experience can in turn recall the smells experienced at the time. Maybe it was nothing more, mused the general, than the kind of obsessive thoughts you sometimes have under the pressure of anxiety—used to bother him as a boy in church, the obsession then that he'd suddenly blurt out something blasphemous—the obsessive thought going around and around in one's head, the brain's way of providing something identifiable around which free-floating anxieties could accrete, the obsessive thought like a worry bone to a dog, something concrete to gnaw on.

"Like a song you can't get out of your head," Catherine had once told him, trying to be helpful.

"No," he'd replied. "A song's pleasant. These nutty obsessive thoughts aren't. Like a song you *don't* like but it keeps going round and round in your damn head anyway." Was this recurring memory smell of onions merely that, a recurring annoyance, or did it have a deeper significance? Resurrected on the day after the MANPAD attacks, it might, he thought, be nothing more than the kind of crazy thought people have in a moment of disbelief, as when over three thousand Americans were murdered on 9/11, the kind of seemingly unrelated thoughts that the brain quickly brings to mind in order to mitigate the horror of the reality before it. Perhaps.

Salvini heard Eleanor Prenty come back on the line. "General, the President says, 'Go!' He's delighted—said it was smart thinking, hitting the terrorists before anyone, especially the terrorists, would expect it. But there is one thing."

Uh-oh, thought Salvini.

"The President wanted to know how you could possibly have organized an strategy plan so quickly."

"I did what Georgie Patton did," Freeman replied, the

blood suffusing his phone hand as he explained how, wherever Patton was, even when he was on holiday in Europe, he would study the topographic and Michelin road maps of the towns and countryside, compiling his own private files of possible contingency plans. And planning for a hit on North Korea, he told Eleanor, was a natural, ever since the Korean War ended in an uneasy, dangerous, nail-biting armistice. "And my *retirement*," Freeman continued pointedly, "has helped considerably. Kept me occupied updating my files. I have a plan on how to attack Buckingham Palace, should it ever be occupied by terrorists. And one for the Élysée Palace, especially if the Frogs are still in it."

Salvini didn't hear the National Security Advisor's sigh, but did hear her ask, "Have you ever thought of joining the Diplomatic Corps, Douglas?"

"Every damn day!" He was getting cocky again, primed to go. "Thank you for speaking to the President so quickly. I know how busy you people are. I've seen three presidents grow old before their time."

"And three advisors," said Eleanor.

"You're as young-looking as you were in college."

"Don't lie to me, Douglas."

"Young in spirit," he said.

"One more thing."

"Yes, ma'am?"

"I assume we can contact you through SOCOM HQ at MacDill. They'll be monitoring the mission, probably via Japan."

"Yes, ma'am," he said clearly, not wanting to go into detail, adding, "Some of my old buddies cut through a lot of red tape. I won't go into mission details with you. That way when we come back with a launcher and missile from Kosong and show North Korea's a terrorist base, you won't be able to give the media any SOCOM details of our mission. You can tell 'em the truth and say you don't know. That way we don't compromise any further DA missions."

"Will your friend Marte Price know?" He knew the National Security Advisor must know of his occasional "liaisons," as he liked to call them, with America's preeminent female correspondent. Even so, Eleanor's question took him by surprise.

"I told her that if I'm given the green light to talk to the press after the mission, she'd be first to know. She's already sniffing about. I asked her not to push it—go public with anything—and in return I'd give her first dibs, if my talking to the press was okayed by the boss. But of course there'd be no classified technical information."

"Sounds reasonable," Eleanor said in a quietly serious and personal tone, which, apart from the general, only Salvini could hear. "Douglas, I have to be honest with you. Although the Joint Chiefs, your buddy *Mikey* included, have done everything to speed up your procurement requests and limit the number of personnel who need to know to a bare-bones minimum, their computer threat assessment analyses have unanimously classified Payback as OTC."

"Officers Training Corps?" proffered Freeman jokingly.

"You know what I mean, an 'Off the Chart' mission— beyond the 'Highly Dangerous' classification. On a scale of one to ten, they concur that it's a minus five."

"That all?"

Well, at least he wasn't lacking in confidence. But she knew it would take a lot more than that to pull it off. "Douglas . . ."

"Yes, ma'am?"

"Godspeed."

CHAPTER ELEVEN

AT MACDILL AIR Force Base, Freeman strode into the office of a harried and surprisingly young quartermaster general. The quartermaster knew nothing about the mission, only that a long-haul aircraft was being requested, this time by a General Douglas Freeman, now listed on the "nonactive" roster. It couldn't be very important. He jerked his thumb back impatiently toward a clump of three C-130s, each with four Rolls-Royce Allison turbo props, over 17,000 horses in all. The C-130 Herk had always been one of America's heavy lifters. Powerful enough to haul five standard pallets or ninety-two troops into action, it could also be an ambulance for seventy-four litter patients and cruise at 33,000 feet with a payload of 40,000 pounds for 2,250 miles. All of which would have made it ideal for transporting what was vaguely designated by the general's team as "the equipment," as well as Freeman, Aussie, Choir, Salvini, Lieutenants Bone Brady, Lee, Gomez, Shark Mervyn, and Chief Petty Officer Tavos, both Gomez and Mervyn listed in SO-COM's nonactive roster as "technician-specialist." "One of those Herks," said the quartermaster impatiently, "will haul all you need."

"I want a C-5," said Freeman.

"You *want*?" riposted the quartermaster, mistaking Freeman's tone for arrogance rather than a measure of the concern Freeman felt for what he knew deep within would be a precarious mission.

"All right," Freeman said agreeably. "I'd *like* to have a C-5."

"I'd like to have Shania Twain," answered the quartermaster. "You know how stretched we are for Galaxies? We've got a hundred and thirty of them. That might seem a lot to you, General, but in case you hadn't noticed, we're spread pretty thin these days around the Mid-East, in South Korea, Kazakhstan, to name a few. We haven't even got enough of the beasts to meet our regular resupply here in the States."

All right, Freeman thought, he'd toned down his demand to a request but he wasn't inclined, nor was there time, to get on his belly and crawl to this Johnny-come-lately, a man who was probably still in diapers when General Douglas Freeman's Third M1A1s had effected the great U-turn attack against the Siberian Sixth Armored and decimated it.

"Call this 202 number," Freeman told the quartermaster, "and tell them I'd like a C5-Galaxy, and I want it now because it's the *fastest* heavy lifter you've got."

The quartermaster scribbled down the 202 area code and number. "Who the hell is this?"

Freeman knew he could have told the Air Force officer outright, but he had to obey his own strictly imposed no-leak policy. "Call the number," he told the quartermaster as they moved outside to the runway. "If you don't, I'll take this to SOCOM HQ, rattle your cage!"

The Air Force officer whipped out his cell, as Freeman later told his team, "quicker'n Wyatt Earp," the quartermaster's officiousness deflated like a slashed balloon. "Yes, ma'am!" Freeman heard him say, the quartermaster coming to attention as he spoke. "Yes—no problem. Right away."

The quartermaster coughed, moving to nonchalantly slide his cell away, but missed his pocket, the cell phone striking hard on the MacDill runway. Freeman bent down and picked it up for him. "Thanks," responded the quartermaster, his voice markedly subdued. "Ah—a Galaxy or Starlifter—whatever you want."

"I'll take the big bastard," Freeman said amicably.

"Right. Galaxy it is, then."

"Good."

"Ah, General Freeman . . ."

"Yes?"

"Ms. Prenty wishes you Godspeed."

Freeman nodded. It was the second time Eleanor had said that. He extended his hand in friendship to the young quartermaster general and smiled. "Thanks. I'll need it."

CHAPTER TWELVE

ONCE AIRBORNE IN the huge Galaxy, Freeman went over his attack plan, every single detail, three times en route to Hawaii with his eight-man team. Aussie, Choir, Sal, Bone Brady, Johnny Lee, and Tavos would do the actual break and entry of the warehouse. Gomez and Mervyn would stay with the insertion vehicle, while Freeman, to his chagrin, but in obeisance to his Commander-in-Chief's express order, would remain at mission control.

Landing on Oahu at dusk, the men, including the general, who set the example, ate a meal heavily laced with kimchi, the fermented Korean mix of cabbage, garlic, hot red peppers, green onions, and shrimp-fish paste that Koreans had as a side dish with every meal and was so strong that Aussie said it should be classified as a WMD. "Know a coupla guys," he said between mouthfuls, "who are on the 'speed bump.'" It was the name that the six hundred Americans and South Koreans who manned the first line of defense along Korea's DMZ gave to Camp Bonifas on the DMZ. They would therefore be responsible for evacuating all noncombatants at Panmunjom in the event of invasion by the North.

"What about 'em?" asked Salvini, his normally open, congenial Brooklyn smile contorted by the sour cabbage mash.

"Well," answered Aussie, pausing to wash down the kimchi with a gulp of North Korean Dear Leader beer, "they say no matter how horny they get, they'd rather jerk off than try to bed someone with kimchi breath!"

Freeman was remembering his embarrassing moment with Margaret. Onions! Maybe that's why he'd been obsessed with onions, an unconscious warning to him to make sure that his attack team would eat only Korean food before the attack, more than one American killed because of his North American smell on the wind.

"I believe it," said Gomez. "I couldn't go near a kimchi breath."

"I'd rather screw Choir," joshed Aussie.

"Nah," said Sal, "he's too tight!"

Chief Petty Officer Tavos shook his head. "You guys!"

"Okay, boys," cut in the general. "Listen up. Our senior boat man, Mervyn here, is about to take us through a refresher of Zulu-Five Oscar techniques."

"No need," joked Aussie. "Just drop out of this big bird, run, and fart. North Koreans comin' for you get a whiff of that kimchi burst and *Mo du da ju got da*—they're dead."

All of them had had to commit key Korean terms to memory, the ability to be "superfast studies," superfast learners, especially of foreign languages, now being mandatory for all Spec War applicants, and not just Green Berets. It was an ability aided in no small degree by Lieutenant Johnny Lee's expert knowledge of Mandarin, Cantonese, and five other languages, which included Korean—one of the reasons Freeman chose him—as well as Japanese, French, Russian, and a dialogue spoken by the Sakhalin Islanders who, as part of the Kuril Island chain north of Japan, had been occupied alternately by Japan and Russia during the last century.

Before Lee took over from Eddie Mervyn, going over useful evasive phrases, Aussie asked him, "What's Korean for 'I would like some pussy'?"

"Don't worry about it, Aussie," Freeman assured him. "You won't have time."

Johnny Lee told him anyway—*Mo Sang gin ssang Yoen*—but didn't explain that it meant "you ugly bitch."

Freeman smiled. Great morale here, he thought; together with surprise it was the essential ingredient for success, as any football coach knew. A surge in morale could spring you a quick goal in the first few minutes, and knock the opposition right out of the game.

CHAPTER THIRTEEN

ARTURO OMURA, HIS wife, and his thirteen-year-old grandson had worked hard to make a living ever since Grandfather Omura had immigrated to the United States in 1936. Grandfather had always been a prescient man, and in 1934 had predicted war was coming with America because, he said, Japan's war minister Tojo's unsmiling face, cruel enough by itself and looking even crueler because of the rimless spectacles he wore, was the face of a man bent on conquest.

Already the Japanese armed services, long emboldened by their stunning naval victory over the supposedly great Russian fleet at the Battle of the Tsushima Strait in 1905, had wreaked havoc upon Russia's army in the east, and Japan's subsequent victory over Chiang Kai Shek's Chinese Nationalist divisions of the Guomintang and against Mao Tse Tung's Communist armies had enabled Nippon to seize the rich mineral resources of Manchuria. But Grandfather Omura had told his wife and grandson Tayama, that the nascent Japanese Empire was still not satisfied. Tojo and his gang of thugs, as Grandfather Omura had always described them, though only in private, were now looking south toward the rubber of Malaysia and the oil of the Dutch East Indies. And the only reason they had not invaded Malaya and the spice-rich East Indies, Grandfather explained, was because of the United States Navy, based in Hawaii, which could thwart any Japanese movement south of Japan, unless Japan were to knock out the American fleet in Pearl Harbor on the island of Oahu. Such talk scared Grandmother Omura because if anyone outside the family overheard and was to report it to the *Kempei Tai*, the thought police, the entire family would be arrested. Her husband, Arturo, replied more than once that it was because of the very presence of such evil organizations as the Kempei Tai that he wanted to move them to the United States, that he had no wish to see his children's children living under the military dictatorship he was sure was going to get a lot worse under Tojo.

Grandfather Arturo Omura had his wish fulfilled earlier than he'd anticipated. He, his wife, and his grandson, Tayama's parents having died several years before, arrived in Honolulu in 1936, courtesy of the Kempei Tai who, having received a tip-off about Grandfather Omura from an Emperor-worshipping neighbor, then hatched a Machiavellian plan worthy of Vladimir Putin in his early days in the KGB.

Rather than sending Omura and his wife to prison in Japan for having criticized War Minister Tojo, the Kempei Tai set up Omura, his wife, and Tayama on Oahu in a little rice teriyaki stand several blocks from Pearl Harbor where U.S. sailors came ashore on leave en route to downtown Honolulu, which was then little more than the pink Royal Hawaiian Hotel with a cluster of smaller buildings spread along Waikiki Beach. The rice stall was fastidiously neat, the rice the very best, the teriyaki beef devoid of the fatty gristle of less conscientious entrepreneurs, and for U.S. servicemen on a sailor's meager pay, many of them coming out of a depression-battered America, it was the cheapest off-base meal around.

Except for every second Sunday, Omura, his wife, and his grandson worked what eighty years later would be called "24-7" as they served up the steaming hot rice and teriyaki.

They listened to the sailors carefully, noting their shoulder-patch ship's insignia. On his biweekly day off, Grandfather Omura would take his long bamboo rod and go fishing around the harbor—not, of course, in any restricted area, but it wasn't difficult to identify a U.S. aircraft carrier or a battleship, the leviathans of the world's navies. And, like any fisherman, he'd try different spots. A good caster for his age, Omura always used a heavy sinker so as to get his line well beyond the rocks. Allowing for the angle of his cast line, he could estimate the depth—always vital information for Admiral Yamamoto's G2 intelligence staff whenever they planned a submarine- or air-launched attack. The Kempei Tai had also provided Grandfather Omura with a German-made wide-angle Voigtlander Vito B camera set into the false bottom of his bait-and-tackle bag, the camera activated by merely reaching down for bait and pressing the shutter button.

The undeveloped film was left under one of the many black, honeycombed volcanic rocks that Tayama passed by on his nightly walk through the park across from Waikiki beach, up toward Diamond Head. Tayama and Grandfather Omura knew that if they did not continue spying for the Kempei Tai, who had "kindly" facilitated their emigration to Hawaii, then Tayama's two eighteen-year-old brothers, one conscripted and serving in Manchuria, the other in Korea as part of the Japanese occupational force, which had been there since 1910, and both his teenaged sisters—all effectively kept as hostages by the Kempei Tai—would suffer the consequences under the hands of the Imperial Army's Unit 736. This secret group of Japanese "scientists" specialized in tying Chinese and, later, Allied POWs to wooden stakes and subjecting them to a plethora of chemical and biological prototype weapons. The unit's doctors, like Dr. Mengele in Auschwitz, who also subjected human beings to unspeakable tortures, kept meticulous records of how long it took the subjects to die when exposed to anthrax, bubonic plague, et cetera, so as to better manufacture the prototype weapons the Imperial Japanese Army were building for use against their potential enemies, the Chinese, Koreans, British, and Americans.

The strain on Arturo Omura proved too much, and a combination of hypertension, fatigue, and guilt at what he was doing against America killed him in the summer of 1940. His wife, heartbroken, fell gravely ill less than six months later, in early January of 1941, with pneumonia. Their grandson Tayama, now eighteen, had to take over the burden from his grandfather, spying full-time for the Kempei Tai, lest his brothers and sisters back in Japan be imprisoned or executed for any refusal on Tayama's part to continue spying.

Once able to share the burden of his grandparents' circumstances, of their American dream gone sour because of the neighbor in Japan who had informed on them, of having to assure the safety of their loved ones back in Japan, Manchuria, and Korea—wherever the Imperial Japanese Army had sent them—Tayama now had to carry the added responsibility of running the rice and teriyaki cart by himself. The Kempei Tai, using the most popular and therefore the most widely distributed American novel of 1939 as the reference for their number-for-letter code, informed Tayama, via the dead-drop stone in the park across from Waikiki, that he would receive money to help pay off his grandmother's bill for what had turned out to be a month's hospitalization at Queen's Hospital before she died. "Big deal," Tayama told himself, using one of the quintessential American expressions he'd learned since being in Hawaii. Was this monetary assistance supposed to be received as an act of Japanese generosity after they had blackmailed him to assure the safety of his family? He also began receiving monthly postcards from his two sisters and two brothers, his sisters' postcards bearing the postmark of Nagasaki. The handwriting was certainly theirs, but the content was bland: visits to shrines, flower shows, et cetera. Nothing that was even remotely political unless, Tayama suspected, the endless postcards of shrines were meant to remind him of one's expected and sacred duty of sacrifice to the motherland. But beyond this, there was no hint of the rapidly growing tension between the United States and Japan as reported almost daily in the *Honolulu Advertiser* over Japan's continuing invasion of and atrocities in Chinese territory and Japan's ongoing brutal occupation of Korea, where thousands of Korean women were viewed by the Japanese Army as nothing more than sex slaves to be used in the service of the Japanese troops of occupation. In an attempt to counter any Western criticism of the army's treatment of these women, they were referred to as "prostitutes" by Japanese diplomats, a complete misnomer, as the women received no reward for providing the Japanese soldiers with sex. Indeed, they were shot if they resisted any son of Nippon, the pugilistic Nippon that the Omuras had sought, unsuccessfully, to escape.

Tayama received money and an assistant, Yoko, a good-looking Nisei, a Japanese-American of immigrant Japanese parentage. In her early twenties, she had been told to assist Tayama Omura in running the food stall. They hardly spoke for the first three days, he confining his remarks to instructions on the need for cleanliness—the thousands of sailors from Pearl Harbor were used to very high standards of hygiene aboard their ships. A food poisoning aboard a ship, some of them had told Tayama, could spread like a "prairie fire." Despite her being born in Oahu, Yoko was not familiar with the phrase "prairie fire" and felt embarrassed that she didn't understand. Tayama's explanation was given kindly, devoid of any of the pomposity she'd had to endure from other male Nisei bosses. She and Tayama worked well together, neither getting flustered by the rush of noonday and dinner customers, most of the crowd being sailors from the big American carriers *Enterprise, Lexington*, and *Saratoga*, which were tied up in Pearl, each of the three big aircraft carriers housing more than four thousand men and many fighters and torpedo bomber planes.

Soon Yoko was smiling and joking with the sailors, which, while it pleased Tayama from a business point of view, annoyed him intensely as a man who was sliding helplessly in love, despite the fact that he thought she must surely be a Kempei Tai operative.

She was.

July 4 was not a big celebration in Hawaii, which, as the Kempei Tai controllers never tired of reminding their agents, was not a state of the U.S. but still a territory, "stolen" from the Hawaiian Islanders by an act of Congress four years after an armed group of businessmen, led by a missionary's son, Sandford Dole, declared itself the provisional government of Hawaii, following which the islanders' beloved Queen Liliuokalani was arrested, tried, and humiliated in her own palace, deliberately referred to as "*Mrs.* Dominic," her American husband's last name. Sentenced at first to five years hard labor, this later commuted to a year's house arrest, Queen Liliuokalani died twenty-two years later in a house ironically called "Washington Place," situated one block away from the palace. But if July 4, 1941 was yet another American holiday despised by the Kempei Tai, it was not so for the 39 percent of the Hawaiian population who were Japanese. For them it *was* a holiday, a day off from hard labor in the rice and pineapple plantations. And for Tayama Omura, it was one of the most memorable days in his life, and Yoko's, as he finally told her he loved her and she confirmed her love for him—and her "blackmail" status as a Kempei Tai spy. It was an enormous relief for both of them. At least they could live together, as long as the Kempei Tai allowed them, free at least in each other's arms, unwilling spies, their horrible secret shared. Occasionally, one of the Kempei Tai's blackmailed Nisei agents couldn't take the pressure any longer, squeezed into an unbelievable psychological space between loyalty to family and loyalty to America, the country that had given them so much, a land of freedom impossible in Japan, from which their parents had fled through emigration. One such agent, a fisherman, had decided he could no longer take the strain and, knowing it was too dangerous to go directly to the Oahu police, wrote a letter to the Honolulu police chief.

Soon gruesome pictures of the man's headless corpse were found by Tayama, Yoko, and Kempei Tai agents at their individual drop-off points.

It was this agent's execution, his body having been dumped in shark-infested waters off Molokini's atoll near Maui, that was responsible for a sudden increase in American counterespionage surveillance of the large Hawaiian-Japanese population. For Yoko, her American citizenship exacerbated her guilt at times to almost unbearable proportions, despite her public face, especially as the Kempei Tai increased pressure on them to spend more time on their days off collecting as much intelligence as possible about the fleet anchored in Pearl Harbor. It was becoming too dangerous for Tayama to use his grandfather's Voigtlander camera.

On December 6, 1941, watching dancers already practicing for next summer's Prince Lot Hula Festival, Tayama and Yoko were stopped by a Japanese-Hawaiian man in his late twenties. Dressed in a colorful hibiscus-patterned shirt and matching shorts, and carrying a tightly rolled-up copy of the *Honolulu Advertiser,* he showed them a badge—police, FBI, Naval Intelligence, they didn't know which—and motioned them away from the edge of a noisy crowd nearby who were watching a hula competition. He led them toward the carp ponds and golden-stemmed bamboo in front of the Gardens'

Chinese hall, where a blush of yellow-orange ilima flowers against the green bowed obediently beneath the gentle, cooling flow of plumeria-tinged trade winds. Yoko, so frightened she felt she could barely breathe, fixed her eyes on the ilima blossoms that cast softly moving shadows along the edge of the pond in which big red-sashed carp glided by, Yoko envying the fishes' tranquillity. They heard the carefree laughter of a group of Nisei boys passing them, shouldering a six-foot koa-wood surfboard, another boy "heading" an even more prized sixteen-foot olo board, once allowed only to Hawaiian royalty, the youths' raucous chatter, and the fact that the boys seemed not to notice anyone else's presence in the park, increasing Yoko's fear.

The government agent stopped in the shade of a multi-trunked banyan tree, well away from the hula spectators. "I'm Lieutenant Suzuki, U.S. Naval Intelligence. You know what that is?"

Yoko looked somewhat puzzled, but answered, "Police?"

"Sort of," Lieutenant Suzuki said.

"Oh," said Tayama, "we have a license for stall."

Suzuki turned quickly, his right hand grasping his newspaper, trying to hit a wasp. "You have a *what*?" he asked Tayama brusquely.

"A license," explained Tayama, "for our stall."

"No, no," said Lieutenant Suzuki, suddenly twisting away from the wasp, smacking at it simultaneously. "Get outta here!"

"Wasp sting very bad," said Yoko with a sweet seriousness.

"What?—oh yeah. Damn things. It's the crowd. Too many people."

Yoko and Tayama waited politely as the wasp came in at Suzuki's head again. This time Suzuki's rolled-up *Advertiser* hit its target, the wasp momentarily flung into the brown grass, where the lieutenant's sandal quickly squashed it.

"Got the bastard!" Suzuki said triumphantly, and turned to Tayama. "You're old Arturo's grandson, aren't you?"

"Yes," Tayama answered, annoyed by Suzuki's easy familiarity with his grandfather's name but trying not to show it. The least this policeman could have said was "*Mr.* Omura's grandson."

"Why?" Tayama asked in as neutral a tone as he could muster, the Kempei Tai always having impressed upon their agents that while it is risky to appear defiant to investigators, it can also be dangerous to roll over like a dog in submission. Confident, patriotic citizens in America, Tayama had been told, and which he'd learned in Hawaii, didn't have anything like the respect for, or fear of, authority that citizens in Japan displayed. Your average U.S. citizen, the Kempei Tai had told him, would just as likely question the questioner with something like, "What's the problem?"

Lieutenant Suzuki stamped on the dead wasp again as if to emphasize his unrelenting nature. "You fish a lot?"

"Fish?" Tayama shrugged—he felt American. "Yeah," he said easily—not "yes," but "yeah." "So," he added, grinning, "there a law against fishing?"

"No," said Suzuki, turning his attention to Yoko, who was looking respectfully at this man who felt the need to kill insects twice. "No law against it. It's just that you've been seen fishing a lot near Pearl." Suzuki was still looking intently at Yoko, the trade wind that was whispering through the profusion of banyan leaves above them gently blowing a strand of hair across her slightly parted lips.

"So?" said Tayama, fighting his anger at how Suzuki was staring at Yoko, the lieutenant's look lascivious in its intensity. "You want me to fish somewhere else?"

"Might be an idea," said Suzuki, without taking his eyes off Yoko.

Tayama was about to say, "It's a free country," but that

would be pushing it. At the same time, he was aware that too easy an acquiescence might confirm any suspicions Suzuki was harboring about him or Yoko. "Okay, but what's the problem?"

"Security," said Suzuki, his eyes shifting suddenly to Tayama. "Navy doesn't like people getting too close to Pearl."

"Okay," said Tayama. "All this trouble with Tojo, right?"

"Yeah."

Tayama nodded thoughtfully. "He's a troublemaker, that one," he said, and he meant it. "They ought to do something about him." Suzuki sensed a hard conviction in the young Nisei's voice, a tone that made it clear that this Omura really did not like the Japanese war minister.

Tayama was feeling increasingly nervous. If Suzuki mentioned his and Yoko's nightly walks through Moanalua Gardens, it would tell Tayama that U.S. Naval Intelligence was doing much more than a simple security check on them.

"Don't take offense," said Suzuki. "It's not just you. They don't want anyone near Pearl."

"Fine," said Tayama.

Suzuki said nothing, and there was an awkward silence before he gave a nod and walked away. Another wasp swooped out of the banyan toward him; the investigator frenetically struck out again with the newspaper.

"He looks so funny!" said Yoko, hand to mouth as if to stem an explosion of laughter.

"Don't!" Tayama said. "That'd really make him—" Taking Yoko's hand, he turned about quickly to look back at the hula competitions, and they both shook with laughter, their outburst exacerbated by the sudden release of tension, the sound of their laughter fortunately subsumed by the clapping of the hula spectators. Tayama told Yoko he would have to find a better hiding place for the concealed camera in his tackle box. No doubt the Kempei Tai would press him to keep photographing Pearl, whether he kept fishing or not. Tayama and Yoko also reaffirmed their decision never to disclose the name of their *shikisha*—controller—to each other. That way, if they were ever caught, neither of them could identify the other's contact. Tayama wondered just how many spies, willing or otherwise, the Kempei Tai had planted throughout these beautiful and, for him and Yoko, dangerous islands.

After they made love the next morning, he showed Yoko where the camera and lenses were, in the event something happened to him before he could move them unobserved from the apartment. It had been during one of the rare times when his snoopy landlady wasn't at home that he'd taken the Voigtlander and lenses out of the false bottom of his fishing tackle box and placed them beneath a floorboard in his apartment. "If I'm not here," he told her, "and you have to get the camera quickly, don't bother fiddling about with the coins I use to lever it up. Go get the claw hammer from the cupboard under the bathroom sink. It's in with the other plumbing tools."

She nodded. They lay in silence together in the dreamy afterglow of their passionate release, and understood each other without talking, so that when she finally did speak it was in answer to a question he had not asked, but which she'd felt. "Don't worry, Tay. I'm strong enough. I could pull up the whole floor with my fingers."

He squeezed her shoulders, looking into the imperturbability of her eyes. "I hope you never have to." He started to get up.

"No, stay," she begged.

He turned his wristwatch toward her—it read 6:20. "Already late, sweetheart. We should have been out of here ten minutes ago. I'll go ahead, set up the stall." He kissed her. She dragged him back down. "Let them wait. No one wants to eat till ten. Everyone sleeps in today."

"You're a seductress!" he said happily, pulling away, unlocking his arms from her. She *was* strong.

"Your body," she said, her eyes fixed on his nakedness, "is showing me you want to stay."

He threw her a kiss. It wouldn't have mattered if it had been pouring rain outside, his mood after making love with Yoko was always upbeat. He felt, as Grandfather Omura would have said, like a lion. The fact that the early sun was shining in a near-cloudless sky, the blue not yet paled, and there was the myriad birdsong of barred doves, mynah birds, and sparrows, amid the fragrance of plumeria, whose white blossoms stood out amid the verdant hibiscus-splashed green of indigenous plants, only elevated his mood that much more. Instead of the downcast feeling that had always accompanied his morning walk to work before he met Yoko, he now had the feeling that with her he could endure. It was true: love did conquer all.

As if it was being performed just for him, sweet music floated across the harbor from Pearl's Ford Island, where colors were being struck as the sailors in their Sunday whites began their day. The approaching dots of planes coming in over the Waianae Mountains to the northwest, Tayama thought, must be some kind of fly-past, the pilots' timing impeccable. As the dots became larger, Tayama saw the blood-red suns painted on the fuselage and suddenly stopped, all his attention riveted on the planes and the black cigarlike appendages slung beneath them. Torpedoes. It was as if a giant's hand had grasped his throat, his larynx paralyzed, unable to utter a sound though his mouth was wide-open.

It was 7:49 as Air Commander Fuchida, breaking radio silence, signaled, *"Tora! Tora! Tora!"*—Tiger! Tiger! Tiger! Received by Admiral Nagumo, commander of "Red Castle," the carrier *Akagi,* 275 miles northeast of Oahu, the message from Fuchida was confirmation that the Japanese spearhead squadrons of forty-three Mitsubishi Zero fighters, forty-nine

Nakajima bombers, fifty-one Aichi dive-bombers, and forty Torpedo bombers had attained complete surprise, catching the Americans off guard not only in Pearl Harbor but at other U.S. airfields and barracks throughout Hawaii, as well. Fuchida joked gleefully with his fellow pilots that they had caught the Americans "with their pants down." Bombs were raining even before morning colors aboard the American ships had been completed, the Japanese pilots struck by how, save for the absence of several U.S. carriers, the layout in Pearl Harbor had been so precisely duplicated by Japanese Intelligence in the pilots' practice mockups in Japan.

Tayama, like so many other inhabitants of Honolulu watching the massive raid unfold, could feel the concussion of the massive explosions in the pit of his stomach, the attack so savage and unexpected that for many the curling palls of thick, black smoke in the distance and the roiling eruptions of orange-crimson fire on Ford Island and belching fire from the docked and anchored fleet seemed surreal at first—it couldn't possibly be happening, not against America's Pacific bastion. It must be Hollywood people making a film.

Those too far away from Pearl to hear the screams and other agonies of the dying sailors and civilian employees who were trying to save themselves and their vessels nevertheless saw the carnage, marked by the great curdling black columns of oil smoke, so thick at times that it obscured the stricken battleships under attack.

Yoko came running down to join Tayama, who hadn't moved since the first torpedo struck. The reek of the oil fires and the death and destruction was so strong, it had overwhelmed the usually flower-scented trade winds, indelibly impressing the pungent odor of the tragedy on the senses of those who saw and smelled it.

Out of breath, Yoko grabbed Tayama's arm, gripping it tightly. "I—I—got rid of the camera. The landlady—" Yoko had to stop for air. "The landlady ran outside with everyone else as soon as the first bombs—Oh, Tayama, what'll we do?"

It was as if he hadn't heard her, his head shaking in stubborn disbelief, yet he could taste the fumes of burning oil. "Yesterday," he told Yoko, "the radio announcer said our people and theirs were having discussions in Washington to avoid any—" Tayama's voice was lost amid a bone-shaking detonation. A battleship had split apart as its forward magazine exploded from a direct hit, what had been its deck now a gaping hole, vomiting flame skyward as gunpowder packs for the leviathan's big fourteen-inch guns blew up and ammunition cooked off amid the blazing infernos. Yoko was crying, utterly confused. "What do you mean?" she asked, shaking. "our people and theirs?"

Tayama didn't answer. Instead, he quietly took her hand.

It was 8:30, just over a half hour after the beginning of the attack, and already seven of the American battleships—*West Virginia, Arizona, Maryland, Tennessee, Nevada, Oklahoma,* and *California*—had been either sunk, run aground, or engulfed in flames from explosions the likes of which few Hawaiians, even those who had witnessed Hawaii's legendary volcanic eruptions, had ever witnessed.

"We have to get into town," Tayama told Yoko. "One of the fishermen I know does a run to Kauai."

Yoko had often dreamed of going there, to the lushly beautiful island, but as a visitor, not on the run. "How long will it take us?"

"I'm not sure," he said, knowing only that Kauai was about 120 miles from Oahu. "Twelve, maybe fifteen hours. If we can leave straightaway, we should be there about midnight."

Tayama flagged down a Waikiki-bound bus. The bus driver was also Japanese-American, the three of them avoiding eye contact. What would the American authorities do? How would they decide who were loyal Niseis and loyal immigrants and who weren't?

Tayama saw a neighbor, also Japanese-American. They exchanged glances nervously. The man, holding tightly on to the back of one of the seats as Tayama and Yoko passed him, suddenly blurted out, "We'll be all right."

Tayama and Yoko said nothing. At the next bus stop an elderly white couple got on, the man glaring at the driver. "I'm not paying *you*!" he said.

"Walter!" the man's wife snapped. "There's no need for that. Pay the man."

"See," said Tayama's neighbor, "we'll be fine. Look at the German-Americans. They're fine." The man's voluble, unsought opinion embarrassed everyone on the bus, especially Tayama and Yoko, the man's public display not at all in the nature of the Japanese-born Americans. And it was delivered in such a tremulous voice that it suggested he was merely trying to reassure himself. "Yeah," he mumbled. "We'll be fine."

As the bus neared the fishermen's wharf a mile or so west of Waikiki, Yoko could see a huddle of a half-dozen or so people by several of the boats off to the right, involved in some kind of altercation with a Navy shore patrol, the latter's highly polished white helmets and black-lettered MP armbands standing out in the bright sun against the surf-fringed turquoise ocean.

"Don't get out," Tayama told Yoko quietly, holding her hand tightly. "I don't see his boat. We'll go on to Waikiki and I'll call his home. He might have anchored somewhere on the island's northwest side, which is better anyway. It's closer to Kauai."

"Ha!" said their nervous neighbor. "All probably drunk. Saturday-night fling. Ha!"

Yoko smiled weakly. Farther on, at the stop a block from the pink Royal Hawaiian, which was one of only a few hotels near what is now the International Market Place, they alighted so that Tayama could use the pay phone in the plush lobby of the hotel. One of the American guests coming out of the hotel glowered at them, a bellboy trying to get the crowd waiting for the phone to form a line along one side of the lobby, where guests, early risers for a Sunday, were spilling out onto Kalakaua Avenue in confused alarm. Someone was yelling that Schofield Army Barracks were also under attack, someone else claimed that a Japanese submarine had been depth-charged off the entrance to Pearl Harbor. Perhaps, Tayama thought, that had been the first explosion he'd heard on the way to the stall.

Tayama and Yoko, avoiding the stares of guests coming and going through the lobby, kept their eyes fixed on the phone queue ahead of them, the hostility in the air so intense that for the first time in her life Yoko was aware that she could actually feel waves of hatred directed at her.

"Hey, Omura!"

Tayama turned his head back toward the hotel's entrance.

"Come here!" It was the Naval intelligence officer, Lieutenant Suzuki.

Even before Tayama and Yoko stepped up into the back of the open khaki-green three-ton Army truck, they saw that their neighbor from the bus was among the dozen or so Japanese-Americans who had already been rounded up.

"Think we'll be all right?" Tayama asked his neighbor as he sat down on the truck's hard seat.

"Shut your face, Omura!" shouted Suzuki.

CHAPTER FOURTEEN

ON THE THIRD night of internment, as the moon slipped temporarily behind thick cumulus, Yoko, blindfolded, was taken by two men to a small, pitch-dark shed toward the rear of the camp. One of the men savagely beat her when she tried to protest, her blindfold slipping. He shoved an oily wad of cloth down her throat. After the rape, they told her if she reported it to anyone, her "Jap boyfriend" would be dragged out of the men's barracks and would "get the shit kicked out of him."

One of her attackers, though she could see neither clearly, given the darkness, was a black man, and the other sounded like Lieutenant Suzuki.

Bleeding, her face throbbing with pain, Yoko crept back to the women's barracks and wept quietly in her bunk, determined not to raise a fuss, put Tayama in danger. The thought that Suzuki, a fellow Japanese-American, might have been one of the men seemed unthinkable until she recalled reports she'd heard of how in Korea and China some of the POWs captured by the Japanese Imperial Army had turned collaborationist, and had become more cruel toward their own kind than their Japanese captors.

Four days later she saw Suzuki enter the camp between two tall white guards and noticed, with satisfaction, that the naval intelligence officer's former swaggering self-confidence had been replaced now with a stare of apprehension.

A few days later the rumor was that while Suzuki was still nominally a lieutenant in U.S. Naval Intelligence, he was being used not as an interrogator but merely as an interpreter and, as a further insult, in the women's, rather than the men's, barracks. He too was clearly under suspicion. She also saw Tayama for the first time since they had been herded into the Army truck. Not being married they, like all the other single men and women, had been segregated and couldn't speak to each other. But Tayama didn't have to be told what had happened to her. He could see the dark bruising on her face and arms, her swollen lips, and while he said nothing, the veins in his neck suddenly became taut, pulsating with rage at what he knew must have happened.

From that moment on, Tayama Omura's one-time admiration for America and Americans froze and transformed itself into a hatred that would never leave him, a hatred increasingly rationalized by the way in which the innocent Nisei and Japanese immigrants in Hawaii would be treated for the duration of the war. Never mind the fact that later Nisei volunteers, many of them who, like Suzuki, had been either downgraded or dismissed outright from the National Guard and who were prevented from joining any of the armed services, eventually formed two segregated Nisei regiments and that one of these units, the 442nd, went into action in Europe, becoming the most decorated combat unit in the history of the United States. Or that one of the Nisei veterans, whose life was saved by a field blood transfusion from a member of a segregated black combat unit and who lost an arm during battle, was not only decorated but later became Hawaii's first senator. For Tayama Omura all that mattered was that his beloved Yoko had been raped by an American.

Six weeks after the assault, Yoko realized her ill fortune had become compounded and drastically exacerbated. She was pregnant, so now she lived with the ever-growing fear— one of the worst to befall a Nisei—that she might be carrying a black man's child. Not even white Hawaiians, she knew, could live with what was then considered a shame worse than death. In Yoko's Japan it had always been accepted that black Americans were no better than savages. They were considered highly potent sexually but almost as low on the evolutionary ladder as the Chinese, those Chinese who had fled their turbulent country to Hawaii now taking a special, if quiet, delight in seeing the Nisei rounded up, receiving what the Chinese deemed the Nisei's comeuppance. It was only fitting, from the Chinese view, that the Japanese pay not only for their attack against America but also for their continuing invasion of the Chinese homeland, memories of Nippon's aggression in Manchuria and the rape of Nanking still fresh in the minds of many Chinese who had fled their homeland to escape the Japanese.

If there was any chance of Tayama's hatred of the U.S. fading in the future, it was dashed forever on the evening of Sunday, March 15, 1942, when Yoko, despite the prohibitions of her deep Shinto upbringing, tried to abort her pregnancy with a coat hanger in the women's barracks washroom. Septicemia quickly set in and soon she went into shock. She was rushed to Queen's Hospital but "expired following abortion of Caucasian/Asian fetus," as the coroner's report put it, "at 0315, March 17/42."

From that day on, Tayama Omura, his hatred further fueled later by the fact that both his sisters were killed, along with tens of thousands of his fellow Japanese, by the A-bomb the Americans dropped on Nagasaki, which ended the war, became an implacable foe of the United States. The subsequent apologies by the U.S. government years later for its wartime treatment of Americans of Japanese descent did nothing to mitigate his hatred, so that during the Korean War of the early 1950s when he was approached by North Korea's RDEI, Research Department for External Intelligence, he was ripe for recruitment to spy on America's strategically vital Pacific base in Hawaii. If revenge hadn't been motivation enough, he was brusquely informed by the Kempei Tai that his two brothers, who had surrendered with the other Japanese divisions in Korea at World War II's end, might be eventually freed and repatriated by Pyongyang. But it was an unnecessary inducement, for what had previously been a resented task of espionage, through blackmail, against the Americans had now become a zealous and ongoing revenge for the death of his beloved Yoko and his two sisters.

And so, by the time General Douglas Freeman and his eight fellow "nonactive" list team members were en route on their black-ops Payback mission, the defiant but ever-cautious, hardworking Omura, the "quiet old guy" who had built up a chain of teriyaki/rice and sushi stalls throughout the islands after the war and who, in his quietude, didn't seem to bear any residual animosity against America for its treatment of Japanese-American immigrants during the war, had developed one of the most sophisticated North Korean espionage rings in the United States.

Following what the international media were calling a "terrorist" attack in America against the three airliners, North Korean Intelligence HQ in Pyongyang issued a red alert to its agents throughout the world. Omura's network was specifically ordered to watch for any unusual U.S. military activity in Hawaii, as it was the most likely stopover and refueling base for any U.S. SpecOps "Asian target" mission launched from America's West Coast—the big U.S. base in Yokohama the most likely springboard after Hawaii.

Omura's espionage ring went into high gear. One of his agents, a worker at the huge military airbase adjacent to Honolulu's civilian airport, saw a huge plane land that same evening. With his folding NVG zoom-lens video camera he got a shot of nine men plus the pilot and air crew who alighted from the huge cavernous jungle-green/khaki aircraft. Ten minutes later Omura's agent was able to take infrared stills of the loading of what he estimated was a sixty- to seventy-foot-long fuselage with six wheels, two at either end and two in the middle. It was encased in U.S. Army khaki all-weather wrap and had three equally spaced bumps, like engine blocks, along the top, the wrap, it occurred to Omura's agent, the same kind in which the Americans had transported aircraft and helicopters from Hawaii to Camrahn Bay during the Vietnam War. But he reported that he could see no rotor blades attached, assuming these, as was usual during transport, had been bundled inside the huge Galaxy.

CHAPTER FIFTEEN

Pyongyang (North Korean Intelligence HQ)

"SOMETIMES," COLONEL KIM said, upon receiving the coded e-mail message, "the Americans wrap the rotors separately from the main body of the helicopter like a collapsed beach umbrella. Unfortunately our agent's NVG camera's angle has obviously not penetrated deeper into the plane's interior."

"It looks to me, Comrade Colonel," suggested his second in command, Major Park, "that it *is* a helo. One of the three bumps, the middle one, is the engine, the other two being rotor mounts, one forward, the other to the rear."

"Like their original Chinook," said Colonel Kim, "only a smaller, faster *lift* helo."

The colonel thought hard, his dour grimace born of the ruthless competition for promotion in a country that prided itself in being the last true Communist stronghold in a capitalist-corrupted world. He looked again at Omura's spy's report. In his mind's eye Colonel Kim was going over the various types of U.S. helos, trying to discern what kind of load the American Special Forces could be carrying. One of the men in the infrared stills, Omura's message informed him, was definitely the legendary Freeman who, Kim remembered, had made a name for himself against the Siberian Sixth Armored. But he was retired, wasn't he? And what heavy load was the helo, if it *was* a helo, trying to deliver? And where? Surely the American marauder Freeman—if he *was* planning an attack on North Korea—must realize what folly it would be to enter North Korean airspace with *any* kind of helo. Even if Freeman was daring enough to fly NOE, nap of the earth, under the radar screen, he would first be picked up by North Korean coastal radar as he flew in from Japan or Okinawa farther to the south.

"Special weapons?" suggested Major Park. "To attack the heavily defended depot at Kosong?"

"Are you sure," put in Lieutenant Rhee of Coastal Defense Unit 5, "the Americans' target is Kosong? Perhaps they are only going as far as Japan?"

Colonel Kim and Major Park looked at their unusually tall subaltern. A young officer's initiative was encouraged up to a point in the Dear Leader's million-man army, as in any other military, but stupidity wasn't.

"Where else could the gangster American and his team of thugs be headed for?" asked Colonel Kim.

The earnest young officer, Lieutenant Rhee of the North Korean Army's East Coast Defense Command, quickly apologized for his presumptuousness, but the fact was that he had more on-the-ground experience than either Colonel Kim or Major Park along the rugged east coast, where the beautiful and massive Taebek range stood as a mighty bastion against the East Sea and Japan 475 miles away. It had been Japan from which the hated Americans had come to aid the detested South in what North Korea had taught its people had been a reactionary capitalist war waged by the United States and its running-dog lackey, South Korea, against the paradisiacal North. By now, this blatant distortion of history was accepted as inviolable fact by several generations of

North Koreans, despite them having gone through such devastating famines in the 1990s and early 2000s that starvation rations had killed thousands and literally dwarfed an entire generation.

It was because of these famines that Lieutenant Rhee, at five feet ten, stood out as among the tallest of his generation, from which Pyongyang had had to struggle to get any North Korean soldiers who could hold their own standing next to the six-and-a-half-foot American giants who manned the DMZ with such impressive physical presence. But the North Korean Army, along with their Dear Leader and his cabal in Pyongyang, were the best fed in a country whose Communist leadership under the Dear Leader had poured all it possibly could into its armed forces. As such, the army of which Lieutenant Rhee of North Korea's Coastal Defense Command was an ardent member came closer to the clichéd "lean and mean" ideal than most professional armies. The meanness was the result of a carefully maintained paranoid cradle-to-grave indoctrination of hatred against America and its "running-dog lackeys," the latter a Communist propaganda expression so old and outworn that other Communist regimes no longer bothered to use it.

It was used again in May 2004 after a train on April 22 carrying ammonia nitrate fertilizer through Ryongchon near the Chinese–North Korean border struck an oil tanker train, which brought down a live power cable, causing a massive explosion that leveled large sections of Ryongchon and killed or wounded over two thousand, most of them children. For the first time in more than thirty years, the Hermit Kingdom requested outside aid, but any coming from the running-dog lackeys of America or South Korea had to be rerouted by sea so that the North Koreans would not think the U.S. or any of its "lackeys" were involved in the aid effort.

For Rhee, the daily propaganda had nurtured a continual sense of vigilance, increased by the undeniable geographic fact of the ruggedness of Korea's east coast. He could think of few other coastlines that were so ideal for covert landings of special forces by North Korea's enemies.

CHAPTER SIXTEEN

ON THE OTHER side of the world, in the Galaxy's huge redded-out interior, Douglas Freeman and his eight-man SpecOp team could feel the change in the deep, throbbing timbre of the Galaxy's four big engines as the giant transport began its glide path from 33,000 feet over the cobalt blue of the far western Pacific toward a verdant sliver of land that was the southeastern coast of Japan. It had been a long haul, both the Galaxy's crew and Freeman's team glad to see terra firma. As they passed over the Japanese coastline, an immaculate green patchwork of rice fields below, no one was happier than Choir Williams, who hated the avgas smell that permeated transport aircraft. This only added to his general aversion to air travel, which was, contrary to all counterargument, based on his firm belief that bad things happen in threes. In all other matters, Choir's SpecFor buddies knew him as the epitome of the nonsuperstitious, commonsense soldier, but on this matter of threes, his belief was as unshakeable as Freeman's conviction, which also amused fellow SpecFor members, that George Washington had indeed stood in the prow of the boat. Those who knew Freeman well, like Aussie Lewis, Salvini, and Choir, saw the general's belief not so much as evidence of his eccentric nature but as a manifestation of his lifelong commitment to exemplary leadership. It was the type of "on the point" leadership that Washington had exemplified: visible and unafraid, the kind

that those who had served under Freeman had come to expect
and which, despite his Pattonesque gruffness at times, was
the reason that even those who didn't like him had to grudg-
ingly admire him.

"Not long now," Freeman advised Choir, as the Galaxy entered a "shelf" of bone-rattling turbulence at ten thousand
feet, the Welsh-American's face having taken on a pucelike
pallor.

"Should've eaten somethin', mate," advised Aussie
loudly, " 'fore we left Hawaii."

"He did," said Sal, winking at Chief Petty Officer Tavos
and the four other SEAL volunteers. "A banana and a slice o'
white bread—you know, the old diarrhea diet."

"No, no," Aussie corrected Sal, "I meant a *meal*—you
know, a mess o' fried eggs, bacon, nice greasy side of fries,
and—"

"You wicked bastard," Choir mumbled weakly.

Freeman smiled at the give-and-take between Choir and
Aussie, their ongoing teasing a measure of his team's
morale. Sal's winking at Tavos and including the four other
SEALs in the joke was the kind of small but deliberate act of
inclusion that the general knew was crucial if the team was
to execute what he, in one of the greatest understatements of
his career, had referred to casually in his airborne briefing as
"pre-mission DOPAE"—deplaning of personnel and equipment. It was an innocent-sounding acronym, which one of
the SEALs, Eddie Mervyn, confided to his colleague multilingual Johnny Lee, must have originated in someone's
dope-smoking mode.

"No way, Eddie," Lee assured him, smiling. "Closest the
general's come to smoking a joint, I heard, was when he
went to a strip joint looking for terrorists in Washington
State."

Eddie Mervyn, checking his weapon of choice, a Heckler
& Koch 9mm with folding stock and laser-dot targeting,

commented, "No terrorists in a strip joint. Muslim fanatics don't drink or watch tit."

"Exactly," said Lee, "but the scuttlebutt is, the general cottoned to the idea that strip joints'd be the perfect cover for terrorists in the States. No one in Homeland Security'd expect that a fundamentalist fanatic would go to the tit shops and hit the booze, right? Perfect cover."

Bone Brady was impressed. "So Freeman figured that out?"

"Yep," said Lee.

The general made no comment, his attention drawn to the six-wheeled equipment that was shuddering in the turbulence. He loosened his harness a tad so he could lean forward from the team's bench and tighten one of the lines.

Aussie, to the four SEALs' amazement, had nodded off, his legs sticking out, his feet resting on his combat pack and almost touching one of the bright orange "glo" Air Force HIBUDs—"hi-buoyancy" drums—that had been lashed down below the equipment's pallet.

"Can see *he's* worried," the loadmaster joshed before he made his way through the narrow space to inform the general that they were fifteen minutes from the carrier battle group *McCain* off the island of Ullŭng.

"Thanks, Sergeant," acknowledged Freeman. "Would you ask the driver to put it through on-screen?"

"Yes, sir."

As the flat screen came alive, they could see the Galaxy's line of descent toward Ullŭng Island, 170 miles east-southeast of Kosong on the North Korean coast, the Kosong warehouse on the SATPIX—satellite pictures—being ten miles north of the DMZ. Whether or not the team would head the 92 miles in to the South Korean coast then head up along the coast, passing over the DMZ, or head instead directly to Kosong would be something Freeman would decide after—or rather, *if*—the deplaning of personnel and equipment succeeded, and after he received updated real-time intel. The latter could be provided only by the Signals Exploitation Space, the ultrasecret "blue tile" room with its "Big Blue" screen located deep in the inner sanctums of the *McCain*, as the carrier steamed at reduced speed off Ullŭng, protected by its battle group's screen of cruisers, destroyers, and two nuclear attack submarines.

The screen's data-block read, "TD2"—time to drop zone—"14 minutes."

"With this headwind that's hitting us now," said Salvini, "I'd say it'll be more like twenty minutes."

"Want to bet on it?" joshed Freeman.

"Bet?" It was Lewis, suddenly awake and sitting up. "Did I hear *bet*?"

Freeman smiled knowingly at Brady, who was sitting immediately to the general's right. "Aussie'd bet on the sun not coming up. Next to watching that so-called football game down under, 'Australian Rules'—an oxymoron if I've ever heard one—Aussies are addicted to beer and gambling."

"Yeah," Salvini called out above the sustained roar of the Galaxy's turbofans. "An Aussie gets wounded, they transfuse him with Foster's Lager."

"Foster's, my ass!" Aussie corrected him, sitting up and assuming the air of an outraged connoisseur. "I only drink Castlemaine. That's Castlemaine Four X to *you*, Mr. Salvini." Aussie turned to look along the bench to the tall African-American. "What's the bet, Shorty?"

"Data-block up there," explained Brady, indicating the screen, "is telling us it's fourteen—no, thirteen—minutes to the drop zone. Sal thinks it'll be longer."

"Ten minutes," came the pilot's warning, the headwind having now dissipated.

"Damn!" said Aussie. "I could have made some money."

The red light was still on but already the Galaxy's ramp yawn was under way, the great plane's huge door lowering like the jaw of some airborne leviathan, the whine and howl of its hydraulic pressure lines mixing with the rush of cold air invading the huge, warm cave of the plane's interior.

Far below, they could see a vast, cobalt-blue sea, wrinkled and flecked here and there by the short-lived whiteness of breaking waves. The loadmaster and another crew member released the tension lines. The crated equipment, which included the team's eight individual eighty-pound combat packs, Freeman not needing one insofar as he'd been ordered by the President to stay at mission control, slid noisily but evenly down over the rows of precisely aligned rollers.

The drogue chute pack attached to the palletized load followed it out into the void in a long taper of bundled lines, the sudden unraveling and reefing of the three enormous nylon conical-ribbon drogue chutes, each 83.5 feet in diameter, sounding like a thousand tents struck by a banshee wind. The noise was so alarming that for several moments, before the tripetal blossoming of the drogues' dazzling white canopies a half mile aft of the plane, Johnny Lee instinctively stepped back—onto Eddie Mervyn's combat boots. Mervyn's obscenity was unheard by his diving buddy, given the combined maelstrom of unraveling lines, slipstream, engine noise, and the racket created by the hundreds of well-oiled floor rollers still spinning, despite their load having exited, descending toward the sea. It was a sea that, given the centuries-old conflict between the two countries, was claimed by both Korea, as the East Sea, and by the inheritors of Nippon, as the Sea of Japan, even before Japan's annexation of Korea in 1910 and its brutal domination of the country until 1945.

"Go!" shouted the Air Force sergeant. The team stepped into space, Freeman and his first four from the ramp's starboard side, Aussie and the remaining three from the port side, the roaring wind so cold, so fast, it took their breath away, heart rates increasing, the dot of Ullŭng Island coming up at them fast.

Then each man felt the sudden jerk, his body rising as his Mach III Alpha—the high-glide tactical parachute—took over. With the best glide-rate-to-descent ratio of any Special Forces chutes in the world and its eighteen ripple-arc panels and independently flexed left/right control cords, it allowed its jumper unprecedented maneuverability, despite each commando's heavy combat pack.

The black basalt pinnacles of Ullŭng Island appeared momentarily to be sliding uphill, an optical illusion caused by the nine men's alpha chutes inclining slightly against the horizontal during a short, sharp buffeting by updrafts. Beyond the island, Freeman and his men now saw the whitish gray slivers of the *McCain*'s 7th Fleet battle group, the carrier battle group out of COMPAC's—Commander Pacific's—base in Yokosuka, Japan. *McCain* was steaming, as expected, in the middle of her protective screen. Not surprisingly, the two attack subs, presumably fore and aft, were nowhere in sight.

Within *McCain*'s screen of twelve vessels, which included four destroyers, two frigates, two guided-missile Aegis cruisers, a replenishment vessel, and the two nuclear attack submarines, was the Wasp-class helo carrier transport USS *Yorktown*, carrying 2,100 Marines of a Marine Expeditionary Unit under the command of Colonel Jack Tibbet. Marines high and low were making bets as to whether the nine parachutists would be able to land on the "boat," as the big aircraft carrier *McCain* was known to her six thousand personnel, the other ships' sole reason for being in the battle group to protect Captain Crowley's flat-top.

"What d'you think, sir?" Executive Officer John Cuso asked Crowley, who, as captain of the *McCain*, was also admiral of the fleet.

The diminutive Crowley, who'd stepped down from the bridge and made his way along the walkway known as "Vultures' Row," from where he had a high and open-aired view down onto the four and a half acres of flight deck, held Cuso's question in abeyance. He watched his orange-vested swimmers drop like black stones from *McCain*'s CM-53E, the Super Sea Stallion's rotors' slap clearly audible for a change, now that the carrier's air arm's ops had been suspended, its eighty-two aircraft chained down to allow as much space as possible for the helicopter's "triple P"—pick up personnel and pallet—retrieval crew to operate. This was a rare event in normal times, but less so in the world war against terrorism wherein U.S. supplies and combatants had to have RO/RO—roll-on, roll-off—capability across ever-shifting fronts, some of which existed one day and were gone the next.

"Depends on how much jump time they've racked up," Crowley finally answered.

Cuso, the black XO, executive officer, recalled the only combat jump he'd made in his life, an "emergency eject" from his shot-up Tomcat. It was an event so terrifying, so fast, Cuso sent hurtling out of the fighter with such force, that initially he'd felt no pain. That came later, together with the naval medical board informing him that the injuries he'd sustained in his lower back and legs would not only end his career as an elite naval aviator, the crème de la crème of combat pilots, but would even deny him the opportunity to be a "bus" driver in commercial aviation.

Cuso shaded his eyes against the sparkling sea. "You know who they are exactly?" he asked Crowley.

"Don't be silly, Commander. We aren't privy to that kind of SOCOM Washbasin information. We just row the boat, do as we're told."

John Cuso smiled wryly at Crowley's disdain for Special Operations Command and Washington, D.C.

"Used to be a time," Crowley continued, "when we were given more than visiting Special Forces' blood type, rank, and serial number. But now—" He exhaled wearily while watching the nine descending dots scattered high above the battle group. "—we're damned lucky to be told where they're going."

The parachutists continued performing what appeared to be random gyrations but which, Crowley knew, were highly individually choreographed maneuvers designed to override and nullify the myriad unseen air currents that formed an invisible tangle of random vectors above the battle group. The sky above as much as the sea below him, the captain knew, was far from a uniform medium, consisting of phantom wind shears, crosswinds, and vicious gusts of air constantly in motion, so that the whole pattern of the invisible sky was ever changing as dramatically as the ceaseless reconfiguration of clouds.

Even before Douglas Freeman had reached the *McCain*'s fantail, stepping down onto it with all the grace of Baryishnikov, what seconds before had been a distant line of towering ice-cream-white on the horizon had already begun flattening out into what *McCain*'s weather office called L3s, shorthand for nascent and threatening thunderheads.

Aussie Lewis, Choir Williams, and Bone Brady touched down within seconds of one another on the port side of the flight deck directly across from the carrier's six-story-high island. Brady and Choir quickly turned to face their chutes, simultaneously running toward the wind-inflated nylon panels, quickly trying to reel in the chutes' lines. In both their chutes, the air-filled panels collapsed obediently onto the hard deck. Aussie's chute, however, broadsided by a sudden and powerful crosswind, one of those invisible demons of dog aviators and flight-deck crews alike, was blown back port aft, the small deck crew assigned to help running after him. Momentarily losing his footing, he tripped, being dragged unceremoniously across the tracks of catapults 3 and 4. In a second he was back on his feet, but unable to stop, glimpsing the black safety net that fringed the flight deck rushing toward him. He hit his emergency release buckle, but simultaneously fresh gusts reinflated his chute and he saw the safety netting flash by. A second later, his chute gone, he plummeted into the sea over fifty feet below, his swearing drowned unheard as he disappeared beneath the waves, his head bobbing up moments later in the carrier's dangerously churning wake.

The Super Stallion, which had assumed its normal position off *McCain*'s aft quarter after having lowered the team's big load onto the flight deck's number 1 elevator, now turned sharply in a U-turn, hard astarboard, its rescue swimmer already at the helicopter's door.

The helo's downdrafts momentarily flattened the carrier's wake into a foam-edged blue pool, Aussie's normally brown hair now a black slick, his face strained as he attempted to look up through a maelstrom of wind and water at the descending orange blur that was the rescue harness. He hadn't seen anyone drop from the helo, so that when the swimmer grabbed his arm, the Australian-born Lewis instantly thought "Shark!" and struck out with such violence that he stunned the swimmer, who in turn slapped Lewis across the face, yelling, "Calm down! I'm here to—"

"Oh, shit. Sorry, mate, geez—"

"Calm down!"

"Yeah, yeah, right. Okay."

"He hit him!" said John Cuso, watching through his binoculars.

"Who hit who?" growled Crowley, watching the last of the nine-man team, CPO Tavos, touch down without incident.

"That Special Forces guy in the drink," said Cuso. "He just clobbered our swimmer."

"Panic?" said Crowley. "Doesn't seem like Special Forces—more like a ninny."

The deck crew gave the chopper's rescue team, and presumably Aussie, a celebratory round of applause, the subdued sound of their gloves further muffled by the Sea Stallion's roar, its downwash throwing up tiny pieces of grit from the flight deck as high up as Vultures' Row, a piece stinging Crowley on the cheek.

"Dammit," grumped the admiral. As captain of the *McCain* he was almost as detail-obsessed about his job as was Douglas Freeman, who as yet Crowley did not know was the leader of this Special Forces drop-in. Crowley immediately ordered his XO to implement more than the normal number of pre-flight "FOD"—foreign debris—walkdowns, in which a long line of deck personnel, shoulder to shoulder, would move slowly down the fourteen-degree-angled flight deck, peering down at the black deck with the concentration of a hobo looking for cigarette butts and coins. Debris as small as a dime could play havoc with a jet's finely tuned engines and so delay an entire launch for a squadron or the 24-7 four-fighter CAP—combat air patrol. And a CAP must always be aloft, its pilots acting not only as over-the-horizon lookouts, but, should it become necessary, as the battle group's airborne "bouncers," as *McCain*'s master chief had called them.

Another piece of grit struck Cuso.

"Have a nice swim?" Sal asked Aussie, who was emerging from the Sea Stallion's downblast. His sodden uniform was so plastered against his body by wind and water that it reminded Cuso of the wrap he'd seen on the Special Forces "palletized" equipment, by now safely stowed below in the hangar deck where the wrap gave the crude rotorless helicopter shape a distinctly ungainly mummified appearance.

"I *said*," repeated Sal as he walked behind Aussie, "did you have a nice swim?"

"Piss off!" Aussie replied, following John Cuso, who was

leading the sodden Aussie below to one of the few shower-equipped two-man staterooms, Cuso explaining, by way of ameliorating Aussie's embarrassment, that the pilots were probably all aft, shooting the bull in their informal "Dirty Shirt" wardroom. But Aussie wasn't in the mood to hear what anyone else was doing—all he wanted was a hot shower, his desire for instant warmth increased by a bone-chilling blast of wind that Salvini also felt as they passed from the gray-tiled section of the carrier's gallery deck into "blue-tile country." Here, the cold air Salvini and Aussie had just experienced came from the computer-cooling fans in the five highly classified command and ultrasecret blue-tiled communications rooms, including the ship's Signal Exploitation Space, or SES.

"Take all the time you need," John Cuso told the still-dripping Aussie, who saw fresh, knife-edge-pressed Navy-issue khakis; a neatly folded, almost blindingly white crew-neck T-shirt next to the trousers, along with a pair of thick, woolen khaki socks and black boots that were so highly polished, Aussie could see Sal's maddeningly smug face on the boot's toe piece, together with a face he didn't recognize.

"Master Chief Schmidt here," Cuso told them, "will take you two gentlemen forward to the SpecOp briefing room. You two can spend the night in this stateroom. The other seven members of your team have been similarly billeted on this deck."

"Don't want to put any of you guys out," said Sal as Aussie, his teeth literally chattering, peeled off his soaked underwear.

"You're not putting anyone out," John Cuso assured Salvini. "No one uses this stateroom."

"Room to spare, eh?" said Sal.

Cuso gave him an enigmatic smile. "You'll have to toss for which one of you gets the upper rack."

Salvini looked at the two-tiered bunk then at Aussie, telling Cuso, "This guy farts wherever you put him!"

Cuso nodded good-naturedly. "Well, the boat's doc tells us there's a study says those who pass wind frequently live longer."

"Geez," said Sal. "Aussie's set to outdo Methuselah!"

"Piss off!" came a voice behind the shower curtain, followed by a hissing stream of hot water, its fog billowing out from the stall.

Cuso grinned. "See you gentlemen at lunch."

After Cuso left, Salvini glanced about the sparsely furnished stateroom. There was barely enough room to contain two curtained bunks and two short-backed Naugahyde chairs, the remainder of this tiny space crammed with a basin, mirror, two storage-space drawers, a Houdini-like shower stall, and two small flip-down writing desks.

Per custom, Freeman, as commanding officer of the nine "visitors," dutifully climbed up the six laddered stairwells to the *McCain*'s bridge to pay his respects to the ship's captain. Unfortunately, Captain Crowley quickly developed a self-induced tension headache, his neck muscles becoming as taut as a dead-lift cable the moment he realized it was General Douglas "George Patton" Freeman who was the CO of what Crowley would describe in his unofficial log as "this covey of misfits parading as Special Forces Rambos."

Crowley knew he was being unfair, that in fact Rambo types were speedily weeded out from potential SpecFor recruits as soon as possible. Rambos were muscle-bound egos on the loose. Or, as he had heard them described by Freeman himself during a CNN interview with Marte Price, "Protein-Powdered-Diet-Dick Wannabes. Wannabes who can't work as a team."

Despite Freeman's disdain for Rambo types, Crowley, no

less a man of habit than Freeman or any of his eight-man team, clung to his prejudiced view of what he referred to biliously as "Freeman et al.," by which he meant Special Forces in general. For Crowley and his generation, SpecFor were still cowboys, and as such provided a convenient repository for prejudices in toto, such as Crowley's privately nursed resentment at having female aviators on his boat. It was a prejudice that, if he ever gave voice to, he knew would end his career overnight. What particularly irked him as captain of the carrier and admiral of the battle group was that if he and other flag officers had been forced by Congress to accept "women fighter pilots"—an oxymoron, in his traditionalist view—why in hell hadn't they legislated women into Special Forces? Oh no, he thought, Congress wouldn't allow a woman to be part of a CHISU—"chute in and shoot up"—against the enemy, but by all means bring women onto his boat and let them fly an $80 million aircraft. It was double dealing, forcing him to accept skirts as fighter pilots and yet allowing Freeman types to pick and choose whom they wanted or, more to the point, to exclude those they didn't want. He was so churned up by Freeman's appearance on the bridge that for several minutes after the general had departed, Crowley remained on a slow burn, ready to morph into Growly Crowley, the sobriquet he'd been assigned by officers and crew who had run afoul of him during the battle group's constant patrols in the dangerous waters between Japan and North Korea. "Dammit," he fumed to Cuso, complaining how the Chief of Naval Operations in Washington, in faraway Washington, had e-mailed him a memo whose very wording further raised his ire in its slavish political correctness. The memo informed him that should his female "combat" helo pilot, Lieutenant Kaymara, call sign "MK"—Mary Kaye—experience difficulties associated with menstrual cycles, that he, and his XO, should effect "appropriate nonpsychologically invasive measures to assure this aviatrix is not required to fly combat missions at that time."

"Avia*trix!*" Crowley rasped, immediately circular-filing the hard copy of the CNO's memo into the bridge's wicker trash basket. "Aviatrix," he grumbled anew as he hauled his diminutive figure up into the admiral's high chair. "She's a pilot, not an aviatrix. Those women already know enough tricks."

Down below, as Freeman, Choir, Gomez, Lee, Eddie Mervyn, and Bone Brady approached Sal and Aussie's stateroom, it appeared to be on fire, the steam pouring from it so dense, it looked like smoke. They glimpsed a ghostly figure emerging. It was Salvini holding his finger to his lips for them to be quiet. Freeman, sensing Sal was up to no good, stayed outside the stateroom as four of the team, Choir, Mervyn, Brady, and Chief Petty Officer Tavos, utilizing their Special Forces and SEAL silent-approach technique, crammed into the small stateroom, the steam quickly swallowing them up. Freeman waited. After this nonsense they'd have to go over the plan for the Kosong mission once more as their transport down in the hangar deck was being unwrapped, readied to go.

The general heard the shower click off, saw the curtain brusquely open, and heard a high-pitched chorus of "Oooh—it's a shark!" upon which Sal, Choir, Mervyn, and Brady, hands held effeminately high, exited on tiptoe. "Oooh—a shark! It's a shark!"

"You bastards!" shouted Aussie. "I'm gonna get you!"

"Shark's gonna get us!" came Sal's voice, high-pitched in mock panic. "Oh, she's so angry, girls. We'd better go!"

"Pricks!" came a rejoinder, Aussie snatching a towel that looked as if it were attacking his head, so vigorous was his rubdown, his mind scanning his memory of payback techniques with all the speed of the legendary Freeman ransacking his mental files for mission-altering minutiae. Choir Williams, Aussie knew, had a phobia about spiders. Salvini, after having related over a beer a story about a horror movie that had haunted him since his youth, had revealed that he harbored a fear, whenever he was on a flush toilet, of being attacked by something primeval that lurked in the sewer systems of the world. About Mervyn and Brady, Aussie didn't know, but he promised himself he'd bloody well find out. The general, being a mere spectator and not a perpetrator in the smart-asses' chorus, assumed an innocent "don't know anything about it" expression, and led Aussie, after he'd changed, to the briefing ready room, where Johnny Lee and Gomez, the last two of the nine to land on the carrier, were already seated, smirking at each other over Aussie's plight and enjoying a soft ice-cream cone given to them by off-duty aviators who were drawing out the long, thick stream of chocolate ice cream from the "dog machine" in the nearby Dirty Shirt room.

"Well," said Aussie, looking at Lee and Gomez, "if it isn't the two fucking stooges!"

"All right, guys," said Freeman. "Listen up."

Freeman was grateful for the morale-boosting joke, but his tone was now all business, and he declined the offer of ice cream because it was cold dairy, a dessert that had a propensity to give him gas, a distinctly unhandy thing to have in any situation and a painful distraction for the leader of a mission, even if the mission was to be overseen by Freeman in the relative security and comfort of the carrier's high-tech Blue Tile rooms. The fact remained that, sitting or standing, the general bore enormous responsibility, not only for his eight-man team, but for the future safety of the millions of Americans, and indeed anyone, who boarded the thousands of commercial airliners that flew daily in American skies.

"Our transport's being readied on the hangar deck," he told the eight men. "I want to go over Payback's details again."

There were none of the usual stereotyped groans emitted by actors in the movies who complain of going over a plan for the umpteenth time. Every one of the eight men was listening intently. For Bone Brady it was like preparing for an examination. No matter how much you'd studied and restudied the outline and computer-generated three-dimensional layout of the ground around the Kosong MANPAD warehouse, and the layout gained from the two-inches-to-the-kilometer scale SATPIX overflights of MAMS—man-made structures—the information constantly updated by human intel, field agents, or by signal intel, there was always the danger of an overlooked detail.

On one practice mission in the kill house at Fort Bragg, Freeman, unbeknownst to the rest of the team, had had Special Operations Command install a LASKAS—laser-keyed alarm system—overnight. Such information about the kill house at Fort Bragg or the warehouse at Kosong was something that a SATPIX recon, even those flights capable of IRI, infrared investigation, would have missed in the interval between overflights. Plus, everyone from the President down was concerned about not making another blunder like President Carter's ill-fated attempt to get the American hostages out of Iran.

With such SNAFUs in mind, Freeman had made sure, even though the Kosong warehouse stood several miles south of the town of Kosong and should not be easily confused with any other building, that each member of his eight-man team knew precisely which quadrant of the football-field-sized warehouse he'd be responsible for. That is, *"if,"* as Eleanor Prenty pointed out in her final Payback memo to Freeman, "your team manages to get in." Freeman had immediately scratched out "if," replacing it with "when."

After they'd gone over the plan in the ready room, including another run-through of Army hand signals and American

Sign Language, Freeman glanced at his under-wrist watch. It was now 1130. "I've told Commander Cuso we'll be good to go at 1630. That'll give you a daylight launch and five hours now for chow, rest, and combat-pack check. The *McCain* serves everything from cordon bleu to your trusty all-American hamburger. You will, however, remember that you're not to eat *any* of it." He glared down at their ice cream with an exaggerated expression of disapproval. "You will, for lunch, resume eating your delicious kimchi." Eddie Mervyn and Brady exchanged glances as if they'd been instructed to eat shit.

"Yummy," said Aussie, ever the contrarian.

"I don't want to detect any American scent," emphasized the general, who, despite his orders to stay at mission control, was wearing his battle-camouflage uniform. Like the team's other seven SpecFor uniforms, it was in marked contrast to the spit and polish of Aussie's Navy officer issue of ironed, knife-edged khakis. "Remember," continued Freeman, "no aftershave, no deodorant, no hair gel. No toothpaste— use bicarb. And no hot chocolate, cola, or beverages other than water or Chinese green tea. Intel sources tell us the NKA have currently purchased tons of cheap black Typhoo tea from China, but as long as you stick to your green tea issue you'll be fine."

To drive home the point, the general told the five newcomers about what had happened to a SpecFor team in a suspect cave high up in Afghanistan's Hindu Kush. The team, assigned the mission with only ten minutes' advance notice, had had no time to prepare "food-wise." It had been a death-trap, everyone but the team leader wiped out. Freeman had always suspected that, like so many incidents in 'Nam, the rush insertion had been betrayed in large measure by the SpecFor's telltale American smells. The al Qaeda terrorists who'd unloaded on them, Freeman told his team, had probably literally gotten wind of the SpecFors before they'd even entered the cave.

"Sir," asked Eddie Mervyn, who'd been selected as chief pilot and whose speech became more rather than less formal as the mission's H-hour neared, "are we going straight in to Kosong or off-angle?"

Aussie Lewis, who was busying himself changing from his Navy-issue khakis into the camouflage battle uniform that had been rushed over to the *McCain* courtesy of Colonel Tibbet's Marine Expeditionary Force aboard the Wasp-class carrier *Yorktown,* looked at Mervyn in surprise. Choir Williams, Salvini, and the burly Tavos did the same. Along with Freeman's fundamental axiom of *"L'audace, l'audace, toujours l'audace"* it was well known among SpecFor types that Freeman's strategy, unless the enemy was actually waiting and looking straight at you, was that the best line of attack was the shortest, the most direct.

"Straight at 'em," said Freeman, adding by way of explanation, "I've always been a big fan of Horatio Nelson. Straight at 'em."

Eddie Mervyn, however, gave good cause for what at first had seemed to be ignorance of Freeman's adage. He indicated the TV in the ready room. Its sound was down, but the pictures from the *McCain*'s TV weather office, always available for its pilots, gave all the visual aid Eddie needed. "Those L3 thunderheads coming down at this battle group from the northwest don't look promising," he told the general, referring to the line of towering white cumulonimbus that were now flattening out into foreboding dark anvil shapes off the North Korean coast, a promise of stormy weather driving south against any straight east-west line of attack against Kosong.

It was Freeman's turn to surprise Aussie, Choir, and Sal. "You're quite right, Eddie," the general said. "There's no doubt we're heading into wild weather to the west that'll be pushing down on our right flank, so I figure the best chance of surprise insertion and extraction is a diamond-shape plan of attack. We head 175 miles northwest from *McCain*'s battle group here off Ullŭng, then 75 miles southwest to Kosong. Even if the NKA expect an attack, which they won't because it's too soon, they'd expect us to come up from the South, either from somewhere along the DMZ or along the coast, certainly not from the north. On the way back, we'll complete the diamond shape by doing the exact opposite—southeast from Kosong, then wheel northeast back to the battle group."

"Wheel" reminded Aussie of the general's famous tank maneuver, and he hoped that the general would have as much success here.

As they dispersed from the ready room, Freeman saw that Choir's face had not regained its normal color. "You still woozy from the plane ride here?" Freeman asked him pointedly. "Brain fog?"

Brain fog? Mother of God, thought Choir, his face flushing with embarrassment in front of his comrades. "No, sir. I'm fine."

Freeman nodded, but did Choir glimpse a lingering doubt in the general's face? The Welsh-American had always known that the kind of air sickness—or, more accurately, the motion sickness—he was prone to could make you "woozy," as the general had put it, temporarily incapable or at least slower than normal. And the last thing that Payback's team needed was a member who was slower than normal. Where they were headed, slower meant dead.

CHAPTER SEVENTEEN

LIEUTENANT RHEE OF the North Koreans' Kosong Coastal Defense Unit 5 had earlier expressed doubts to Colonel Kim and Major Park as to whether or not the American gangsters would dare launch a Special Forces attack against North Korea for fear of enraging the NKA's Dear Leader Kim Jong Il. Rhee had also suggested that if the Americans did attack North Korea, the MANPAD warehouse at Kosong might not be their target. But now he was reconsidering the opinions he'd given to the colonel and major, in part because such individual initiative was not encouraged in the highly trained and well-equipped NKA, its organization a mirror image of the old Sino/Soviet military structure, where any thinking "outside the box" was immediately suspect, especially when it involved junior officers and the lower ranks. Individuals such as Rhee who strayed in thought from the party line implicitly challenged the infallibility of the Dear Leader.

Still, Rhee knew intuitively that the key to success, as so often demonstrated in the West, was to occasionally demonstrate the willingness to take a risk. And so he thought he might adopt another concept from the decadent West in the same daring spirit the Dear Leader had shown when he'd ordered North Korean special forces to kidnap a capitalist South Korean film director in 1978 to make movies for him. Lieutenant Rhee decided that he would take out some insurance, sending fifteen of his Coastal Defense Unit 5's fifty-five men to Beach 5, the relatively small half-mile-long crescent of sand near the Kosong warehouse and the sector for which the unit was named. He would split the remaining forty men into three five-man patrols north, south, and west of the warehouse, in effect fanning them out to form a semicircle around the warehouse and the beach directly below, leaving the remaining twenty-five men in Unit 5 to form a "mobile rush" platoon, each soldier mounted on a Chinese-made three-wheel "Red Dragon" vehicle. The powerful off-road runabouts, with their thick, tough, gripping pneumatic tires, were ideal for the cart tracks that augmented the coastal road that ran south past the North's moodily beautiful Diamond Mountains, the latter an extension of South Korea's equally rugged south Taebek range.

This vitally strategic road linked Kosong to the North's port of Wonsan sixty miles to the north, the road overlooked by the towering, snow-covered crags of Mt. Kumgang, which sat majestically just north of the deadly demilitarized zone.

Rhee had "done his time" on patrols along the 2.5-mile-wide, 148-mile-long swath of land mines and high razor-wire fences of the DMZ. DMZ "incidents" following the armistice had caused the death of another 1,638 Koreans and Americans, and so he doubted that the imperialists and their South Korean lackeys would launch any kind of retaliatory attack across the DMZ. It was too carefully guarded. The only problem he had now was waiting to get the signature of Colonel Kim for the release of the twenty-five dragon vehicles he'd ordered, Kim in turn having to receive the written permission of the commander of IV Corps, the latter constituting the NKA's easternmost deployment of troops, south of the east-west Pyongyang-Wonsan axis.

Rhee, like every other North Korean, had been born and raised in the Hermit Kingdom, so called because of its seclusion and the ludicrous irony of it being the only hard-line

Communist state in the iron grip of a royal family–like succession. And so he was used to the extraordinary amount of red tape involved in getting the most minor things accomplished in the military's bureaucracy. Even so, the lieutenant found it difficult to mask his annoyance with Colonel Kim, who, as CO of the nine-hundred-infantryman battalion to which Unit 5 was assigned, had not yet obtained Pyongyang's release of the necessary vehicles. It wasn't as if, Rhee pondered, he'd requested an upgunned laser-sight and snorkel-equipped Chonmaho tank for some mad dash across the DMZ.

Pondering the delay, Rhee wondered if IV Corps HQ, who knew him only as a number, suspected him of wanting the all-terrain vehicles not to bolster his defense of Beach 5 but for a darker, more nefarious reason. Was he a closet *kotchebi,* one of the so-called Fluttering Swallows, who, in Pyongyang's words, had turned their back on "the glorious people's republic of our Dear Leader, wanting instead to flee to the decadent capitalist cesspool of America's running-dog lackeys in the South"?

In fact, it had never occurred to Rhee to defect. Not only would it mean torture and death if you were captured, but the journey usually involved long, dangerous treks north through mountain hides into China, the DMZ to the south being simply too heavily mined and defended. It meant keeping well away from any kind of road, and if you managed to escape the NKA patrols, there was the treacherous crossing of the wide Yalu River into China where, in all likelihood, government officials would promptly arrest you and return you to North Korea. Of course the swallows could try to escape across the Tumen River in the far northeast into the Chinese and Russian "boot on its side" area south of Lake Khanka, where there were Chinese and Russian border patrols everywhere.

He was thinking more about the *kotchebi* because of the

danger they posed to his sector. Some of them, he knew from personal experience, had tried to escape on small, homemade boats, intending to rendezvous off the coast with South Korean smugglers who dared to make a quick nocturnal dash across the 38th parallel at night to pick up their human cargo. Rhee's own Unit 5 had foiled the attempted escape of fourteen would-be "fluttering swallows" in the last nine months, a high number for the relatively small patrol area around Kosong and Beach 5.

Indeed, several of his Unit 5 men had been part of a rocket-propelled grenade and small-arms sinking of a smuggler's boat off Kosong. The smuggler was not as forthcoming about revealing the names of his contacts in the North, and Rhee promptly ordered the man's legs broken. The Unit 5 squad, using their rifle butts to execute the lieutenant's command, had gone into a frenzy, their blows a chance to vent their hatred and envy of their Southern neighbors' affluence and degenerate American morals, evidenced by the centerfolds of naked women that South Korean patrols routinely dropped here and there along the DMZ to goad Rhee's men. The smuggler, writhing in agony, screamed that the swallows he'd picked up were wanting to go north to the toe of the 20-mile-wide, 150-mile-long "boot" which provided the only direct land access north of the Najin-Sonbong Free Trade Zone to Russia's far east. Here, in the crowded free-trade zone, surveillance of possible American infiltrators must be difficult. American Special Forces posing as traders might be able to slip through.

Colonel Kim, studying the battle maps at Unit 5's barracks, his hands clasped behind his green uniform, his red colonel stars on his stiff shoulder boards catching the light, was preoccupied, not with the far north around the Free Trade Zone but rather with possible entry points to the South along the DMZ. Major Park saw the colonel's fingers closing and opening like a claw in spasm, a telltale sign of his superior's irritation with Rhee's concern about the Najin-Sonbong FTZ. "That's absurd," the colonel snapped at Rhee. "Look at the map, Comrade. From Najin-Sonbong Free Trade Zone to the warehouse here in Kosong is over 250 miles."

"Helicopters," said Rhee, his tone bordering on insubordination. "The Americans have helicopters."

Major Park flushed angrily. "You think the gangsters would fly all the way down from the FTZ because it is easier for them to use the FTZ as a base? If they come at all—and it's too soon—they will come by helo from the sea. Straight in from the sea, not on such a ridiculous, roundabout way. The Americans only know one way. Our Intelligence files tell us that the U.S. gangster Freeman prides himself on it. 'Straight through,' that is his strategy. Americans by nature are too impatient for any other way."

The colonel, the only one of the three officers whose rank made him privy to Omura's agent's report about the all-weather-wrapped equipment that had been loaded onto the Galaxy in Honolulu, leaned forward, fingers drumming irritably on the map table. "Inchon," he said simply, and Major Park lapsed into an embarrassed silence, while Rhee found new respect for the colonel.

Inchon, Rhee had realized, had happened way back in 1950, but was it a salutary lesson in the present circumstances? None of the three men had been born, let alone been a soldier in the army when the present Dear Leader's father, Kim Il Sung, had unleashed his million-strong Communist Army, his seven Soviet-equipped North Korean Army divisions hurling themselves against the South. As Kim, Park, and Rhee grew up, they, like all of North Korea's children, had learned the story of the eighty-thousand-strong NKA invasion force which, spearheaded by an armored division of over 250 tanks, had surged across the 38th parallel early on the early morning of June 25, 1950. Seoul, the South Korean capital, had fallen in seventy-two hours, its fleeing, terrified population caught by Movietone cameramen, the sweeping black-and-white images of the South Korean collapse flashed across the world, the prospect of yet another world war threatening barely five years after the cataclysm of 1939–1945 had ended with the hope that a United Nations could prevent war.

Rhee remembered the exhilaration in his great-grandfather's voice as he described how his platoon, indeed all the NKA platoons, ran, not walked, behind their Chinese-built Soviet T-34 main battle tanks as the NKA armor crushed Seoul, mercilessly routing and rolling over the terrified outgunned, outtrained, outplanned, and panic-stricken South Korean troops. U.S. troops were rushed from U.S.-occupied Japan to hold the line. They couldn't. Though many were veterans of the fierce fighting of just a few years before in Europe and the South Pacific, having been blooded in the horrific close-quarters combat from Saipan to Iwo Jima and Okinawa, many were now out of shape, having enjoyed the long postwar furlough in Japan and carrying "spare-tire" stomachs to show it. And they were out of practice, their positions overrun as they joined the millions of fleeing South Koreans.

Through sheer luck, the Soviet member of the five-member-country Security Council had stormed out of the U.N. headquarters in New York in a fit of pique the day before the invasion and so wasn't present for the crucial emergency Sunday Security Council vote as to whether or not the U.N. should send U.N. forces to assist the South Koreans in their hour of dire need. Without the Soviets, who would have had the power of a veto, the Security Council vote was unanimous to assist South Korea. And so U.S., British, Australian, Canadian, Turkish, and other troops, under overall U.S. command, embraced that euphemism for war, "police action," on the Korean Peninsula. Like all civil wars, from before Athens and Sparta to the massive slaughter of the American Civil War and the equally savage Russian Revolution of 1917, the war between North and South in Korea was unforgiving, members of one American division machine-gunning unarmed NKA POWs in the dread-filled tit-for-tat nature of the "police action." In less than twelve months, the NKA, as Rhee's great-grandfather had told him, had managed, with the help of the Chinese, to force the U.S.-led, blue-flagged U.N. troops to retreat over 175 miles to the southern end of the "limp dick" as U.S., Australian, and British soldiers insultingly referred to the drooping-phallus-shaped country. The U.N. soldiers were fighting for their lives in the ever-shrinking Pusan pocket, a sixty-mile-diameter enclave of burning buildings and exhausted, dying men.

It was an extraordinary victory for Kim Il Sung's armor-led Communist legions. And a massive humiliation for the U.N. forces, especially for the U.S. Army, the once-great capitalist army that as recently as five years before had boasted a strength of millions but which now stood, very unsteadily, at only a fraction of that. America, Rhee's great-grandfather explained, was so typical of weak, democratic countries. It had demobilized so rapidly in 1945–1946, after the Nazis and Japanese fascists had surrendered, that all the U.N. force had now, apart from the relatively few tough British Commonwealth brigades, U.S. Marines, and the Turks, were what Rhee's great-grandfather's generation called overfed, "degenerate Americans" shipped over in haste from Japan.

The NKA's noose of steel, Rhee recalled his great-grandfather telling him, had tightened around Pusan, forward NKA officers consolidating their forces and making wagers with one another about who would be the first officer to have the honor of seeing the first U.S. flag of surrender.

Kim, seeing how the young lieutenant's concern about a

possible Freeman attack from the Free Trade Zone had been stymied by the mention of Inchon, reminded Major Park and Rhee in an uncharacteristic moment of levity that the joke at the time around the Pusan perimeter was that many South Koreans and some Americans had torn off their white T-shirts and underpants, so desperate were they to surrender. But it was not easy to see them, given the thick, roiling black smoke that had resulted from the U.N.'s forces' ad hoc scorched-earth policy, and in the chaos that ensued from the South Korean forces' massive abandonment of arms and matériel during their rout to Pusan.

Lieutenant Rhee knew the rest: it had been drilled into him and his comrades at school how his great grandfather's generation of North Koreans had continued to close on Pusan along the 150- to 200-mile-long semicircular perimeter, the NKA's disposition of forces looking from high points along the banks of the Naktong River on the evening of September 14 like a predator's open mouth about to snap shut on the beleaguered American and other U.N. forces, their backs to the East Sea. U.S. fighter bombers were swarming overhead, but all along the perimeter, as had often been the case during the U.S. and South Korean retreat from the 38th parallel, the confusion created by the flood of refugees intermixed with fleeing soldiers, the NKA in hot pursuit, made it impossible for the pilots to distinguish friend from foe, scores of the U.N. soldiers being killed or wounded by "friendly fire."

"Then it happened," Rhee's great-grandfather told him. "Inchon." Rhee remembered that whenever his great-grandfather came to this part of the story about the Americans being exhausted, about to be pushed into the sea, the old NKA soldier's face became a bitter mask. "The American gangster MacArthur landed at Inchon."

Lieutenant Rhee recalled the story of how the seventy-year-old legendary American general, risking all, had done something that, to even some in the U.S. Pentagon itself, seemed at best ill-conceived, at worst insane. Withdrawing the vitally needed 1st Marine Division from the Pusan pocket, MacArthur used the Marines to spearhead an amphibious assault by the American X Corps against Seoul's port of Inchon, well over two hundred miles to the northwest of the Pusan pocket. The sheer audacity of it, a long, overextended Marine, air and naval left hook deep *behind* enemy lines, at a place where both natural and man-made port obstacles made it markedly unsuitable for any such landing, astonished the world. It had stunned the NKA troops, and severed their already overextended supply line.

Now Colonel Kim and Park were, like Rhee, remembering the landing. Every graduate of the harshly disciplined NKA staff college was required to study MacArthur's strategy. The American general, Colonel Kim reminded Major Park and Lieutenant Rhee, had snatched victory from defeat by forcing the NKA on the defensive at Inchon. With the NKA having suddenly to throw all it had into trying to contain MacArthur's brilliant landing, the beleaguered Eighth Army in the Pusan pocket was not only able to hold its ground but to effect a breakout. Suddenly the pursuing NKA was the pursued. Which was why now, all these years later in Kosong, Kim's mention of "Inchon" had so quickly nullified Major Park's initial disdain for young Rhee's reminder that the American gangsters "have helicopters." Park realized that if there was to be an American reprisal for the terrorist attack against the three airliners, it might not be a direct line of attack but very indirect, like MacArthur's deep thrust behind the NKA's front line.

In any event, the three men took comfort from the hope that the Americans, despite their opulent logistical capability, would be unable to make any attack, direct or indirect, for at least two to three weeks, given the formidable line of rapidly approaching thunderstorms. The rain in them would blind even the most sophisticated helicopters, except perhaps for the renowned Pave Low. Besides, the coast north and south of Wonsan fairly bristled with NKA radar posts.

"I have to go," Kim announced abruptly. "All we can do is stay sharp."

It was 1600 hours, the earlier Prussian blue of the East Sea now a brooding expanse as the line of thunderstorms moved ominously southward down North Korea's sullen east coast as the three officers dispersed from their meeting, Colonel Kim on an unannounced inspection in the tense, tight air of the DMZ's Panmunjom, Lieutenant Rhee to his Beach 5 unit, and Major Park to Wonsan Harbor, sixty miles north of Kosong, where he was liaison officer between the army and east coast elements of the North Korean East Sea Fleet, whose 236 combat vessels were responsible for the defense of North Korea's rugged east coast all the way north from the DMZ to the Yalu, Amur, and Ussuri rivers on the border with China and Russia.

At 1620, Rhee radioed the five section leaders of his Unit 5 patrols. Although, as Colonel Kim had said, it would take the American gangsters a while to prepare any assault they might be contemplating, the lieutenant wasn't going to be so foolish as to slacken off from sending patrols fanning out into the hills around the Kosong warehouse. It would keep his men on their toes, though he did admit to himself that there was a problem, something that every military and civilian leader knew about, namely that if you place people on *constant* alert, they become blasé. The Americans were discovering this, even with their graduated five-stage color-coded Homeland Defense warnings. Rhee knew that it wasn't that people became lazy, but rather physically and emotionally tired of living in a state of maximum readiness.

To alleviate the strain on his fifty-five-man defense unit, he told them about the twenty-five off-road vehicles he had requested, through Colonel Kim, from Pyongyang. For soldiers burdened with long garrison duty on their feet, the possibility of gunning through the hills around Kosong, mounted on a brand-new—well, used—Red Dragon all-terrain vehicle was a treat to look forward to.

CHAPTER EIGHTEEN

GENERAL DOUGLAS FREEMAN and his small but heavily armed eight-man Special Forces team were carrying out a final weapons check on "the beach," the steel strip three decks below *McCain*'s island on the open-to-air section of Elevator 2, where on occasion *McCain*'s personnel sunbathed in the warmer climes. Here a ten-man launch party, selected by XO John Cuso and classified "top secret"—no other ship's personnel allowed—carefully removed the khaki-colored all-weather plastic wrap from the long triple-hump "equipment" and saw that what they and Omura's spy on Oahu had assumed was an improved Chinook chopper with its two rotorless mounds and a centrally positioned engine or radar hump was instead a sixty-five-foot-long tear-shaped gray craft, nine feet wide at one end tapering to a six-foot-wide wedge at the other end.

To XO John Cuso, gazing down at it from the control bucket of the hydraulic arm that would slowly lift the craft from the "beach" in a stork-and-baby canvas sling and lower it to the sea's surface, the top-secret ALWAC-XP—Advanced Littoral Warfare Craft, Extra-Powered—that had been loaded in and flown from Hawaii with Freeman's eight-man team on the Galaxy and then drogue-chuted on its pallet to *McCain*, resembled the outline of a giant, polished gray cigar tube, one end spherical like a nuclear sub's, the other end tapered—or rather, pinched—into a wedge-shaped bow. Cuso's initial

impression, however, like that of the others in *McCain*'s
launch party who had been privileged to have laid eyes on
the craft, had to be somewhat modified by the fact, as explained by General Freeman, that once this top-secret naval
"surface" craft dived below the surface, its revolutionary
lightweight composite V-shaped hull became the hull not of
a surface ship any longer but of a submarine of only sixteen
tons displacement.

"Two in one," Freeman told Cuso proudly. "And," Freeman continued, his outline, like that of the ALWAC, only
dimly visible in the sick, yellowish penumbra of the hydraulic arm's sodium arc light, "sixty miles an hour on the
surface, fifty below. That's revolutionary technology with a
capital 'R.'"

Cuso took advantage of Freeman's attention on the launch
to edge away from the legendary general, whose kimchi
breath was as eye-wateringly pungent as that of Tavos
nearby and the other seven men in Freeman's team. The general, without taking his eyes off the big hydraulic crane and
its canvas sling that cradled the ALWAC-XP craft as it was
being lowered, further explained to John Cuso how the unusual shape was the result of pioneering work done by
American naval architects and engineers in Greenport, New
York, who had been given the task of designing a compact,
fast, air-transportable, clandestine craft capable of carrying
an eight-man Special Ops team and 2,200 pounds of ammo
and provisions for at least 450 nautical miles.

Apart from the extraordinarily light weight of the craft,
due to cutting-edge carbon fiber technology, there were another two unglamorous but vitally revolutionary aspects of
the surface-planing-cum-submersible vessel. First was its
MUSCLE—massive unit small cell lithium energy—system,
whose batteries were markedly better both in power and full-
capacity life cycles than the normal silver-zinc systems, and
second was the craft's rounded carbon composite stern,

which became its bow once the XP—extra-powered—craft was submerged. This metamorphosis of bow becoming stern, and vice versa, gave rise to the ALWAC-XP's less formal name of reversible-submersible, or "RS," as Freeman, Aussie, Salvini, and Choir called the craft, whose steering computers would be operated by the two SEAL technician specialists, Gomez and Eddie Mervyn. Not only was the RS a dry-delivery vehicle, unlike the prototypical surface-planing *wet* submersible, but it had superior maneuverability, akin to the experience of an automobile driver who, having had to work a standard shift, now had the luxury of automatic. In the RS, this left the pilot and copilot of the aerodynamically contoured craft more time to deal with what the general referred to cavalierly as "minor impedimenta." The latter included enemy submarines, acoustic mines, antisubmarine nets, and North Korean gunboats, which, manned by paranoid crews and driven by high-powered Chinese engines, patrolled the North Korean littoral 24-7 all the way from the DMZ just south of Kosong to the Chinese/Russian/North Korean "boot" in the far north. Such patrol boats were looking for everything from American vessels to "fluttering swallows" who continued to rendezvous with Korean and Chinese smugglers, whose only loyalty was to the portrait of Benjamin Franklin on hundred-dollar U.S. bills.

"Doesn't look like steel," opined Cuso.

"Correct," answered the general. "State of the art, Commander. A Stealth craft if ever I've seen one. Low silhouette, some steel but mainly epoxy carbon composites all over. Effectively nonmagnetic and sonar-absorbing. Even its flip-out stabilizer fins midships, forward diving planes, and its bow-cum-stern stabilizer fins are composite material. Anyway, damn thing's so small, we'll be lost in the sea clutter to any shore radar."

The tall African-American was impressed. Even so, Commander Cuso, whose home was a 95,000-ton, technologically sophisticated Nimitz-class carrier, had his doubts. "It looks—," he began, then paused. He saw no point in injecting any negativity during the highly classified "eyes only" launch.

But Freeman completed the commander's sentence. "Looks unstable, right?"

"Well, yes," answered Cuso. "Seems as if it'd roll in an early-morning dew."

Freeman's response was a jocular grunt in the darkness, only the midship section of the long gray craft clearly visible, caught in the hydraulic arm's spotlight, which now abruptly shifted, sliding off the RS like a circular white sheet that was now undulating up and down the swells that had pushed the craft momentarily under the carrier's launch platform as the *McCain* rose slightly in a big surge.

There was a thump, six inches of cable arm having suddenly unraveled from the hydraulic arm, the sixty-five-foot-long craft, despite side lines, swinging precariously, its tear-shaped bow barely missing the folded starboard wing of an S-3B Viking refueler and antisub aircraft. "Careful!" Freeman bellowed.

"Son of a bitch!" yelled Aussie, previously preoccupied with going over his combat pack. "That's all we need. Crush the fucker before we even start." But it was too late; the RS's stern, momentarily in free swing, struck one of the launch party. There was no other sound than a sickening thud on the steel deck as Chief Petty Officer Tavos collapsed and was quickly "stretchered" away to the ship's hospital for first aid or more if necessary.

"Murphy's everywhere," cursed Sal, simultaneously reminding Aussie that none of the three exit/entrance collars on the RS was made wide enough for a man with his control pack on to pass through.

"Won't be a problem, Brainless," joshed Aussie, while saying a quick, silent prayer that Tavos wasn't seriously injured. "You pass the pack down to one of our drivers. Right?"

"*Drivers?*" said Eddie Mervyn, feigning resentment. "Cheeky bloody Aussie. We are ALWAC *pilots*!"

"Bullshit!" said Aussie, sucking his Camelback's tube, then spitting the first mouthful out as he released the hold-back string on the water tube's clamp. "You're wankers. Friggin' idiot could drive this whore. Computerized to the max. GPS, SatNav 'tronics." Aussie glanced over at one of the carrier's Marine contingent, whose job it was to guard such "eyes only" launches and, in general, assist in maintaining good order and discipline on the boat. "Reckon," continued Aussie, "that one of these Leathernecks could drive it."

The Marine grinned, trying to adopt the pre-launch levity that all of the SpecFor team, except General Freeman, were using to quell the inner anxieties that always accompanied such clandestine "direct action" missions behind enemy lines. And one man already down. How serious was his injury? Would he be good to go? Freeman's uncharacteristic shift in mood, however, was not caused solely by the RS bashing into Tavos or by any second thoughts by the general about his selection of the reversible-submersible for the mission. Indeed, he was confident that, the accident with Tavos notwithstanding, the RS would safely and swiftly transport his team, either on the surface or submerged, to the enemy shore. What had triggered the worry lines not visible to the others in the darkness but which he felt creasing his forehead was the smell memory triggered by the fleeting yet distinct odor of sizzling onions from one of the carrier's dozens of "short order" kitchens, where the ubiquitous hamburger ruled. It was the succulent aroma of the *sweet* onions—not the stronger, cheaper variety, but the much milder eastern Washington Walla Walla variety his mother used to insist on and fry for his dad, who, like many other onion lovers, would at times, as he'd told Margaret, eat the Walla Wallas raw, so gentle was the taste on the palate.

It had been the reason Freeman's dad had earned the nickname "Costanza," after the *Seinfeld* character who, having lost his spectacles, took what he thought was an apple from the fridge and began to eat it, his pride refusing to admit the mistake, so that soon his eyes were streaming with tears. But rather than the smell memory, triggered by the mouthwatering aromas of the carrier's short-order chefs, reminding Freeman of the hilarious *Seinfeld* scene and its association with his beloved dad munching away contentedly on the seasonal Walla Wallas, it disturbed him, just as it had when— God only knew why—the general had found himself thinking of onions while watching the horrific videos of the man-portable missiles attacking the three airlines.

Or was it that the whiff of the frying sweet Walla Walla onions now on the carrier was merely a reminder of the MANPAD attacks, of how one experiences the most absurd random and often inappropriate thoughts at times when you would expect yourself to be focusing solely on the tragedy or the dangerous job at hand?

Perhaps, Freeman mused, such random thoughts were simply the mind's way of escaping from a deluge of sensory input, in this case drawing him away from the horror of the MANPAD murders, away from, however temporarily, the strain of the external event on the mind in the way that one's crazy, uninhibited night dreams vent the tensions of our necessarily inhibited, civilized days. Or, dammit, was the smell memory trying to tell him something quite rational, even banal, yet important? *Onions, his dad, and MANPADs.* What in hell was the connection? He felt as if he were working a crossword: parents, onions, MANPADs, and—

"General?" It was Aussie.

"Yes?"

"Bad news, I'm afraid. Tavos got clobbered worse'n we thought. Doc's just sent down word that our boy's got one hell of a gash at the base of the neck, hemorrhaging like a bastard. He's out. We can't take him. I'd say you're it, General. You can use Tavos's pack. Blue Tile can keep their satellite eye on us." He paused, waiting for Freeman's response. But Aussie knew what the answer had to be. No matter that the President had preferred the general to stay back in *McCain*'s Blue Tile rooms, the hard fact was that one man less than planned on a mission such as this was like a coach taking out his first baseman.

"You good to go, General?" asked Aussie.

"I'm ready," said the general, bracing himself against the bulkhead, palming the ten-round mag into his "blued" 9mm HK sidearm, grabbing his personal combat pouch and lowering it to Sal, who was already up in the RS's midship hatch, holding Tavos's full pack. "How's Choir doing?" he asked.

"Green," said Sal.

"He'll be right as rain," said Aussie. "It's all this slopping about on the surface that bothers him. Once we're submerged, out of the chop, he'll be okay."

For Choir's sake, Freeman was tempted to order Eddie Mervyn and Gomez to head straight for Kosong, due west, to reduce the time they'd be planing through the chop, but he stuck to his planned route, a tight-angled dogleg approach, northwest then southwest, which he was confident would be the least-expected line of attack.

"I'm fine," came an unconvincing Welsh accent. "I've taken a Gravol."

"Yeah," cut in Aussie as they began the "close hatch and secure" drill. "But don't nod off on us on the beach."

"It'll have worn off by then," Choir tried to assure him.

The general said nothing, which surprised John Cuso, who would have pigeonholed the legendary commander as a strict, no-drugs commander. And he was right, but Freeman trusted his men and knew none of them would take anything that would endanger the others or undercut their chance of success. He trusted himself to do the same. He asked John Cuso to look in on Tavos. "Wish him well."

"I'll do that, General. Good luck."

As the twin exhaust pulse-jet-thrust engine surged to life, the RS's wake footpath-thin, unlike the usual road-width wakes left by most craft of its size, Cuso was struck by how quiet it was, no doubt the composite construction of its cigar-tube-shaped superstructure baffling and containing the sound as it rose on an incoming swell under its own soft-throated power, then disappeared into the dark valley of the next trough.

CHAPTER NINETEEN

RHEE SHOULD HAVE been much calmer than he was at this moment above Kosong's Beach 5. He had done a six-month high-stress stint on guard duty at Panmunjom, face-to-face with the American and South Korean sentries, where the air fairly crackled with the tension between the two armed camps, the so-called armistice since the uneasy truce of over fifty years ago having done nothing to reduce the mutual hatred.

It was on the DMZ that Rhee had learned how to stare unblinkingly, as did the Americans and South Koreans, for abnormally long periods, like schoolyard foes standing toe to toe, never losing their *Gun nae ju ne*, what the Americans called "cool." Rhee thought of his time on the DMZ now because he could feel his chest muscles tightening in anger, lips firmly closed, the torque exerted by his temporal mandibular joint sending a bone ache through his sinuses and around to the back of his head, in what would soon be a full-blown tension headache. Pyongyang's rudeness in not even responding to his request for Red Dragon all-terrain vehicles for his twenty-five-man rush platoon didn't help, angering him so much that he could feel his temples starting to throb. He spotted one of his Unit 5 five-man patrols fifty yards away from the beach that lay directly below Kosong's MANPAD warehouse.

She bal!—Shit! He should not have been able to see any-

one in the patrol, but he'd spotted a clump of grass that
seemed to be levitating.

"*Megook-saram imnida!* I am an American!" he shouted
into his throat mike. "I can see you a hundred yards off. Report to me immediately!" With that, Rhee began walking
through the damp-smelling coastal brush toward the offend-
ing soldier, a short, slim man. He was so thin that his vest load
of grenades, flares, and ammunition created the impression
of a stick insect afflicted with protruding goiters, the camouflage net on his helmet festooned with dead grass on a background of green coastal vegetation. Rhee's anger increased as
he realized it was Sergeant Moon, one of the veterans who, as
a very young man, had volunteered as one of the secret North
Vietnamese's foreigners' brigade formed by Pyongyang to
gain vital field experience in fighting the Americans.

"You should know better!" Rhee snapped at Moon. "Since
when does paspalum grass grow at right angles?"

"Sorry, Comrade Lieutenant."

Rhee nodded, immediately accepting Moon's apology,
and Moon knew the lieutenant was motivated by his annoyance with Pyongyang over HQ's failure to provide the all-
terrain vehicles, preventing him from training a rush platoon
to the level of proficiency Rhee wanted in preparation for
any American or South Korean infiltration. Moon, who, as
Rhee's most experienced noncommissioned officer in Unit
5, did most of the paperwork when not on patrol, reassured
Rhee that he had personally forwarded the requisition for the
vehicles. "Perhaps, sir," Moon said encouragingly, "headquarters have already dispatched them."

"Hmm—," began Rhee, pleased that at least he had someone in whom he could confide his frustration with HQ, a
frustration that was very dangerous to share, Pyongyang's
political commissars swooping down on the slightest sign of
complaint or discontent. "—maybe. But we have heard nothing yet. Not even a radio acknowledgment."

Moon nodded his agreement, the paspalum grass falling from his helmet's camouflage net as he did so. "No, sir, but atmospherics have been sabotaging our communications. Solar flare activity's almost as bad as it was in 2003. The signals officer in Wonsan told me the surges of ions from the sun have even been knocking out American satellite signals and radio traffic."

Rhee appreciated his sergeant's efforts to reassure him, but there'd been no interference whatsoever with the radio signals from their allies, the Chinese, who were a lot farther north of Kosong than was Pyongyang. And Rhee pointed out that the traffic from the boot had been as clear as a Korean temple bell. Sergeant Moon was struck by the fact that the lieutenant had used the word "temple." In the rigidly enforced atheistic state, it was a measure to Moon of just how much the lieutenant trusted him.

"Yes," agreed Moon thoughtfully, "the traffic from the boot is clear, despite the mountains between us and the flat land along the boot's toe. Perhaps," he suggested, "it is an especially powerful station up there, like some of the Japanese-American stations on the west coast of Hokkaido. I have heard a lot of traffic between Pyongyang and the boot. Maybe the solar flaring will die down soon and we'll get a radio message that the Red Dragons are already on their way."

"Maybe," said Rhee, realizing that while Moon was merely trying to placate him, there *was* a chance, given the hodgepodge that the ionosphere had made of radio communication, that his requisition had been received and acceded to, that a message had been sent to Kosong, with Pyongyang annoyed that it had received no confirmation from Rhee's Unit 5.

"I'll call them again," said Rhee, but there was hesitation in his tone, and Moon knew it was well advised, junior officers in any army knowing that they do well not to become a pain in the neck to their superiors. Nevertheless, Sergeant Moon encouraged the lieutenant to call, suggesting, "Perhaps our requisition got lost?" Anything was possible. The sergeant had heard that even in the so-called highly efficient capitalist societies, important messages were sometimes inexplicably delayed and went astray. An old NKA major had once told him that when the arch enemies of Korea, the Japanese, had attacked America on December 8, 1941, December 7 in the United States, at the beginning of the great imperialist war in the Pacific, the vital message warning the American admiral Kimmel, commanding Pearl Harbor, of the impending Japanese onslaught had been sent from Washington, D.C., by regular telegram.

"Yes," said Rhee. "I'll call Colonel Kim on the Trace." The latter was an American word for the DMZ.

Moon nodded his assent but said nothing. This way if there was a sharp retort from Colonel Kim, the sergeant could say that he hadn't verbally agreed to press the colonel on the matter.

Rhee took out his cell phone. The static was worse than the previous day. He would have to go into Kosong and use a landline. At least there was no need to use code; a request for twenty all-terrain vehicles was hardly a national secret. Besides, even if the Americans intercepted the message it would simply be another in the flood of millions of signals that were scanned by American fleets and other listening posts that America's National Security Agency in Maryland assiduously monitored every second of every day.

NSA did not pick up the signal directly but received it as a "pass-on" from D2, one of the CIA posts on Japan's central Honshu Island. This request of Rhee's for twenty-five all-terrain vehicles was in turn rerouted through *McCain*'s blue-tiled Signals Exploitation Space to "Alfa Lima Whiskey Alfa Charlie," the Advanced Littoral Warfare Craft now designated by Special Operations Command as "RS."

CHAPTER TWENTY

THE SEA WAS a vast blackness, and aboard the speeding RS, Douglas Freeman was worried.

He had the kind of feeling students get when they finish an examination question, with five minutes to go till pens down, then suddenly realize in the pit of their gut that they might have entirely misread the question, but know that because of the time factor they've now irretrievably committed themselves. In Freeman's case it was slightly more important than an examination paper; he was carrying the responsibility for seven other lives than his own and taking the risk that if Payback went sour, the United States, already overextended in its World War III commitment against terrorism, might suddenly find itself in a full-blown war with North Korea.

Freeman, both hands on the grips, perspiration beading on his forehead like drops of blood in the redded-out interior of the craft, stared at the point, the apex on the chart, where the adjacent side and hypotenuse of a right-angle triangle met.

"Apex ETA?" he shouted at the RS's pilot Eddie Mervyn, while trying to retain his usual matter-of-fact tone, evoking calm, giving no hint of the rising panic that attended his thoughts of what might have been a fundamental blunder on his part. *What if the warehouse near Kosong had nothing in it but regular military stores? No MANPADs?* The chest-tightening sensation that the legendary commander was experiencing was exacerbated by the ear-dunning noise of the

RS racing through the juddering surface chop at fifty miles an hour. The corrugated impacts on the foam-cored composite skin as the craft smashed through one wave crest after another rattled even the most securely stowed combat packs against the aluminum ballast tanks and fiber-woven aluminum compressed-air storage flasks, the clatter inside the redded-out craft so loud that anything said below a shout went unheard by pilot Mervyn, copilot Gomez to his right, or by the other five team members.

"One hour, twelve minutes to the apex point, General," answered Mervyn. The weather was becoming so rough, it would soon be time to dive.

For the first time in years, since Iraq, the general felt a hard, acidic burning sensation in his throat as the bile of a sudden anxiety arrested him. What were the onion smell and the video pictures of the MANPADs' exhaust trails trying to tell him? Memories of his father telling him ad nauseam, in the way all parents bore their children with repetition, how much he loved the soft, sweet vegetable were haunting him. Why? And what of the videos of the missiles' exhaust? Why were they bugging him?

The general hated feeling confused, but he was feeling it now. Should he share his concern with the team?

Throughout his career, ever since his first lieutenancy, one lesson had been relentlessly driven home to all those young men and women like him who'd earned their first bar: No officer should ever lead his troops into a foolhardy attack. The concomitant lesson was that no matter how detailed, extensive, and expensive the operation's preparations had been, no mission should proceed if anything hitherto unknown, either through HUMINT or SIGINT, alerted the officer in command that the situation had significantly changed. Freeman well knew that history was replete with terrible examples of raids and massive offensives that should never have gone ahead. The fact, however, that such missions kept happening was largely due to the failure of leadership nerve, the natural tendency of all leaders at times—from a sporting team's captain to a general—not to order a halt to a maneuver once it had been set in motion, especially when such an action could be interpreted as cowardice.

Freeman apprised his team of his sense that, for reasons he said he couldn't articulate beyond a gut feeling, something might be amiss, and that while he couldn't put his finger on it, it was perhaps, he told the team, a foreboding, a warning.

It was really all he could say. He could hardly tell them that it had to do with onions and videos—they'd wonder if he was cracking under the pressure. Indeed, for a fleeting moment, he dared ask himself the same question.

Despite the ear-dunning noise of the RS's high-speed planing after he had told the men of his late-hour reservations about the mission, he had the sense of a sudden, prolonged silence in the craft.

In fact, it was only seconds before Aussie answered, "So? We'll fuckin' find out. Our job's to waste the warehouse. No fuckin' house, no fuckin' wares. Right? They were NKA MID numbers on those friggin' launchers."

"Right!" came a chorus, so thunderous in its intensity that momentarily it drowned out the sound of the maelstrom created by the fastest littoral warfare craft in history.

"All right," responded Freeman. "We go on as planned." He turned to Gomez and ordered, "Hard left! Course two seven degrees."

"Hard left!" confirmed Gomez, moving his control yoke briskly to port, the wedge-shaped craft slowing before making the abrupt turn.

The resulting slosh effect during the turn sent hundreds of gallons of roiling seawater surging over what on the surface was the round, bulbous stern of the surface-planing craft, creating a sudden, gut-dropping sensation in everyone except pilot Eddie Mervyn and his copilot Gomez, who were used to the maneuver from their training runs at Greenport, New York.

"Submerge the boat!" commanded Freeman. "Sixty feet."

"Submerging the boat," said Mervyn.

In the thirty-seven seconds that it took for the RS to descend from the noise and fury of the storm-whipped surface to the world beneath, Choir Williams passed from the realm of incipient seasickness to a calm so profound that not even the unending washing-machine pulse of the jet-thrust engine, the hissing of air from the ballast tanks, and other assorted noises, perturbed the SpecFor warrior.

"Sixty feet," Gomez informed the general.

"Reverse configuration," Freeman told him.

"Reverse configuration," confirmed Eddie Mervyn. With that, the Reversible-Submersible underwent its metamorphosis, turning through an arc of 180 degrees, so that what moments before had been its bulbous stern on the surface now served as the craft's bow, and what had been its six-foot-wide, wedge-shaped, V-hulled bow on the surface now became its stern, thus reducing the drag resistance of water over the sixty-five-foot-long superstructure.

The overall noise level was drastically reduced. Gone was the constant buffeting of wind and wave against a fast surface-planing craft. In their place there was now only the soft winking of red-orange instrument lights, the calming green waterfall of the vertical sonar lines, and the dime-sized blues of the Quad, the four five-foot-long homing torpedoes.

The only other steady electronic sound was the gentle whirr of the VCC's—Vane Control Computer's—backup computer. The computers, like their predecessors aboard the inherently unstable Stealth Nighthawk fighters, constantly made nanosecond adjustments, in this case to the RS's recessed diving planes, stabilizers, and midship canards, without which the revolutionary craft would have been as unmaneuverable and as unstable as a floating bottle.

There was virtually no sense of motion inside the redded-out craft, its forward movement evidenced only by the persistently low throbbing of its jet-pulse-thrust engine, but even this sounded now to Choir not so much like an annoyance but rather the reassuring constancy of a heartbeat.

"Turn about," said Gomez, and all eight men unlocked their swivel bucket seats and moved them through 180 degrees as the RS sped, with a current assist, to a submerged speed of 47 knots, 53 miles per hour, faster than any attack sub now extant, Aussie shaking his head in silent admiration.

But the fear of the unknown was still upon the general. In a team as small as his it was the custom of the leader, as he'd just done, to confide any serious doubts that might affect the other members. His fear, however, was not one of those normal apprehensions that grip anyone who stands on the edge of the unknown, but a leader's haunting dread that he might be about to attack the wrong target, an empty warehouse. But then, every commander, he reminded himself, every boss, no matter how high or low, had an equal obligation to weigh last-minute fears or intel against the demoralizing effect of repeating them.

Amid this fear that he might be risking the lives of his men, including his own, in a FUBAR, Fouled Up Beyond All Recognition, op against an empty shed, the general recalled the fiery deaths of over two hundred children and hundreds of other airline passengers. He weighed that certainty against a doubt that the North Koreans were somehow involved, unscrewed his combat compact, and began putting on his camouflage war paint. For all the electronic wizardry that surrounded him in this revolutionary war craft, he anticipated he would end up having to do what every soldier since David had faced Goliath had done: engage his enemy face-to-face. Even, perhaps, hand to hand. Which was why, for the first time since his legendary "sojourn in Siberia," as another old soldier had so wryly described it, the general elected to carry an AK-47 rather than his Heckler & Koch MP5 submachine gun or a composite M16 with grenade launcher, as Mervyn and Gomez were carrying. The Russian designer, Mikhail Timofeevich Kalashnikov, had deliberately invented his weapon with a solid wooden stock in mind, for in tests the AK-47's wooden butt proved to be a formidable club, unlike its Western cousins which, though much more accurate, like the latest Russian AK-74, had neither the cement-blasting hitting power of the AK-47's big round nor the bone-crushing power of the Russian weapon's heavy stock.

Sal, though as tense in the preattack mode as everyone else in the RS, idly asked Gomez, "How come the order to take her down is 'submerge the boat'? I thought it was 'dive.'"

"'Dive' is for emergencies," said Gomez, his eyes watching the green waterfall, alert for any of the vertical black lines that might suddenly squiggle, which would signal an anomaly within the RS's hundred-mile passive sonar listening range.

"Huh," responded Sal. "How fast can we go down if we have to?"

"You wouldn't believe," said Gomez. "In eight seconds we can— Hello, what's this?"

"Anomaly?" cut in Freeman.

Gomez, his combat green/sand camouflage taking on a dark bruised color in the craft's dimly lit interior, stared at the foot-square waterfall, each of whose dozens of vertically parallel lines represented a sound print picked up by the craft's "stingray" tail, a passive array of small microphones in series that were strung out astern from a drum reel hose in the keel, the transparent hose filled with an amber-colored oil stabilizer fluid that contained the quarter-sized microphones.

Gomez indicated the suspect sonar trace, a few-millimeters-thick black line that looked to Aussie as if it had suddenly developed delirium tremens.

"Was it our engine noise?" asked Freeman. "During the turn?"

Gomez shook his head, answering slowly, "No, sir, we played our stingray's tail out to—"

"Three hundred feet!" cut in Eddie Mervyn impatiently. "'Sides, we calibrated a baseline for that."

"The baseline," Johnny Lee explained, unasked, to Bone Brady, who looked confused, "is like having an electrocardiogram. Pilot gets the engineer's sine wave on the computer, punches it in as a normal parameter so sonar doesn't mistake it for a bogey."

"I know that!" said Brady. "You white guys think all we do is play basketball and join the fucking Army?"

Johnny Lee's jaw dropped, appalled that his team member could even *think* he was racist.

Bone, one hand holding his SAW, Squad Automatic Weapon, smacked Lee on the shoulder, laughing. "Hey, man, I'm just pulling your leg!"

Johnny Lee's face crumpled into a smile. Bone leaned closer to him. "You ain't even white!"

The linguist was nonplussed again, and for a man who was not only multilingual but also knew how to think in a variety of languages, he was momentarily stymied as to what to say, yet felt impelled to say something. "Why do they call you 'Bone'?"

"'Cause," said Aussie, one eye on the squiggly sonar line, "he'll bone anything that moves. Right, Bone?" Before Brady could answer, Aussie Lewis added, "That's why he volunteered for this job. He heard the NKA have women as regulars. Use a lot of 'em on guard duty. So if we come across a *Yo-bo*, a honey, Brady'll bone her while we do the Break and Enter. That right, Brade?"

"That's right!"

By now, Gomez had transferred the suspect trace on the waterfall into the computer's TML—Threat Memory Library—a register of thousands of ships' sound prints, each ship's engine or engines giving off its own distinctive "voice" print.

"Searching," Gomez informed Freeman. An orange bar light lit up on the TML computer's console, indicating a ship type match, the printout:

> Submarine. ChiCom HAN class. 345 feet. 5,500 tons dived at 25 knots. 90 Mega Watt. Nuclear attack boat. Armament 6 × 533mm torpedoes or mines. CC 801 surface-to-surface missile. Radar-Snoop Tray surface search sonar with Trout Cheek active/passive array. Tasked by PLA for patrol in North China Sea and Chinese littoral. Modifications include baffle plates and hull extensions post-2002, making individual vessel identification uncertain.

"What are we hearing?" pressed Freeman. "His pump?"

"Not sure," answered Mervyn, his brows knit in concentration.

The computer's red warning box suddenly flashed

"POSSIBLE HOSTILE BY NATURE OF SOUND."

It caused no alarm, the U.S. Navy automatically classifying all ChiCom and Russian war vessels as potential hostiles, as it did *any* ship that approached U.S. Navy vessels. The only exceptions to the rule were ships belonging to NATO core countries, such as the Netherlands and West Germany—but not France—and the highly trusted CAB—Canadian, Australian, and British—ships, the Australians in particular having earned a "triple A" rating with U.S. forces for having long ago decided to hold fast with the United States from World War II, Vietnam, and Korea up to and including Afghanistan and the two Iraqi wars.

Gomez separated out the Possible Hostile trace line and amplified it on the screen. "That's its sound print."

The RS having to stop and listen to the HAN added to the tension surrounding the general's dilemma as to whether or not he should proceed. The delay caused by his having to stop and sort out the possible hostile's intent meant that the Payback team's evac time from Kosong would be perilously close to dawn. Dawn was ideal for attack, a time of indistinct shapes not yet fully delineated by the sun, but it was *not* a time for withdrawal, with the enemy able to see movement with or without benefit of night-vision goggles.

The TTT—Time to Target—readout was twenty-eight minutes.

"He's closing," Gomez advised Freeman. "Ten thousand yards."

"Five miles plus," intoned the general. Too damn close. He turned to Eddie Mervyn. "Pilot. Tubes ready?"

"Tubes ready, sir."

"Status?"

"One and two tubes forward warshot loaded. Number three astern warshot loaded. Number four astern decoy loaded."

"We're between a rock and a hard place, boyo," Choir told Aussie. "Old man fires a live fish, we could be at war with China."

"Yeah," said Aussie. "And if he doesn't, we could be flatter'n a fucking pancake."

Eddie Mervyn's gaze shifted from the anomalous "print" squiggle to the four transparent safety covers over the torpedoes' Fire selector buttons.

"Nine thousand yards!" reported Gomez.

Time to Target was twenty-five minutes. Everyone was

tense, save Choir, who, so grateful he was no longer suffering the torture of unrelieved seasickness, calmly accepted the fact that they could not expect any assistance, any help whatsoever, from the battle group. He and his seven comrades were not officially here. The only thing that bothered him was whether the Chinese sub, clearly venturing well beyond the North China Sea, had been tipped off about them and was doing the NKA a favor, or whether the HAN's captain, as sub captains of all waters were wont to do, was merely on a "fishing" expedition. In any event, the important question was, Had the HAN locked on to the RS's engine pulse or a noise short from any other part of the RS?

"Eight thousand yards."

Would the general, Choir wondered, elect to evade or to fire if the HAN got too much closer? He knew that Freeman's natural disposition was to follow the dictate of *L'audace! L'audace! Toujours l'audace!* But in a sub, once you opened the tubes, an enemy sub immediately would know your intention, would counterattack, and the mission would be compromised. Yet not to fire was to let the HAN, over five times bigger, get too close with its six big Russian-type 533mm explosive HE torpedoes, which would be suicidal for the RS.

Time to Target read twenty-three minutes.

"Range?" Freeman asked Mervyn.

"Three thousand yards and closing."

Thirty seconds later, at precisely fourteen miles from target, Freeman ordered Eddie Mervyn to down-gear the RS's electric underwater motor and take her slowly toward the bottom of the littoral's continental slope, the general emphasizing "toward." To allow the RS, now known officially as the RS-XP, extra-powered, to actually touch the mud-sea interface would risk having the sixteen-ton craft sink into the gelatinous green ooze, burying the prop in the accumulated sediment of eons and the detritus of massive slides triggered by shifts in the tectonic plates around the Pacific's rim of fire. Plus, should the craft become bogged down, the strain on the MUSCLE battery system and shaft as the RS tried to extricate itself from the mud would not only emit sound, but the bubbles of putrid-smelling hydrogen sulfide would race to the surface, exploding in a telltale profusion of iridescence. Bubbles might not be seen by the HAN unless it was right over the RS, but they soon would be visible if the HAN kept on its present course, and heard if the ChiCom Navy's hydrophone mikes were halfway decently maintained. Any noise "shorts," such as the whines of a straining electrical motor, would most definitely pinpoint the Payback team's position.

CHAPTER TWENTY-ONE

ABOARD THE *MCCAIN*, over eighty miles to the east, an EWO, electronics warfare officer, in the blue-tiled Signals Exploitation Space looked around at XO John Cuso, whose black skin and graying hair were usually in marked contrast but were now bathed in the subdued blue light emitted from the SES's flat screens. "Sir, I've got a ChiCom trip S PL radio loop between a ChiCom sub, eighty-four miles west of us, and Qingdao."

A triple S, ship-to-shore-to-ship, communication loop between a Chinese Communist vessel, merchantman or warship, in the Sea of Japan and its Chinese or North Korean port wasn't unusual. A Chinese sub had as much right as the American *McCain* to be passing through the Sea of Japan. What *was* unusual, however, was that the communication between the HAN sub and the Chinese naval base at Qingdao was in PL, plain language, uncoded Mandarin. And neither the ChiCom submarine, nor Qingdao, HQ of China's North Sea Fleet, had used a "burst," a superquick nanosecond, transmission but rather regular snail-mail low frequency. Using a low-frequency transmission, John Cuso and everyone else knew, had cost more than one submarine captain a court-martial for having given an enemy's surface warship or submarine time to triangulate—zero in on your position—a violation of any submariner's first commandment: "Thou shalt not be heard."

The only reason that *might* be cited for using plain language would be if your vessel, sub or surface craft, was on fire and quick assistance was an imperative. Cuso recalled the Cold War Soviet Kilo-class sub that had burned and sunk rather than risk giving out the location of its battle group by sending an SOS to its fleet HQ.

"You think the RS would have picked up the HAN sub's transmission to Qingdao?" asked Crowley.

"If the HAN had its pop-up antenna deployed," said Cuso. "That's the million-dollar question, Captain."

The older man, diminutive though he was, had the worry-creased face that, as he sat in his admiral's high "Mikado chair" in the SES, somehow made him appear taller, infinitely wise. "If that HAN's on fire, we should be hearing noise shorts."

The EWO nodded. Old Growly was right—you could hear a fire from hundreds of miles away but only if conditions were favorable, and they weren't. The storm now barreling down into the Sea of Japan, or East Sea, from the Sakhalin Island chain north of Japan and past Vladivostok to the east was churning up the sea's surface like some massive Mississippi paddleboat with a jet assist.

"But you could hear the son of a bitch's radio message to Qingdao?" Crowley asked the blue-hued EWO.

"Yes, sir, we heard him—and Qingdao responding—because the big Chinese sub was transmitting from the surface."

"The surface?" said Crowley, glaring down from his Mikado chair at Cuso as if it were Cuso who had committed the indecency of a sub skipper radioing from the surface.

Then the import of the intercept between Qingdao and the nuclear-armed HAN sub struck John Cuso, cutting through the fatigue of overseeing *McCain*'s launch of his country's ultrasecret Advanced Littoral Warfare Craft, or so he thought. "That HAN *wanted* us to hear its chatter with Qingdao!"

Crowley said nothing, but was scratching his crotch, the

itch a habitual manifestation of uncertainty in the old warrior. A ChiCom nuclear sub squawking from the surface and in plain language rather than code was something so—so blatantly *nontraditional* that he found himself regarding it as a personal affront by one fellow sea captain to another. It reeked of change, at the very least of spontaneity, which battle-group commanders did not like. There was enough uncertainty in the world already, enough aboard his boat of six thousand souls who could make *McCain* work only if they operated as a team, by the book, by unchanging, reliable routine, not by some cowboy like Freeman or this Chinese joker whose sub, indicated by a red X on the SES's big blue screen, was, the data block said, 3.68 miles north of where the electronics warfare officer calculated Freeman's RS should be.

"That's it," Cuso reiterated to Crowley, wondering if the captain had heard his hypothesis of a few moments before. "They must have wanted us to hear."

"Admiral," cut in the EWO responsible for monitoring Japan's listening posts, "our ears in the three nearest Japanese ports are also reporting hearing a PL loop."

Crowley shifted uncomfortably in his Mikado.

"He's gonna rip his balls off," whispered a hard-copy gofer.

"He hears you, bud, he'll rip *yours* off!"

"Quiet! Goddammit!" To their surprise it was Cuso's voice, not Crowley's, the captain's worry lines dark furrows in the eerie blue glow from the big screen showing red X's and white squares representing all "real-time" warships across the five-eighths of the world that was salt water.

"Question is, gentlemen," said Crowley, his soft quietude in marked contrast to Cuso's enthusiastic problem-solving, "what did Qingdao and the sub say to each other? Who's on the translation?"

"ICT suggests that—," began the EWO.

"ICT—balls," cut in Crowley, his voice rising but still not

as grumpy as earlier. "Initial computer translations read like some of these modern-day Bibles. They miss out on all the colloquialisms of the language, so they miss the guts of the message. We need a human being on this one. Where's Oakley?" She was the senior translator on the *McCain*.

"She's in the security bubble, sir. Should be done in five."

"Be precise," Crowley admonished impatiently. "Five hours, five days?"

"Five minutes, sir."

"Good." The admiral turned to his XO. "John, let's get a Viking up there with JSF quad cover along with the Hawkeye."

"Yessir," said Cuso, heartened by what he considered to be a smart decision by Crowley, to get the Viking antisub chaser aloft to join the already airborne E-2C Hawkeye as soon as possible. The four Joint Strike Fighters would ride shotgun should an attack on the "possible hostile" HAN be deemed necessary in order to run interference for the RS, which, by the chief EWO's reckoning, should be only fifteen minutes away from its mission's target—which, for reasons of high security, aboard *McCain* was simply referred to in SES as "the shed."

"Rhino" Manowski was excited but trying not to show it as he snapped off the return salute to his plane captain, the latter's identifying brown shirt barely visible in the subdued yellow glow cast out onto the flight deck by the light at the base of the carrier's island.

"Good hunting!" Manowski's plane captain shouted up, his voice all but lost in the noise of the approaching storm, the "gonads-dropping" thud then whine of the carrier's Elevator 2 as it descended to bring up the next Joint Strike Fighter, and the hum of the yellow tow tractors—or "donkeys," as they were called aboard *McCain*—adding to the din of the carrier's pre-launch operations. The 95,000-ton "boat" turned into the wind so as to gain maximum lift for the quad of Joint Strike Fighters, which would constitute a fluid "fingers four" shield protecting the S-3A Viking twinjet sub chaser as well as the Hawkeye.

Rhino Manowski had been the wingman for celebrated fellow veteran aviator Lieutenant Commander "Chipper" Armstrong when the F/A-18F Super Hornets had been the carrier's primary Strikers, both men distinguishing themselves in America's most recent "referee action" over the Taiwan Strait, trying to prevent the Beijing-run People's Republic of China and Taiwan's Republic of China from further savaging each other. Manowski and Armstrong were among the very few to have mixed it up and destroyed two of the Soviets' revolutionary designed MiG-29 Fulcrums. In Manowski's case, he had not only escaped the Fulcrum's legendary backward tail-slide-overshoot trap, but had downed the MiG in the process by getting off a quick Sparrow slap shot from his Hornet's starboard recessed well, Manowski seeing the missile literally disappear up the Fulcrum's tailpipe, blowing the MiG apart with such violence that it had sent a rain of white-hot debris into his Hornet's port intake, shutting it down.

When Manowski had landed his injured bird, he'd missed the 3 wire, his tailhook snatching the 4 wire instead, but at such an oblique angle that it had slipped off just as quickly. The Hornet's surviving starboard engine, as required, was not yet off full power, the setting needed in case a plane missed the wires and had to "bolter"—go around for another try. But on one engine instead of two, and heavy ordnance not yet expended, the Hornet was too heavy to take off again. Manowski had ordered, "Eject!" heard the explosive bolts fire, and thanked God and the ACES' ejection seats whose "zero-zero" capability assured that he and his radar-intercept officer would be thrown high enough for their chutes to deploy. Manowski's chute, like his RIO's, opened, both men having had a split second, amid the traumatic shock of literally being blasted out of their Hornet, to appreciate the genius of whoever it was, in May of '52, on the USS *Midway,* who had first tested the feasibility of using an angled flight deck, now standard on all U.S. carriers and which, at 14 degrees off center, ran from the stern to an abrupt sawn-off-looking end back from and left of the bow. It had meant that as their disabled Hornet careened down this landing deck–runway, it was not coming in behind other planes waiting for takeoff on forward catapults 1 and 2.

As Manowski had floated down toward the sea, before *McCain*'s "Jolly Green" rescue helo had picked him up, he was relieved that his new multimillion-dollar junked airplane hadn't clipped any of the parked aircraft that jammed the available deck spaces. It didn't matter to his RIO, who, unlike Manowski, had not landed in the ocean but had slammed headfirst into the huge warship's port bow. Despite his helmet, the RIO was knocked unconscious, and by the time the helo's swimmers located him, after he had been swept aside in the bow's push wave then sucked astern, his body had been mangled by the carrier's prop blades.

It was testimony to Rhino Manowski's toughness, as well as his skill as a naval aviator from Top Gun that he was as excited to fly this night as he had ever been. Yes, night ops were scary as hell—someone had said it was like being shoved in a dark closet and having the door slammed on you. But it was the greatest rush he knew. Besides, tonight there was a special reason for Rhino, Chipper, and Quad 3 and 4 to be geared up. This would be their first nontraining op in their wonder of wonders, the F-35C, the Navy's version of the Joint Strike Fighter.

As Chipper Armstrong's plane captain was guiding his JSF to its takeoff position in front of the jet-blast deflector on the forward starboard catapult, he smelled the strong fumes and watched the green-shirted cat 1 crew attaching the hold-back bar to the fighter's nose gear. This restraint, together with the plane's brakes, would allow the "35," as the JSF was being called by all involved in *McCain*'s flight ops, to have its Pratt and Whitney engine at full power, building up thrust like a caged stallion eager to be free.

Chipper saw a green shirt sprint forward, holding up his chalkboard with the takeoff weight written on it so both Armstrong and the "shooter"—or catapult officer—could see that total weight of the F35-C was 30,168 pounds plus fuel and ordnance. If the shooter failed to pump enough saturated steam from *McCain*'s reactor into the cat's pistons, the sudden and enormous jerk forward would end up tearing the 35's nose-wheel assembly out of the fighter.

On the other hand, too little steam to drive the pistons would throw the plane off the deck with insufficient force, toppling pilot and plane into the sea, whereupon the carrier's enormous V-bow would slice it in half, not even giving the pilot, as Rhino Manowski had had in his injured Hornet, time to eject. And the monolith that was *McCain* would not stop. Even if Crowley wanted to, he wouldn't. Such an interruption would be a dangerous pause in what to the casual observer appeared to be organized chaos on the flight deck, but this "chaos" was, in fact, an intricately and minutely choreographed ballet of war. A single error by any of the yellow-shirted plane directors, shooters, arresting gear officers; blue-shirted elevator and tractor operators; green-shirted crews; brown-shirted plane captains; or the red-shirted weapons and crash crew could, in a nanosecond, turn the flight deck into a jet-fuel-and-ordnance-fed inferno, as had happened aboard the *Oriskany, Forrestal,* and *Enterprise* in the late '60s, killing 205 crew.

Manowski, like Armstrong, could smell the astringent odor of jet exhaust fumes that had risen up over the jet-blast deflector behind Armstrong's plane, the fumes driving off the bracing smell of sea air, and he saw that Chipper Armstrong and his shooter, who was hunkered down in the bump on the deck known as the "pod," both signaled agreement on the green shirt's chalkboard takeoff weight. Manowski, impatient to be airborne, watched the green shirts dash about Chipper's Joint Strike Fighter, doing their last preflight check. With no problems reported, the shooter signaled Armstrong he was good to go. Chipper set his engine control to "afterburner" and gave the shooter a sharp, definite salute, remembering how *McCain*'s XO had grounded a nugget, a new pilot, for having given what Cuso had characterized as "a sloppy, indifferent wave" rather than a salute that was an "unambiguous signal" to the catapult officer. Seeing Armstrong's no-nonsense salute, the pilot's hands off his plane's controls, the shooter pushed the launch button in his pod, ungating—that is, releasing—the pressure-driven pistons, jerking the fighter ninety yards down cat 1, hurling it aloft, the rapid acceleration from zero to 120 miles per hour in under two seconds shoving Armstrong's eyeballs back into their sockets before he took hands-on control of the aircraft.

Ninety-five seconds later Manowski clipped off his salute and felt the tremendous rush that unfailingly gave him an erection, "like a pipe cleaner pulled through your ass," as the pilot of the big twin-jet Viking sub chaser had indelicately described it to the newest member of his four-man crew, the S-3C being the latest upgrade of the original Viking S-3. As a precursor to this mission, the S-3C's pilot unfolded his Viking's wings aft of the jet-blast deflector on cat 2, waiting for the last two of the JSF quad who would protect his crew and the team of five in the carrier's E-2F Hawkeye. Though the already airborne prop-driven Hawkeye was relatively slow, it was the eyes and ears of the American battle group, its long-range electronics and raised two-thousand-pound rotodome capable of detecting bogeys more than 250 miles away from *McCain* and the carrier's shield of ships.

The ability of the Hawkeye's three "moles"—radar operator, combat information officer, and air controller—to have their systems simultaneously track more than 654 targets, while controlling in excess of 45 strikers and interceptors, dazzled any newcomer, nuggets and deck crew alike. The flying "dish on a stick" Hawkeye was an awkward-looking aircraft with none of the sleek "you talkin' to me?" assurance of a fighter, but its effectiveness as an airborne early-warning station was unquestionable.

Although the sub-chasing Viking was carrying Harpoon antiship missiles and retractable MAD—Magnetic Anomaly Detector—in its tail, and sonobuoys that could, like RS's waterfall of black lines on a green surface, detect noise shorts and other sounds emitted by submerged submarines, *McCain*'s SES had already pinpointed the ChiCom HAN. It was assumed that the four Joint Strike Fighters swooping down through the bruising, bulky clouds of the storm front at Mach 1 plus would serve notice to the ChiCom skipper that he should indeed follow the Mandarin plain-language directive from Qingdao to withdraw *post haste*!

The problem was, as SEAL and RS "pilot" Eddie Mervyn told Freeman, the HAN had not moved.

"It's still on the surface?" asked the general.

"Yessir."

"Disobeying orders?" opined Bone Brady, whose black face, unlike the war-painted Choir Williams, Salvini, Freeman, Eddie Mervyn, and Gomez, Aussie, and Johnny Lee, needed little camouflage, only the lively gleam of his eyes visible in the RS's redded-out interior.

"Son of a bitch *could* be disobeying orders," Freeman conceded, "or this whole plain-language gig could be a setup to give us false confidence, encouraging us to move faster than we should, to surface and plane it flat out to the beach." He thought for a moment. "Scope depth!" he ordered, and they could hear the ballast tanks releasing air for the RS to rise to sixty feet below the surface.

"Search or tactical, sir?" inquired Eddie Mervyn.

"Ah—search," answered the general in what for him was a rare moment of embarrassment. His momentary pause had demonstrated that the legendary leader of conventional and SpecOp warfare perhaps hadn't realized that the RS had two scopes, one for long-distance scanning, and the tactical scope for closer-in torpedo and evasive maneuvers. Or had the general, famous for his attention to detail, merely forgotten it in the tension, shared by all eight of them, caused by not knowing whether the possibly hostile HAN was willfully or unwittingly disobeying orders from Qingdao because of nothing more than a mechanical malfunction?

The SpecOp team heard the soft whine of the larger search scope sliding up through its sheath, Aussie watching the six-by-four-inch flat screen that was forward of copilot Gomez and pilot Mervyn, immediately to Gomez's left.

"It's raining," said Gomez, his source of this information not the scope, which was only now breaking surface, but rather the RS's foot-square sonar "waterfall," the "fry wave" of the falling rain creating a narrow vertical band of static on the screen whose green color had been drained of much of its luminescence by the RS's "rigged for red" lighting. The latter would help the team's six-man hit squad once they landed—*if* they landed—on Kosong's Beach 5, Eddie Mervyn and Gomez remaining behind on the RS for the exfil—exfiltration.

On the computer, pilot Eddie Mervyn could see nothing on the scope's relayed computer-screen pix but a heaving rain- and wind-lashed sea of whitecaps as the Force 9 storm pushed south from Siberia.

On *McCain*, over a hundred miles east-southeast of Kosong, the SES's meteorological screen clearly showed that the storm had rapidly picked up speed ever since its front had passed over the natural brake of the land situated a hundred miles west of Vladivostok, the storm now having only the unobstructed "flat" surface of the sea with which to contend.

The "Pan 'n' D," as the quick pop-up-and-down search-scope scan was referred to by the Navy submersible instructor who had trained SEAL technical specialists Gomez and Mervyn, confirmed nothing more than it was pouring rain in the darkness. The difference in temperatures between the rain and seawater was creating a crazy dance of phosphorescence and "rain-scratch" on the screen, Gomez assuming that the island of Ullŭng and *McCain*'s battle group southeast of Kosong were probably not yet hit by the full fury of the Force 9 gale winds.

"Waste of time," said Freeman by way of apologizing for having risked a search-scope scan and thus the RS possibly being spotted by a fishing trawler, or even the HAN.

"Not really, sir," Gomez assured him. "I mean, it wasn't a waste of time. With our radio aerial breaking surface with the search scope, we've picked up clearer plain-language radio traffic between the HAN and Vladivostok."

Freeman looked nonplussed. "You mean between the HAN and Qingdao?"

"No, sir. Vladivostok's getting into the act. Seems that the Russian fleet there is getting ticked off with the ChiCom sub encroaching in their patrol zone."

"Why?" asked Aussie. "The Russians go where they want. Why shouldn't the Chinese?"

" 'Cause," said Salvini, "Russia still thinks it's a superpower—like when it used to tell China and the Dear Leader that the Soviet Navy ruled the waves. Besides, Beijing and Moscow are having one of their tiffs."

"Tiffs?" challenged Brady. "That's a Limey word."

"So?" said Salvini. "I must've picked it up from Aussie or Choir."

"You've been hanging out too long with Brits and Aussies," Brady joshed. "Tiff—you mean Beijing and Moscow are having a *fight!*"

"Yeah," said Salvini, "a row. Flexing their muscles. Staking out their territory."

"*Their* territory!" said Johnny Lee. "It's international waters. And any further west, the HAN'd be within North Korea's two-hundred-mile economic zone."

Freeman ignored the others' patter. The legal niceties of maritime law were fictions of academe insofar as underwater operations were concerned. Every man in the team understood this, and all of them had known at least one SEAL who, during the Vietnam War, had participated in the clandestine "officially deniable" missions into North Vietnam's Haiphong Harbor. From the littoral, they had made their way undetected into the very sewers of Hanoi, where sudden unexplained explosions, suspected by NVA officials of being caused by gas leaks, occurred in the vast subterranean system beneath Hanoi.

The question now for Freeman was, had any vessel—warship, surface, or commercial—"pinged" the RS and alerted the North Korean coastal guard? One of the general's better traits, as recognized by all who had served close to him, was his readiness to consult subordinates, his willingness to ask advice ironically only adding to his reputation as a leader who knew more than most. Aussie Lewis, Salvini, and Choir, who had served with Freeman the longest and so could read him quicker than the others, sensed that the general was wrestling with uncharacteristic indecisiveness. But they understood why—there was nothing quite as unsettling in an RS or any other submersible as the feeling of having been pinged by a possible hostile. It meant having your range of possible reactions thwarted by the fear of massive retaliation should you "jump the gun," react too quickly. In so doing, you'd give your potential adversary the inestimable advantage of knowing your precise latitude and longitude, not to the nearest mile, as in the days of World War II, but, in a world of global positioning satellites, to the nearest foot.

"We've got state of the art in this tub, General," said Aussie encouragingly. "I'd bet ten to one no one zaps us with their sonar. Shit, we're no bigger'n a fucking killer whale. Fuckin' rocks on the bottom are bigger'n us."

Freeman nodded appreciatively, his impressive build seemingly bifurcated by the search scope's sleek column. "Thanks, Aussie," he said. "But you'd bet on it raining in the Sahara!"

There was a burst of laughter, more because they all needed to vent what some SpecFor types referred to as "impan-itis"—impatience anxiety.

"I wouldn't bet on rain in the desert, General," said Eddie Mervyn. "But I'm with Aussie on this one. This 'tub,' as he calls it, has gone through more SDTs than—"

"Speak fucking English!" cut in Aussie.

"What—oh, SDTs—sonar detection tests—out of Green-port. Scores of 'em, and not one rebound. Not one. This baby's CR, composite rich. Not enough metal in her to fill your tooth." Eddie's exaggeration, gross as it was, neverthe-less got the point across.

"I agree," added Gomez, whose right eye was becoming irritated by a dab of camouflage paint that had worked its way into his cornea, causing his eyelid to blink, creating the bizarre impression that he was winking madly at Eddie Mervyn. He closed the eye momentarily, hoping to wash away the foreign matter and resenting the fact that all this "war paint" might be unnecessary if they didn't execute the mission they'd spent so much short-time, high-pressure preparation on. In any event, Gomez's usually even-tempered nature was aggravated by both the great decisive general's present indecisiveness and by the fact that if they did go in to Beach 5, he and Mervyn would have to stay aboard the RS as the getaway drivers. So why the hell did they need war paint? "All dressed up and nowhere to go," he muttered.

"What?" Freeman's voice was sharp, unforgiving.

"Ah—nothing, sir. I—ah, just making a joke."

"I'm not in the mood for goddamn jokes, Gomez. If you've got anything to contribute, contribute. Otherwise, keep quiet."

Gomez swallowed hard, but surprised everyone by tapping the waterfall screen and immediately adding, "Sir, the weather topside's so bad that even down here at sixty feet we're still in subsurface turbulence. Even if that HAN, or anyone else, was pinging us—which I can't hear at the moment—incoming sound waves are in 'extra rinse' mode. Everything's scrambled—long as we don't go deeper below the turbulence."

Freeman nodded and placed his hand on Gomez's shoulder. "Thanks. I think you're right." The general paused and looked around at his team, his gaze resting on Choir Williams. "One thing, Gomez—" The general grinned slightly. "If we're still in subsurface turbulence, how come Mr. Williams here is not bringing up his breakfast?"

"He's fuckin' drunk!" joked Aussie Lewis, always one to press the humor envelope despite, or rather to spite, any official instruction not to.

Gomez indicated the four-inch-square data block left of the waterfall that showed all four retractable stabilizing fins not out to their full length but extending and retracting in response to the water flow probes that were sending a steady stream of data to the stabilizer's computer. "It's only a matter of nanoseconds," Gomez explained, "between data inflow and stabilizer adjustment—so fast, our bodies don't even register it."

"Thank you, Mr. Gomez," said Choir with mock solemnity. "And no, I am not inebriated, as my vulgar antipodean friend has charged."

"Good," said Freeman. "Then we're good to go." It was stated as a decision, not a question. Time to push all jitters aside. He had pitted his concern for his men against the possibility that the HAN or some other vessel knew of their presence, now only eight minutes away from what the computer's chart told them was Beach 5's surf line, and he was convinced that the HAN's presence was merely coincidental. It was a big sea—bound to be other traffic. Even if NKA intel had got a heads-up of him and his team en route to Japan, even if somehow one of their field agents had been lucky enough, or "tinny" enough, as Aussie would have put it, to have spotted the Galaxy in Hawaii, what would they have reported? It was against this possibility that he had ordered the three foam-plastic mounts be duct-taped equidistant apart on top of the RS before it was shrouded in the opaque khaki helo wrap. Anyone spying this shape would most likely see the outline of a long Chinook-like chopper with forward and aft rotors and an engine mount in the middle. And the general would not let his recent obsession with the "damn onions'" low sulfur content and the relatively high sulfur content of Russian missile propellant stand in his way. He knew ever since his days as a young officer that human nature in war, just as in peace, often seeks reasons to postpone action rather than risk entering the unknown. A good leader knew when one should no longer take counsel of one's fears, Freeman recalling how FDR had led his nation out of the dark with his fearless statement "All we have to fear is fear itself."

"Beach, four thousand yards," Mervyn said matter-of-factly, though he knew that they were approaching the point of maximum danger, when the general would have no option but to raise the search scope on infrared to see the beach. So paranoid was the Hermit Kingdom, the Dear Leader's coastal defense troops had the unsettling habit—as long confirmed by SATPIX recon—of stopping their searchlight trucks along the coast road and sweeping the beaches and rocks with their 2,000-watt beams.

"Slow to two knots," ordered Freeman, Gomez's hand already poised to do so in accordance with the detailed plan that all eight men had only recently committed to memory, so much so that each of the six-man hit squad was confident that should the storm obliterate any chance of moonlight, he could still make his way from Beach 5 up the stem of the Y-shaped trail then turn left, following the southern branch to the warehouse, which, running north to south, lay at the top of the Y between its two arms, the north-south Kosong-DMZ coastal road just fifty yards west of the warehouse. Indeed, Freeman had insisted they all go through the mock-up without the benefit of night-vision goggles. The unknown factor, of course—the latest SATPIX intel notwithstanding—was how heavily the warehouse was guarded. Would the NKA's night watch be your regular flashlight, check-the-door walk-by, as you might expect if the NKA wasn't expecting location-specific attack? Or had there been an intel leak on Freeman's side, and now a full-blown NKA reception awaited them?

CHAPTER TWENTY-TWO

THE SHEETS OF rain drenching the fairly nondescript North Korean beach were both a "plus" and a "negative," in Freeman's words. The rain was so torrential, it would provide a veritable curtain between them and the beach during what the six-man hit squad, as well as Eddie Mervyn and Gomez, knew from personal combat experience would be the most vulnerable part of the mission. Exfil was tricky too, but you could always leapfrog each other's position during withdrawal while your swim buddy laid down covering fire—if the enemy had detected your presence before you could get back to the craft.

The rain, of course, could be a negative factor going in, Freeman cautioned, adding that even the team's thick-tread Vibram rubber soles could slip once rain-sodden earth and gravel filled the boots' grip spaces.

For a moment Aussie was concerned that Bone Brady, preoccupied with loading his weapon, hadn't heard the general.

"You asleep, black man?" he asked Brady in his typical upbeat, precastoff humor.

"Whatta you mean, milk face?" said Brody, palming in the chubby triangular box mag for his M-249 SAW, the hit squad's automatic weapon, affectionately known by its operators as "Minimi." "I ain't been asleep, gringo."

"Huh," said Aussie. "Do you remember the general telling

us how the Y track to this fucking shed has been covered in crushed gravel?"

"Yeah," said Bone. "So?"

"So no slippin' an' slidin' on the trail, big boy."

"Well, y'know," said Brady, "sometimes Charlie doesn't stick to the trail. Sometimes he goes off trail and blindsides you when you're all following the tourist path to and from the beach like good little Boy Scouts."

"Point taken," said Freeman. "Final weapons check."

Each man gave him a thumbs-up, Sal's raised so high and ramrod straight that Aussie told him yet once again how during his youth Down Under, such a gesture had been the equivalent of giving someone in America the finger.

"That's the hundredth time you've told us that," said Sal, his tone edgier than usual.

Everyone wanted to get out of the RS's two hatches, whose "lids" were flush with the craft's superstructure to decrease drag at high speed underwater. But now the RS was crawling toward the beach like some metallic slug, its electronic probes absorbing such a flood of incoming data that, like the driver of the latest computerized auto or the pilot of a brand-new Joint Strike Fighter, Eddie Mervyn and Gomez felt simply overwhelmed by the cascade of information. Right now, two hundred yards from the surf, the RS's computers were giving myriad readouts of wind speed, outside temperature, inside temperature, fuel remaining, electric motor range using MUSCLES system only, jet-pulse range, humidity both inside and outside the RS, and the sea's salinity content, the computers accordingly making the necessary algorithmic corrections for possible torpedo or decoy firing. Ballast tanks' status, circuitry verifications, and aerial and hydrophone arrays status were also being integrated to calculate the course of least resistance amid the myriad crosscurrents and rips of the surf. Most of the displayed data was being ignored by the RS's pilot and copilot, except for four readouts: the precise distance to beach, the angle of beach incline, the water's decreasing depth, and the graph line showing the exact point at which the RS would become visible. When they reached that point, Eddie Mervyn, with Gomez double-checking, would lift the hard black plastic safety guard over the zebra-striped button that would deploy the RS's tractorlike treads. Like the wheels of a light aircraft suddenly descending from their previously fuselage-covered wells, the RS's two forward and two rear miniature oval caterpillar tracks would allow the RS to keep moving forward *without pause*, taking the team beyond the surf surge, allowing the hit team to deploy dry and so not be weighed down by sodden combat pack or no-name fatigues.

Sal tore open a Trojan packet, took out the condom, and stretched it over the end of his shotgun's barrel. The reversible-submersible was designed to take them in very close, from the sea's continental slope or littoral into shallows no deeper than three feet, but Sal's motto for such amphibious landings had been taken from a sign he'd read as a young boy on holiday in Maui: "All Waves Are Dangerous." He'd seen more than one SEAL accidentally "baptized by full immersion," as the instructors called it, the SEAL at the point of disembarkation necessarily turning his back to the sea, loaded with full combat pack one second, underwater the next, felled by a wave that normally wouldn't have challenged a ten-year-old.

On the infrared search scope's flat screen they could see the phosphorescent dancing of surf and rain, the rushes of foam going farther than usual across the sand of Beach 5 because of the gale-force winds. Immediately beyond the undulating line that marked the dip and rise of sand dunes was another line. This varied in height from 50 to 130 feet, delineating the jagged crest of steep, scrub-covered cliffs. The latent heat of the land, relative to the colder sea, was emitting tendrils of mist that spiraled up here and there, resembling the vapor columns from hot springs, of the kind SATPIX intel had revealed in the Nine Moon Mountains southwest of Pyongyang.

"Tracks deployed," announced Eddie Mervyn, the small Kit-Kat-sized SOC—status-of-craft screen—informing them that they were now 138 yards from the lacy foam of exhausted surf. The SOC's data block also informed them that in precisely one minute and forty seconds, the top of the teardrop bow would be visible to "EXT VWS"—external viewers—at a point between two of the big X-shaped beach defenses, meant to be an impediment to the big American Wasp-class LHDS'—Landing Helicopter Dock Ships'—landing craft.

"Hope any external viewers are in bed," said Aussie.

No one answered him. Mervyn checked the data block again and announced, "Hatches opening in two minutes. I say again, lids opening in two minutes."

"Hatches opening in two minutes," acknowledged the general, adding, "Aussie, you and Choir follow me through hatch one. Sal, you lead Bone and Johnny through two. Confirm."

Aussie and Choir gave a thumbs-up, answering in unison, "Follow you through hatch one."

"Good," said Freeman, upon which Sal, Bone Brady, and Johnny Lee answered, not in unison but in staggered response, "Hatch two."

"Very good," said Freeman. They'd rehearsed this confirmation drill at least a dozen times en route to *McCain*, but dammit, neither Sal, Bone, nor Lee had been able to answer in unison, each of them slightly out of sync with the other two. All right, thought Freeman, he'd say nothing about it. First, it would sound tendentious in the extreme, like a frantically obsessive schoolteacher he once had in high school who had routinely gone ballistic if you didn't recite a sonnet error-free. "No, no, no, no, *NO!*" the general remembered her chastising her students, and then abruptly brought himself back to the present.

The only thing that mattered was that he, Aussie, and Choir, upon exiting through one, and Sal, Brody, and Lee through two, remembered every detail of the attack plan. Speed and precision were paramount. Five minutes after "hatches open," the general, Aussie, and Choir should be racing up the Y's stem and turning left on the Y's southern arm, Salvini, Bone, and Johnny Lee swinging right, onto the Y's northern arm, the general's trio responsible for entering the warehouse at its southern end. At the same time, the plan called for Bone to position himself on a SATPIX-chosen rise closer to the coast road, near the northern entrance of the warehouse. There, he should be able to provide covering fire for teammates Salvini and Lee at the northern end of the building and be able to sweep the coast road with his squad automatic weapon should any PITAC, pain-in-the-ass civilian, be up and around on the predawn road between Kosong, a mile to the north, and the DMZ, ten miles to the south. Meantime, the general's trio at the building's northern end would also be provided with suppressing fire from Choir Williams's SAW.

However, whatever happened, aboard the RS Gomez and Eddie Mervyn had been told by Freeman to allow no more than twenty-five minutes for the operation: "Five minutes up, ten minutes to shoot and loot evidence of MANPAD storage, five minutes back to the beach. Five minutes max for unseen contingencies." If they weren't back at the RS by then, Gomez and Mervyn would reverse from their submerged though shallow surf-hide into deeper water, execute a quick 180-degree turn, and head back to the *McCain*'s battle group at full speed. The humiliation of a botched attack would be tenfold if the NKA somehow managed to either damage or capture America's most highly secret combat watercraft.

CHAPTER TWENTY-THREE

THE GENERAL'S NIGHT-VISION goggles were jarred by his leap from the RS's roughed "step-off" that Gomez had dutifully deployed starboard below hatch one. But the blur caused by the jarring was quickly countered by the NVGs' MEDs—microscopic electronic dampeners—and he had as good a picture of the half-mile-long banana-shaped beach as he was going to get. Its foreshore was littered by gale-blown flora, including bushes and ghostly tree trunks whose bark had been stripped, the trunks tossed and driven farther south from Siberia in the storm's surge. Aussie, gripping his Heckler & Koch submachine gun, and Choir, his SAW, followed the general out of hatch one, and off the RS's starboard side Salvini led Bone and Johnny Lee off the port side of hatch two, the six men crossing the beach, linking up in single file at the base of the Y, a fifteen-foot gap between the first three, led by Freeman, Salvini's trio behind.

The only sound was that of surf and the steady pouring of rain, the Vibram-soled combat boots of the six men barely audible in the soft, course sand, then the slightly noisier footfalls on the crushed-gravel yard-wide stem of the Y trail and—they weren't sure.

Freeman didn't hear it, the legendary general loath to admit that in recent years his hearing in the 2,000-plus hertz range wasn't what it used to be in the days when he could hear the squeak of a Soviet tank's treads in soft snow a mile away in the taiga. But Aussie Lewis heard something other than the rain pelting down on the hard leaves of camphor laurel trees and the sustained roar of the sea a hundred yards behind them. He stopped, tapped the general's shoulder, and gave the hand signal for the others to halt.

With the sound of their footfalls silenced, everyone in the two three-man squads of the hit team could also detect the faint yet distinct two-stroke lawn-mower-like whine, whose persistence could be heard above the sound of the unrelenting rain upon the dense bush of the slope and the pounding of the surf. A blur dashed across the trail in front of the general—a hare. Now the noise was not confined to one engine but a number of them. "Motorbikes," Aussie whispered to Freeman in front of him, then signaled the same to the four men behind by using the American Sign Language Freeman had insisted they all learn.

Bone Brady nodded, recognizing the sound of all-terrain vehicles, reckoning there must be at least half a dozen of them, or more. Were they one-rider ATVs, Freeman wondered, or two-man vehicles? If the latter, the odds were already two to one against the team if the ATVs, which sounded to the general as if they were about a quarter mile away, were heading in the direction of the beach. Or maybe they were just passing by on a regular ATV patrol along the coastal road. Indeed, the noise seemed to be abating.

Freeman knew there were only three choices: wait, abort, or attack. He'd already used up fifty seconds of Payback's precious twenty-five-minute window. His pause was only a few seconds long, but seemed like an eternity to Johnny Lee, just down the slope behind him. The general signaled the team to proceed slowly in crouch position.

The first North Korean they saw through their rain-slashed night-vision goggles was an unusually tall soldier, a lieutenant, given his helmet insignia, the man standing atop a molehill-shaped rock with an evil-eye slit across its seaward front. A bunker. The NKA lieutenant, standing about two feet above the machine-gun's redoubt, did not have night-vision goggles, Freeman noted, but was staring out to sea through big ChiCom-issue IR binoculars. Freeman could see that behind the Korean there was a clutch of about eight ATVs, a final duo of the machines arriving, cutting their engines, the ghostly wooden warehouse twenty yards or so beyond. Suddenly there was no more ATV noise.

Lieutenant Rhee turned around in the pouring rain to admire the last arrivals of the complement of what were now ten Red Dragon ATVs, not quite half the number he had requested, but, he mused, better than nothing. From habit on the DMZ night patrols, he sniffed the air for any sense of alien presence, but all he could smell on the wind was the faint aroma of kimchi—no doubt, he thought, coming from his machine gunner and the gun's ammo feeder in the bunker directly below him.

In about three seconds, thought Aussie, the North Korean lieutenant was going to turn his head back toward the ocean and see them. What in hell was the general—

A fierce, choking rattle rent the sodden air, as one-in-five white tracer rounds erupted from Freeman's AK-47, taking down the tall Korean and thudding, with their peculiarly brutal sound, into the clump of surprised ATV riders. An instant later another long burst of AK-47 rounds whistled through the air, this enfilade fired by the Koreans at the general's trio, who quickly dispersed left of the trail, going to ground as the NKA's submachine-gun bullets whistled over their heads before thumping and chopping into the surrounding brush. The overwhelming temptation for Salvini, Bone, and Lee was to do the same as Freeman's trio, only to move right of the trail instead of left, taking up defensive positions in the thick cover. But the tactic the general had so meticulously planned was for him, Aussie, and Choir to attack the southern end of the MANPAD warehouse, Salvini, Bone and Lee to attack the northern end. The general wasn't averse to changing plans midstream if circumstances warranted it, but the heavy rain and the fact, which he and Aussie had already noted, that the North Koreans seemed not to be wearing night-vision equipment argued against any radical departure from the plan.

"Go!" yelled Freeman, dispelling any doubt the other five might have had about whether or not they should dig in. The sound of his stentorian voice overriding the storm's own assault sent the team into overdrive. It was in these rushing moments that Freeman's SpecFors' endless physical training resulted in what Aussie Lewis had once described as the team's ability to run "faster'n a fucking Enron accountant," *and* with full, C4-loaded packs. It was a bad analogy, Choir had told him. Enron ran *from* trouble, SpecFors ran *into* it, like the firemen on 9/11.

The second burst from Freeman's AK-47 as he ran forward from the brush wasn't aimed at the wounded NKA lieutenant, who'd dropped behind the cover of the bunker, but into the bunker, from which he could hear the screams of the two men within as Freeman's next burst of AK-47 fire ricocheted noisily inside the bunker, the burst's white tracer rounds whizzing about like bits and pieces of white-hot metal, chopping up everything and everyone inside even before the general drew level with it, Aussie popping in two high-fragmentation grenades as the coup de grace, Freeman's AK-47 now sweeping the ATVs, most of whose drivers hadn't yet had a chance to bring their "back-slung" weapons to bear.

Several of the ATVs' fuel tanks were spewing gas, the remaining tanks already spouting leaks as Choir Williams discharged his SAW, its rounds ripping the Red Dragons' seats apart, creating a kapok snowstorm in the rain, puncturing the remaining gas tanks with multiple perforations. Surprisingly, what Aussie expected to be spurts of gasoline coming from the Red Dragons' shot-up tanks were nothing more than trickles, indicating that the tanks were near empty, some barely leaking at all. He tossed another grenade at the clump of three-wheeled vehicles. There was an enormous, jagged purple X that momentarily lit up the ATVs in a surreal flash of light, and the crash of the grenade, immediately followed by several of the Red Dragons' gas tanks exploding, threw the NKA into further confusion.

But the NKA's return fire, wild at first because of their surprise, quickly became more focused, and Bone Brady, sprinting toward the strip of coast road that ran by the warehouse's northern end, was knocked clean off his feet by a rocket-propelled grenade explosion, as were Johnny Lee to his left and Salvini on his right. Ironically, it was the thorn-thick brush that had threatened to impede their advance up the slope from the beach that now saved them, the tangled mass of roots and thorn branches absorbing the fragments of RPG that had exploded only feet away. As Brady fell, his SAW clattered noisily to the ground, despite the cushioning effect of the rain-soaked path. His obscenities, heard only by Salvini, were lost to the others in the deafening noise of the firefight. Johnny Lee, his ears ringing from the explosion of the RPG and feeling nauseated from the gut-punching concussion, nevertheless managed to get off three cartridges of number 00 buckshot at the RPG duo huddling by the northern entrance. The twenty-seven pellets blew the two Koreans back with such force into their two Red Dragons that they seemed to be executing backflips from a standing position.

By now, Freeman, Aussie, and Choir, to Freeman's left and right respectively, were past the mauled ATV group and Lieutenant Rhee, who, hit in the left thigh by Freeman's AK-47 in its first sweep, lay bleeding profusely. Having sought cover quickly, Rhee had dragged himself so close to the rear of the bunker, which Freeman and Aussie had silenced, that in the darkness, swirling with curtains of rain and sea spray, he couldn't be seen. But *he* could see three of the attackers running past him toward the warehouse only seconds away, most of the NKA defenders having withdrawn into the building itself to protect its stores against the assault troops, who, despite their lack of insignia, Rhee was sure must be Americans, because of their size. They looked like giants. Of course, he realized the fact that they wore Kevlar American-style helmets meant nothing, because, like the ubiquitous Russian-made AK-47, the American "Fritz" was readily available to terrorists et al. in the underground arms and armor bazaars worldwide. He heard the sound of splitting wood, his enemies presumably already at the sliding doors at both the southern and the northern ends of the building.

Rhee saw six or seven of his remaining ATV soldiers returning fire from several gun ports situated in the door, but he knew that without the advantage of what obviously must be the enemy's passive night-vision goggles, his men could aim only at the muzzle flashes of the enemy commandos. Growing weaker and realizing that the round he'd taken in his thigh had probably done more damage than he'd first thought, he knew that if he didn't hurry and rig a tourniquet, he'd die. Perhaps he could use one of the two dead bunker crewmen's belts.

Under cover of the noise of a group of his ATV men, who'd remained bunched up outside the building, using the gutted hulks of their three-wheeled vehicles as an ad hoc defensive barrier, he dragged himself a few feet along the rear of the eye-slit bunker rock. With enormous effort, biting his left hand to mute his involuntary gasps of pain, his nervous system going deeper into shock, he pushed against the bunker's small but craftily camouflaged rabbit-hutch-like iron door, but it wouldn't open. Mustering all his waning strength, he pushed again, and felt it give way, though there was still considerable resistance. Finally he managed to squeeze himself through the partial opening into the protective rock cave of the bunker, from where he was determined to command his counterattack, and where he felt the attackers would least expect him to be.

In the pitch-black interior he found it difficult to breathe, and the stench of feces and urine from the grenade-gashed night pail was suffocating. He managed to rig a tourniquet by using one of the dead men's belts without, he hoped, being seen by the marauders, who had seemingly come out of nowhere. Despite the agony he was in, the Korean lieutenant never doubted for a moment that the enemy would be either killed or captured. Every one of them. Though he felt nauseated from the cloying combination of spent cordite, body odor, and defecation, and despite the noise of the battle raging outside, Rhee willed himself to concentrate, pulling out his cell to call in the remaining thirty of his men who formed the crescent-shaped patrol zone around Beach 5. And he was especially keen to contact Sergeant Moon, to make sure that the ten men stationed on the beach itself would cut off any escape down the Y from the warehouse by the enemy—Americans, South Koreans, or whoever the attackers were.

There was a loud *bang,* which Rhee heard even in his rock-encased gun pit. He guessed it was one of the warehouse doors giving way.

The big reinforced-brass warehouse lock, however, hadn't yielded to the two HAL rounds Choir fired at near point-blank range into the doors' "Dear Leader" lock. The HAL, a hardened lead slug, encased in its polyethylene sabot, had become as legendary in its effectiveness against hard targets as Freeman's leadership was in the matter of tactics, the HAL a favored assault round in SWAT and SpecFor teams fighting terrorists from Kentucky to Kabul. But, as Freeman was first to see through his NVGs, the lock was still intact. The famed slugs, though capable of passing clean through an engine block, had proved no match for the lock's double casing and reinforcing rods behind the two sliding doors at each end of the football-field-sized warehouse. Disappointed, Choir saw that while the lock's keyway had been blasted out by a HAL, its all-important casing, though scarred, was infuriatingly intact, its horseshoe-shaped shank still holding the two sliding doors together.

"Give 'em the Play-Doh!" Choir yelled to Aussie. Having already decided that this was the only alternative course, Aussie was ready with a beige baseball-sized glob of Semtex C4 plastique, which he pushed hard against the lock, the Semtex's adhesive, doughlike consistency making it a malleable recipient of the black-striped, reddish-orange det cord that Aussie pushed into it.

"Back!" he shouted, sticking another detonator into the soft explosive to reduce the one-in-ten chance of a fail to one in a hundred. He lit the two det cords' fuses, stepping back smartly with Freeman and Choir behind the southwest corner of the warehouse as each cord's firing-train sequence began, each ignition charge setting off the aluminum-shelled intermediate charge and then the base charge against the lock. The explosion shook the entire building, and sent up a huge cloud of dust that immediately became sodden in the downpour and turned to mud.

Freeman's trio could hear windows blown out, shouts of alarm, and then the anticipated volleys of fire from within the warehouse. The fact that relatively few rounds seemed to be striking and passing through the explosion-charred doors meant most of the bullets were merely "swiss-cheesing" the doors, the NKA's indiscriminate aim seldom hitting the fist-sized hole that a second before had been the top-of-the-line "Dear Leader" double-cased lock. This told Freeman, Aussie, and Choir that the voluminous but erratically aimed enfilade coming from within the warehouse was "piss-pants firing," as Freeman called it, the kind of shooting routinely encountered by newly drafted recruits in every army since the world's first volley of musketry.

Rhee, his tremulous hands covered in the blood and feces-splattered mud, whose slime he couldn't see but felt and smelled, found it difficult to breathe. The astringent fumes of cordite and the odors from the smoldering, steel-reinforced doors plugged his sinuses, causing a pounding headache that was rapidly spreading back from his cheekbones and temples to the base of his neck. Nevertheless, Rhee again pushed the numbers on his cell phone and waited again for Sergeant Moon. And again there was no response, only static, not even the usual snooty Pyongyang operators who informed callers that the "comrade you are calling is either away from his phone or unavailable at this time." Rhee told himself to calm down. He was a lieutenant, wasn't he? An officer. The Party expected him to stay "cool," an expression he detested but one that was still used by younger NKA conscripts who had unfortunately picked up the "migook," or American, slang from the propaganda programs beamed in via satellite from the hated "Voice of America."

Though having temporarily staunched his loss of blood, Rhee felt himself sliding toward unconsciousness, only the pain of the bone-embedded round keeping him awake. So what if he couldn't reach Moon? He suddenly remembered that Sergeant Moon was off duty now, in Kosong. But by now, surely the whole of Kosong must have heard the noise—if not the small-arms fire, then certainly the resonating bang of the enemy now blowing the door lock on the other, northern, end of the warehouse as well. Moon would surely be roused by the noise of the fighting and would quickly rally the three five-man patrols north, south, and west of the warehouse, forming a crescent-shaped defense line into a "crab-claw" pincer movement, sweeping toward the road, across to the warehouse, trapping the invaders, one of whom Rhee could hear shouting in an unmistakable American accent.

Rhee was wrong about Moon hearing the firefight. The sergeant *was* off duty at the time, but Moon, like most who lived on the southern outskirts of Kosong, had been oblivious to the small-arms chatter a mile or so to the south of the town, the chatter and rattle of small arms and the distant *boomp* of the Semtex explosions subsumed by the more dominant sound of the Force 9's wind and rain, as well as by the persistent crashing of the sea against the coastline of the Wonsan-to-DMZ coastal defense sector. Moon, a deep sleeper even during the loud sirens of Pyongyang's oft-pronounced "high alert" times, became aware of the attack only when the young son of the fisherman next door who hung his nets out near Beach 5 unit's HQ heard the big Semtex explosions and alerted the sergeant.

Once awakened, Moon, though still sleep-drugged and careful not to switch on the single overhead light lest it wake his wife, moved quickly, plunging a hand into one of the water-filled glasses for his dentures, and dispensing with his usual habit of upending his boots and thumping their soles to evict "crawlies," as his son called unwanted insects.

Within five minutes, speeding along the wind-and-rain-whipped coastal road in a Chinese-made Bohai jeep with Unit 5's driver and one of his marksmen, the latter hanging on to his hat, Moon dialed in the patrols, which should be able to morph, as practiced, from a crescent to a pincer and close on the enemy within fifteen minutes at the most. But all he got was static. Next, he called the Beach 5 patrol. How in hell, he wanted to know, had they not seen the attackers land? There was no response, only a surging of white noise, like that of a distant sea, and the fierce crackle of lightning, which had probably knocked out the big microwave relay antennae high atop the hills around Kosong, and Wonsan over forty miles farther north.

He heard another explosion, this convincing him that the invaders had definitely gained high ground above the beach, meaning they must be about to attack the warehouse—perhaps they had already reached it? If only Colonel Kim and Major Park had paid more attention to Lieutenant Rhee's warning of a possible attack.

"Faster!" he ordered his driver, who now had the Bohai up to seventy miles an hour, the rain so torrential that the vehicle's wipers couldn't contend with the gale's deluge. Moon called the beach patrol again. No answer.

"Nothing on the cell?" shouted the driver, his voice all but lost to a roll of thunder.

"Nothing," Moon replied. "Nothing but static."

He was trying the jeep's radio phone. More static.

The harried driver was confused; he was too busy trying to concentrate on avoiding the potholes in what had once been the Dear Leader's well-paved coast road to fully grasp the sergeant's comments about the enemy apparently not being seen on the beach. "You mean," he shouted again above the howl of the force 9's winds, "that the enemy weren't on the beach—they came by air?"

Sergeant Moon swore, a pothole juddering the vehicle so hard, his thermos cup of *insam cha* spilled the hot ginseng tea onto his thigh. *"Kapshida!*—Let's go!" he shouted at the driver. "You're driving like a peasant! And what do you mean, they came by air? In weather like this?"

"The Americans have good aircraft," said the driver. "Some of their helicopters—"

"Yes, yes!" cut in Moon impatiently, "but we would have heard them."

"Maybe not," countered the driver. "I remember in Vietnam their Pave High—"

"Pave *Low!*" Moon corrected him tendentiously. "Yes, yes, they're on you before you know it and can fly low. I *know.*"

"So low—," began the driver.

"Be quiet. We'll see." Moon was thinking of parachutists.

He hated the West as deeply as any other Korean, but it hadn't blinded him to either the West's technological brilliance or the bravery of its running-dog lackeys. Americans or British, for example—they had courage, enough to try a low-level infiltration, riding tough through the violent storm down to seven hundred feet in order to launch the kind of quick, brutal commando assault that was now under way, then helicoptering out. A submarine was out of the question, for how could one of the American attack subs, or one of their huge Trident "Boomers," even if they got to the coast, off-load commandoes in such violent weather? A small boat would never make it to shore.

The long burst of one-in-five red tracer from Bone's Minimi flitted across the coast road like a stream of fireflies. But the effect of the 5.56mm rounds had decidedly more punch than any insect, shattering the Bohai's windscreen and killing the driver, sending the vehicle into a precarious roll toward Bone's firing position on the opposite, eastern side of the coast road. Brady heard and felt a tremendous *whoomp*, which was the concussion wave from Sal and Johnny Lee having to hit the lock on the northern end of the warehouse a third time in order to literally punch out the "Dear Leader" 's casing.

The big African-American felt the ensuing rush of hot, charred wood and singed grass passing over him, and instinctively closed his eyes against the airborne debris. And this despite his having the protection of his NVGs and Kevlar helmet. He was mad at himself. "Stupid, stupid, stupid!" He had every right to be angry at his action, instinctive though it may have been. In Freeman's SpecOp preparations you trained ad nauseam to protect yourself but to curb certain instinctive reactions that endangered the team. In his firing position Bone was facing directly away from the warehouse, his Fritz and NVGs protecting his eyes. With his target rolling toward him from the road at virtually point-blank range, he knew he should have kept his "eyes on the prize," as Freeman had drilled them. Instead of the Bohai jeep sliding to a stop in a hail of gravel and mud, it could have easily jumped the road's shoulder and slammed into the knoll from which Brady had been firing, and with his eyes shut he wouldn't have had time to react, his death depriving the team of its major road-covering fire.

Brady was confirmed in his self-criticism in the next instant, when through his NVGs he detected a figure emerging from the jeep. The white blob of infrared radiation that was Moon pulling himself out of the burning wreck was dripping infrared radiation, which Bone realized was blood. Brady squeezed the SAW's trigger. Nothing. It had to be a jam, because the Minimi was being fed from one of its preloaded 200-round plastic magazines, and a quick visual of the transparent plastic casing showed he still had plenty of rounds remaining. With no time to clear it, he dashed toward the oncoming Korean, whipping out his K-bar from its shin sheath, slipped on the rain-slicked road, and fell, his impact against the wrecked Bohai's front bumper temporarily stunning him, which gave Sergeant Moon time to reach in his canvas holster for his 9mm Makarov and fire.

Although half blinded by broken-glass granules and the pouring rain, the NKA sergeant got off three shots in rapid succession. The first went wild and the second struck Bone's Fritz but ricocheted off, the third smashing the American in the left shoulder, fracturing the clavicle as Brady, recovering from his fall, got up and charged the Korean.

The impact felled both men. Brady's right hand grabbed Moon's gun wrist, banging it furiously against the pavement until the Korean lost his grip, the 9mm Makarov skittering noisily across the road, the sparks it produced appearing as transient pinpoints on Brady's NVGs. Moon had never been so close to an American before, and the stereotyped NKA picture of the huge, black basketball champions of the world, despite the man's familiar kimchi breath, did nothing to help the Korean NCO. But he was tough too, and, despite *his* wound, was determined to give as good as he got, holding off Brady's knife hand with all the strength and knowledge he'd gained as a Tae Kwon Do Black Belt.

While the two men were locked in their mortal combat, both ends of the warehouse had been entered, by Freeman, Aussie, and Choir at the southern end, Salvini and Johnny Lee at its northern. All five of them had preceded their entrance with concerted cones of fire, making sure that none of their own off-the-shelf, team-designated IRIs, infrared identification dots, was caught in the enfilade.

In the frenzy of his struggle, Moon was aware of an ominous burning pins-and-needles sensation spreading across his chest as he fought the man who had killed his driver and aborted his attempt to reach the Beach 5 turnoff barely a hundred yards away. The big African-American had his knife point at Moon's throat. Then, with the sweat coursing down his rain-drenched spine, Brady suddenly felt the Korean's body go limp. He pushed the knife into the man's throat, but the Korean was already dead. A heart attack, guessed Brady. Whatever, thank God for it. He got up and, though gasping for air and feeling decidedly weak with the intense pain, he immediately began the quick procedure to unjam the Minimi. Brady's action manifested the kind of determination that under high stress and strain was mute testimony to the outstanding level of physical and mental conditioning that Freeman had insisted upon in his Special Forces throughout his career.

Inside the warehouse, battle was joined. The North Korean defenders, having rallied from their initial panicked surprise, had set up two defensive lines across the middle of the warehouse, one facing south, the other north, using short, stubby boxes, which Freeman guessed were crates of ammunition, as barricades. The general admired the Koreans' initiative, but if the ammo boxes were full, it was extraordinarily stupid—and not the kind of thing that he would have expected from the vaunted, supposedly highly trained NKA. But this was also the country in which millions continued to starve because paranoid ideology had ridden roughshod over common sense. Within seconds, the football-field-sized interior was literally buzzing with what appeared to be chaotic small-arms fire but which in fact was being carefully directed by the American Payback team in the relatively confined space so as to avoid blue on blue, or so-called "friendly fire."

The impact of Freeman's AK-47 and Aussie's HK 9mm parabellum rounds against the Korean southward-facing line was mixed. Freeman could tell from the sound that some rounds were clearly hitting bodies and fully packed boxes of either ammo or other stores, while others were striking hollow or empty munition boxes. To his enormous relief, he caught a glimpse in the flash of one of Aussie's stun grenades of the outline of several two-foot-square-by-six-foot-long boxes. "Johnny!" he shouted into his throat mike, "that Korean writing say what I think it says?"

Johnny Lee had to wait for another stun grenade, this one thrown by Salvini, to catch sight of the boxes Freeman was asking about.

"MANPADs!" Lee confirmed. "We got 'em, General. We got 'em!"

"Not yet, Johnny. Gotta get one of those outta here!"

Freeman feared that if one or two errant rounds penetrated any live ammo stored in the boxes, there would be—

No sooner had he had the thought than two quick 9mm bursts from Aussie's HK set off a round of link-belted ammo in one of the stubby boxes, the box "blooming" in the team's NVGs into an intensely white blossom of light, only Choir in Freeman's trio and Salvini at the far northern end managing to flick their NVG filters down in time to prevent the short-lived but blinding flashbulb effect on their eyes.

"FUBAR!" came Aussie's unbidden situation report. He was right—the exploding ammo box set off others, the ammunition "cooking off" in several of the stubby ammo boxes producing crazy fusillades of fire through the huge, darkened warehouse, shots coming and going in every conceivable direction in a strangely beautiful but deadly display of red and white tracer arcing and crisscrossing through the deafening chaos of both the intentional and unintentional pyrotechnics. Earsplitting crescendos punctuated the small-arms fire every time a purplish flash and crashing sound of an exploding grenade or RPG joined in, filling the huge interior with a lethal lace of white-hot metal that emitted a buzzing sound that could be heard above the pandemonium of deliberately and accidentally discharged weapons, shouts, murderous battle cries, and the incessant drumming of the storm, which now had the coast firmly in its grip.

Thunder could be heard everywhere, so intense that it reminded Freeman, Aussie, and Choir of the massed cannonades that had rolled over them years before in the Russian taiga. But while the thunder was all around, the flashes of lightning that gave birth to the storm's basso-profundo sound could be seen only through what few windows the warehouse had, because the Payback team had immediately closed the doors behind them the moment they had gained entrance to the building. Freeman's insistence that the doors must immediately be shut after they entered the building had seemed tendentious and time-wasting, even crazy, to Gomez and Eddie Mervyn during the team's initial planning session. But if there had been any doubt about the wisdom of the general's "door" decision among the other team members, it had been rapidly dispelled once the gunfight in the warehouse had erupted. As a young officer, Freeman had been struck by

Hitler's axiom that war is like walking into an already dark room and closing the door, and long experience had taught him that closing the door after you had entered fast *always* panicked those inside. Trapped. It was an overwhelming message to the enemy that there was no escape, that either they surrendered or they were going to die where they stood, especially given the ferocious speed of the Payback team's attack.

Having cleared the SAW's jam, Bone Brady, the gaping wound in his left shoulder not bleeding as profusely as he would have expected, was nevertheless in terrible agony. The pain had been there all the time but had been temporarily overridden by the surge of adrenaline he'd needed fighting the now-dead North Korean sergeant. Pulling out a morphine "jab," he thrust it into his thigh, cradling his injured arm inside his battle tunic, his wide fireman-issue suspenders serving as an immobilizing strap. He'd no sooner clipped one of his six unused "feed boxes" of 5.56mm ammunition onto the SAW than he heard the sound of trucks coming south from Kosong, toward the warehouse.

Soon slit headlights were faintly visible in the downpour, the rain so cold he was beginning to shiver, the body heat of his life-and-death struggle with the stocky little Korean sergeant now replaced by what he felt was approaching hypothermia. In the euphoric rush of the painkilling morphine, he had no time to realize how the freezing rain had probably saved his life, the resulting vasoconstriction stemming the flow of blood from his wound.

The roar of a motorcycle and sidecar caught him off guard as its lumpy infrared blob in his goggles slid over the summit of the hill barely three hundred yards to his right, beyond the northern end of the warehouse. From the 3-D computer SATPIX mock-up of Beach 5, the warehouse, and environs, Bone had expected to see any newly approaching traffic as quickly as he'd spotted the NKA sergeant's jeep, but the motorcycle and machine-gun-mounted sidecar combo had no headlamp, and he would have missed it altogether had it not been for the high-intensity "strobe" flare stuttering away to the east, casting the warehouse and the robotlike figures of the combatants caught moving around it in a macabre, bluish white light. But the motorbike combo driver and gunner saw him too, and opened fire. Woozy from his wound and the morphine, Bone was a second late, but here again the North Koreans had come up against one of Freeman's crème de la crème—the men whom he so dubbed knowing that first to fire didn't necessarily win the day. The warrior who won, no matter how outnumbered, was the man who fired for effect, this discipline imposed upon him not by his commander nor even by his will, but by the mundane, finite supply of ammunition and provisions he carried, from the time of the Grecian phalanx to the war against terror. It was a truth that terrorists, from those who had come up against Freeman's trained men in Afghanistan to those operating as far away as the Arctic, were learning as they came into contact with the painful reality of American and British SpecFor firepower.

As quickly as the firefight inside the warehouse had begun, it ended. "*Hwang bok A-ni meun jun neun da!*—It's surrender or death. Now!" shouted Freeman in the Korean phrase that Johnny Lee had taught him. The general's announcement, so faultless in its syntax, so loud and commanding in its tone, cut through the cacophony of battle like a salvo from a man-o'-war, and almost blasted Salvini's earpiece apart.

The general's ultimatum was immediately supported by an awesomely concerted barrage from his team, whose automatic, shotgun, and grenade fire was orchestrated via mike with Salvini and Lee, and was so fiercely well aimed, killing at least a third of the remaining defenders, that it convinced enough of the North Koreans that it was indeed either surrender or death. After a few desultory shots from the direction of the long boxes Freeman had glimpsed earlier, he could see a white cloth being waved frantically side to side in the middle of the warehouse. The flag of surrender was difficult for Aussie to see, given the pall of dirty white fog in his NVGs as the heat and acrid reek of cordite rose into the air and made eyes water to the point that Choir Williams almost felt obliged to don his gas mask. He thanked God and the stunning surprise of their attack for not necessitating its use earlier, the NKA having no time to use tear-gas canisters, which in the enclosed environment would have been as much, if not more, a difficulty for them as for the Americans.

But if it was over in the warehouse, as Johnny Lee concurred with Freeman, this wasn't the case on the coast road. Bone Brady's squad automatic weapon, though taking out the motorcycle and sidecar combo with one accurate burst as opposed to the NKA machine gunners' wildly inaccurate spraying, became so hot firing at the ensuing three-truck convoy, taking out two of the half-ton Chinese-style vehicles, that the SAW was steaming in the rain and he had to change to the backup barrel. He made the switch in under three seconds, a remarkable achievement, given the appalling weather and his injury, but it wasn't fast enough to stop the third truck.

Unlike the first two, which had burst into flames, sending their occupants, many engulfed by the gas tanks' explosions, fleeing into the rain-soaked brush, this third truck, though stopped, was discharging its unharmed occupants. Through his NVGs Bone saw at least twenty heavily armed NKA regulars spilling out of the truck, down into the road's drainage ditch, so that now the truck formed a barricade between them and Bone twenty yards away across the road. By now he was coming under incessant rifle fire, added to now and then by the telltale rattle of AK-47s and what sounded like several more up-to-date AK-74s.

"Aussie!" shouted the general, "go help Bone. Back here in five. We have eight minutes."

"Back in five!" confirmed Aussie, clipping a fresh thirty-round mag into his HK MP5, grabbing Choir's SEMTEX parcel with his left hand, his HK in his right, then hightailing it through the length of the warehouse, leaping over several bullet-popped ammunition boxes, which seconds before had constituted the NKA's "city wall." The flashes of white streaking past him were the body heat from the defeated defenders of the warehouse who, under shouted directions from Choir Williams, Lee, and Salvini, were throwing down their weapons. The clattering of their discarded steel sent a medieval-like ring through the huge, prefabricated warehouse, which, ironically, Freeman discovered on noticing the imprint of a U.S. Marine I-beam during the careful but fast surrender, had been built by the U.S. Army's Corps of Engineers for the South Koreans before the Korean War had ended and the DMZ line was drawn farther south.

For all their expertise in assembling and disassembling *any* firearm known to man, Choir and Salvini, who had the job of deactivating the North Koreans' weapons while the general and Johnny Lee ordered their prisoners to remove their boots, didn't have sufficient time to spike every single NKA weapon.

"Seven minutes!" shouted the general, who now rapidly distributed his pancake-sized lumps of SEMTEX among the growing pile of surrendered weapons, which included several of the rocket-propelled grenade launchers and the prisoners' boots. He then stuck multiple short lengths of ten-second det cord into the pancakes of plastique, as Johnny Lee herded the single line of bootless POWs, about fourteen in all, out of the warehouse via the southern door, after which he told them that they had ten seconds to run the last few yards of the Y's left fork and to cross the road. "After that," he told them, "*Da ssa bo ryo*—we'll open fire." As he hustled the last of the prisoners out the door, his voice took on a wry tone, a habit he'd picked up from Aussie Lewis and the Welshman Choir. "*Kochang-kapshida*—Please go straight!" he said.

The prisoners needed no encouragement, for already they were quickly, if awkwardly, making their way along the last few yards of the gravel pathway toward the road's shoulder at the top of the Y, which they scampered up, several slipping on the shoulder's rain-slicked slope until they got to the road, Lee informing Bone and Aussie via his throat mike not to fire on them, as they were unarmed and now bootless, which was evident when they began to cross the badly potholed coast road. Unused to traveling barefoot, they were hopping about in the rain like apprentice firewalkers. Never had one of the best-equipped armies in Asia been so disabled, driving home the fact to Johnny Lee how once again Freeman had proved worthy of his legendary status in the history of American arms. Having experienced the same humiliation himself during a South Asian mission years before, he had subsequently made it a fail/pass test for any of his SpecFor members. If you couldn't hump a regular combat pack of seventy pounds, the same weight that the Grecian hoplites in the age of Troy had had to carry into battle, for twenty miles, in bare or "stockinged feet," as the SAS boys in Wales put it, you could not be a member of a Freeman team.

Bone and Aussie, Aussie holding the remote detonator for the SEMTEX packs, saw the POWs crossing the road a hundred yards south of them, the POWs' tenderfoot progress across the rough bitumen providing Aussie with the only moment of levity during the attack. "Look," he told Bone. "Fucking Bolshoi Ballet—fairies in transit!"

But Bone Brady didn't have time to look south, because

he'd just seen an infrared "bloom" in his NVGs, which, even given its blurred outline in the rain, was clearly recognizable to him as a Chinese-made T-55 main battle tank with NKA markings. It was an old model, but both men could see it had been upgunned.

"Fark!" said Aussie. "That fucker's loaded for bear, Bone. Time to go, mate."

The sight of the tank not surprisingly emboldened some of the NKA soldiers across the road who'd been hunkering down behind the three-ton truck, and now their small-arms fire increased from the occasional pot shot and wild burst, most of it coming from under the truck itself.

For a moment Aussie and Bone had been so well dug in with the SAW that the first glimpse of the tank didn't bother Bone, but the moment he and Aussie heard the T-55 slewing its turret, the big, ugly 115mm upgunned cannon swinging in their direction, they exited the gun pit after throwing five high-explosive grenades across the road. It would buy them at least ten, maybe twenty, seconds before the NKA could bring their tank-led attack to bear.

Running back to the warehouse, Aussie tossed the last two smoke grenades he had, and heard Freeman's voice: "Five minutes!" which meant that that was all the time they had to race back down to the beach to the RS. The plan was to do it in a quick, staggered-dash withdrawal, but Salvini, the designated MANPAD-box carrier, had taken a bad fall halfway down to the beach and still hadn't reached the RS. They'd have to buy him time. Aussie pushed the detonator button. The earth shook behind them and belched flame as the warehouse exploded in a giant orange-red ball of splintered wood, ammo casings, and ammunition, momentarily illuminating the barefooted Koreans in stark relief.

As pilot and copilot aboard the RS, Eddie Mervyn and Gomez were exercising what the instructors of Germany's

Spec Op Grenzschutzgruppe 9 routinely referred to in joint
NATO Ops as "professional patience." It was yet another
military term for "staying cool," or rather, trying to, in an increasingly stressful situation. The RS's Zulu clock showed
them that the team had only four minutes to reach the RS before castoff, the reversible-submersible sitting on the sandy
bottom of the crescent beach's surf line in two fathoms of
water, and rolling in the storm surge despite the craft's computerized stabilizer fins that were constantly moving in and
out from their recessed sheaths.

"Choir's not going to like this rockin' and rollin'," said
copilot Gomez.

"No," said Eddie with uncharacteristic brevity and final-
ity. His temptation as pilot was to risk a quick "up scope,"
but he dismissed the idea. Even in the twelve feet of water
that afforded the RS at least a three-foot "hide" margin, they
could hear the firefight moving ominously closer to the
beach from the slope beyond, which meant that the team
must be coming down the Y, laying suppressing fire behind
them.

The team was doing just that, to allow Salvini time to re-
cover the MANPAD box, from where he'd dropped it off
trail among the stiffly resistant bushes and nettles, and reach
the beach.

Raising the search scope would enable Mervyn to see what
was going on, but rather than aiding Salvini in any way, the
"up scope" might identify the craft's position to any pursuing NKA troops, who by now, Mervyn guessed, were coming pell-mell down the Y.

"What the hell's that?" Gomez asked, indicating the passive sonar's waterfall. It looked as if the wafer-thin waterfall
screen of sound lines had suddenly been violently kicked,
the normally placid cascade of vertical lines broken up into a
high-pitched, sizzling static. But this was not the jamming

static purposely emitted by the powerful generators aboard *McCain* and its battle group to support the Payback team mission. It was clearly coming from a local source.

The source was the extraordinary vibrations caused by the NKA's upgunned T-55. Having rolled past the warehouse, it was now descending the Y astride the Y's flooded track, the tank belching coal-black exhaust from its twelve-cylinder diesel engine and spraying a hail of both 7.62mm and higher-caliber rounds from its coaxial and independently fired machine guns as it lumbered down toward the beach. Crushing all in its path, mashing stout brush and tangled vines into the rain-sodden earth, the tank's vibrations shook the electronic life out of the RS's waterfall screen, the RS itself now no more than seventy yards away as the behemoth dipped then climbed up the western side of the last sand dune between it and the hard, wet sand at the surf's edge.

"They're out of the shed," John Cuso quietly informed Admiral Crowley as they watched the latest satellite pix's infrared readout on *McCain*'s Big Blue. Officially, Cuso was off duty, but no one in SES or on the bridge wanted to be caught sleeping during one of the most exciting *McCain*-launched missions in the carrier's long and illustrious career. What made it especially riveting for the relatively small number of men and women who'd been selected to participate in the highly secretive launch of the RS was that they knew, together with the other nearly six thousand souls aboard the boat, that this had been the officially sanctioned retribution—"media deniable," of course—for the horrors unleashed in the murderous MANPAD attacks against American civilians.

Up till now, the fury of the Force 9 charging south from Siberia into the East Sea had clouded SATPIX infrared surveillance, but, through a break in the deceptively calm eye of the storm, the big blue screen, or rather, the state-of-the-art computers that fed its data blocks with information relayed by the satellite, had enough clear weather to pick up the action 22,300 miles below the satellite's orbit.

"Looks dicey," commented off-duty air boss Ray Lynch. "What's that big job with the camouflage net over it?"

"A *tank*," said one of the twelve electronic warfare officers who sat reverentially beneath Big Blue.

"Upgunned T-55, we think," put in another, to ameliorate his fellow EWO's sarcasm. "A hundred and thirty-five millimeter."

"Laser guided," proffered another EWO.

"Possibly," said his colleague.

Air boss Ray Lynch shook his head and moved back a little from the screen, nursing his thick mug of java. He didn't say anything, but some of these Navy guys knew squat when it came to tanks. Before he'd become air boss and was a fighter jock during the Iraqi wars, he'd been in action against tanks, particularly the ubiquitous T-55, of which Russia alone had over 25,000, and he'd never seen a 135mm T-55. Putting that size cannon on a 36-ton T-55 chassis would be like mounting a howitzer on a pickup. Fire a round and the recoil'd kill everyone aboard. But he didn't say anything— just stood there, watching the screen.

Lynch was already violating the strict Blue Tile prohibition against smoking and bringing food and beverages into the SES, but he was allowed to get away with it because of the extraordinary stress and awesome responsibility of his job. Managing the equivalent of four metropolitan airports at peak hour simultaneously, and all this on a four-and-a-half-acre slab, required lots of coffee and the nerves of a quarterback. And he'd just brought in the entire "Snoopy Gang," as *McCain*'s aviators referred to both the roto-domed early-warning Hawkeye and the magnetic-anomaly-detecting sub hunter Viking, the two of these relatively slow, fixed-wing aircraft having been protected by Chipper Armstrong, Rhino Manowski, and the other two pilots of the Joint Strike Fighter quad. All eleven men had been talked down through the violence of the Force 9 by Ray Lynch, who hadn't considered his job done until he'd personally observed that the Hawkeye's pilot, copilot, Combat Information Center Officer (CICO), air control officer, and radar officer, the latter three known as the plane's three moles, had been safely deplaned.

After hours of being cooped up in the Hawkeye's windowless, equipment-stuffed section of the fuselage and staring at nothing but their banks of computer screens and data blocks, looking for the HAN-class sub and losing contact with her in the lightning rage nor'nor'west of Ullŭng Island, the moles, as was usually the case, were blinded by the dawn's early light, weak though it was in the storm's eye. Only after Lynch had seen the three moles linking hands and led child-like from the plane by a white shirt did he allow himself a coffee break.

As he was watching the drama of Beach 5 unfolding on Big Blue, the hushed tones of *McCain*'s EWOs unintentionally only adding to the tension rather than ameliorating it, Ray Lynch reaffirmed his conviction that no matter how heart-stopping it could be to be a fighter jock, such as aces Armstrong and Manowski, flying the most lethal war machines man has ever made, or how stressful it was for him to be the man who had to bring them safely down on the boat's roof, surely nothing could compare with the hard, brutal work of warriors killing other warriors face-to-face.

Ironically, the white IR image of the T-55 appeared much sharper on the screen, because of the clarity of Big Blue's computers, than it did in the NVGs of Freeman, Choir, Lee,

Aussie, and Bone as they poured concerted fire through a 180-degree arc at the IR blobs of white that were the NKA soldiers using the brutish tank as protection.

Again, Freeman's hard-driving physical training was paying off, enabling his small band of warriors to maintain a highly accurate *and* concerted fire on their NKA pursuers. As opposed to the excited, wild shooting by the NKA regulars, the bursts of directed fire from Freeman's AK-47, Aussie's and Lee's HK submachine guns, and Choir's and Brady's SAWs were a rapid-moving IR study in "effective fire," wherein no round was wasted. "If you can't see it!" went the general's axiom, "you can't hit it," and so none of his trainees ever got away with the excuse that they were merely laying down suppressing fire. "A waste of ammo!" would be the general's terse reply. "You're not on a Hollywood set!"

The team had taken out eight NKA before the T-55 reached the base of the big fifty-foot-high dune, the supra-athletic ability of Payback's five shooters enabling them to move with remarkable agility in and out of the sodden brush and sea grass that covered the dune like rain-matted hair on some enormous scalp. Their extreme physical fitness also meant that when they took aim, either stationary or on the run, their heart rate was so comparatively low, around 50 per minute, that, like any champion triathlete, their "shakes" factor was at a minimum, their kill shots usually within an inch of the aiming point.

As Salvini reached the hard-packed sand at Beach 5's shore, with the six-by-two-by-two-foot-long box marked "MANPAD" in Korean, Eddie Mervyn, hearing his harsh, dragging footsteps via the fine, catlike "nose-hair" sensors on the RS's bow, down-geared the craft's treads to slow ahead, and Gomez prepared to exit the hatch. "I'll help 'im. Sounds like he's haulin' something heavy."

* * *

Back in *McCain*'s Blue Tile, Air Boss Ray Lynch held his breath, his mouthful of java unswallowed.

"Son of a—," began one of the EWOs. "Tank's on top of the dune!"

"Wish," said John Cuso, "we had our Strikers overhead now, Ray."

Ray Lynch hadn't realized the *McCain*'s XO was aware he was still in the room. "So do I, John."

"And start a war," said Admiral Crowley.

"We're already in one," rejoined Cuso.

"I meant widen it," retorted Crowley grumpily. "We've got enough mad Muslims to deal with." There were lapel-pin-sized red crescents, possible hostile sites, all over Big Blue, from Kabul to the Russian Far East and the Russian Near East. "Last thing we need," he said, indicating the inset map of Korea, "is an all-out brawl with these jokers on the Prick." He saw a young EWO—a woman—glance around at him, then back at the screen.

"Holy shit!" said Ray Lynch. It was a sight to behold for those watching Big Blue and for the six Americans—Freeman, Choir, Aussie, Lee, Sal, and Brady—on the beach, for as the RS's bulbous, cigar-tube-shaped bow became visible in the third surf line of the storm-driven sea, dawn was breaking. Bone, his loss of blood and energy causing him to falter, was struck by two succeeding ten-foot waves, going under, Salvini dragging the six-foot-long, steel-band-wrapped box. Gomez, his left hand on the RS's forward starboard stabilizer wing, lunged out to grab the rope handhold of the box that Salvini was dragging. Gomez knew it probably weighed no more than thirty-five pounds, *if* there was a launcher and missile inside, but whatever its weight, it was hard to handle in the surf.

For a moment, visible via satellite to all in Blue Tile, but

ironically not to those on the beach, Gomez lost his grip as he
tried to help Salvini, the box tumbling about so rapidly in a
wall of surging foam that he could have sworn it was empty,
until Salvini, straining and up to his waist in the surf, body-
pressed the box over the foam's crest, where Gomez took
hold of it again and felt its weight on his left arm, a deep gash
in his bicep, unnoticed by him till now, having been caused by
one of the box's metal binding straps, but noted by the EWOs
and others in Blue Tile hundreds of miles away whose computers were being fed the SATPIX's IR camera relay feed.

Mervyn, the RS's state-of-the-art computers notwithstanding, did a superb job keeping the craft stable enough to
allow Sal and Gomez to haul the long box down through
hatch one.

Back on the beach, because of the storm's residual force,
Freeman, Aussie, Choir, and Lee became momentarily hidden in a thick fog that, had they not been temporarily caught
in the windless eye of the storm, the wind would have blown
asunder and revealed them naked, as it were, on the beach,
trying to reach the RS. The fog didn't stop the NKA's pursuit, but in the early dawn the pale sunlight diffused in the
thick fog created a glare that defeated all efforts of the NKA
pursuers, except for Lieutenant Rhee, to see the escaping
Americans.

Rhee, having spent the last twenty minutes in pain and anguish at not being able to contact his troops because of the
Americans obviously jamming the NKA frequencies, and
unable to take part in the fight, now dragged himself up to
the eye slit of the stench-filled bunker and with considerable
effort raised his head and the big ChiCom IR binoculars level
with the bunker's slit. He almost blacked out from the effort.
Pausing a moment to get his breath, Rhee focused on the
down slope that led like a bushy apron to the beach. The fog
that had swept in to fill the vacuum of the storm's eye natu-

rally obscured his field of vision, but failed to entirely blanket out all infrared radiation, most of this appearing to him in the IR lenses of the ChiCom binoculars in the form of short spits of light as weapons were fired by his pursuing NKA comrades and by the withdrawing Americans, but as to who was whom, he couldn't be sure, exacerbating his frustration. He sat, hunched and wounded, behind a 79G "Sky Arrow," the clumsily nicknamed but extremely hard-hitting NKA version of the ChiCom's 12.7mm antiaircraft machine gun, which could and often did double up against South Korean state-of-readiness patrols across the DMZ as a heavy infantry machine gun, which, as Rhee well knew, was capable of meting out horrific damage to any ground target within a mile of the shoreline.

When he glimpsed an umbrella of radiant heat hovering just above the roiling gray wall of the surf, he felt his throat contract, his tongue dry and rough as sandpaper, the stench of his two dead comrades momentarily evicted by his excitement. The umbrella of heat above the water had to be a U.S. helicopter, whose noise was either baffled by the plastic, sound-suppressing blisters that the Migooks often used in SpecOps or was being drowned out by the feral roar of the T-55, which, in spite of the sound of its throaty menace, was achieving little more, it seemed to Rhee, than being a fifty-five-ton shield for the twenty to thirty NKA infantry trying to stop the Americans, the tank's machine-guns' fire traversing the beach, but as yet apparently not hitting anyone.

Seeing a tank in such a mode, Rhee quickly recalled NKA officers such as Colonel Kim and Major Park referring to ineffective T-55s as *"Kofi Annans"*—all noise and little action. Now even NKA infantry fire was falling off for lack of targets. Then he heard the guttural cough from the tank's cluster of grenade/flare-popping tubes firing a salvo of high search flares into the Americans' fortuitous fog cover. The flares burned with such intensity as they descended beneath their chutes that their light "bloomed" out Rhee's binoculars, the latter's filter to no avail.

While swearing at the stupidity of the T-55's commander for, albeit unknowingly, whiting out his ChiCom binoculars' IR capability and making his eyes water copiously in the backwash of the astringent phosphorus, Rhee saw something with the naked eye at about the point where his IR binoculars had picked up the umbrella of heat. It looked for all the world like a huge, truncated cigar casing, a massive version of the cigar tubes that held the NKA senior officers' Havana cigars. Then he saw two—or was it three?—figures by it. Given the fog-curtained dawn, it was impossible to make out whether they were swimming or hanging on to the thing. Then as quickly as he'd cursed the tank commander, Rhee was praising his commander in arms, the phosphorus flares so hot they were creating burn holes in the fog over the beach and surf, one of these holes providing Rhee with a temporary window through which he plainly saw the bulbous bow of the craft and its strange back-to-front appearance, as if its bow was its stern and vice versa.

It didn't matter to Rhee exactly what it was. All he knew was that it was well within range of his bunker's heavy 12.7mm machine gun. The weapon's mid-gun sight was warped, but the target was only about two hundred yards away at most. If he couldn't get one or two rounds into it with the 700-rounds-a-minute Sky Arrow, he should be put on public latrine duty where everyone from old NKA veterans to young girls had posters of the current American President plastered on urinals and in toilet basins to aim at.

He flicked off the safety and, using the palm of his left hand to steady the gun's stock, squeezed the trigger. If the blowback noise took *him* by surprise, it also startled Freeman and Aussie, the last of the six-man Payback team to reach the RS as fog rushed in again to fill the temporary vacuum that had been created by the phosphorus flares' burn-off of oxygen. Worse, while most of the big 12.7mm antiaircraft slugs chopped futilely into the cold and angry surf, at least two rounds struck the bulbous bow.

"Jesus!" shouted Aussie as he momentarily lost his grip, while helping the wounded Bone. Brady, despite having managed to jerk down the pull tab on his Mae West earlier with his free hand before being knocked under, was having to struggle to stay upright long enough for Freeman and Aussie to help pull and push him up to the RS's starboard retractable stabilizer canard, which doubled as both handhold and footstep up to hatch two, hatch one having been ordered closed by Eddie Mervyn to prevent more of the kind of flooding that had followed Salvini and the MANPAD box in as it was dragged and bullied down at a near-impossible angle through hatch one into the RS's belly.

"C'mon, Bone!" Aussie yelled. "Shake a leg, mate, or we'll be fucking *paté*!"

Freeman retrieved Bone by grabbing his left shoulder, Brady's scream so loud Gomez thought his wounded comrade was done for, but then Bone was knocked from the general's grasp by a wave and disappeared.

Rhee fired again, his left hand sliding inadvertently on the rain-slicked stock, unwittingly depressing the barrel's angle of fire. On the beach there were other screams and shouts as an errant burst from the fog-shrouded bunker fell short of the RS, chomping instead into a squad of NKA infantry. The latter, having become suddenly impatient with the T-55's cautious progress on the wet sand, had rushed forward toward the roaring but fog-hidden surf, afraid that the enemy might slip away due to one of those incidentals that civilian know-it-alls find inexplicable but which men at arms experience more often than is ever recorded. For the moment that the tank commander, now doing an Israeli, standing up for better vision in the tank's cupola, his only protection that of the

ribbed leather helmet, saw the infantry squad's bodies being
literally butchered by very heavy machine-gun fire, he sur-
mised that his tank and its attendant infantry were coming
under a rearguard fire from the bunker. The cagey Americans, he had assumed, had left one or perhaps two of their
number in the bunker to delay—or rather, ambush—the
NKA's progress down the slope and onto the beach, buying
their fellow gangsters time to get away. In a second the tank
commander slewed the T-55's turret 180 degrees, shouting
to his crew that they were taking fire from the rear. "*Cha-
ja!*—Find it!" he shouted into his mike. *"Cha-ja!"*

Though he couldn't be heard over the tank's internal radio
circuit, all NKA frequencies continuing to be jammed by
Blue Tile's satellite-directed down-beams via the E2-F
Hawkeye, the commander's voice was so loudly urgent that
it cut through the howl of the tank's twelve-cylinder 580 hp
diesel in the rear of the tank's hull, both the cupola's 115mm
and its slaved 7.62 coaxial machine guns opening up on the
tongue of flame from Rhee's Sky Arrow barrel.

Rhee, his cell phone useless, yelled frantically, waving the
cell, hoping that at least its plastic casing would be glimpsed
by either the tank's commander standing up in his cupola or
the driver, through his vision slit. The big V-12 engine
coughed out more filthy exhaust, which, while exiting seaward, washed back over the cupola, the airborne hydrocar-
bon fumes momentarily engulfing the commander as the
tank, having used its coaxial machine gun as a subcaliber
ranging gun for the T-55 main gun tube, bucked hard and
belched bloodred. The fume extractor halfway down the barrel was still smoking, as the tube's second shot erupted, sending a HEAT—high explosive antitank—round streaking up
at over a thousand yards a second toward the cunningly concealed slit-eye rock bunker 180 yards to the west, striking it
with 200-tons-per-square-inch pressure.

Rhee, in the fetal position, was unable to hear anything, not even the normal sounds of silence, as he was flung about the ten-foot-long bunker like a doll, his helmet smashing into the far rock wall with such force that the concussion stunned him into a sense of nothingness, only a suggestion of feeling throughout his body, as if he'd been inside some huge cement mixer but no longer knew where the exit was amid the warm, smoking debris in the pitch-black darkness.

He could barely move—he must be covered in rubble, the only sound now distinguishable being that of the sea. His lack of pain tempted him to think he had escaped any additional injury. Or perhaps it was such a massive wound that feeling had deserted him altogether in the throes of death? He sat there in the stone-cold darkness, peering into what, he wasn't sure—a mixed debris of dank earth and shattered rock? He guessed he'd been there for five, possibly ten minutes—his watch was smashed. It was only a cheap Dear Leader II—but its loss made him anxious and angry. On his meager salary it had been a major purchase. He could not hear any firing. Either it had stopped down on the beach or he was covered by so much rubble that he couldn't hear it.

The fact was that he had been there for only less than a minute, his body in shock, his mind trying to catch up, but knowing he was dying.

Down on the fog-shrouded beach, the NKA, now more circumspect, had gone to ground, or at least into any depression they could find at the base of the big dune, the tank having dug into defilade position. With only the tortoiselike curve of its cupola showing, its machine-gun fire hosed back and forth along the crescent beach while the tank popped more flares high into the fog, trying to relocate the craft several of the NKA infantry had claimed to see and toward which they had tried to direct the tank's fire. Without their radios working, however, it was more a waste of ammunition, despite the lucky hits on the RS's bow, which, while not penetrating the specially rolled high-tensile composite and steel casing of the craft, had pulverized its forward sonar sensors.

"Shit!" complained Gomez to Salvini and Johnny Lee, who were working frantically inside to pass the MANPAD box aft while pilot Eddie Mervyn stepped up to hatch two, ready to assist in getting Bone, if they found him, aboard, the chunky noises of the thick 12.7mm slugs nearby doing nothing for morale.

A dull *whoomp* invaded the maelstrom of combat in the surf-thick air, then another and another, the Payback team immediately recognizing the sounds as those of stick grenades being tossed, if not accurately, at least in the near vicinity of where the NKA had seen the team's boot marks, still visible on parts of the fog-shrouded beach.

"Shite!" Aussie said, actually catching sight of an excited NKA soldier throwing one of the stick grenades in his direction, the NKA were getting that close. Aussie couldn't fire because, having just spotted Bone floating away, he had swum after him and was now fighting the current to get him near the RS fifteen feet away. Bone's gasps of pain were so loud they could be heard by Aussie in the raging surf that seemed intent on capsizing the RS, only the reversible-submersible's computer-slaved stabilizer fins keeping it right side up. A stick grenade exploded no more than ten feet away. Aussie and the general, the only two Payback warriors apart from Bone outside the craft, felt the impact as a sickening punch in the solar plexus and below. Kevlar vests could stop a bullet and some shrapnel, but such vests didn't cover one's genitals unless, like Brady, you'd had a Kevlar cup custom-made to protect your privates, or what the big, black warrior referred to collectively as his "Bone"—the real derivation of his nickname.

The general unloaded his penultimate mag of parabellum, cutting down the would-be pitcher, another NKA behind the first not even getting his grenade from his brown khaki vest before he was riddled by Freeman's AK-47's bursts, collapsing in the waist-high surf, where his grenade went off.

By now Aussie had, with the strength of a SpecFor warrior and the will of a mule, managed to stand his ground in the punishing surf, left hand gripping the stubby, winglike stabilizer, his right hand having gained equal purchase on Bone's Kevlar collar, pushing him up against the RS, Aussie's body acting as an ad hoc breakwater on the less-exposed side of the RS, which pilot Eddie Mervyn had brought about as he'd seen Bone drifting. Instead of the RS's bow facing the shore, Eddie had worked the thrust engine on MINPUS, minimum pulse setting, to turn south through approximately 90 degrees so as to use the RS like a big, floating log, its seaward side providing protection for the general, Aussie, and Bone.

"C'mon, Bone!" Aussie shouted yet again, his voice lost to anyone but Freeman and Bone in the roar of sea. "You can do it, Bone!" Aussie gave Bone's collar a mighty push, which shoved Bone's head level with the stabilizer-cum-step, Aussie's strength almost pushing the Kevlar vest clean off Bone's torso. Brady's vest momentarily hid his head as he mustered all his remaining strength to lunge and grab hold of the step with his good right hand, Freeman giving him the "bum's rush," pushing his butt upward in concert with a collar push from Aussie.

The machine-gun rounds, which Aussie initially thought were evidence of the heavy 12.7mm antiaircraft gun opening up again, were in fact from an AK-74, the first round hitting Freeman's Kevlar vest, one or two zinging off the RS's rounded hull, the other two blowing Bone's scalp off.

The wound was so horrendous there was no indecision— the protocol of ancient warriors from earliest times was clear in such cases. Comrades-in-arms may wish to save the man's body if religious rule or political expediency or, as in the Marine Corps, tradition dictated, but there was no question amid the swirling maelstrom of blood, surf, and enemy fire in the fog. Freeman handed his AK-47 stock-first down through hatch two into the hands of whoever had reached out to help, then he grabbed hold of the edge of the stabilizing fin over which Brady's jerking body was draped, Brady's head oozing gray matter into the foam-crazed surf. As Aussie Lewis, his right arm tightly around his brother's shoulder, steadied Brady in the crash of a wave that broke over them and the RS, the general quickly drew his HK sidearm and shot Brady point-blank in the temple. To pull the dead weight inside would be to risk everyone to more fire, and the fog seemed to be lifting.

"In!" Freeman told Aussie, who released the dead man then scrambled into hatch two, followed by Freeman.

"Where's Bone?" In the ear-dunning noise of the storm, whose eye was now passing over them, they hadn't heard the general's 9mm.

"Dead," said Aussie.

"Move out!" shouted Freeman, buckling into his seat's H harness. The RS reeked of sweat, and hot oil from the guns.

Eddie Mervyn gave the thrusters their head in a tight forty-five-degree turn, and hit the Full Power Submerged button, everyone but Mervyn and Gomez slammed back into their seats by the sudden acceleration. It reminded Johnny Lee of seeing the naval aviators taking off from a carrier.

Within thirty seconds, the RS's digital readout was registering 30 knots, the fast craft already a quarter mile out from Beach 5. Freeman ordered the RS's MUSCLE-driven engines to be geared down to Slow Ahead, then Stop, prior to Reversing Mode, wherein, as the RS turned through 180 degrees, the bulbous, tear-shaped aerodynamic bow of the sub became the surface craft's stern, while what only seconds before had been the submersible's stern now, as the craft surfaced, became the water-slicing V of the RS. As the craft's speed rose dramatically from MUSCLE-powered electric power to full-thruster diesel-jet power, the craft planed through wave and trough in a fast-moving shroud of spray that looked like gossamer from a distance but which to the seven men inside—especially to the wounded Johnny Lee and motion-sickness-prone Choir—sounded like a hailstorm of unprecedented fury. What was worse, it felt as if they were going over the speed bumps of wave crests at more than a hundred miles an hour, when in fact, as Gomez unhelpfully pointed out, they were doing only a mere sixty miles an hour.

The noise and juddering they experienced, despite the NASA-developed foam rubber that had been specifically designed to better distribute impact shock on the astronauts' bodies during the shuttle's reentry, was, in Salvini's understated phrase, "fucking unbelievable," every bone in their bodies feeling as if it would shake loose from their worldly frame.

"ETA at *McCain*?" Freeman asked brusquely, ignoring Salvini's complaint.

"At present speed," said Eddie Mervyn, "1014."

"May—be," began Choir, his voice shaking like his bones, "we—can reduce speed a bit, General?"

"Why?" snapped Freeman in an accusatory tone. "You going to throw up?"

"Not if I can help it."

"Then help it." He paused. "They may be scrambling fighters. We'll be all right once we're into the battle group's perimeter."

"We could submerge," Eddie explained to Choir. "But those bastards blew out our sonar mikes. We'd be driving blind."

"Huh," said Choir, in a surprisingly combative tone, certainly one that neither Aussie nor Salvini had heard from the Welshman when he spoke to the general. "We're driving blind *now*. Can't see dick through all the spray and shite hitting us."

"Our GPS computer is still on track," Eddie assured him,

pointing to the screen. "There's our course home. East nor'east. A straight line."

Aussie had said nothing. He was disgusted with himself. He'd wanted to give Brady a heartfelt good-bye from one warrior to another, to a man he'd grown to like and respect, but he'd held back even in the moment of his comrade's death. It had been a spineless surrender and right now the normally ebullient warrior didn't want to be with himself. God forgive him for his cowardice.

"You okay, Aussie?" asked the general, but Aussie couldn't hear him for the noise. Salvini dug him in the side. "General wants to know if you're okay."

"Yeah, I'm okay," Aussie called out to Freeman.

"Good," replied Freeman, who then called to Lee, "Can you hear me?"

Johnny Lee could just hear Freeman, the explosion of the rocket-propelled grenade near him, Bone, and Salvini at the northern end of the warehouse having permanently damaged his left eardrum. Freeman told them what had happened to Brady, what he, Freeman, had done. No one had anything to say. It was understood.

After a few more minutes, during which the juddering of the waves against the RS seemed like an endless attack by the sea, Salvini asked, "You want to undo the box?"

"Are you kidding?" said Gomez. "It's hard enough keeping in my seat."

"Shove it alongside me," persisted Sal, tapping the knife that he wore strapped to his thigh. "I'll cut those metal straps like they're butter. Bone didn't get it for nothing."

"Not in this turbulence," said Freeman. "Besides, we don't want to destroy anything that CIA forensics can use—"

He stopped, grabbing the RS's midline roll bar, so violent was the next set of ten-foot-high speed bumps through which the RS passed like a flying fish between troughs.

It wasn't that they were heartless men talking about the

box, forgetting about Bone's death, his corpse now floating facedown somewhere in the crescent bay of Beach 5. But once in action, like any professional at work, work came first, lament or regret later when the present danger or problem had passed. Already Gomez had said his Hail Marys and called upon the Holy Mother to be with the soul of his late comrade-in-arms, and Aussie had silently said the Lord's Prayer. Now Freeman led them all in the Twenty-third Psalm, though he knew Sal, his Catholic upbringing notwithstanding, and Aussie, a lapsed Episcopalian, wandered between agnosticism and qualified catechism.

"Amen," said Gomez, his eyes having been open throughout the prayer, watching the flat-screen radar display relayed from the pop-up "doughnut" radar just behind the V-shaped bow, all of them depending now solely on the radar because of the unreliability of the smashed mike-fed waterfall screen. "Surface vessel, three thousand yards," he said. "Bearing zero four four."

Any prop signature reading was out of the question, the sheer noise of the RS itself negating any input from the damaged sonar mikes.

"Friend or foe?" asked Freeman.

"No flag reading," replied Eddie, who, with Gomez, was watching the flat screen.

"Dammit!" said Freeman. "Merchant or warship?"

"Looks like *a* junk. I say again, *a* junk. About a thousand-tonner." An assistant RS pilot in training in the international waters of the South China Sea once made the mistake of referring to flotsam seen floating on the surface as "junk," triggering a massive coordinated fleet action that had consumed thousands of gallons of fuel in response to the word "junk." Hence Gomez's emphasis on the article "a."

"Must be bobbing around like a cork," said Aussie.

"It is," said Eddie.

"Steer zero niner," Freeman ordered.

"Steer zero niner," confirmed Mervyn, who, Sal noticed, had quickly put on his Navy-style watch cap, a move that Eddie made when he anticipated possible trouble.

"Shifting!" Eddie warned them, but nothing had quite prepared them for the hard right to the new course, Sal and everyone else intuitively grabbing hold of their H harness seat belts, the box sliding abruptly toward Johnny Lee, who was sitting right of Salvini.

"Goddammit!" shouted Freeman. "Secure that fucker!"

"Sal or the box?" said Aussie. Everyone was uptight—the mission, with only one fatality on Payback's team, had gone well, all things considered, thanks in part to the fog along the beach, but no one was in the mood for sharp evasive actions against a fishing junk that might well be a ChiCom listening ship bristling with electronics behind its deceptively fragile-looking bamboo superstructure, each man acutely aware they could yet lose what they believed was the prize.

"Shit!" It was Eddie Mervyn, seeing the smaller blips on the radar's screen. "They're putting over RIBs—two of 'em." He meant rigid inflatable boats.

"Retrieving fishnets?" proffered Choir.

"In this fucking weather?" riposted Aussie.

Freeman wasn't going to gamble with the team. They'd got the box—*a* box—and whatever it contained they were taking it home to *McCain*.

"Engage at will," he told Mervyn.

"Engage at will, aye, sir," said Mervyn. If those two RIBs could be seen clearly retrieving nets from the angry sea, fine. But if not, he was going to unleash everything the RS had. "Submerging," he announced. "Hold on."

There was a deafening hiss as ballast tanks blew, filling now with a rush of water like scores of cisterns filling at once and quickly, the RS coming to a near full stop. During this eight-second "gut rush," as it was known, when Payback's complement underwent sudden deceleration, Choir threw up, the craft, as if on cue from his vomiting, sinking rapidly, bulbous stern first, which now became the bow of the RS's submersible mode, the entire back-to-front, or as Aussie called it, "ass-up," maneuver causing Choir to further throw up what little remained in his stomach. "Sorry—," he said weakly. The automatic swiveling of seats activated by Gomez so they'd all be facing the direction in which the sub was heading drove Choir into a paroxysm of dry retching.

"Up search scope!" ordered Eddie Mervyn, and Gomez complied, the sleek column rising up, Eddie busy punching in DACS, the decoy torpedo's attack codes, and, as possible backup, the TACS, or the torpedo's attack codes.

"Scope on-screen," said Gomez, adding with deliberate emphasis, "It *is* a junk we're seeing."

"Where are the RIBs?" Eddie asked Gomez.

Aussie, in the reverie that more often than not fills one after such a mission, whether it be crossing dangerous borders in a cold war or a live-fire incursion, couldn't suppress a grin at Eddie Mervyn's question. He thought "Where are the RIBs?" was the funniest question he'd heard in months.

"Where are the damn ribs?" Eddie again asked sharply.

"On the barbie!" said Aussie.

"What?"

No one laughed, especially not the general, who was making a mental note to upbraid Lewis as soon as they were safely back aboard *McCain*—*if* they got back to *McCain*.

"One RIB zero two five approaching. Second one— behind us—on two seven zero."

"Drums!" yelled Gomez. "They're rolling drums!"

"Go deep!" shouted Mervyn.

They felt more than heard the gurgle of water as Mervyn opened the torpedo tubes' lids during the graceful descent, the meter needle in the fathometer spinning backward. They were going down like a stone. At three hundred feet there was a rush of compressed air.

"Decoy away," said Gomez. "Tube one."

"Decoy away," confirmed Eddie. "Tube one."

"Tubes two and three ready," Gomez told him, the Spec-For warriors all watching the search scope's screen. They were at 350 feet, approaching their crush depth at 450, Mervyn slowing the rate of descent now, the pictures of the storm-tossed surface being relayed to them via the long fiber-optic thread whose buoyant eye, no larger than a human one, surveyed the heaving surface. Because of the profusion of storm-tossed waves, however, the "rolling visibility" pictures were hit and miss, in that one moment they'd have a glimpse of the junk, the next a wall of foam, the next nothing but angry gray sea.

"Aircraft!" shouted Lee.

"It's a seagull, for fuck's sake," said Aussie.

"Oh."

The general's voice conveyed the kind of quiet authority that everyone knew would brook no interference. "I want everyone here to calm down. Messieurs Mervyn and Gomez are in charge. Now, shut up!"

A series of sonar tones like a player piano surged into the RS's vomit-stinking interior. Part of being a good leader, Freeman knew, was the ability to delegate authority, and right now, countermeasures against what seemed to be an impending enemy "drum" or "depth charge" attack were in the hands of the two men in the team best trained to deal with it, pilot Eddie Mervyn and copilot Gomez. The best thing his team could do was be quiet and pass the freezer bag of Arm & Hammer baking soda that the general had taken from the red fiberglass first-aid kit affixed to the RS's midships rack, Salvini, Lee, Choir, and Aussie dutifully passing along the Ziploc, pouring liberal amounts of the baking soda on what Aussie softly called Choir's "generous contribution" to the mission, the odor-eating molecules of baking soda absorbing the smell of sick, at least enough to make the atmosphere more tolerable.

The musical tones increased in pitch and volume as the RS decoy, a pack of miniaturized state-of-the-art electronics crammed into a six-foot-long, fifteen-inch-wide steel "fish," or torpedo casing, flashed through the sea. Already it was drawing hostile fire, as witnessed by the Payback team via the plethora of red data lights flashing and alarm bells ringing on the main computer's console.

"Son of a bitch!" said Gomez. "Look at this!" He was watching the luminescent trace that snaked quickly through the superimposed grids of the seabed, the decoy giving off what the RS's designers referred to as "one-man band" signals, the "band" not referring to a one-frequency band but to the kind of one-man circus ensemble so popular in Europe, where one person behind a curtain simultaneously operates kettle drum, base drum, saxophone, cymbals, et cetera, creating the impression for the listener that there are many more players involved. The RS's decoy was emitting a cluster of pulses that would, it was hoped, convince the junk and its two rigid inflatables that the decoy was the RS.

It seemed to be working, the voluminous thumps of depth charges, which momentarily caused the RS's screen to shudder and grid lines to meet, coming not from directly overhead but at some distance from the RS, which was now in ultra-quiet mode, all but immobile at 580 feet, and over a mile away from the decoy. Still, Eddie Mervyn expressed surprise, pointing out to Gomez an apparent discrepancy between the distance to the depth-charge detonations as registered by the RS's passive mikes astern and the "bang index," the informal name given by RS operators to the data block on-screen, which registered concussion waves of enemy mines, torpedoes, and other weaponry. "Should be louder trace than that," Eddie told Gomez.

"Yeah," agreed Gomez. "But our stern mikes must've been damaged too. Meaning our bang index is probably way off too."

"What do you think, Aussie?" asked the general, less interested in the answer than in reestablishing morale.

"I don't give a rat's ass," said Aussie, "long as those friggin' drums aren't rolling on *us*. Decoy's doing its job, that's all that matters."

"You're right there, boyo," said Choir. It was the first time he'd spoken since he'd been sick, the RS's smooth running underwater allowing him to regain his sense of equilibrium. There was another depth *boomp* farther off, and Freeman could sense the lessening of tension among his battle-fatigued team. The computer screen shuddered again, but this time they could see the blossom of light on the radar, the explosion the size of a silver dollar on the screen.

"They got the decoy," said Gomez, but the question on everyone's mind was would the junk and the RIBs give up now, convinced they'd got the Migook raiding party?

Quietly, yet distinctly, as if the enemy above might hear him if he spoke too loudly, the general told Eddie Mervyn to release "wreckage." Slowly Mervyn opened the vent to allow a mix of prepacked hydraulic oil, rags, and lumps of PVC insulation foam, the first kind of debris you'd see on the surface after a sub was hit, to drift up.

"Won't that go straight up?" asked Johnny Lee. Lee knew a lot about SpecFor warfare on land, and at least seven foreign languages, but on matters of oceanography he was, as Aussie not so gently reminded him, "a dumb ass," Aussie explaining how because of currents, salinity layers, upwelling, and the storm's crosswinds, the flotsam they were jettisoning to fool the junk would probably surface at least a mile away—maybe more.

"Yeah," Johnny Lee told him. "I know that, you convict. But will they buy it?"

"We'll see," said Freeman. "We'll wait, see if they move off."

"Better pray," said Salvini, "they don't see our eye."

"Nah," said Gomez. "Shit, it's only yea big." He made a circle with his forefinger and thumb. "No bigger'n a golf ball."

"We'll see," said the general.

"I hope *they* don't see," quipped Aussie Lewis, a comment that Johnny Lee thought particularly morbid, especially given Brady's savage demise of only a short time ago, and the fact of his own wounds, a ruptured eardrum caused by the concussion from the RPG, and what had at first sight seemed only a flesh wound on his arm but which was now throbbing with the intensity of an unlanced boil.

"Anything from our eye?" asked Freeman.

"Heaving swells," replied Mervyn. "No traffic visible."

"Bring her to periscope depth," ordered Freeman. "Slowly. We'll take a closer look."

"To periscope depth slowly, aye," continued Eddie, who was as anxious as his seven comrades to get moving again after the half-hour wait on the gelatinous ooze of the sea bottom. Of necessity it had to be an "ultraquiet" wait, no one moving lest he create a noise short that would betray their position to the spy ship junk and its two deadly runabouts, which might still be around despite the silence, using the sea clutter that had now obscured the RS's radar waves, as cover. It was hard on all of them—men of action forced to wait, exercising all the techniques to fight boredom that they'd been taught from Brecon Beacons on exchange programs with the British Special Air Service in Wales to Fort Bragg in North Carolina. Even so, Aussie and Salvini especially detested the long waits, whether they were in the leech-infested jungles of Southeast Asia or in the relative comfort of the RS, Choir's "upchuck" notwithstanding.

The RS continued to burp air bubbles from its ballast tanks

as it rose from the black ocean depths toward the faintly lit upper layers of the Sea of Japan's international waters.

"Cut red light to white—it's daylight upstairs."

Upstairs, Freeman knew, was by now international waters, its rules penciled out meticulously by bureaucratic gnomes in Geneva, Zurich, and Berne, rules that every blue water navy promised to abide by. But for Aussie, Salvini, Choir, and the others, the reality of international relations in the deep blue oceans that covered three-quarters of the world, hiding the great mountain ranges of the Mid-Atlantic Ridge and the deeps, such as the 28,000-foot-deep Marianas Trench to their south, could best be described as Saltwater Dodge where, like the Wild West's infamous frontier town, the right of way belonged to the most powerful. The chaos was made worse by the stupid brown-water, that is, riverine and continental slope, "close-to-Mommy" navies, as Freeman called them, who, after the Cold War, when they had welcomed either the blue-water U.S. or Soviet navies to protect them, were now trying to move away from being mere local and regional powers to blue-water status overnight.

In a hurry, combatants in any navy who hadn't thought their plans through could be dangerous, and that's what Freeman was worried about now. If the junk's skipper had thought this cat-and-mouse game through, he should have already left the area, because no matter how important it was for the Payback mission to be kept under wraps until it was over, until Freeman got the box back to *McCain*, Freeman knew, as the junk's skipper should have realized, the U.S. Navy would never permit such a revolutionary vessel as the RS to fall into enemy hands, either damaged or captured. He knew that if Ray Lynch and the others in *McCain*'s Blue-Tile supersensitive Signals Exploitation Space closely monitoring the RS's infil onto and now its exfil from Beach 5 thought for one second that the RS might be captured, its crew perhaps already depth-charged into insensibility and unwitting surrender, Admiral Crowley would act quickly. His entire carrier battle group of thirteen ships would unleash everything in their considerable arsenals to destroy the RS so utterly that it would be nothing more than carbon fiber.

"Sixty feet, periscope depth!" reported Eddie Mervyn.

"Scope depth," acknowledged the general, adding in a hurried but nevertheless carefully measured and modulated voice, "Pilot has the con." At this, Mervyn became OOD, officer of the deck, and instructed Gomez, "Up search scope. Closing the eye."

"Up search scope. Closing the eye," said Gomez, as Freeman watched his distorted bean-string image in the oil-polished sheen of the search scope's column.

"Ten to one they've buggered off," said Aussie.

No one would take the bet.

"Relay visual to screen," Gomez informed Eddie.

"Relay to screen. Magnification?"

"One point five."

"One point five. Very good."

Everyone was watching the screen, the shutdown of the eye resulting in a momentarily blank screen before the search scope's circle came online to show, they hoped, a magnified vista of the surrounding waters. Instead, all they saw were foam-riven gray walls of water crashing in on the scope, visually highlighting their vulnerability. Nothing but an angry sea.

"Reducing magnification," said Eddie Mervyn. The never-ending walls seemed less intimidating but just as relentless. The important thing was that there was no sight of the junk or its two depth-charging rigid inflatable boats. Gomez cursed the malfunctioning sonar, which was unable to confirm their conclusion, based as it was on nothing more than their search scope's digital pics of a heaving ocean. A ship, junk, or other vessel could easily be missed, as Freeman well knew.

Given the crazy change in vectors involved, one second the scope would be atop the crest of a huge wave, giving a 45-degree snapshot of the ocean for miles, the next all that would be seen was a solid wall of water, as trough replaced crest. But as yet, no junk was in sight. What made it worse for Freeman was that, as confident as he was that the junk had withdrawn, he was able to only partially concentrate on the intermittent views of the search scope. The reason: things weren't right. The grip of his obsession about the sweet onions and the MANPADS had not been cast off by his frank acknowledgment of doubt to the crew. It was bad luck that the HAN sub showed up before the attack and the junk shortly after, but was it pure chance? The littoral waters *were* vigorously patrolled by the PLA and NKA navies. Or had someone somehow got a fix on their course? Someone at the beach who'd seen them racing off, at least the RS's wake, and quickly extrapolated from the straight-line course? It was impossible to tell.

"Clear through 180 degrees," Eddie Mervyn informed the team. "Beginning second 180 now."

Freeman was sure that the scope's 360-degree sweep would be clear as well, because his suspicion was growing. During the half-hour wait, he'd had time to chew over several other things that had also surprised him: the lack of any NKA beach patrol, which every member of the Payback team half expected to be there, near such a high-priority target, and there was only *one* tank. You used tanks in platoon sizes—maybe a pair, one covering the other, and more often three, but rarely only one tank. And how come there were no more armored vehicles, Chinese-made armored BTR-60 and BMP amphibious personnel carriers?

"All clear through 360," came Eddie Mervyn's assurance.

"Run CC check," said Freeman.

"Running counterclockwise sweep," confirmed Eddie. "Through 360."

"Three-sixty" made Freeman think of another absentee. With the vital MANPAD storehouse relatively close to the DMZ, how come there'd been no Deng-type fast attack vehicles with the roof-mounted 360-degree-sweep 23mm chain gun and pintle-mounted 7.62mm up front? If he remembered correctly, the Deng 355 FAV had a 24-7 day-night-sighting sleeve above the chain gun. And a T-55 instead of the ChiCom 98 laser-guided missile tank. Or was his glass-half-empty mood feeding on itself? Maybe with the storm lashing the coast, Pyongyang had put out a "Defend the Fatherland" alert, which braced all their units along the 148-mile-long DMZ for an impending all-out U.S./South Korean breach of the line? And he knew that such an alert used up the NKA's liquid gold, as Johnny Lee referred to the NKA's expensive oil, which they'd received as payment from Middle-Eastern terrorists in return for MANPADs and other weapons.

And of course the boys in Blue Tile country on *McCain* had jammed every damn frequency the NKA had tried to use, and how long had the Payback team been ashore? Twenty-five, maybe twenty-six minutes maximum. It had seemed a lot longer to the team—always did when you were being shot at—and so what time did the NKA have to rush reinforcements to Beach 5 when for starters they were unable to talk to one another?

Ah, thought the general. He was Monday-morning quarterbacking, his mood understandably mordant because of the loss of Bone. The fact was, he reminded himself, that the storm was so ferocious it would have grounded any NKA antisub aircraft, and the seas were so high that any sonar echoes the NKA spy junk might have hoped for had probably been degraded by the storm-churned tumultuous sea.

"All clear on countersweep," pronounced Eddie.

"Thank the Lord for that," said Aussie.

"Amen," said Sal.

"All right," said the general. "What's ETA for *McCain*?"

"Forty-three minutes at maximum underwater speed," replied Gomez.

"Sir," put in Mervyn, "with our sonar mikes shot, I'd rather plane it. It'll be rough, but with more speed and maneuverability we'll—"

"I agree," said Freeman, his mood more upbeat. He looked at Choir Williams. "Sorry, Choir, but if we go faster we'll get there quicker."

"In twenty-five minutes," added Eddie encouragingly. "Two-thirds max surface speed."

Choir nodded.

"Op's over, Choir," said Aussie. "You can pop a Gravol."

"I have."

The general turned to Salvini. "Moment we're aboard *McCain*, Sal, you can open the box, but not in this turbulence. Besides, as I said before, we can't disturb anything that CIA forensic might be able to use."

"Roger that," said Salvini, trying to hide his impatience and annoyance. Yes, yes, he knew the old man was right, but "stone the crows," as Aussie would say, hadn't they earned the right to have a peek? All right, he told himself, he'd be a good little boy and wait till they reached *McCain*.

Eddie was already making the turn, the seats reversing in concert, with the RS's wedge end becoming the bow once more. But Salvini couldn't shake the conviction that the general, the cool legend of the Siberian taiga, was having an attack of nerves, delaying opening the box as long as possible, as if he was afraid there mightn't be anything worthwhile inside after all. Sal didn't say anything, but his eyes, looking down at the box, told Aussie what he was thinking.

"Tighten your harnesses!" ordered Eddie, who still had the con. "This mother's gonna be an ass-busting ride, old buddies."

When the RS surfaced in a blow of dense spray that struck them like a car wash's opening deluge, all seven men were tight in their H-harness, their heads cushioned in the dense "memory foam" cranial cushions, with a broad foam head strap immobilizing each commando for the series of body-slamming hits that ensued as they raced at 50 mph through a confused chop made up of residual Force 9 surge and vicious crosscurrents. Maximum speed in this witches' brew would have caused multiple contusions and even fractures, had they not been restrained. Even so, the general had a headache, brought on not by the severe juddering caused by the RS's high speed but rather a question that was gnawing away at him after the nearly disastrous depth charging, namely, had somebody alerted the PLA navy about the Galaxy and its palletized cargo? Even if they didn't know exactly what that cargo was?

CHAPTER TWENTY-FOUR

"WE HAVE THE RS-XP on radar," announced Blue Tile's OOD.

"I see it," said John Cuso, the white blip on Big Blue pulsating along a line over a hundred clicks east-northeast of Kosong.

"Man," said one of the junior EWOs, his eyes fixed on the RS, "that thing's doin' fifty or I'm a duck."

"You're a duck," said the OOD on the main console. "Data block says he's clipping near sixty miles an hour."

"Oh, that's what I meant, sir. Fifty *knots*."

"Yeah, right!"

The ripple of laughter that ran through the Signals Exploitation Space bespoke high morale, but captain of the boat and admiral of the carrier battle group Crowley didn't join in. He was doing morning rounds and as usual there was much on his mind. He was purportedly in the short list of admirals for the next CNO, the United States Chief of Naval Operations worldwide, one of the most powerful offices and officers in Washington, and rumor had it that he and Admiral Jensen, COMSUBPAC-GRU 9 (Commander Submarine Pacific—Group 9) at Bangor, Washington State, were in a dead heat with COMSUB Atlantic. It was a matter of honor among carrier proponents that Crowley win out against the "pig-boat duo," the latter's derogatory name derived not from the reputed pig-style conditions of life aboard the old water-rationed, nonnuclear subs, where the only two men allowed to shower daily were the cook and the prop's oiler. In fact, the term "pig boat," as Freeman knew, originated from the scenes of the relatively small subs all gathered about a tanker and/or replenishment vessel like so many piglets around a sow.

"Old man has a few more wrinkles this morning," Air Boss Ray Lynch quipped to John Cuso.

XOs made it a career-saving habit to be noncommittal about their bosses, and so the tall, slim officer said nothing.

"Well," continued Ray Lynch, "he should be smiling. Scuttlebutt is that they found COMSUB Atlantic in flagrante delicto with a SIG skirt." He meant a female signals officer.

"Really?" said Cuso disinterestedly.

"Yeah," said Ray Lynch, not so tired from launching another Combat Air Patrol that he wasn't up to more idle chitchat. Despite his general fatigue, his demeanor changed into a rather good imitation of a Brit naval officer of the kind he'd had to cooperate with during joint NATO fleet exercises: "No, not good at all, old boy. Waylaying young damsels on the high seas. My spies tell me his executive officer *did* knock before barging into COMSUB Atlantic's stateroom with a 'Most Urgent' form—" Ray Lynch affected a slight mental lapse, finger on lips, brow furrowed. "—from the base at Bangor, Maine, but alas, said admiral was apparently all the way up channel and didn't hear his exec because of huffing and puffing and attendant 'ooh-ahs' from said skirt."

"Haven't you got some planes to park?" Cuso asked wryly.

"Oh, all chained up in the hangar. Brown shirts down there are swearing like that Australian Black Ops guy—Stewart?"

"Lewis, Aussie Lewis," said Cuso, glad to change the subject from gossip about the rivalry for the CNO, though secretly he welcomed the news if it was true. If Crowley got the CNO spot, Cuso, God willing, should be on the very short list to have his own command. Suddenly the ejection from the F-14 Tomcat that had almost killed him seemed as if it might have been a blessing in disguise. He'd always pooh-poohed his mother's old Southern Baptist conviction, which she held to this day, that God listens to us but doesn't answer prayers right away, that the answer comes in different guises. He still was an atheist, a paid-up member of the glass-always-half-empty society. But, John Cuso mused, if he got command of the "boat," one of the greatest ships afloat, maybe he'd write a special thank-you letter to his mom.

"Heard about the MEU?" asked Lynch. MEU was the battle group's Marine Expeditionary Unit.

"No," said Cuso, straining to be polite but growing weary of Ray Lynch, who, he figured, was about the best air boss in Pacific Command's six carriers but was definitely on the short list for CNG—chief naval gossip. John Cuso understood it. After the hair-raising business of landing 80-million-dollar planes on the roof for four hours, the need for relief, the temptation to talk about anything other than flight-deck ops, was too strong. "What about the MEU?" he asked dutifully.

"It's throw-up central over there. Crew says you can see 'em hanging over *Yorktown*'s side. Looks—" Ray began to laugh. "—like it's covered in flies."

The *Yorktown* was the battle group's Wasp-class LHD-26B, Landing Helicopter Dock ship, part of the U.S. Marines' "Gator Navy," so called because of the potent amphibian force the Marines had proved to be in the great and bloody amphibious landings from Guadalcanal to Saipan. It was a measure of the storm's ferocity that even the 45,000-ton carrier that housed a 1,700-man battalion of Marines, 45 assorted choppers, several of the hybrid Ospreys, 2 F-35s, and 3 LCACs, or Hovercraft Landing Craft, was rolling and pitching enough in the storm to make so many Leathernecks ill. In fact, only 150 or so Marines had felt the urge to deposit their breakfasts into the Sea of Japan, but the crews in the battle group's protective screen took perverse pleasure in seeing their indisputably tougher and, from the point of view of the women aboard *McCain*, aggressively politically incorrect Marines on the receiving end of things for a change.

"Serves 'em right," chortled Ray Lynch. "*Yorktown*'s old man should be keeping her into the wind 'stead of beam-on, for cryin' out loud."

Cuso shrugged noncommittally. He'd seen a radar zoom shot of the Marines on the big blue screen. It told him why the skipper of the LHD *Yorktown*, the ship named, like all new LHDs, for an illustrious World War II forebear, was not heading into the wind. The skipper was probably giving the Marines, his men, and a few women, a taste of what it was like to be readying to go forth in a relatively light 160-ton hovercraft while taking the big Pacific swells broadside.

CHAPTER TWENTY-FIVE

THE RS WAS fourteen minutes from docking with the *McCain,* or, as Gomez was suggesting, given the rough weather, being picked up by the special girdle-equipped helo from the *Yorktown.* But already General Douglas Freeman had the sinking feeling of a man about to meet his Waterloo. Deep within the general's psyche there arose the conviction that just as another military legend, Napoleon, had lost it all, albeit by the skin of his teeth, in what the victorious Wellington had called a "damn near run thing," Douglas Freeman would lose it all. He felt that he'd been convinced, or rather had convinced himself, that he might be the victim of an Intelligence ruse that would heap humiliation on top of failure if there was nothing in the box after all. "After all" included the loss of Bone Brady, who'd committed himself to Freeman's command largely on the basis of the general's quick thinking and to-date successful derring-do. What had he, Freeman, always said? *"L'audace, l'audace, toujours l'audace!"* He had gone in with audacity, banking on surprise, and he'd succeeded in blowing the target to smithereens and grabbing what he had told the team would be the prize of a shoulder-fired launcher and missile. In short, he had convinced himself that, following Gomez's suggestion, when he and the team reached the *Yorktown* and the world wasn't the eye-juddering experience it was here as the RS planed the ocean swells like a Hummer on a corrugated speed-bump road, he would find nothing but a pile of rocks or dirt, the box's only resemblance to that of a real MANPAD box being that the ingredients weighed the same. Clever bastards. No doubt their purpose was to achieve an enormous propaganda victory to accuse the U.S. of blatant aggression and the U.S.'s running-dog lackeys of Britain, Australia, and the like that there was no evidence whatsoever of North Korean involvement in terrorism.

"Don't worry, General!" It was Aussie shouting through the nonstop hammer blows of a furious sea. "It's in there. I'll bet ten to one." He paused. "Anyone in a betting mood?"

No one responded. Did that mean, Freeman wondered, they believed Aussie, or that they didn't want to risk their hard-earned pay?

What negated any positive spin that Aussie might be putting on the situation was the general's realization that if it had been that obvious to Aussie what he was thinking, the whole team probably sensed his self-doubt as well, and self-doubt was *not* the stuff of legend.

Choir had his eyes shut, so did Salvini; Gomez and Eddie Mervyn's eyes were glued to the monitors. At this speed, a hit against a floating log or any other debris churned up by the storm would be a head-on collision at 50-plus miles per hour with no airbags. Johnny Lee, despite another jab of morphine, was grimacing in pain. Finally, Eddie Mervyn said something, but his voice was so quavery from the battering of the sea that Freeman had to ask him to "say again."

"Force 9 dropping to Force 8," Mervyn repeated.

Choir looked whey-faced, as if he was about to make yet another contribution to the mission.

"Slowing, five minutes," said Eddie. "I say again, let's go for pickup by girdle."

Freeman didn't take long to consider the option, which was to try to bring the RS alongside *Yorktown* in the storm-lashed ocean. As they slowed, everyone could see a clearer picture on the flat screen now that the spray sheath had abated with their decreased speed. The view was of a rolling blue ocean, white-veined with spindrifts. "Concur," he told Eddie Mervyn. "Pickup by girdle from *Yorktown*."

The engine's jet-pulse noise subsided, Eddie warning them, "I'm gonna have to bring in the stabilizer fins, otherwise they'll get stuck in the girdle net."

"What fucking girdle?" said Aussie.

"It's too dangerous to try to side-dock in this Force 8. We'll have a helo come get us with their net sling. Divers'll go under and sling us."

"Piss on that!" said Aussie, with his usual eloquence. "This fucker'd roll in an early-morning dew. Could slide right out of the friggin' net!"

"They done this before?" asked Salvini.

"Yeah, NASA uses them to retrieve any fallen satellite debris off Cape Canaveral." He meant Cape Kennedy.

"Debris?" It was Salvini, looking as alarmed as Aussie.

"Oh come on," said the general. "What's the matter with you guys? Going out of a Herk is far trickier than girdle retrieval. Should I call your mommies?"

"The Galaxy," said Sal. "It wasn't a Herk."

"Oh all right, smart-ass," said Freeman congenially. "The aircraft."

He has guts, this general, Aussie told himself. In another fifteen, maybe thirty minutes he could be welcomed aboard *Yorktown* holding nothing more than his dick from the Payback raid, but here he was, indisputably a leader, chastising them despite what must be a hard moment for him. One man dead and the steel-strapped box still unopened. Aussie prayed that as soon as the big flat-headed bolt cutters on *Yorktown* cut the steel straps off the box, the general would have yet another victory to his credit, not a Waterloo but a moment like seeing Old Glory atop Mt. Surabachi, and no one to tear it down.

"Firing flares for pickup girdle," said Eddie, and there were two loud bangs.

Choir's eyes opened slightly, his voice groggy, barely audible. "What's goin' on, boyo?"

"You fucking dork," joshed Aussie. "We're in Las Vegas. You just missed the biggest pair of tits—"

"Shush!" said Eddie loudly. "Can't hear Blue Tile. Static."

"Amazing," Aussie whispered sarcastically. "Blue Tile can pull in a damn signal from a Mars lander but a mile away from us all we get is static."

"It's the storm," said Gomez quietly, holding up his hand in a sharp signal for Aussie to stop bitching, Gomez's face creased with the effort of listening to Blue Tile's instructions for the RS to maneuver itself into the wind.

"We've already done that, Einstein," Aussie answered Blue Tile's instructions anxiously. There was something amusing to Freeman in the fact that one of the best warriors he'd ever seen, a privilege to have on his team, was getting nervous.

"It's simple, Aussie," the general assured Aussie and Sal. "You've seen pictures of how they lift out those aquarium whales in those big canvas slings for transport."

"*I* haven't seen 'em do that," Aussie riposted, turning around to look at Choir behind him, the movement an awkward one, given his tightly strapped H harness. Despite the RS's stabilizer fins having been withdrawn, causing the craft to roll like a *stunned* whale, the Welshman's mood was suddenly upbeat with the prospect of being transported to the 45,000-ton *Yorktown*, a craft much more substantial than the 16-ton RS. He winked reassuringly at Aussie, giving his comrade-in-arms the thumbs-up.

"Oh, look at this," said Aussie. "The rough rider from

Wales is giving us the old A-OK sign. That's reassuring. He's whacked out on Gravol and dehydrated from up-chucking for the last four hours. It's affected his fucking brain."

Johnny Lee couldn't suppress a laugh, though it sent a piercing pain shooting through his arm. The PMS—postmission syndrome—as SpecOp leaders, tongue in cheek, described the release of tension and concomitant surges of euphoria and general silliness that followed hot on the heels of a near-death experience, was palpable inside the RS after the firefight, where they were outnumbered by at least ten to one. The odds Aussie was now giving were that there would be a MANPAD in the box.

The general was having his own surge of optimism, wit-nessed first by his jocular inquiry whether the team wanted him to call their "mommies" to reassure them that the girdle lift was safe, and second by the shift in his mood that oc-curred when he realized that there was a very straightforward explanation for the NKA's lone T-55 and lack of any fast ar-mored fighting vehicles during the total of the hellish twenty-five to twenty-six minutes they were ashore and try-ing to get Bone back into the RS.

The straightforward answer was the very thing the general had been so careful to plan. His own ruse—telling the Presi-dent, his National Security Advisor Eleanor Prenty, and the Joint Chiefs that his SpecOp team would need at least six weeks' preparation time—was a well-intentioned lie, so that should news of the planned Payback mission leak out and the North Koreans' Intelligence relay it back to Pyongyang, the Dear Leader's military would figure they'd have at the very least a month to reinforce Beach 5 to annihilate the U.S. raiders. That this was clearly the reason for the lack of a so-phisticated NKA trap reminded the general once again how often people, such as himself, who lived in a dangerous world in which there was so much intrigue, habitually sought intriguing or conspiratorial answers when the obvious was staring them in the face. *You idiot,* he told himself as he heard the approaching *wokka wokka* sound of one of the *Yorktown*'s heavy-lifting Super Stallion transport helicopters. You set up a six-week wait time, lull the NKA into a sense of security, giving them what they think is lots of prep time for a possible U.S. attack, then you turn into a worry guts because your plan *worked*. What's the matter with you, Freeman? Georgie Patton would've had your guts for garters. Get a grip, you're renowned for leadership cool. Show it. Bone would expect it. Freeman's strong will notwithstanding, however, what had been a kernel of suspicion was growing, and the more he tried to suppress it, the more it demanded attention.

"If you start barfing again," Aussie warned his wan-looking Welsh swim buddy, "I'll throw you in the drink!"

"I just burped, you Aussie bastard!"

"Ah!" cut in Freeman, smiling. "Feeling better are we, Choir?"

"Yes, sir," said Choir. "I'll be even better when I put my two feet on the old terra firma."

"Holy shit!" cut in Aussie. "What the hell—"

"Relax, Aussie," said Gomez. "It's the sling hitting the hull." The sound of tackle and cable block they heard was quickly followed by two loud splashes outside the spun-carbon composite skin of the RS. The noise was that made by the two JRDs—jump-rescue divers—from the Super Stallion, the transfer of the RS to the *Yorktown* getting under way once the divers had completed shackling the starboard and port-side hooks of the rubberized Teflon sling to the U-bolt that was now dangling from the end of a cable being played out through the block-and-tackle arm that stuck out from the big Super Stallion's belly.

The "wire," as Eddie Mervyn was told by the Stallion's pilot, was "barge haul" tough, but for Aussie, who glimpsed the wire on the search-scope's flat screen, it looked no thicker suspended from the hundred-foot-long helo than a piece of black cotton thread. The SpecOp, SpecWar warrior, who had distinguished himself from Siberia to Germany's Dortmund Pocket and the hard desert of two Iraqi wars, had no trust whatsoever in the cable. "I've seen the bastards snap."

"Thanks a lot," said Eddie Mervyn. "That helps."

"No BS," said Aussie. "I've seen 'em snap, go across the deck like a cattle whip—cut a man clean in half."

"It's not gonna snap!" said an irritated Gomez, who was nevertheless crunching in the numbers for torque-to-angle ratios. But the RS, he noted uncomfortably, despite it being much lighter than the prototype, weighed sixteen tons, fully loaded with men and gear. The Super Stallion's external sling capacity was 16.7. No doubt, like the crush depth of the RS or any other sub, specification tolerances always had an inbuilt safety margin, but the swells they were slopping around in in this Force 8, even with the RS into the wind, would mean it wouldn't be a lift from a stationary position. One swell over the craft would momentarily add tons of water to the weight.

"He'd better make the pull on a crest, not in a fucking trough," opined Aussie.

"Aussie!" It was General Douglas Freeman speaking in his rare stentorian tone. "That's enough!"

Aussie was watching the screen intently, so much so that Gomez and Eddie Mervyn wondered whether Aussie had heard the general. Sal and Choir knew he had; they also knew better than to say anything right now. The three of them had been with the general longer than Lee, Gomez, Mervyn, or Bone. Sal and Choir had been with Aussie in Iraq—they'd seen the aftereffects on Aussie of the terrible street by street, building by building, room by room fighting. It had marked them all with memories that stayed repressed until times of stress.

Apart from Aussie's wife, Alexsandra, Choir and Sal had been the only ones who had also witnessed the softer paternalism of the warrior who'd made his way from the Australian Outback, where few Australians ever venture, down through the then hard urban seafront of the Rocks area in Sydney, before it became yuppified, working with down-and-outs prior to his starting on what was going to be a working holiday to America but which ended up in a love affair with the Australian-style openness of the United States.

They heard a series of loud, splitting noises as the hitherto slack U-belt of the sling tightened into a noose around the RS's midships, the sea rushing by them like a torrent. "Splitting noise is fine," said the general, as if casually assuring everyone in the craft about the reversible-submersible and not just Aussie.

"Yeah," added Sal. "Just the dried salt on the cable. Gets between the strands and spits out when you put any weight on it."

There was a surge of static on the flat screen, and outside another roaring of water as the Stallion's crew chief, operating the winch, quickly dunked the RS back into the water, giving the cable slack rather than "torquing" it during a sudden "wash over" by a rogue cross-wave. No one in the RS could see any sign of the cable on the flat screen anymore because of the spray generated by the big helo's seven titanium-sparred rotor blades. Incongruously, or so they thought at the moment, the Yorktown's Blue Tile SES was feeding their flat screen with cable TV signals, the color washed out, giving only sepia-toned, jerky, documentary-like shots of a group of Arabs talking to some woman.

"What's going on?" asked Choir. "I know that woman's voice, but I can't see her."

"You know squat," Sal joshed, hoping to lessen Aussie's anxiety about the wire, whose spitting had quite frankly scared Sal too. He'd never heard it that loud before.

"Edward," said Choir, addressing Eddie Mervyn in a good-mood imitation of a British lord, "turn up the volume, there's a good chap." This little bit of theater, he thought, might draw Aussie's attention away from the possibility of an errant strand giving way.

"It's Marte Price," said Aussie. "I'll be damned. What's the leader strip say?" he pressed, his attention and that of the other seven, especially the general, shifting to the flat screen where *Yorktown*'s own Signals Exploitation Space was linking the wallowing RS to an Al Jazeera/CNN broadcast.

"Oh shit, shit, shit!" It was Gomez, looking away from the screen at his six comrades, as if pleading with them to tell him it wasn't true.

"Be quiet!" said Freeman. "Listen!" He had no sooner given the command than they all felt the sudden jerk of the wire and heard the sound of the Super Stallion's three engines howling to full power and the noise of the huge canvas sling gripping the RS around its belly. This created a teeth-grating sound, as of hundreds of broken chalk pieces on a blackboard, making it impossible for them to clearly hear the SES feed on the flat screen, the sound of their weapon rack creaking as the Super Stallion took the full strain doing nothing to improve matters. All that Gomez and Eddie Mervyn, closest to the screen, could hear through the continuous groaning of the RS, its composite carbon skin protesting against the tight canvas, was "American attack...White Hou..." Aussie heard it too, the picture on the screen now scrambled.

"The White House has been attacked?" he asked.

"No, no, no!" It was Gomez, almost beside himself with anguish. "*Dios mio!* Didn't you see? My God!"

"No, I didn't!" Aussie yelled sharply to be heard above the racket of wind, stormy seas, and the giant helo's constant roar.

Mervyn, preoccupied with the controls so that nothing would be inadvertently switched on during the crucial lift, had had his eyes off the screen, leaving Gomez to deal with what he had seen, which had all but struck the SEAL technician-specialist dumb. The usually sallow complexion of the Spanish-American had turned to what in the light of the flat screen's bluish hue seemed a grayish, seasick pallor.

"It's Bone," he said. "The—"

"C'mon, man," said Freeman, who so far had heard only a word or two from whom he, like Choir, was sure was Marte Price of CNN. "Spit it out, Gomez. What the—"

"They—they know all about the attack," said a shaken Gomez.

All eight felt a sudden bowel-chilling drop, profanities breaking out in and outside the craft, including one from Johnny Lee, his fear of the wire snapping momentarily shoving his pain aside. There was another shout—this time muted—from outside the craft, or rather on top of it.

"Must be a diver riding atop us!" said Lee, his voice cracked and dry.

"Fuck the diver!" said Aussie. "What about Bone, Gomez?"

Gomez was bent over, both hands white on the roll bar. "They've got Bone. Saying he confessed the attack was planned by the White House. White House is denying—it's an Al Jazeera feed to CNN."

What had been Aussie's expression of tight-faced shock now relaxed, his incredulity overriding his fear of loss of control that had manifested itself on the wire, over which he had no control. But with the assertion that not only was Bone alive but confessing as well, he had regained control. Aussie had been there, had seen Freeman shoot Brady to put the poor bastard out of his misery.

"Yeah, right!" said Aussie, his tone so pregnant with contempt for what he'd heard, it cut through the maelstrom of noise, penetrating even the noise of the Super Stallion's engines, which were now in feral roar mode as it strained and picked up the RS. As the craft rose above the chaotic, wind-whipped seas, the RS's bulbous bow nosed forward toward *Yorktown*. In the RS, a loose combat pack, Lee's, which should have been stowed, tumbled forward, thumping hard against the composite bulkhead, dangerously close to the flat screen.

"Stow that fucking pack!" shouted Freeman, the fury in his tone reminiscent of his outburst when in '93 he'd heard about the slaughter of the Rangers and Delta Force men in Mogadishu when two Blackhawks went down. Eddie Mervyn grabbed Lee's pack. "Whose is it?" he shouted angrily.

Choir jerked his head around, checking that his own pack was in the rack, as if the accusation was leveled at him. Everyone aboard, including the legendary boss, seemed to be losing it.

"Approaching *Yorktown*!" It sounded like the voice of God, a booming authority from on high from the sky outside and beyond the RS. Probably coming, Choir thought, from the *Yorktown*'s flight-deck horn. "I say again, approaching *Yorktown*."

"Yeah, yeah," snapped Aussie. "I heard you the first fucking time. *Hooray* for the *Yorktown*. Fucking idiot—where the fuck's he think we're heading to, fucking North Korea? Gomez, stop worrying. All that shit about Bone, it's Al Jazeera—fucking A-rab station. They made it up."

"But it was a CNN feed," protested Gomez, while at the same time wanting desperately to believe Aussie.

Aussie's contempt wasn't abating, and he was resorting to his childhood epithets. "Ah, stone the bloody crows, mate.

Just because it's C an' fucking N doesn't make it holy. One of those bastards did a deal with Saddam's son, remember? Prick told the CNN guy he was going to have one of his own relatives whacked when he came back to Iraq. Did the CNN guy tell what he knew? No, sir. He had too cozy a deal for CNN exclusives from fucking Baghdad with Saddam's boy. They're all in bed together, Gomez. Wake up, they don't want the truth. All they want is more viewers like you. That Marte Price bitch, she's no diff—"

"Aussie!" thundered the general. "You get a grip! That's an ORDER!"

No one in the team remembered *that* tone. The general's face was boozy red. "You!" hollered the general above what was now a din of cables slacking—they were on *Yorktown*'s flight deck, "keep your damned opinions to yourself. I don't know what Gomez heard, but whatever—" He stopped mid-sentence.

The SES feed was now coming in beautifully, full color, showing Marte Price, mike in hand, the info block reading NARITA, JAPAN. "...an attack," Marte was saying, "against North Korea, which the White House will neither confirm nor deny, and the photo of this man—" Bone's face stared out of the screen. Marte's voice faded for a moment, then came back full volume. "—who North Korean officials claim is an American and who they say confessed that he was part of the attack led by retired, and I want to emphasize that, *retired,* General of the Army Douglas Freeman. Erin, over to you."

They felt the RS bump softly onto the *Yorktown*'s deck. Shortly after, there was a sharp rap on hatch one.

"No one," added Freeman, "says anything. Got it? No comment. I'll do whatever talking's necessary *after* we debrief. I'll go out first, check that the media isn't anywhere near this tub."

There were muffled "yessirs" from the seven other commandos. "Lieutenant Lee, you follow me if I give the all-clear. You need to see about that arm straightaway."

"Yessir. Sorry about the loose pack."

"Don't be sorry. Be contrite." The general actually smiled. For a moment he was like a forgiving uncle. "And don't do it again!"

"No, sir."

"All right, open the hatch." It was a soft command by a dour Freeman, his voice having lost all its anger, an emotion he was afraid was about to flood over him again as he heard just what half-truths the NKA had been able to propagate.

"Yes, sir," said Eddie Mervyn smartly. "Opening hatch one."

Freeman looked up, saw a diving-masked face peering down at him. "Admiral sends his regards, sir, and the captain welcomes you aboard. I'm to tell you, General, that you can take all the time you need."

"How do you know I'm a general?"

"Ah, well, I just saw you on the TV."

"When, precisely? When?"

"Umm—" The man was thinking, seawater dripping from his shiny black wet suit. The sun was shining! "Ah, just 'fore we got on the helo."

"Very well. Are there any media aboard?"

"Media? Don't think so, General."

"I want you to go make sure no media's been flown in. I don't want my boys having to contend with some cap-backwards camera loony poking a goddamn lens in their faces. They need rest."

"Yessir. I'll go check."

"You do that, son. And close the hatch. That wind's cold."

"Yessir."

"SES feed is gone, sir," Eddie Mervyn told a disconsolate Freeman.

There was a rap on hatch one again.

"Open it," Freeman told Eddie.

It was the diver again. "No media, sir—yet."

"Very well," said Freeman. "We'll be out in about ten minutes. Some hot coffee would be appreciated."

"How about some Krispy Kremes?" said the diver.

"Sounds good to me. But—" He pointed to Aussie. "—*no* Krispy Kremes for my Aussie friend here. He's on a diet."

"Got it," said the diver, giving Aussie a sidelong glance, before closing the hatch.

"Son of a bitch!" Aussie objected. "No Krispy Kremes!"

Salvini laughed. "The guy believed you, General."

They all laughed, and the team feeling was back, previous remarks made in heat forgiven, but the general's serious tone returned as he addressed the team.

"Before we exit this RS, I want to share a couple of suspicions with you—get your input. Something that's been bothering me since before the mission, ever since the terrorists unloaded those three shoulder-fired missiles on the three planes and murdered all those folks—children especially— is the color of the missiles' exhaust. It had a markedly bluish tinge, a fingerprint of high sulfur content. I won't bore you with what led me to that conclusion." He forced a smile. "Sounds crazy, but it has to do with onions. Maybe I'm just a worrywart here. Maybe I'm just taking counsel of my fears, never a good idea, I know. But I'm at a dead end with trying to figure out the connection, if there is any, between the color of the exhaust and anything else." He sighed before adding, "But we're not children, and sometimes you never get clean-cut answers to life's mysteries, things that you see, things that you dream. The second thing that's been bugging me is more tangible, however—more disturbing. I'm talking here about the presence of the HAN and the junk. Was it pure *coincidence*?" He left the question hanging in the air for a moment, before adding, "Maybe it *was* coincidence.

After all, we were traversing one of the busiest sea routes in the world, between the North Korean and Japanese coastlines."

Aussie, however, saw the general's concern. "I don't like coincidences."

" 'Cept," joshed Sal, "when you win a few bucks on the nags."

"Nags?" said Choir disingenuously, adopting a confused air to lighten the sudden dark mood that the general had brought upon them. "*Nags?* Are we talking about women or horses here?"

"I'll tell Alexsandra you called her a nag," said Aussie.

"Ah—in that case," said Choir, "I withdraw my question. My apologies. Nevertheless, I think you'll find that the HAN and our unflagged junk were nothing more than patrol vessels who happened upon us. Just think of how many patrol craft *we* have back in the States along our coasts."

"Point taken," said the general. "We probably would have seen more if it hadn't been for the storm."

"Oh, c'mon, guys," Aussie challenged them. "Gimme a break! Storm, shorm . . . those two buckets were looking for an echo—not a surface ship but a submersible. What I mean is that someone must have seen us en route, via Hawaii. You can't miss a friggin' Galaxy landing in Honolulu. It's the biggest bird we've got—can carry three Apaches fully armed and ready to go. So whoever saw us down their intel chain figured that that pallet drop—you know, the big fucking parachutes you can see for about a hundred fucking miles?—meant that something special was going aboard *McCain*. No one knew exactly what we had strapped to that pallet, not even the guys on *McCain*, because of the general's neat mock-up job on the RS. But anyone who saw those big drogue chutes would have suspected that something out of the ordinary was going on aboard *McCain*. And if they don't have a spy on that fucking Ullŭng Island, I'll dance with Choir."

"Then there *has* to be a spy on that island," said Choir, "'cause I'm not dancing with Aussie."

The others laughed, and even Aussie allowed his Welsh-American buddy a grin, but he was holding fast to his no-coincidence theory like a Jack Russell terrier.

"So a spy on Ullŭng," continued Aussie, "sees the big drogue chutes but no choppers coming off the carrier."

"'Cept," interjected Sal, "for that one that had to save you from drowning. You know, when you saw that *big shark*?"

"Oh, ho ho ho—very droll, Sal. I'm still not even with you, you prick!"

Aussie looked across at the general and tried, amidst the post-traumatic relief of the mission, to reinvigorate the discussion about whether or not the presence of the HAN and the junk had been coincidental. "So, if someone was watching the battle group and didn't see any SpecOp chopper leaving *McCain*, only the regular combat-patrol quad, they would've twigged to the idea that whatever came down on the big pallet was a boat to be put over after dark. So they alert the NKA, who dispatches the HAN, courtesy of the PLA, and then the junk, who are already at sea because the rest of the coast patrol boats have had to run into port or get the shit knocked out of them by the Force 9." Aussie paused. "Make sense?"

"Possible," conceded Freeman. "You're right about someone seeing the Galaxy. That was my main fear too. That's why I went to so much damn trouble to get those fake engine mounts put on the RS under the all-weather wrap to make it look like a helo."

"But," contested Johnny Lee, "they wouldn't have known exactly what to look for."

"You're right, Johnny," interjected the general, "but

Aussie's point still holds. The HAN and junk would have been traversing the sea lanes not looking, but rather *listening* for us with their sonar. That's how they got on to us, even if they didn't know exactly what kind of craft we were in."

Now a few of the other team members were starting to pay more attention to the general's and Aussie's doubts about the odds for or against coincidence.

"I think Aussie's right," said the general, "about someone probably having spied on us. In that case the crucial link in the spy chain would probably have been in Hawaii, where some NKA or affiliated agent who saw the Galaxy saw the RS being loaded, made me as the mission leader, and put out an all-points advisory, including any agents on Ullŭng Island, to look for the Galaxy."

The general, unconsciously and uncharacteristically, was biting his lip before he added, "That island's so damn strategic. There has to be a spy or spies on there."

Sal was nodding his head in agreement now. "You got a point, General, and you too, Aussie, I have to admit. But hey—we got the job done, didn't we?"

"Yeah," said Aussie. "We aced the bastards because they didn't expect there'd be a payback so soon after their bloody triple play. And," Aussie continued, "they had no idea about our beautiful machine's speed."

"So then, what's the problem?" pressed Sal.

"Excuse me," put in Aussie, "but did you fall on your fucking head comin' down that trail? The problem, *boyo*, as my Welsh warbler here would say, is what about next time we, or some other SpecFor team, has to go into the Dear Leader's Hermit Kingdom? We need to root out that spy ring—all down the line."

They all agreed, and Freeman said he'd start the wheels moving on it immediately, though the actual spy-busting job would be one for the FBI and Homeland Security.

"All right," said Freeman. "I'll make sure it goes out as an 'Urgent' to our intel guys in Honolulu. Ask them to do a frame-by-frame examination of the airport's perimeter IR cameras the night we passed through. They might pick up something."

"Yeah," said Eddie Mervyn. "But Honolulu Airport's so open, General. I mean, it's so close to the civilian runways, anyone on a plane-haul tractor or in a mechanic's uniform could wander around and take an infrared zoom shot. They sure as hell wouldn't use a flash either."

"So," enjoined Freeman, "we'll get the FBI and Homeland to do a check of all IR zoom lenses imported and sold in Honolulu. That kind of stuff, especially infrared and other night-vision equipment, has been carefully recorded since 9/11. And being an island, it's a hell of a lot easier to keep track of what's coming in and going out. If they can catch someone in Honolulu, it'll break the chain." The general paused. "The only other thing, gentlemen—and it's concomitant with the question of coincidence—is that the NKA could have guesstimated from our first reported sonar position that we were heading for the area of Kosong, the warehouse, even though I had us on an indirect dogleg course for Beach 5. The question, then, is whether the North Koreans at the warehouse had time to fake us out."

"Well, hell," said Eddie Mervyn. "There was nothing fake about that firefight, nothing fake about that round Bone took."

"I *know* that," said the general testily. "I'm talking about them maybe, just *maybe*, having had time to switch the—"

"You mean," cut in Johnny Lee, "you don't think there's a MANPAD in the box?"

Freeman's jaw was tight. "I just don't know, Johnny."

"Well, shit," said Aussie. "Let's go open the friggin' box."

"Right," said the general. "But in one of the *Yorktown*'s armories. We'll need a big pair of cutters. No rough-and-ready

job, though. Remember, we don't want to contaminate anything for the CIA's forensics."

"We're outta here," said Aussie. "Give me a hand with this
damn—" He paused, his voice taking on a markedly ironic
tone. "—this MANPAD-*marked* box. And Eddie, ask
Yorktown's master chief if they have a good pair of flat-
headed bolt cutters."

"Flat-headed bolt cutters, roger."

Eleanor Prenty's phone rang, and her assistant, Flax, answered. He was a flaxen-haired "brain" from Harvard, or
was it Yale? All she remembered was his paper on post–Cold
War international relations. He'd warned that globalization—
the global village—had its upside, but that if you thought
nationalism was on the wane, watch the news. You could
wish for Rousseau's uplifting general will if you wanted, but
at the end of the day it was Thomas Hobbes—he of the life
of man, without a tough government, being nothing more
than "poor, nasty, brutish, and short!" or, as one clock-
harried Oxford Ph.D. candidate hurriedly scrawled on his
exam, "poor, nasty, *British*, and short." In any event, Eleanor
had liked her flaxen-haired assistant, whom she'd nicknamed "Flax," to his hidden displeasure, because he understood that this world war against terrorism couldn't be
fought according to the rules of World War II, that *all* terrorists were people who, like the worst of the Nazis, would
wave a white flag to coalition troops as if to parley when in
fact all they would really do would be buy enough time to re-
load and kill the coalition messenger. No, you had to do what
the Israelis did in '04: go after the head of the snake and kill
them any way, anywhere that you could, and Eleanor had
spent a great deal of her time as National Security Advisor
convincing the President that he must make it clear to all
other countries that the United States would go wherever

necessary to kill the snakes, and it wouldn't bother with time-wasting legalese.

Yorktown's TV studio was setting up a scramble-phone conference with her and the general, but it would take a half hour to get it done unless she elected to talk to Freeman in plain language. Admiral Crowley was advising that, given the carrier group's position off North Korea and, effectively, China, he thought it best to wait for scramble.

"I agree," Eleanor told Flax. "Tell them I'll wait. Last thing we need is to be overheard by—" She stopped herself. She'd almost said "Beijing," which was presently locked in yet another bitter intellectual property and copyright battle over illegal use of Microsoft and U.S. software programs. "Tell them I'll wait for the scramble."

Aboard *Yorktown*, Freeman's team, though still wet through from the rain during the firefight on Beach 5, took no time in getting to the box. Freeman, thorough as usual, didn't rule out the possibility of a booby trap, and had requested time in one of the big steel- and ceramic-lined armories down on the 04 level. Here, the armory doubled as a bomb disposal bay deep within the Wasp-class carrier.

Whereas Sal had been itching to open the box during the run back from the North Korean coast, now he, like the others, wasn't in any great hurry to find a box of dirt or a bomb.

When Lee arrived, his arm bandaged, the general asked, "Break anything, Johnny?"

"No, sir. Not a pension wound. I'll be okay."

The general smiled at Lee's "no pension wound," but the others were so burned-out, as one of the Marines had observed upon their crawling out of the vomit-reeking RS, that even with the best will just now they couldn't find anything to smile about. What made the mood even worse was that the huge ship, filled with 1,600 Marines and over a thousand of-

ficers and crew, was alive with computers, not only desktop
military operational computers but hundreds of laptops, being used by on- and off-duty crew, and "every damn one of
'em," as Freeman had observed somewhat sullenly, was
showing the CNN/Al Jazeera feed. Until they'd entered the
creamy white, ceramic-lined armory, none of his team, except for Gomez, had seen the TV picture of Bone. That had
changed a second after Johnny Lee had entered the armory.
The armory's computer, on a swivel mount for armorers to
check weight-to-power loads for *Yorktown*'s VTOL—
vertical takeoff and landing—aircraft, as well as for the big
ship's helicopters, was now showing the latest CNN/Al
Jazeera feed. The team fell into a gloomy silence when they
saw Bone's bandage-wrapped head filling the computer
screen. He looked bruised, though with his black skin this
was difficult to discern, his eyes bloodshot and fixed in a
thousand-yard stare, which the team, but not the public at
large, knew was the stare of a dead man. Gomez still
couldn't bring himself to look, averting his eyes from the
screen, fixing his gaze instead on the armory's bright red fire
axe.

"Yes, Erin," came Marte Price's voice on CNN. "That's
the only picture Al Jazeera has of the man whom the North
Koreans claim is an American Special Forces soldier. It's a
photo, I believe—a still shot, not from a video."

" 'Course it's fucking *still*," snorted Aussie. "He's *dead*,
you twit!"

"They must've dragged him out of the surf," said Sal.

"Which is more than we did," confessed Freeman, but it
was said not in a tone of guilt but more in the manner of acknowledging a bad tactical error. The Marines, he knew,
wouldn't like it. They had a code: they never left their dead.
Even during a terrible winter rout, such as the fighting withdrawal from the Chosin Reservoir in October 1950, with
120,000 Chinese coming down at them from either side of

the snow-covered valley, cutting off their retreat to Wonsan, they had fought carrying their dead. What would they think of the general, General Freeman, leaving one of his own behind off Beach 5?

But SpecOps was a different ball game. In an "INDIO"—in, do it, out—op, as many out of Fort Bragg's SpecOp school called such missions as Freeman's attack on Beach 5, everyone understood that if you took a "lethal" or were otherwise fatally wounded, rather than let you be taken prisoner it was your comrades' responsibility to think of the team.

The NKA were calling Bone an "imperialist lackey, cannon fodder for American imperialist aggression against the freedom-loving people of the Democratic Republic of Korea."

"Ever notice," said Aussie, "how all these bloody dictators call their countries the 'Democratic Republic'? Whenever you hear that, you know they're fucking tyrants."

Sal grabbed the big flat-headed bolt cutters after Gomez and Eddie had gone over the box for any signs of a trip mechanism wire or of tampering with the box's sides, bottom, or lid. He found it impossible, however, to even slide the head of the big cutters far enough under the first of the four metal straps to get a grip.

"Fuck forensics!" said Aussie irritably, striding over and heaving the red fire axe out of its holder. "Here, let me have a whack at it. Stand back."

The other seven tired men, including the general, did as he said, and Aussie brought the heavy fire axe down hard on the first metal band, which sprang apart, its zinging sound echoing in the armory. He whacked the second band, and they heard the wood splinter along with the vibration from the first band still reverberating. Aussie paused. None of them had slept after the grueling eight-hour mission, and the high adrenaline rush had been replaced by what Aussie habitually called the "three-ton-truck" that weighs anyone down after their body has been on a high-alert, high-stress job, made worse by people trying to kill you.

Aussie paused for breath, then whacked the box twice more and pried it open. "Well, I'll be screwed!"

"Not by me, you won't," intoned Sal dryly.

"Nor by me," said Choir—Johnny Lee, Gomez, Eddie, and the general all grinning like the proverbial Cheshire cat.

"It better not be fake," said the general, looking down.

It wasn't, the launcher sky blue, and, cradled by its side, the Igla 2C, its brownish translucent nose shining brightly against the armory's white ceramic dazzle. And on the launcher's shaft, the small yet distinct Korean lettering and MID number.

"Son of a bitch," said Sal softly. "You did it, General."

"*We* did it," the general corrected him. "Only wish that Bone were here to see it."

"Maybe," said Gomez, "he is."

Freeman shrugged noncommittally, then added, "Well, I know for sure who *is* going to see it—those lying sons of bitches in Pyongyang. They're going to see that we caught them with the smoking gun. We'll get it on CNN *and* Al Jazeera."

"The American-haters," put in Aussie, "won't believe it."

"You're right," the general replied. "But they're not the ones we need to see it. We need every American and ally and potential ally in this war to see it—to see just what we're up against—child-murderers." The general paused and looked from man to man. "We, gentlemen, are going to do what JFK did when he gave those pictures of the Cuban missile sites to our U.N. ambassador, Adlai Stevenson, to take to the U.N." Freeman smiled at the thought. "Stevenson asked the Soviets whether they had put any intercontinental ballistic missile sites within ninety miles of American soil. The table-thumping Soviets denied it, then Stevenson had his assistants uncover the map stand with all the photographs of the Cuban sites. Commie sons of bitches had to 'fess up, and Kennedy got their missile-loaded ships to turn back and dismantled the missile sites in Cuba. U.S. lost some good men getting those U-2 pix of the sites, like we lost Brady at Kosong. But we nailed the bastards."

"Give 'em shite, General," said Aussie.

"Rest assured, gentlemen," promised Freeman, "I will. And I have a hunch that the White House isn't going to want this ad hoc phone conference on scrambler at all. I think that they'll want to hear about the contents of this box quickly in—"

"Plain bloody language," cut in Aussie.

He was right. The White House did want to hear it in plain language. But not as bloody as that which normally peppered a soldier's battlefield vocabulary, and so the *Yorktown*'s skipper, under the CVBG's commander, Admiral Crowley, instructed *Yorktown*'s TV room's satellite-to-ship-to-shore producer to put the general on a seven-second delay with the White House in order to delete any "impolitic rhetoric... vis-à-vis the North Koreans."

The director of ship's signals aboard *Yorktown* had to bleep Freeman four times in as many minutes as he "unloaded" and, as Marte Price would later report to the world, "lit into the North Korean Communists and their 'running-dog lackey' terrorists"—using the Korean phrase Johnny Lee had quickly tutored him in. The general also lit into "those damn closet Commies who still lie *waiting* in the new Russia to seize power, republic by republic"—a comment that struck everyone as odd, but the general wasn't convinced North Korea didn't have some "old commie supporters" abroad, as he told Aussie.

A sanitized version of the general's *Yorktown*–White House conference, albeit with him standing in front of *Yorktown*'s camera, his sodden uniform stained by Brady's blood, was broadcast on the networks an hour later. But even with the editing, the force of his words, fused like armor-penetrating rounds by Bone's painful absence, still electrified America, along with the MANPAD evidence the team had uncovered, and the general's explicit warning that for as long as America and her allies had been fighting terrorism, it was unfortunately, as the British had so persistently cautioned, "early days yet."

"Muslim fanatics," said Freeman, "are like any other. They are unrelenting. And to defeat them, the American-British-Australian coalition, and all those who have the guts and political will for the long haul against terror, must be just as unrelenting in our determination to exterminate the vermin. To do this we must spill our treasure and, what is much worse, our blood. But there is no other way."

And so the general continued to give them "shite." What the general habitually and contemptuously referred to as the "Useless Nations" for once became useful under the glare of not only the American public but anyone who even contemplated boarding an airliner in the future. The U.N.'s Secretary General endorsed a General Assembly motion to immediately stop all technical aid to North Korea, but under the urging of the United States, food aid for the suppressed people of North Korea, especially for children, was to continue.

CHAPTER TWENTY-SIX

ALL THROUGH THE Pentagon, clutches of officers were watching a tape of Marte Price's "exclusive" interview with Freeman, the audio gaps caused by the bleeps in this tape resulting in a segmented sound track that Freeman would subsequently describe to Marte Price as having been sabotaged by Big Brother.

"Which Big Brother?" Marte had pressed in the pre-broadcast interview, the kind of question that endeared her to him. "They're everywhere, Douglas."

"Marte," he'd told her, "next to mass murder, the worst thing, the very worst thing, these bastard terrorists have done to us is to excite those who love bossing other people around, spying on them, cutting into freedom of speech, freedom of movement. Hell, I never used one profanity in my teleconference, but the White House had to go and bleep me."

"You did call the North Koreans scumbags, General."

"Well, dammit, they are. Any creep who makes missiles to use for the express purpose of blowing children and other civilians out of the air is a scumbag, and needs to be bagged as scum!"

"Can I use that, Douglas?"

"You betcha."

She used it, and the Pentagon saw the interview. Halfway through, General of the Air Force Michael Lesand was shaking his head as he heard Freeman's epithets for the North Ko-

rean leadership, the epithets, articulately spoken, clearly calculated to tell the world just what General Douglas Freeman
thought of those "gutless child murderers in Pyongstink who
provided shoulder-fired missiles to terrorists."

Of the three terrorist "duos," one pair, the Guatemalans at
Dallas/Fort Worth, killed themselves and several passengers
with what the FBI now determined was their backup Igla 2C
in the map case, the first Igla having been the missile that had
brought down the Brazilian airliner.

Of the other four remaining terrorists, two were run to
ground, found at JFK, as Freeman had postulated to Eleanor,
toweling themselves down in one of the international terminal's "Executive Class" bar-equipped suites. At LAX, the
two Army of Palestine terrorists were cornered in one of the
circular waiting rooms, screaming in Arabic, until they were
felled by the SWAT team's shotgun-fired nonlethal bean
bags and taken away.

Ironically, had the Dear Leader and his North Korean
henchmen kept quiet about the Kosong raid, they might have
gotten away with their lie that the missile and launcher displayed by Freeman were fake, or that the Americans had
bought them to try to frame the NKA. But all the histrionics
of denial with which Pyongyang initially greeted the "blatant attack on our freedom-loving people" were undone the
moment they'd tried to make propaganda out of a false con-
fession from Bone. By showing Bone Brady's face to the
world, admitting the American attack had taken place, they
were now caught utterly off guard when the launcher and
missile with the Korean MIDs were presented by Freeman,
the rest of the SpecFor team's faces being blacked out on
Freeman's orders—not to deny them the glory of their moment, but to protect their identities.

CHAPTER TWENTY-SEVEN

HOMELAND AIRPORT SECURITY, quite independent of Freeman's message to search their infrared tapes at Honolulu Airport had, as a matter of post-9/11 standard procedure, already done so. They could see two possible intruders who had crossed from the civilian section of the huge airport into the "Restricted—Deadly Force Authorized" area between 2200 and 2247 hours on the night during which the big SOCOM—Special Operations Command—Galaxy had landed with its cargo of all-weather-wrapped equipment aboard.

Facial ID was impossible, the infrared cameras recording merely two "bleeds"—white thermal blobs on a grayish background. One figure, a tall individual, seemed to be wearing what looked like coveralls, like so many mechanics at both the civilian and military ends of the huge complex of runways. His ID badge, which he wore around his neck, was giving off a civilian employee's IR dots, the same kind of stick-on, off-the-shelf IR dots as had been used by Freeman's team. This told Homeland Security Agent Johnny Suzuki and FBI Agent Jenny Osaka that whoever it was holding the big IR binoculars and what appeared to be a small camera was almost certainly a spy who had guts, for there were random Humvee night patrols, especially after 9/11 and the triple hit against the airliners. But whoever it was also seemed to know the location of the invisible laser beam that would trigger alarms at the military airport's headquarters, should they be trespassed.

The second intruder was a figure who was not bleeding IR radiation but was surprisingly cool and had recognizable Navy IR dots—probably one of the Navy SEALs from Pearl Harbor honing his "infiltration and exfiltration of enemy bases" techniques.

There seemed to be no doubt that the taller individual was the primary suspect, but neither Homeland Security's Johnny Suzuki nor FBI's Jenny Osaka could be 100 percent sure. When Johnny Suzuki, at Homeland Security headquarters in downtown Honolulu, did the computer search for all those registered in Honolulu and the rest of Oahu who either owned or had bought zoom IR binoculars and IR cameras, it took only three and a half minutes, something that would have astonished his Nisei great-uncle who had worked as a military policeman until he was interned during World War II.

Of the seventeen names that popped up on the computer, two were now deceased, three in old-age homes, and only one of the remaining twelve—information that Johnny had been able to acquire by using the man's Social Security number given at the time of purchase of the binoculars—was over six feet tall. It was now easy to identify the man from the civilian airport's photo ID security files. His name was Yudah Ulama, a Muslim of South Asian descent, originally from Indonesia, who had been granted U.S. citizenship in November 2004.

General Freeman, more used to tactical and strategic maneuvers than to counterespionage, nevertheless made what Aussie described as a "bloody good suggestion" to Homeland Security and the FBI—namely, to be a little lax, though nothing *too* obvious, regarding airport security on the return flight of the Galaxy, with the RS, again all-weather-wrapped and bearing the three bogus helo engine mounts, to Hawaii.

The plan worked, up to a point. That is, intel must have been passed from Yokohama, from where the Galaxy took off, to Hawaii, regarding the departure of the plane loaded with what seemed to be a triple-engine helo or boat in all-weather wrap. In any event, the intruder showed up again near the military/civilian airport perimeter, obviously trying to gather more information about the strange craft hidden under the wrap than he'd been able to garner when he'd first seen it being loaded aboard the Galaxy on its way to Japan.

But what could Homeland Security or the FBI arrest him for? Trespassing? Instead, they put the suspect under 24-7 surveillance. The next day, he worked a long, twelve-hour shift as a food dispenser in a small teriyaki/rice concession stand *outside* Honolulu's domestic terminal, which would explain, as Jenny Osaka pointed out to Johnny Suzuki, why they had been unable to identify him *inside* either the international or domestic terminals.

For both Johnny and Jenny, the intruder and his teriyaki-stand cover seemed as good a connect as they were going to get. His religion and height—six feet, two-and-a-half inches—in a predominantly short population only added to their certainty. But he had still not met anyone, though both Homeland Security and the FBI now knew he had a dark-room in the small bungalow he rented in Chinatown, and must be developing the photos of the Galaxy and the RS. Besides this infraction of the Patriot Act, not registering his lab, he had not committed any more serious a crime than trespassing in a DoD-restricted area.

The break for Johnny Suzuki and Jenny Osaka came on the second day, when, on what was obviously his day off, the man, Yudah Ulama, took the beach bus to Hanauma Bay, where he left a can of Coke beneath a rock well back from the beach's concession stand, after which he changed under cover of a beach towel and went swimming, joining the hundreds of others who were enjoying watching the myriad marine life in the crystal-clear waters of the horseshoe-shaped bay.

He had been gone no more than a minute before a young Japanese-American youth emerged from the water, went to the open showers, and quickly toweled himself down as he walked casually to the rock, retrieved the Coke can, and then mounted a mountain bike for the steep, hot ride up to Kalanianaole Highway.

The mountain biker, in his early twenties, rode to the post office a couple of miles away at Hawaii Kai, where he was arrested in the process of mailing a canister of film from the fake piggy-bank Coke can to a post-office box on the island of Kauai. Yudah Ulama was arrested as he was about to board the Waikiki-bound Beach Bus.

Johnny Suzuki and Jenny Osaka identified themselves to the postmaster at Hawaii Kai, and a quick computer search told them that the post-office box in Kauai was rented by a Tayama Omura, who, a concomitant computer search revealed, was now nearly ninety, living in an apartment block down above Brennecke's Beach near Poipu on the southeastern end of the Garden Isle.

Jenny Osaka told Johnny Suzuki that it was kind of sad to have to arrest such an old man, but Johnny would have none of it. "Just like a woman," he said, knowing it was clearly a blatant sexist remark. "I remember my grandma saying that they shouldn't have hanged Tojo after the war because he was 'getting on in years.' You think those Nazis, those child torturers like Mengele, hiding down there in South America, shouldn't have been taken out by the Israelis just because they were 'getting on in years'?"

"I just think it's sad," responded Jenny. "I just think of a woman holding a baby in her arms. What happens?"

In a moment of unpleasant revelation, Johnny replied, "Look, my great-uncle was in Navy Intel here during the war, but *he* stepped over the line. When they were interning the Nisei after Pearl Harbor, he and an older black guy raped a young woman in the camp. He was demoted, and they put him in the stockade. This Omura, whoever he is, is old, but he's probably been working against the U.S. for North Korea—and who knows who else?—for years. Probably cost a lot of our guys their lives." Johnny pointed to the computer screen. "Says here he was interned during World War Two. And now we've got him as the owner of the post-office box in Kauai that would have received that dead drop at Hanauma Bay. He's a ninety-year-old spy, Jenny."

"I know," she said.

When Tayama Omura, after doing his midday Tai Chi stretches, called his two stringer agents, twice, between the contact time of 3:00 and 4:00 P.M. and didn't get a response, he assumed both had been arrested. One of the stringers, the mountain biker, might have been in a traffic accident—it was gridlock in Honolulu these days, which was why Tayama had moved to Kauai—but *neither* of them responding was a bad sign.

En route on the twenty-six-minute Aloha flight from Oahu to Kauai, Johnny Suzuki received a call on his cell from Honolulu headquarters. "Johnny, those two jokers we have in cells have both received calls on their home phones from the same number. We traced the calls back to the P.O. box guy in Kauai. Be careful."

"Thanks," said Johnny, then informed Jenny Osaka, who was now tying her shoulder-length black hair into a ponytail so that it wouldn't interfere with her firing if she had to.

"Hope he comes quietly,' she said.

"Listen," Johnny warned her. "This guy's a pro, right? A

ninety-year-old can pull a trigger same as a nine-year-old,
only with better aim. So when we get there, have your
weapon drawn before we get anywhere near his apartment.
I'll enter first."

"Don't worry, I'll be fine," she said.

"I know."

Tayama Omura's face had none of the serenity that long
life sometimes brings those who have endured and have
peacefully turned their backs on the mad rush of humanity in
the congested places of the earth. His countenance was more
like that of an angry mask from one of the early Tahitian
warriors. The effect of a mask, however, ironically caused
many a warrior to assume the personality of the mask, frightening their owners more than their enemies.

As Omura had aged, his life force had been kept strong by
the ever-increasing need for revenge against a generation,
most of whom were now dead. He hated what he had become, and knew deep beneath the mask of the spy against
America that the spirit of Yoko would be saddened by his de-
cline into hatred. In using it to kill so many Americans by giving secret information to the North Koreans from the Korean
War on, his hatred had overwhelmed the power of her love—
in avenging her he had undone himself. So that when he knew
they were coming for him, his habit of revenge was so powerful that he viewed their approach as nothing less than an un-
warranted attack on him and Yoko that must be repulsed.

He already had the .45 that he had taken from the Intelligence policeman, Suzuki, who'd been a party to the rape of
his beloved and whose throat he had cut one night in Honolulu after the internment had ended in 1945. The .45 was an
old weapon, but he had routinely cleaned and oiled it, and he
had no reason to expect any of the big .45 bullets would fail,
having kept them in an airtight urn next to the urn of her
ashes.

His apartment was in a cream and brown-trimmed block built high on the rocky cliff just east of Poipu's Brennecke's Beach, whose body-surfing waves were among the world's best and most dangerous, waves that, like allied intelligence, Tayama Omura had never turned his back on.

As he saw the unfamiliar sedan pull up outside the apartment, and the man and woman get out, he noted how there'd been no flashing lights, no sirens. No doubt they didn't want to alarm any of the tourists, not so soon after his North Korean paymasters had killed so many Americans and when everyone holidaying on the islands had to catch a plane back home. Some tourists in the apartment block had canceled their return flights and signed on for another week in the complex or elsewhere on the island until, they said, they'd feel confident that all airports in U.S. territory had been secured against missile attacks. All the lead articles in the *Honolulu Advertiser*, Omura recalled, had been about the growing demand by consumer groups for expensive cutting-edge technology to be mounted on all passenger planes, like the Israelis did, and also on FedEx and other major airline courier planes that carried so much of the nation's business.

Omura took down a hollow gourd helmet/mask from his collection on the wall. As a spy, he had a predilection for masks, the hollowed-out gourd one that had been worn by warriors long before Queen Liliuokalani's reign. The hardened, sun-baked gourd helmet had only two hockey-puck-sized holes for the eyes and seven hide tapers dangling from it like a segmented beard. If he didn't get the first shot in, the gourd would offer some protection.

He unlatched the door then walked back to the sofa by the window through which he had watched a thousand sunsets. Lying down on the sofa, he drew the *Advertiser* up over his masked face as if he'd dozed off while reading, the gun in his right hand, by his side between his right thigh and the sofa's back. He wasn't going to go meekly. He'd take at least one of them with him. To add authenticity to his dozing-off pretense, he let his left leg slide off the sofa, its black rubber sandal resting idly on the carpet.

He heard the knock and didn't stir, but breathed deeply so they'd see the rise and fall of the old man's chest as he slept.

"Mr. Omura?"

No answer.

"Maybe he's deaf," Jenny, her gun drawn, whispered.

"Maybe he isn't," said Johnny softly. "Mr. O—?"

Omura fired, the force of the impact punching Jenny back through the doorway, the second shot, from Suzuki, hitting the old man as he fired his second. Suzuki's body flung back, like Jenny's, but against the wall. And it was over, Omura's throat, though he was dead, gurgling like one of the tiny, man-made streams said to have been dug by the Menehunes, another kind of outcast in Hawaii, who had also been conquered.

"You okay?" a winded Suzuki asked Jenny Osaka, who, after being hit by the .45 slug and slammed back rudely against the hallway wall, had slid down, her breath knocked out of her. "I think I'm—" She paused, looking about for her sidearm. She was still holding it. "I think I'm okay. You? Oh, Lord—" She'd just seen the gruesome gourd helmet, the blood gushing from beneath it.

Suzuki walked unsteadily toward the grotesque mask and, after checking for a pulse and getting none, gingerly removed the hollowed-out gourd. He frowned, unconsciously creating a transitory image in his face of the old man's, its wizened-up skin so cleft with anger that it reminded Suzuki of a small papier-mâché map of deep, dry desert coulees devoid of any suggestion of life. It was as if Suzuki's bullet hadn't killed him but that he'd died years ago.

"Well," said Jenny, picking herself up, already feeling the bruise on her left breast from where the .45, fired by Omura at virtually point-blank range, had been "stopped hot," as they said on the police shooting range, by the newly arrived Hagvar vest, "thank God for that new Hagvar stuff."

"Hagvar," said Suzuki as he covered Omura's face with the blood-soaked newspaper. "What kind of a name is that? Sounds like some Nordic god. *Hagvar*!"

"I don't know exactly what it is," said Jenny Osaka. "Some fish stuff and new Kevlar. Whatever it is, we owe our lives to it."

"Amen to that."

CHAPTER TWENTY-EIGHT

UPON HEARING YET another news clip of Freeman calling the North Korean government "scumbags" and "the gutless child murderers of Pyongstink," General Lesand, amid a group-viewing by the Joint Chiefs, shook his head again. "The President better put a leash on that man."

"Yes," agreed the Army Chief of Staff.

"No," demurred the Chief of Naval Operations, surprising his colleagues. "Not yet." The CNO was a wiser, older man than the Air Force, Army, and Marine Chiefs, and he reached back in memory to the unbleeped words of a sound tape of the inimitable Winston Churchill, who, in his speech to celebrate the first substantial victory against the Nazis' vaunted Afrika Korps at El Alamein in 1942, warned his already weary and blitzed population, "Now this is not the end, this is not even the beginning of the end, but it is, perhaps, the end of the beginning."

There would be battles yet to come and, Freeman's diplomatic failures notwithstanding, there would be more paybacks to come until the scumbags' nests were found and destroyed, as many as possible per one hit but, if necessary, as Aussie said, "one by bloody one until the job is done."

On the *Yorktown*, as earth passed into night and a translucent blue haze lay over the East Sea and the Sea of Japan, the sun a disc of beaten gold, Freeman, a sheaf of e-mail hard copies in his hand, climbed high up the stair ladders to find a place on the ship's Vultures' Row, not because it afforded him a vulture's view of the dangerous, accident-prone business of combat aircraft taking off and landing, but because it afforded him a private place where he could be alone and think upon yet another victory in his legendary career. He thought of Bone, for whom a memorial service, with a recovering Chief Petty Officer Tavos attending, would be held on *Yorktown*.

The general read the congratulations from the President, the Congress, and the Joint Chiefs, as well as the news story sent to him by his son about the fierce citizen-lobbying in Congress for a law requiring all commercial aircraft using U.S. airspace to install Israeli-type anti-MANPAD technology. Most important to him was the e-mail from Mr. and Mrs. Jason Brady. It told the general of their pride in a son who had served so gallantly, and thanked the general for the first e-mail he'd sent—to them, assuring them that their son had died in combat, that the North Koreans had not captured him at all, that he had *not been* tortured, as the "donkey press" had first reported.

The general thought too of his fears, of the persistency during his nocturnal sleep of the faces of men and women with whom he had served, some of whom had been killed. What place his obsession with sweet onions and blue exhaust had to do with anything he didn't know, and was too wise to pursue it now, for it was like trying to make sense of any complex array of thoughts and images that populate our conscious and unconscious dream hours. He knew there must sometimes be connections—perhaps there was more to the sweet onion odor he had detected coming from the kitchens aboard *McCain* prior to the launch of the RS. And maybe not. Only time would tell, he mused: yesterday is history, today is a gift, tomorrow a mystery.

The next message, and the last before he and the team would go to bed before the media frenzy that was awaiting them at the end of their two-stop flight to San Francisco via

Hawaii, was from Margaret. She said she had gotten a new DVD but didn't know how to work it. "Would you help me, Douglas?" she wrote.

"I will," he murmured to the wind, smiling to himself as he remembered their time in bed before he'd left on the mission, how she'd giggled at his talk about Walla Walla onions. Then suddenly, like a name you've been trying for days to recall, Freeman made the vital "connect" between the low-sulfur sweet onions and the bluish-tinged, high-sulfur exhaust from the missiles. It was the answer to what had been bugging the general ever since he'd spoken to the President before the mission, when he'd been talking about how "a grain of sand in your sock" keeps irritating you when "you can't find it." The onion-missile connect had meshed with one of sociologist Riefelmann's *Zusammenschmelzen* moments, the fusing of two initially unrelated thoughts, in this case onions and missiles, into a third. The latter was Freeman's realization that it might, indeed it *should*, be possible for CIA forensics to analyze the burned sulfur detritus from the Guatemalan-triggered explosion at Dallas/Fort Worth, where the backup MANPAD had been detonated in the relatively confined space of the waiting room. And then to match the chemical fingerprint of the sulfur's unique structure with that of sulfur mines in North Korea or elsewhere in the world, and to trace the *transportation* of the sulfur from the mine to where the missiles were actually *being made*. Then the U.S. could send in a team to execute an in, do it, out mission, or what Aussie would call "a little mine demolition."

Exhilarated by the thought, the general was also exhausted, as were his men. Right now, he and the team needed rest. Even so, when it came time for him and his team to disperse at LAX, to return to their women, see their children, and get back to Monday night football, to take time to live—sort of—the general had yet another surprise for the team.

EPILOGUE

AT LOS ANGELES Airport, Freeman shook each hand, looking straight and clear into each man's eyes. His eyes watered, he explained, because of "all the crap and dust blown up here around LAX from the hot Santa Anna winds.

"I'm going to need you guys when I plan our next mission—wherever that'll be." The team looked at him in astonishment, but Freeman didn't blink, adding, "It could be sooner than we think, the way this world is. So I want one sure way of contacting each of you at any time. I don't want to try chasing someone down because they're out shopping with Mommy at Wal-Mart." He grinned at Aussie. "Got it?"

"Got it."

"Good."